HARRY GETS WISE

A novel

Michael Vines

Copyright © 2023 Michael Vines

All rights reserved

The characters and events portrayed in this book are fictitious. Aside from recognizable historical figures (and members of the author's family), any resemblance to persons living or dead is purely coincidental.

No part of this book may be reproduced, or stored in a retrieval system, or transmitted in any form or by any means, electronic, mechanical, photocopying, recording, or otherwise, without express written permission of the publisher.

ISBN-13: 979-8-8600-3235-4

Cover design by: Jenna Davis Design

Printed in the United States of America

In loving memory of my mother.
And, of course, my grandfather.

MICHAEL VINES

1

Cutting off his big toe was the best decision of his life. He could live without it. In fact, it was probably the only way he could live. Just six years older than the brutal young century itself, he made the sacrifice at age sixteen to avoid the constant skirmishes over a partitioned land waged by one rapacious monarch or another. Most feared were the Czar's terrible Cossacks who always seemed to show up at the worst possible time.

The missing toe on his right foot also allowed him to sit out the Great War. As a result, even though illusions, like the bodies and minds of the men who had survived the trenches, had been broken and shattered all over Europe, his were still intact.

But his surviving illusions did not apply to Europe. Even after the war he saw no future for his kind—reviled interlopers on that crazy continent—and he made an even bigger, riskier decision. He would leave his wife and two daughters behind in a shtetl called Sokolova in newly autonomous Poland and set out, in 1919, for the New World, certain he would send for them soon, once he got settled and could earn a living. In a land overflowing with milk

MICHAEL VINES

and honey—this new Promised Land—how long could it take for him to get a small portion of his own? It's not like he needed freight loads or barrels, even. A few cups would be plenty. A thimbleful would be a step up. He'd be happy with a drop.

When the ship carrying him in steerage entered New York Harbor after a cold, cramped, disheartening voyage, he saw the Statue of Liberty for the first time. The immensity of her features, her outstretched arm and torch reaching for the sky made an impression on him, reinvigorating his hopes. After a false start in Collinsville, Illinois, to which he had followed the tracks of distant relatives he barely knew, he finally ended up on the north side of St. Louis where a tailor he knew from the Old Country named Goldstein was doing all right, so he figured, why not? He opened his own shoe repair shop around the corner named in honor of the verdigris colossus in the harbor and, while he was at it, gave himself an honorary degree proudly proclaimed on the shingle he hung over the door: The Liberty Shoe Doctor, Harry Becker, prop.

Yet he never entirely shuffled off the shroud of the Old Country. Even thirty-five years later, in 1954, long after he'd called for his family and they all had settled safely in America, vestiges remained.

When Harry Becker locked the door to his shop, it stayed locked. His technique began with closing the door tightly. Then he inserted the key and turned the bolt of the lock till it clicked. Solidly, like it meant business. Next, he pressed down on

HARRY GETS WISE

the thumb latch of the handle and pulled, making sure that the door wouldn't open, that it was locked but good. Then he did it again, just to make doubly sure. And here's where Harry's door-locking shtick really kicked in, making it a ritual that was his and his alone: he did it again. And again. And again. He repeatedly pulled and yanked on the door, so hard you'd have thought he was trying to tear it off its hinges. And he made such a racket that if Officer Keegan, the cop on the beat, didn't know Harry and his routine, he'd have thought he was trying to break into the shop rather than lock it up.

Harry still marveled that here, the police were not secret. They weren't here to spy on you or hurt you, but to protect you. The rule of law incarnate right on the block. When Keegan saw Harry locking up the shop, he would sometimes play along.

"Need any help there, Harry? Want me to give it a tug?" No brogue.

Keegan was a towering figure who loomed even larger in his uniform, which he filled out like he was wearing shoulder pads beneath it, and Harry was happy to have this official *shtarker* lend his muscle for an extra guarantee of security. Keegan made a big display of trying to open the locked door, as if he were prepared to pull the whole building down with it if that's what it took—and he looked like he could almost do it—before finally giving up in fake exhaustion.

"Whew! I think we got it, Harry. I'd rather try to

MICHAEL VINES

break into Fort Knox."

Harry went through this whole rigmarole every time he locked his door. As if that would have stopped anybody determined to storm in. Especially since the door was composed of a glass window in a wooden frame. Harry hadn't seen any Cossacks around lately, but old fears die hard. However much faith he had in the goodness of this great land, however much his rational mind knew that the old threats were far away, an atavistic, visceral anxiety told him that he wasn't entirely off the hook. That it could happen here. That never went away. Maybe that's why he made a point of introducing each of his grandchildren to Officer Keegan.

"Marshall, this is Officer Keegan."

"Hi."

"Hello, young man."

"Officer Keegan is a good man. He's your friend. Always listen to him. You need help, go to him. You can always trust Officer Keegan."

Harry didn't say so explicitly, but somewhere, deep in his subconscious, he was thinking, "He will keep you safe from marauding hordes on horseback that gallop out of the morning mist waving sabers over their heads. He will protect you from the Nazis."

For his own part, Harry made sure Keegan's shoes were always in the best repair and always had a reflective shine as bright as the brass buttons on his blue tunic. On the house, of course.

HARRY GETS WISE

* * *

Harry's entire extended family lived directly across the street from the shop. Goldie, his oldest daughter, lived with Sam and their two kids in one of the four flats of the building on Warne Avenue that he bought years ago. Tillie and her husband Sid lived in another with their two boys. Harry, Lena, and Libby, his youngest, shared the entire top floor.

There was too much traffic on Warne Avenue for the grandkids to cross it on their own. Goldie's son Marshall was only eight now, two years older than his sister Sandy, who was three months older than their cousin, Marty, Tillie's boy. Joey, Marty's baby brother born a couple of months ago, obviously wasn't going anywhere.

They could have asked their mothers to help them cross, but they wanted their grandpa, so they stood on the curb, sometimes alone, sometimes as a pair, sometimes all three together, and chanted in a kind of cantorial cadence, "O-o-oh, Grandpa, take me o-o-o-ver-r-r," holding each syllable of the last word separately in a dramatic crescendo.

Harry always dropped whatever he was doing to answer their call, and they'd wait as patiently as kids that age could while their grandpa went through his whole door-locking shtick—which seemed a little over the top even to them—before he crossed the street to fetch them.

The kids loved hanging out in Grandpa's store with him. They loved the tools and the signs, particularly the free-standing red and black metal Cat's Paw sign that Harry kept outside when the shop was open. But most of all they loved the smells emanating from the shoes—earthy and organic wafts of leather, the vestigial equine scent of glue, other people's feet. The place brimmed with the smell of life.

Once inside, each kid went right to work. The boys got hammers to hit soft nails into worn-out soles that Harry saved for the purpose, or they could use the awl to punch holes in scraps of leather. Sandy sat at the sewing machine spinning its wheel—her feet couldn't reach the treadle—pretending to stitch up remnants in distress.

When it was time for lunch, they waited outside while Harry went through his door-locking routine, put up his sign that said, "Back in 20 minutes" (though it would be more like forty-five or an hour), walk about a block and a half to Florissant Avenue—bustling at midday with traffic, streetcars, and pedestrians—make a right turn and walk past Woolworth's, Bertie's Hats, and Buster Brown Shoes to the Warne Grill, a name of curious provenance, since it was on Florissant. But whatever it said on the small neon sign outside above the door, to the cognoscenti, like Harry and the kids, it was always Lucille's, its alluring aroma drifting from fifty yards away into nostrils helpless to resist the promise of the greasiest, most delicious burgers and fries you could get at any price. They didn't know it at the time, but Lucille's would be the standard to which all other burger joints would be compared for the rest of their lives—and never equaled. Sometimes, as they grew older, the smell coming from a new-found greasy spoon might tantalize them with high hopes, but it was fool's gold. As burgers and fries went, it was all downhill from Lucille's.

When they walked in, the kids basked in the halo of their grandpa's celebrity and bonhomie. He was greeted by fellow patrons like a goodwill ambassador from another country, which, in a way, he was. He always got a special greeting and a big smile from Lucille, a small woman with a round face that was all but overrun by the thick pile of dark curly hair spilling over her forehead like grilled onions over a burger. After Harry and the kids ate, he sometimes treated them to the pinball machine in the corner that Lucille had put in not too long ago. They could continue to enjoy their burgers and fries well after they left because, even with the vigorous hand-washing performed under the intervention and supervision of their mothers, the redolence of their lunch would linger on their little fingers for the rest of the day.

❋ ❋ ❋

Harry bought a TV with a seventeen-inch screen in a walnut console at the RCA Victor Store around

MICHAEL VINES

the corner, next door to the Circle Fountain. It was his entrée into the nascent national community being forged by the new medium. Most evenings, the whole family crowded into the front room, as they called it—never the living room—and on Wednesdays and Fridays tuned in to *Coke Time with Eddie Fisher*, a fifteen-minute show where Eddie would put down his glass of ice-cold Coke —distinctively curvy and emblazoned with the sponsor's cursive logo—long enough to croon a few popular tunes of the day. A favorite went like this:

> *Oh, my papa, to me he was so wonderful,*
> *Oh, my papa, to me he was so good.*
> *No one could be, so gentle and so lovable,*
> *Oh, my papa, he always understood.*

To everyone else in the family, the song described Grandpa to a T, but Harry never related it to himself. Instead, it brought back heartbreaking memories of his own father who, despite Harry's begging and beseeching, had refused to leave Sokolova and instead stayed behind with his brothers, cousins, aunts, uncles, and all the rest to be consumed by fire. At least his mother had been spared that, having died years before, when Harry was only nine. As things turned out, perhaps there had been mercy hidden behind his childhood loss.

They were also big fans of Dinah Shore who, like Eddie, was Jewish. And she, too, was watched and admired by millions of Americans just the same. What a country. Of course, most Americans would have had no inkling that she was a Jew. It would never have crossed their minds.

"Is he Jewish?" was a big question for Jews, always had been, asked with hope for one who would bring them favor, and with trepidation for one who would bring them shame. With so many Jews having changed their names—the better to assimilate—it wasn't always easy to know. Especially for showbiz types, like Dinah Shore, whose homespun looks were not dispositive; whose schnoz gave nothing away; who was a blonde and had been a cheerleader at Vanderbilt University, somewhere in the South, no less. She could have passed for a *shiksa* any day of the week. To know better, you had to be in the loop, an underground network where that sort of knowledge was shared with Harry and Lena, and about every other Jew in America. They all knew she was one of them.

And the songs she sang? Probably half of the hits on *Your Hit Parade* were written by Jews—as were classics like *Easter Parade* and *White Christmas*. What was Tin Pan Alley, what was Broadway without them? And when Dinah sang "See the U.S.A. in Your Chevrolet," she was singing a tune composed by a pair of circumcised men named Leo Corday and Leon Carr, obviously changed from something else. If Jews were going to write the songs, it seemed only right that they should sing them too.

From the first time Harry heard Dinah belt out the pitch for her sponsor accompanied by film cutting between gleaming new Chevys cruising across America, he was smitten. So was Lena.

MICHAEL VINES

"I'd like to see the U.S.A. in a Chevrolet myself one of these days. Being driven like a lady," she said.

Harry would like that too, so he learned how to drive and got a license in the hopes of one day buying such a machine (as he called all automobiles), thereby attaining that next level of freedom that was the birthright of all Americans, whether they were born here or not: the freedom to go—wherever he wanted, whenever he wanted. And no one would stop them. He imagined driving Lena out to a nice little hotel somewhere not too far away and spending a romantic night together.

Harry purchased that freedom in the form of a brand new 1954 Chevy Bel Air, a two-tone beauty in baby blue and white. Adding to Harry's pride of ownership was the fact that the Fisher Body plant, which contributed to its manufacture, was located on Union and Natural Bridge, about a ten-minute drive from Warne in his new car. Sometimes he'd drive by just to honk his horn "hello." "Body by Fisher," he'd tell people when he showed off his machine, echoing the plate that was riveted to its door sill, proof to Harry that it was solidly built, dependable, American quality.

When Lena saw the car for the first time, she said, "They didn't have a convertible?"

Harry bought his car just one year before automakers added those magnificent tail fins—the nonfunctional flying buttresses of automotive design. Sleek, aerodynamic, streamlined. Those

11

models were the stuff male fantasies were made of. The '55 Bel Air had not only that fabulous futuristic behind, but her two front headlights protruded like perky boobs, bolstering America's image as the embodiment of the things the world most coveted: great sex and a better tomorrow. They symbolized for all the world that America was the place that the future was heading, if anybody still needed convincing. Harry's machine, the '54, wasn't as sleek as those, but that was fine by him. It was cute and cuddly. Like he was.

Where did they go? For a ride. Usually on Sundays. Maybe to visit the relatives in Collinsville. Or the Shermans who had moved to U. City. Or Harry would load the grandkids into the backseat and they would get their kicks on Route 66, a leisurely, meandering two-laner where they'd stop for another American original—frozen custard at Ted Drewes on the city's far South Side, a destination that might as well have been on the moon without the machine.

Most people love and pamper a new car, keep it clean, and are terrified of getting the tiniest ding on it. Harry was no exception, only more so. If he saw the smallest spot or a smudge on the gleaming chrome trim or shiny steel body of his Bel Air, he'd go straight for the *schmatta*-in-waiting he kept in the glove compartment to rub it out.

❋ ❋ ❋

MICHAEL VINES

Harry was the Lone Ranger of litter. If he was walking down the block and saw an empty pack of Lucky Strikes on the sidewalk, or a wrapper of Bazooka bubblegum some kid carelessly threw to the ground, or a greasy brown paper bag once filled with Lucille's fries, he would bend over, pick it up, and carry it to the nearest trash can, never hanging around to be thanked by the town folk for his good deed. He just did it. He took his responsibilities as a citizen seriously.

On a beautiful day following a pleasant evening of being entertained by Jews on television, Harry gazed out the window of his shop and noticed on the sidewalk in front of it a single windblown page of the *St. Louis Post-Dispatch*. It wasn't unusual that he stepped outside for a moment to pick it up, then came right back in to throw it in the trash. What was unusual was for him to find two men he had never seen before settled comfortably on a couple of chairs, making themselves perfectly at home. Like they owned the joint. How they managed to sneak in during the brief time he was outside with his back turned, he had no idea.

The first thing Harry did was look at their shoes. The tall, young guy's were in good shape, like new, well made, probably in Italy, and expensive. They didn't even need a shine. The short, heavyset guy's were dull and had seen better days. The two men were mismatched, like individual shoes taken out of random boxes to make a pair.

The short, thick guy was world weary, heavy-lidded, in need of a shave, the brim of his fedora snapped over his brow. He looked like someone just woke him up in the middle of the night and gave him some terrible news. His suit looked like he was wearing it at the time.

The tall, young guy could have been the showroom model his crisply tailored suit was fitted for. He was good looking, fresh-faced and trim, no lid covering his hair, which was slicked back by more than a little dab of Brylcreem. And he was loaded with energy, as if he had gotten enough sleep for both of them the night before. The toe of his left foot never stopped tapping.

Harry greeted them as he did all customers. "Good afternoon, gentlemen. How can I help you?"

"The question, Harry," the short one said, "is how we can help you?"

The man knew his name, but that wasn't surprising—Harry was known to everyone in the neighborhood. Besides, it was written on the decal that now ran the upper length of his storefront window: "Liberty Shoe Doctor, Harry Becker, prop."

Harry assumed the obvious. "You're selling something?" he asked. "I have suppliers."

"Oh, we're not sellin' supplies."

"What then?"

"Insurance."

"I have insurance."

"Not the kind we got." That was the tall one, speaking for the first time. The short guy gave him

MICHAEL VINES

a sidelong glance that said essentially, shut the fuck up.

Harry was far from obtuse, but this proposition required a little explanation, and even then he didn't understand. Or at least, he couldn't believe it. Oh, he'd heard of protection rackets, but that was in the movies—Warner Brothers films about gangsters pushing booze during Prohibition. He loved those old films, like *The Roaring Twenties* and *Little Caesar*, which he had seen for a nickel at the O'Fallon, the neighborhood theater across from the park of the same name. Usually, he'd go with his friend, Meyer Goldstein, the tailor. Lena wouldn't go with him. She saw *Public Enemy* with Harry way back when, but in that last scene, when James Cagney was sent home to his mama, his head wrapped in bandages, a blanket tied around his body with a rope, and dropping into the house like the dead weight he was when his brother opened the front door while his poor mother was blissfully fluffing pillows upstairs in anticipation of her dear boy's arrival—that was it. She'd never see another.

Harry wasn't exactly naive, but he thought the kind of thing these thugs were talking about was all made up in Hollywood. He could no more imagine himself being shaken down than he could imagine a big black car driving by with hoods standing on the running boards and hanging out the windows shooting up his shop with Tommy guns. Harry wasn't sure that these guys would go that far, but the short one made it clear that he meant business.

"You know," he said, "there's a guy over on Washington near Grand, had a shop a lot like this one. Very nice, did a good business. Until it caught fire."

Harry braced as the short one continued in no uncertain terms. "From now on, you're gonna pay us in cash every week. You unnerstand me?"

Harry nodded. He wasn't asking for a lot of money, but enough to put a dent in his Profit and Loss. Not that Harry had a handle on his P and L or even thought in those terms. That sort of thing was in Lena's bailiwick. But even though Harry didn't know from generally accepted accounting principles, he could put two and two together. And he knew he was in trouble.

But the short guy had one piece of good news for him. "Tell ya what, Harry. We got a special, today only. First week is free. We'll see ya next week."

As they turned to walk out, something hit the floor with a clang. Harry looked down and saw an iron pipe about a foot long and as thick as Officer Keegan's baton. The short one bent down to pick it up.

"Must'a fell," he said, holding the pipe in front of Harry's face to make sure he got the picture. Then he slammed it into his open palm with a loud smack before slipping it inside a makeshift leather holster that he wore under his arm beneath his suit jacket. No one could have missed the enormous star sapphire bulging from the ring he wore on his pinky.

MICHAEL VINES

But few others would have paid much attention to the leather holster that held his pipe. Poorly made, thought Harry. Shoddy workmanship. Not up to his standards.

Harry was scared in a way that he had never been since he arrived in America. He had no idea what to do. He couldn't tell Lena. He couldn't do it to her—fill her with fear and anxiety over something she couldn't do anything about. But what could he himself do about it? He was just as helpless.

And then he realized: Officer Keegan. The rule of law. Those bums couldn't get away with this. Not here. Not in the neighborhood. Harry would tell Keegan all about it, and the law would protect him. The whole precinct would come down on those hoods so fast they wouldn't know what hit them. So Harry closed up shop, locking the door even more vigorously than usual, then walked Keegan's beat looking for him.

But Keegan was nowhere to be seen. When Harry passed Lucille's, he thought he might catch him there having a cup of coffee or a burger, but no dice. He asked Lucille if she'd seen him, but she hadn't. Giving himself a break, Harry took a load off on a red vinyl-covered stool at the counter and ordered a cup of coffee.

It was easy to see that Harry was not himself, so Lucille asked him what was on his mind. Before long, he found himself confiding to her.

"Have you ever heard of such a thing?" he asked.

"How can it be?"

But Lucille, a tough-talking, worldly broad, knew the score and was unfazed.

"Welcome to the club, Harry," she said, her tone softening a bit, probably for his sake, but still streaked with anger.

"What do you mean?"

"They're takin' over the neighborhood, Harry. It's their territory. Tony the Pipe, they call him. He's their muscle. A real sweetheart. The kid's Carlo Barnini. Green as a bottle of 7-Up, but in tight with the boss, I hear. You know, Benny the B Apicella."

"And you they've threatened too?"

"See that pinball machine over there, Harry. That's not mine. It's theirs. You think I want it in here? This is a restaurant, not an amusement park. And it's takin' up one o' my four-tops. It's costin' me, Harry. I don't see a nickel outta that thing."

"Who else?"

"Anyone they can squeeze a buck outta. You're kinda late to the party, truth be known."

"We'll go to the police. All of us together. We'll tell Officer Keegan."

"Ha!"

Harry didn't like the sound of that. It reminded him of the tone Lena sometimes took with him, and he knew exactly what it meant. That he was an innocent. A naïf.

He'd always taken care of Keegan, of course, fixed and shined his shoes any time for free. And

MICHAEL VINES

he knew he wasn't the only one playing that game. Dependahl kept an open tab at his tavern for him, and the cop made good use of it. He was a regular at Lucille's, too, but come to think of it, he never saw him stop at the register on the way out. It was always understood, on the QT, that Keegan's job came with a few perks. Add it onto his city salary and he was doing pretty well. But Harry had no idea how well. Until Lucille told him.

"Keegan's in on it, Harry. He's on the take."

And this, more than anything that had happened to him all day, shattered him. If Keegan's on the take, that means he was gonna be taking from Harry. Taking money right out of his pocket, like a thief. If Keegan was in on it, there was no law.

"No. I can't believe it."

"Believe it."

"How can it be? They can't do this. This is America. We can't stand for it."

"Harry, you watch Uncle Miltie, right?" Lucille asked.

Of course he did. In fact, like millions of people, the main reason he bought his TV was to watch Milton Berle (Jew) every Tuesday night on "The Texaco Star Theater."

"Sure."

"Okay. So you know what his secretary says? Max, right? Her name's Max? On the show. She says, 'It's bigger than both of us.' That's what she says. To Milton Berle." Lucille then launched into a dead-on impersonation of Ruth Gilbert, the actress who played Max on TV. "Don't fight it, Mil-ton. It's bigger than both of us."

She broke into a little laugh, and despite the weight he was carrying, Harry let it go for a second to appreciate her performance. He smiled back at her. "That's pretty good, Lucille. Maybe you should be on the television too."

"Sure. They got a Lucy, why not a Lucille? They're lookin' for me in New York. But that's the way it is, Harry. You can't fight it. It's bigger than both of us."

The lift she brought to Harry's mood passed quickly, and his face turned solemn. "No. I don't believe it. There must be something. Something we can do."

"Well, you wanna take on Tony the Pipe, Harry, good luck. But I don't think anyone's gonna sign up for that with ya."

Lucille went back to her other customers, leaving Harry at the counter staring into his coffee cup. What could he do? he asked himself, again and again. The last time he was in thrall to a ruthless, overwhelming force, he ran away. Now, from these hoods, these Cossacks in America, there was nowhere to run. He thought of his relatives, lost in the camps. He'd often wondered what he would have done in their situation. In the face of a malevolent power that has come to take everything from them —their dignity, their humanity, their property, their very lives. Now he was going to find out.

2

When Harry first arrived in America, he understood that the streets couldn't literally be paved with gold, though many of his landsmen did not. He wasn't surprised to see that they weren't, which was fine with him. He wasn't looking for gold anyway. Of all the foreign things on offer in this foreign land, all he wanted was that most foreign thing of all: a taste of freedom. To be left alone, at last. As for opportunity, you could hardly take a step without tripping over it. Even a man like Harry, who spoke little English when he arrived and would always have a Yiddish accent thick as schmaltz that might have been mocked and ridiculed—or worse, much worse—anywhere else in the world, was welcome and given a chance to make a go of it. Nobody seemed to care.

As his English improved, he realized that most of the people in the neighborhood had one kind of accent or another. There were your Germans, the majority, but most of them, especially those with a few bucks, lived on the South Side; your Irish, but their stronghold was close by in crummy Kerry Patch before they descended in a pack on Dogtown south of Forest Park, and lived in tumbledown

HARRY GETS WISE

wood-frame shotguns that did justice to the neighborhood's humble moniker; and some Italians, who mainly lived just south of Dogtown in squeaky clean two-family houses or bungalows on Dago Hill, in the accepted parlance of the day; plus a few fellow Yids, like Goldstein, Chervitz in dry goods, and Hersch the hatter. But his tribe congregated mostly on the far west side of town, near, and sometimes in, the closest suburb west of Skinker Boulevard— University City, abbreviated to U. City, aka, Jew City.

Even though they might refer to each other as Krauts, Micks, Dagos or Wops, Kikes or Jews —somehow meant pejoratively—they would never use those slurs to the other's face. Whatever they thought deep down, they accepted each other as fellow travelers who all arrived in the same place for pretty much the same reasons. And they had a sense that they were all in this together. This thing called America. All anybody asked for was a chance, and they all got it. Except the Blacks, of course, for whom nearly every neighborhood in town, except slummy Mill Creek Valley, was off limits. They came here for different reasons altogether, and every other ethnic group had an epithet for them all their own.

So Harry's neighbors happily became his customers. In those days, when your shoes started to wear, you didn't just pitch them into the bin and take the streetcar downtown to buy yourself a brand new pair at the Grand-Leader, as its name implies, the city's grand and leading department store on Washington Avenue that carried so much

MICHAEL VINES

stuff it needed nine stories covering an entire square block to hold it all. Harry went down there just to see it with his own eyes—he couldn't afford to buy anything—and if he had even the vaguest doubt that his new country was indeed the Land of Plenty, which he did not, the cornucopia that was the Grand-Leader, a veritable cathedral of commerce, set him straight.

But even though the shelves were stocked, not everyone could be so cavalier about tossing out their shoes the second the sole started tearing away from the welt. That kind of profligacy would have to wait until after the second big war, when the U.S. was about the only country in the world that wasn't reduced to rubble and didn't have to build itself back from the ground up, and everyone was so flush they didn't know what to do with it all.

But back in the day, when a person bought a new pair of shoes, he'd have Harry the Shoe Doctor nail on some taps to help forestall their inevitable decline, which, when it occurred, they'd go back to Harry, and he'd glue and hammer on a new sole or heel, or stitch them up like new on the Singer 29-4 Cobbler's Sewing Machine that an optimistic banker had lent him the money to buy. And a sound investment it was, for both parties. Harry regarded it with the pride you might expect for a firstborn son. His first American-made shiny object, though it never shined. It was wrought iron and had a black matte finish, but it was as strong and sturdy as the lady in the harbor for whom his shop was named, built to last forever. Harry would sit before the machine, place his foot on the treadle base and his hand on the wheel, and say to himself, "America."

Harry fixed his neighbors' old shoes or, for a nickel, just shined them up. And he saved every one of those nickels, almost. His one indulgence was the cheap cigars he started to smoke. It was always with reluctance and a little guilt that he reached into his coin purse to fish out a nickel for his stogie, but what the heck? He worked hard, made every sacrifice. For the cost of a single shine, he deserved it. He'd just have to do an extra pair tomorrow.

Alone in the one room he rented from Mrs. Aschenschmidt, a flinty German schoolmarm widowed before her time who taught second grade and wore bright red lipstick and kept her auburn hair in a bun as tightly wound as she was herself, Harry had only his cigar to keep him company. It helped him focus on his English lessons for the night class he had signed up for. Its smell wasn't reminiscent of anything from back home, which was mostly an earthy mixture of straw, manure, milking cows, goats, and chickens. And when he apprenticed with the cobbler in the village—the man who not only taught Harry his trade but the rudiments of English, which he picked up when he had tried America on for size, but found it didn't fit —the smells were of leather and glue, much like his shop today. Nevertheless, his cigar's charred bitter taste and the acrid plume that lingered in the air and seeped into his clothes were somehow a comfort to

MICHAEL VINES

him. He couldn't tell you why. Maybe he was getting addicted to the nicotine. Maybe he just liked the buzz.

Other than the stogies, rent, and a few basic necessities, just about every cent went into the bank, and in just three years Harry managed to salt enough away to send for his family in Sokolova. When he went to New York to collect them, first thing he did was to look up his old lady friend again. She hadn't changed a bit, hadn't budged and, though as wearily expressionless as ever, seemed, in his mind, at least, as pleased to see him as he was to see her. Gratified, even, to see that he had gotten along, scooped up his thimbleful of the American Dream. Harry imagined Lena and the two girls seeing her the next day for the first time the way he had a few years before as he sailed into the harbor, and it gave him chills.

He stayed at a Y overnight and got to the pier early in the morning. Waiting for the boat to arrive, and for his family to be processed through Ellis Island, he wondered if little Goldie—she'd be six now —would even recognize him, or he her. And what would she make of him? Tillie would be almost four and have no memory of him at all. Harry had left before Lena even knew she was carrying their second child. Would she love him instinctually or would he just be some strange man stinking of cheap cigars, as unknown and frightening as this strange land itself?

Harry had no idea how he would be received, but

HARRY GETS WISE

when he saw Lena on the deck of the ferry clutching its rails, searching desperately for the man who left her behind, his apprehensions slipped away. He waved wildly and shouted himself hoarse, to no avail. It was all he could do to keep himself from jumping into the harbor and swimming out to the boat, and a good thing too—he didn't know how to swim. Who had time for that kind of thing in the Old Country? There were cows to milk, barely arable little plots of land to till, Cossacks to flee. Here in America, they had public swimming pools. Not a pond or lake or some hollow in the ground that naturally filled up with water, but enormous excavations paved over with concrete by men who knew what they were doing, and filled with clean water, filtered and chlorinated, if you can imagine that, so everyone should stay healthy and not spread germs and make each other sick in an epidemic that wiped out half the town. And they went to all that trouble for recreational purposes only.

The largest public pool in the entire world was right over in Fairground Park just a short stroll down Warne Avenue from Harry's shop, where people could go for a dip and cool themselves off on a hot summer's day. And Harry had never seen hot summer days such as those in St. Louis in August. It was like a jungle, not that he'd ever been in a jungle, but he could imagine. He'd make sure he would take the girls to Fairground Park where they'd learn how to swim like every other American kid. Except for the Blacks, of course. The public pools were for

MICHAEL VINES

whites only. Lucky for Harry, Jews counted as White.

Harry wanted to grab all his girls at once and hold them close, but he had to make a choice, and his first choice was always Lena. He felt her tears moisten his cheek and she buried her face in his chest, hoping to muffle her sobs so the girls wouldn't hear.

"I missed you so," Harry whispered to her. "I need you so."

When they let go, Harry bent down to the girls. Tillie plunged herself into her mother's long coat, then turned for a quick peek to take her measure of this man before going back into hiding. Goldie let her father pick her up and she squeezed her arms around his neck till it began to hurt him, but he wouldn't stop her.

"Is this America Papa?" Goldie asked in Yiddish.

"Yes, Goldie. America. We're home now."

Harry had brought a welcome gift for everyone, which he picked up that morning on his way to the pier—a bunch of perfectly ripened bananas, the exotic fruit he had been in love with since he arrived. He handed one to Goldie and she looked at it like it was from another world, which, of course, it was.

"Banana," he said, and made a big show of peeling it open, like it was a magic trick. Nature's most perfectly packaged creation. He took a bite and then invited Goldie to do the same. She did so tentatively, but once the taste settled in, it seemed to send her eyes into orbit. Harry said "banana" again and Goldie repeated it with gusto. Tillie was intrigued, but wouldn't bite, continuing to cling to her mother instead.

They couldn't linger. Much as they wanted to let the moment last, feeling, touching, holding each other after all this time, they had a train to catch. They dashed to Penn Station to board the *St. Louisan*, namesake of a proud, bustling metropolis, the sixth most populous in the nation, renowned throughout the world as host of the dazzling 1904 World's Fair, and home to two of the nation's sixteen major league baseball teams.

After more than twenty-four hours on the rails, catching sleep in their seats in fits and starts, mesmerized by the never-ending landscape flying past their windows—"This isn't even the half of it," Harry boasted—they finally pulled into Union Station in St Louis. New York's Penn Station was certainly a sight to behold but they hurried through so fast to catch their train, its grandeur blew by in a blur. But they didn't have to rush through Union Station, and they gazed up in wonder at the vaulted ceilings of its Grand Hall from which descended a wrought iron chandelier that seemed big enough to illuminate all of Sokolova, and then some. Warsaw's station was a wooden shack by comparison.

"Who's got money for all this?" Lena wondered. "Just for trains?"

Harry beamed with knowing pride as if the magnificent station were his very own. He well

MICHAEL VINES

understood its symbolism as a monument to a nation on the go, moving fast with purpose and direction, ahead, always ahead, although no one, certainly not he, could say exactly where it would wind up. But wherever, it would be a better place, of that he was sure.

It was no problem getting the kids to sleep that night. The new flat that Harry had rented and furnished came with a marvel or two. Harry turned on the faucet to demonstrate that clean, potable water came flowing out on demand. And the toilet was indoors, right under their roof. It had only one bedroom, for him and Lena, but he put a double bed in the front room for the girls to share.

On this first night, despite their excitement and trepidation, the girls were so exhausted they could have slept soundly on a bed of hard red bricks, one of their new hometown's most prized exports owing to the abundance of high quality clay in the earth on which it was built. With a mattress and pillows as soft and cottony as those that Harry had provided them, they fell asleep instantly.

Harry was happy about that. It had been a long time. He had resisted all urges, and for a healthy man in his prime, that was no small feat. There was no shortage of attractive women who came into the shop with a broken heel or something, and they never escaped his eye. He had a sharp one for the ladies, Harry did, particularly, as a shoe man, for the well-turned ankle. He was quite an attractive guy himself, in a compact package with a ready smile,

29

a lustrous head of hair, and a sturdy if not exactly powerful physique. That continual *klopping* with those hammers of his helped keep his arms toned.

But more than his appearance, he had a winning way about him, a quick, gentle wit and a natural sweetness that coated him like the congealed red sugar on the hard candy apples they sold in the fall at Horne's Candy on Florissant Avenue, around the corner from his shop. And he knew how to crack a joke and tell a story with the best of them. One of his favorites was his unembellished account of Caleb the traveling salesman who dropped by the shop shortly after Harry opened it on Warne Avenue.

Caleb had gotten lost driving from Davenport back home to Louisville and, passing Harry's store, decided to stop in to have a pair of badly worn heels replaced. Hearing Harry's fractured English, Caleb pegged him as a recent immigrant and he thought he'd give the young shoe doctor—as he was billed on his shingle—some friendly advice to help him make his way in America.

"You're new here, I see."

"Yes," said Harry.

"Well, you're a young man, so let me pass on a little tip. Findin' a lady in this country is as easy as pie. All it takes to get her in the mood, so to speak, is to sit her down and offer her a drink. Not just any drink, mind you. But one special drink. Wanna know what it is?"

"Yes."

MICHAEL VINES

"Well, you start with some good ol' Kentucky bourbon. Got to be *Kentucky* bourbon. Ain't no substitute. Got that?"

"Kentucky bourbon."

"That's right. Not too much, now. Just 'bout this much." He held his thumb and index finger about one shot apart. "Now, you pour that in a glass over one cube of ice. Don't wanna water it down. Just cool it off a little."

"One ice."

"One ice. Then, you mix in the secret ingredient. You ready for it?"

"Ready," said Harry.

The man leaned forward and whispered, "Sweet talk."

"Sweet talk?"

"That's right, Doc. You just add a little sweet talk. Kentucky bourbon and sweet talk. The most reliable concoction ever devised by man. Ain't never failed me yet."

The salesman was getting a kick out of himself, but Harry didn't quite get it.

"What is 'sweet talk'?" Harry asked.

"Sweet talk? Why that's just talkin' real sweet, Doc. Sayin' nice things to 'em, things that make 'em feel good. You hear me? Mix that with a shot of Kentucky bourbon and that's all you need."

"Bourbon and sweet talk," Harry said.

"*Kentucky* bourbon."

"*Kentucky* bourbon and sweet talk."

HARRY GETS WISE

While he waited for his shoes, Caleb began extolling America, telling Harry what a great country it is, the envy of the world, and how much it needs people from all over to come here, to take advantage of the opportunities, and help it grow. As if Harry needed to be sold.

"No matter where you come from, Harry, you're welcome in this country. The whole passel o' you. We need people like y'all. Hard workin' men who know how to get the job done. Immigrants. That's what makes America strong. Why, when I see someone like you, I don't see a greenhorn fixin' shoes. I see the father of captains of industry, doctors, lawyers—Nobel Prize winners, goldarnit— stretchin' out as far as the eye can see. So welcome to America, Harry. We're happy to have you."

Harry thanked him and when Caleb's shoes were ready, he handed them to him across the counter.

"That's some fine work, Doc. I thank you. You'll do good in America. Real good," he said as he laced his shoes. Then he stood up, paid a fair price, and said, "Well, I'd best be on my way now. You know which way to Louisville?"

"Me? No."

"Well, I found my way here, guess I'll find my way back."

As the salesman was departing, Harry said, "Good luck, Caleb. And thank you for the sweet talk."

Harry wasn't sure why, but Caleb laughed like that was the funniest thing he ever heard in his life.

MICHAEL VINES

"Sweet talk. That's good, Doc. Very good. Thanks for the sweet talk," he chuckled as he went on his way, with new heels and a new tale to tell his customers.

Harry loved that story, and not just because he got to be the punch line. It said something about America, this big, rambunctious clamor of peoples, accents, and regions, each with its own identity, each with its own character. There was pride of place for them all, like Caleb's for the Land of Bourbon, yet, unlike Europe, where every state wasted their energies warring with every other, they all came together to create something bigger, stronger, more inventive and ingenious than they could ever have done on their own. And their largest portion of pride was saved for this whole. They were indeed the United States of America. E pluribus unum.

In another time, another place, Harry's personality might have gotten him elected mayor. He certainly had what it took to chat up a woman if he wanted to and, especially after having learned the secret mix of Kentucky bourbon and sweet talk, might have had his pick of the flock. But Harry was not so inclined. Oh, he had his fantasies, of course. His imaginary sex life cast a net wide enough to ensnare even the widow Aschenschmidt. Severe as she was, she was not without her allure in that solid Teutonic sort of way where you'd just about need an armor-plated bodice to hold that bosom at bay. And on extremely lonely nights, he'd have to admit that a quick ride through the primeval forests of Deutschland may have crossed his mind. But that's as far as it ever went. Not even the farthest reaches of his fertile imagination could encompass the idea of kissing her with anything resembling passion.

His favorite and most frequent fantasy, however, was for this reunion night with Lena, and now, at last, it was a reality, one for which he had planned and prepared. It was the first purchase he had ever made at the Grand-Leader. A gift for Lena on this special occasion. He handed her the box and when she untied the blue ribbon and opened it, she found inside a pair of silk stockings. These? For her? It was unimaginable. Lena always had a natural appreciation for the finer things, so they appealed to her right away, and she held the silk up to her cheek, caressing it to feel how soft and smooth the fabric was.

Harry took the stockings from her hands, got on one knee, and Lena, wearing only a full cotton slip, extended her leg and let him slide the stocking up to the thigh. He also had for her a package of roll garters, which were all the rage among the smart set, but which left Lena perplexed. So Harry, having been bold enough to ask the salesgirl how they worked, showed her the ropes. He glided it up her leg, folded the hem of her stocking over the garter, and rolled it down to just below her knee.

There was one more gift Harry had for his wife, perhaps to be expected from a shoemaker: a new pair of shoes. Well, not new exactly, but like new. Pre-owned by a young woman who had dropped off her stylish French heels with a T-strap in perfect condition. All she wanted were tiny taps on the heels and toes. She was in a hurry and couldn't wait so she left them with Harry and said she'd be back later in the afternoon. She never showed. Harry pondered endless scenarios to explain her disappearance. They usually didn't end well. In any case, it was a year already, and there was no way he could find her. So Harry wrapped the shoes in tissue paper, put them in a new box, and presented it to Lena.

He was taking a small chance. He didn't know Lena's shoe size. No one had shoe sizes in Sokolova. They were lucky to have shoes. Heck, some of them were lucky to have feet. Not to mention all the toes they were born with. But Harry remembered Lena's feet quite well and in his professional opinion these unclaimed heels just might be the ticket.

Lena gasped when she opened the box. Who could imagine shoes so lovely? Like Prince Charming, Harry slipped the first one over her right foot and voila! She was Cinderella. For the record, a perfect size 7. After he slid the other one on, Lena stood up, two inches taller now with her elongated, well defined legs, and walked gingerly about the room, modeling for her husband.

"Is this what you like?" she asked, in Yiddish.

"Yes."

"Me too."

Harry knew she was too modest to go out dressed like a flapper in those stockings. And where on earth would she ever wear shoes like that? But indoors,

HARRY GETS WISE

after an initial moment of discomfiture, the look seemed to embolden her. Harry had never seen her more alluring, more desirable, and the simmer in her eyes told him that's exactly how she felt.

Even though he didn't need it, Harry also had on hand a bottle of Kentucky bourbon and a vast store of sweet talk. After regaling her with both, the shy shtetl girl opened herself to her husband with a wanton freedom she had never shown before. It would become an unspoken custom between them that whenever they made a date to be alone together in their bedroom, Lena would dress for the occasion. Harry would always make sure she had something nice to wear. And they'd kick things off with their favorite mixed drink.

Harry had gotten his family here just in time. Just before the new immigration laws were passed that would slam the door shut on people like them. He knew he had been lucky, but just how lucky he had no idea. No one could have imagined. That night in bed with Lena, he felt like he could want for nothing more. But more was yet to come. As he and Lena consummated the start of their new life together, they were also conceiving the last of their three children. And the first and only one who bore the label, Made in America.

They named her after Harry's deceased Aunt Leah, preserving, at least, the first initial, as was the custom. But primarily Harry had another woman in mind when he came up with the name—the one who greeted him and his family upon their separate

MICHAEL VINES

arrivals. Lady Liberty. And so, she became Libby. A name she would live up to.

3

Long before buying his television and his car Harry had already punched his ticket as an authentic American and was ushered in by the game of baseball. He had felt a visceral connection to the sport early on and made a conscious decision to adopt it, just as he had its native land. He became a student of the game, immersing himself in its rules, its intricacies, its arcana. He talked baseball with his customers, who explained to him the hit and run, the stolen base, the squeeze play, what it meant to load up a ball, and, though none of them had a grip on it, the infield fly rule. It would remain a mystery for years to come. His favorite play of all was the sacrifice—the bunt, not the fly. With the fly, you were still trying to get a hit. But when you laid one down solely to advance the runner, you gave yourself up for the greater good. That he could relate to.

Sportsman's Park was only about a mile and half from Harry's shop, and, in the years before his family arrived, he began going to games with Meyer Goldstein. He didn't consider the nickel it cost him for a seat in the bleachers to be an extravagance. Didn't feel a trace of guilt about spending it. For this

MICHAEL VINES

was no idle indulgence; it was a rite of passage. For no reason whatever, Harry went with his gut and decided the Browns, rather than the Cardinals, were the team for him—a fateful choice.

Every day during the season he checked the *Post-Dispatch* to see who won around the league. Even before he could read all the words, he could recognize the names of the teams and cities, and he got himself a little geography lesson while he was at it. In time, he even learned to read a box score. On good days, he could lose himself in it—the black ink on the paper adding a final layer to his already polish-and-dye-stained fingers—envisioning the play by play in his head. "SB: Sisler," it read. Pretty cut and dried. About as exciting as the pale, pulpy newsprint it was written on. But in his mind Harry saw George Sisler in a flash of color going with the pitch and sliding into second in a swirl of dust ahead of the throw.

Once Lena arrived, Harry tried to share his passion with her—passion being something that ran deep between them—but she resisted.

"You don't do anything. You watch others do."

"You'll see, Lena. You fall in love. Come. I'll show you. We'll go to a game."

Lena went. Once. She couldn't wait for it to be over.

"No, thank you." she said. "I don't want to sit and watch. I want to do."

So Lena set about doing. It turned out that she

had a head for business that her husband lacked, and at her encouragement, Harry invested in a new shoe repair finishing machine—a mechanical riot of belts and nibblers and sanders and brushes and buffers that was so big he had to move to a larger space down the block so it could fit against the wall. The new shop also had a storage area in the back where Harry kept supplies and the inventory of inexpensive shoes he started to sell, also on Lena's advice.

Had he gone along with Lena's most ambitious idea, who knows what might have been? She wanted Harry to start thinking big—forget about shoe repair and start thinking about shoe manufacturing, on a grand scale. And why not? They were in America now where anything was possible. Look what Kantor, the *schmatta* man had become. He was just a rag collector in the Old Country, and used his haul to make cheap, lumpy mattresses. When he came to America, he bought the equipment he needed to make mattresses with the latest technology—inner springs—and became a big *macher*, the millionaire Mattress King. Those were Kantor mattresses that were waiting for Harry's family when they arrived from Poland. If Kantor could do it, so could he. There was the Brown Shoe Company in St. Louis. Why not the Becker Shoe Company? Lena even went so far as to come up with a marketing line to try to sell Harry on the idea: "*Becker Macht Besser.*" Becker Makes Better. It even had a ring to it in English.

But Harry wasn't interested in becoming a millionaire shoe *macher*, or anything of the like. It just wasn't in his nature.

"We already have everything, Lena. What would we get that we don't have now? *Tsuris*, that's all."

"In America, anyone can get rich, Harry. But you, never."

"We get by, Lena. Nobody bothers us here. For me, that's plenty."

But Lena wanted more and was looking for ways she could get it. Perhaps she could make herself useful around the shop. When she saw that Harry kept his records in only the most informal, haphazard way—indecipherable letters and numbers scribbled on scraps of paper left scattered about the counter, tucked into drawers, or stuffed in his pockets—she knew she had found her calling. She took a night class in bookkeeping and started keeping the books at home.

She came by the shop often, and, as she strolled there with Libby while the other girls were in school, a four-flat apartment building right across the street on Warne Avenue caught her eye. It was just an ordinary building, like many others in the neighborhood, typical of its time and place. But Lena became obsessed with it. When she pointed it out to Harry, he saw a home, its solid red bricks glowing in the sunlight as if they were still afire in a kiln, then taking on darker, rusty shades as they slipped into shadow. It was beautiful. But Lena saw something else, besides—a profit center. And she explained to Harry the advantages of becoming property owners and earning rent from tenants to help pay off their investment.

The owner—already an old man at sixty, creaking with rheumatism—had no intention of selling. But Lena was persistent. She baked a batch of rugelach, brewed a pitcher of iced tea, and offered them to him as they sat on a hard bench he had placed on the concrete porch— a porch he had difficultly climbing the four steps from street level to reach. It was Lena's way of showing him how sweet life could be if he didn't have the building to worry about.

"At this stage of your life, you should be taking it easy. Have another rugela."

"Delicious. You made this?"

"Sure. This is how you should live. Have a little sweet. Relax. Enjoy life. Enough already with the headaches. One day the furnace breaks down, the next day the roof is leaking, the next, a tenant runs out on you. Who needs it? Better to sell and live in peace, am I right? You earned it."

"Let me think about it."

It took only a few batches of rugelach to soften him up, and soon she closed the deal.

The apartments were small, but Lena had a vision. They broke through the wall on the top floor and combined two apartments into one so it was big enough for the whole family. Lena served as

MICHAEL VINES

landlady, renting out the other two units, managing the property, and keeping the books.

Years later, when the girls had grown into women and started families of their own, they became the tenants, each taking one of the two flats on the ground floor and getting a sweetheart deal on the rent—just enough to cover a proportional share of the mortgage. They all lived literally on top of one another.

Libby continued to live with her parents while she attended Washington University, the only sister to go to college. Lena didn't understand why a girl needed to go to college in the first place, least of all to study art. Bookkeeping in night school, fine. But art in college? To be what? An artist? It was beyond her comprehension.

But Goldie and Tillie said, "Don't worry, Mama, she'll get her MRS and quit soon enough." Once they explained to Lena what they meant, it made perfect sense to her. What better place to find a man who could earn a living?

Libby never got her MRS and had to settle for a BFA, which was fitting because she was still a bachelor, female variety, even as she closed in on the worrisome age of thirty, the line demarcating maiden from spinster. Why such a *sheyne meydele*— and she really was by far the prettiest of the three girls—couldn't find a man was a mystery to them all. Not that she didn't have her share of guys chasing after her. She was way too picky, if you asked Lena.

It was time to settle already and have a family of her own.

But Libby was Libby. None of them ever understood what made her tick. Harry sometimes wondered if something might be missing in her nature. Or maybe she had too much of something she would have been better off with less of. Whatever the cause, she was different from the others, that's for sure. For one thing, she was left-handed. Maybe that had something to do with her being such a free spirit. Then again, what else would you expect from the only native-born American among them?

* * *

Harry had been given a one-week reprieve, but the two hoods showed up the very next day, not with a demand for money, but for labor. Carlo was carrying two boxes full of shoes in need of various repairs and dropped them on Harry's counter.

"A little somethin' to keep ya busy," said Tony the Pipe. "Have 'em ready first thing tomorrow."

"Yeah, by three."

"Shaddup, will ya?" Tony said to his partner. Then to Harry, "Just have these fixed up good as new. We'll pick 'em up tomorrow."

"There's what—at least ten pairs here. This will take some time. I don't know if—"

"Don't make me no excuses. Just get to work.

MICHAEL VINES

And, uh, put it on my tab, yeah?" Tony said with a joyless laugh.

"The crew can't go barefoot for long, Harry." Carlo's laugh was genuine.

"Will you keep your fuckin' trap shut, already?" Tony turned his back to Carlo so he didn't see him roll his eyes. And a good thing for that. But Harry did. "Tomorrow. First thing," Tony said to Harry, and the two men strode out the door.

Stealing from him was bad enough, but now this—forced labor? The demand was a familiar one to Harry. Not to him personally, but familiar just the same. Could this really be happening? Here in America?

It was another betrayal to add to the others that had been accumulating. And they seemed to be coming to a head at the same time. Harry reflected on them all, betrayals of greater or lesser magnitude and significance, but betrayals nonetheless. He started small.

There were the Browns, for one. Maybe he should have seen it coming a mile away, but he didn't, and it broke his heart. After the '53 season, the Browns bolted off to Baltimore, forsaking their very name to become the Orioles. It was all that nogoodnik owner's fault, Bill Veeck, sounds like drek, Harry said.

Lena couldn't care less. Goldie and Tillie took it in stride. But Libby, though commiserating with her father, was otherwise pleased to see them go. She had gone her own way, as usual. When she was just a little girl she fell for the two red birds perched on opposite ends of a black bat spanning the players' chests. How smart those uniforms were. Besides, the Browns stunk.

After having loved and lost—and rooting for the Browns, Harry was well acquainted with loss—he was wary about giving his heart again. But he was primed. You might say that he had been two-timing his team even before they left him because he, along with everyone else in St. Louis, couldn't help falling for a young Cardinal outfielder named Stan Musial. Even when the Brownies met the Cards in the '44 World Series, the only one they ever appeared in, Harry would have been happy to see Stan hit a home run as long as the Browns won. Stan did, but the Browns didn't. Stan "The Man" as he was known to everybody or, to Harry, Stan "The Mensch." Now here was a true American hero. And Harry fell in love again.

The betrayal of the Browns was *bupkes*, though, compared to others buffeting Harry at around that time, all of which challenged his faith in the things he valued and took for granted.

This Joe McCarthy, for example, hauling people before Congress, pressuring them to testify against each other, to name names, and all that are-you-now-or-have-you-ever-been *mishegas*, as if there were no such thing as the First Amendment—that didn't sit well with Harry. In fact, it frightened him. He had gone to a few meetings himself, in the 30s

MICHAEL VINES

with Meyer Goldstein. So did a lot of people. What was wrong with that? He never carried a card, like some of them, but he read a Yiddish commie rag called *Morgen Freiheit* once in a while and still read *The Forward*, which never exactly hid its Socialist sympathies.

They were for the worker and so was Harry. Who wanted Wall Street to have it all? Not to mention those union-busting *goniffs* like, it so happens, Brown Shoe, which filled Harry with particular outrage and a pang of regret for not having listened to Lena and starting the Becker Shoe Company. He could have taken them on and stood up for the little guy. *Becker Macht Besser*, indeed. He could have made it all better. He would have permitted no one to take advantage of workers. It wasn't the American Way. The American Way was everyone deserved a fair shake. You pitch in, you play by the rules, you get your share. Even-steven, as Harry always said. That's what America stands for, isn't it?

He knew this not from some dream or fantasy about America that he brought with him from the Old Country, but from studying the founding documents for his citizenship test. After he passed, he was always eager to show off what he learned —what made America great. What made America special.

"The three branches of government: Executive, Legislative, Judicial," he spouted to his children, and later, when they were old enough, to his grandchildren. "It's in the Constitution. Checks and balances. Bill of Rights. Rule of law." Harry's speech would always be laden with that schmaltzy Yiddish accent, so it would have come out more like, "Ze zchree brchanches uv govument." Or something like that.

No one took more pride in his status as a naturalized American citizen, or took it more seriously, than Harry. To his dying day, he never missed a chance to vote. "Straight Democrat all the way," he would say. He was strong for Roosevelt, obviously. To him, the New Deal was the pinnacle of America's ideals.

And Joe McCarthy the nadir. As Harry saw it, the disease personified by this man bored into the nation's core like a worm into a prelapsarian apple.

Harry often crossed the street to have lunch at home with Lena at the white Formica kitchen table and sit on one of the blue vinyl chairs with chrome legs that came with it as a set. During the Army-McCarthy hearings, he'd eat in front of the TV—a pioneer in that regard—and watch what was billed as gavel-to-gavel coverage on the DuMont Network. It was hard for Harry to take. A lot of times, he'd barely touch the *vursht* sandwich on rye with a slice of onion, or anything else that Lena made for him. He had no appetite. Not even his favorite spicy brown German mustard—which Lena had stopped buying, along with anything else of German provenance—would have made a difference. Harry was more forgiving. He missed that mustard and would have bought it, but he didn't insist. He settled for a bland American brand called French's.

"Eat, Harry. Drink. Here," Lena said, spritzing seltzer into a glass for him from one of the bottles they had delivered in a wooden crate every week. Harry nibbled, sipped, and sighed.

"I never thought such a man could happen in America," he told Lena.

"What? You think everybody here's so perfect?"

"Not perfect. But this? I never thought."

"You got *mamzers* everywhere, Harry. You can't escape them."

"But not like this. Not here."

"No? Ha!"

Harry was familiar with Lena's tone—a touch of impatience mixed with a dollop of condescension. He knew he sometimes came across as a sweet but innocent child, always trying to see the best in people, even when they didn't deserve it. And it made Lena feel sorry for him. As if to take back her cynical "Ha!" and her dismissal of his obvious despair, she put a consoling hand over his, leaned into him, and said, "It's a young country, Harry. It's still got a lot to learn. But it will. It's America."

Of course. That made sense to Harry. And it gave him hope—America's most abundant commodity. It was still young, still learning, and deserved the benefit of the doubt. So he made excuses, the way a parent would for a high-spirited son who sometimes crossed the line. Boys will be boys, and all that. Whatever problems America had, it would outgrow them. Whatever its faults, it had a good heart and only the best intentions. America wasn't perfect, but what was? At least it tried. Tried to be more perfect, just like it says in the Preamble.

Libby was suspicious of her father's boundless hope and made no secret of it. She had read Greek myths in a humanities course she took at Washington U. and, as she and her father strolled down the block together picking up litter they found in their path and throwing it into the trash, she told him the story of Pandora's Box.

"You see, Papa, the story says that Pandora opened this urn the gods had given her, and all the evils of the world flew out. By the time she closed the lid, the only thing left inside was hope."

"Thank God for that, then."

"Maybe not. 'Cause if hope was in that urn to begin with, with all the evils, doesn't that mean hope might be an evil too? It lets you hold on to something, just to make you feel good. Like everything's gonna work out in the end. But it doesn't. It can be false hope. An illusion."

"You got too smart for me, Libby, in your college. I believe in hope. We wouldn't be here if I didn't. We wouldn't be anywhere."

So Harry clung to his hope. But it went only so far. This McCarthy was still tough to swallow. A *shanda* on America. And not the only one. There were the Rosenbergs too. Jewish spies sent to the chair just a year earlier. And all the others involved

MICHAEL VINES

—Gold, Greenglass, Fuchs, Cohen—so many Jews. A *shanda* for the goyim, as expression went.

Once in a while Harry and Goldstein went bowling in the afternoon, before the leagues started at night. The Florissant Lanes was just south of Harry's shop—on Warne, oddly enough, not Florissant (the Warne Grill, on Florissant; the Florissant Lanes on Warne. Go figure)—its location marked by a tall neon sign on the side of the building that spelled out "BOWLING" from the top down in glowing green letters. They climbed to the alley on the second floor up a narrow flight of stairs, its creaks and groans no match for the resounding crash of pins and the rumble of hard rubber balls rolling towards them on lanes made of maple and old-growth pine.

They both smoked cigars and bowled with more indifference than skill, though Harry wasn't bad. He had a good eye and a fine touch. Goldstein drank a Griesedieck beer and Harry a Budweiser, which, among the many brewed in his adopted hometown, he'd been faithful to ever since Gussie Busch had a team of Clydesdale's parade down Pennsylvania Avenue to deliver the first legal case after Prohibition to Franklin Roosevelt at the White House. If it was good enough for FDR, it was good enough for Harry.

"We needed this with the Rosenbergs like a hole in the head," Harry said. "They weren't suspicious of us enough already? We had to give them something new. Selling secrets to the Russians. Atomic secrets, *noch.*"

They both agreed that if the Rosenbergs had tried for a million years, if it were their intention all along to hurt the Jews, they couldn't have done a better job. They couldn't have found more fertile ground to sow the seeds of antisemitism in a land where it had never really taken root, beyond the normal amount, anyway.

And to make matters worse, the spies were prosecuted by this Roy Cohn, who was also the big deal lawyer for McCarthy. So no matter where you stood, left or right, there was a Jew for you to hate. Another Jew to blame for everything.

Still, the Rosenberg affair—threat to the nation and Jews, in particular, though it may have been —never challenged Harry's faith in America. In a way, quite the opposite. There was no hint of antisemitism in their prosecution. They had a fair trial.

"You sure as hell wouldn't get that in Russia or the Soviet Union—whatever they want to call themselves. The Czar, Stalin, take your pick. You weren't getting any fair shakes from either one of them. Just get on their wrong side, say one wrong word, and I feel sorry for you." That's the way Harry put it.

Harry had experienced some garden-variety antisemitism since his arrival, some dirty looks, some whispers and snickering behind his back, but he brushed them off as a minor nuisance compared to what he knew from the Old Country. And since he never applied to Harvard or Princeton, or tried to join the St. Louis Country Club, or attend the WASP's high society Veiled Prophet Ball, he never felt outright discrimination firsthand.

It was a particularly painful kick in the gut, then, for Harry to see the ancient inextinguishable hatred come crashing down here, in America, on his own grandchildren. Goldie's oldest, Marshall, was still an innocent, even though Harry had him doing booze runs for him to Dependahl's Tavern down the block. He would send him over there with a one-quart bucket and a dime, and Dependahl would fill it up with beer and send it back to Harry with the kid.

On one of these runs, a couple of years before, when Marshall was about seven, he came back without the dime, an empty bucket, and tears streaming down his flushed cheeks. He'd been ambushed by a tag team of dizygotic twins named Jack and Jill, familiar to him from the concrete playground of the Harrison School, where they were a year or two ahead of him, but whom he would not identify for fear that if they found out he ratted on them, he'd be in for more of the same. He did, however, tell his grandpa that they whipped him with a jacket they had twisted into a scourge, its zipper lacerating his arms.

"Why? What did you do?" Harry asked in Yiddish, simple words and common phrases of which Marshall understood. Marshall answered in his native English, the only language he could speak fluently.

"Nothin', Grandpa. I didn't do nothin'."

"Then why'd they beat you?"

"They kept calling me Jew. And to go back where I came from."

It was far worse for Harry to hear this than to have suffered the attack himself. Marshall told him he fought back, but it was two against one. It wasn't a fair fight. It never was for the Jews. At least not in those days. Harry was glad to hear that the boy had stood up for himself, but it made him wonder if he would have done the same against an overpowering force, like the one that confronted his family that had remained in Poland. He couldn't imagine any of them offering much resistance, but what was the alternative? He knew that only too well. Still, even if they had fought back, what chance would they have had? Just ask the Jews in Warsaw.

Harry did his best to console Marshall. He closed up shop, put his sign on the window that said "Back in 20 minutes"—no matter how long he'd be gone —and took Marshall to the Circle Fountain where they sat side by side in a banquette the color of Granny Smith apples. Feeling helpless, Harry took the path of least resistance, like many before him. He shrugged it off, got on with his life, and sought comfort anywhere he could find it, in this case, chocolate sodas with vanilla ice cream. And while Marshall sucked the last of his down through a straw till he started making gurgling sounds, Harry gave

MICHAEL VINES

him his spiel for the thousandth time. As much to reassure himself as his grandson.

"Executive, Legislative, Judicial." As if to say, in America, we are safe. We have the Constitution and the rule of law. Here, we have nothing to fear.

Or so he hoped. Though Harry was still proud to pledge allegiance to the flag, he was a little wary when people started pushing that "under God" part. God was everywhere in America, was on our side, as they said, had pretty much immigrated here himself and, having broken up with his first choice —as evinced by what he allowed to happen to them in Europe—Americans were his new steady. His new Chosen People.

But Harry also knew that in America when most people talked about God it was pretty obvious whom they meant. Just look how the city lit up at Christmastime. And Harry was not only a Jew, but one who had his own questions about that all-powerful, yet incredibly thin-skinned deity of the Old Testament. So what about people like him— Jews, agnostics, or atheists, even? Wasn't this their nation too? Couldn't we just be one nation, period? The way we used to be.

Goldstein had a son, Lenny, an outspoken lefty with a beard, who was an associate professor at the University of Chicago. He was just a couple of years older than Libby, and Harry and Lena had always thought they'd be a good match. Not anymore.

"What's he teaching up there?" Lena said. "I'll tell

you what. Communism."

"He's a good boy," Harry said, coming to his defense, as he did most people's.

"Not good for Libby, that's for sure. I wouldn't have him on a silver platter. They'd both wind up like the Rosenbergs before it was over."

Lenny Goldstein was out of the running now. He was in Chicago anyway, so Lena didn't have much to worry about. Besides, Libby never showed the slightest interest. But on a visit back home, the hairy firebrand told anyone who would listen that the whole "under God" business they were pushing to legislate into the Pledge, and would succeed in doing that summer—almost a year to the day after the Rosenbergs were executed—was really nothing more than a backdoor slam against "godless communism," words he slathered with a mocking sneer.

He made his case very well. And if he were right, the country was playing right into the hands of Joe McCarthy and all the rest of what Lenny called the "running-dog lackeys" for whom capitalism was itself a god, and they wouldn't allow themselves one minute's rest until they deracinated every last socialist shoot of the New Deal, nullifying the presidency of Harry's revered Roosevelt—their devil incarnate—once and for all.

Despite how troubling all this was to Harry, it was abstract, complicated, and Harry was a simple man, an uneducated man. What did he really know about such things? Washington, Moscow, and all the forces over which he had no control were far away. After crossing half the globe to get here, his whole world was now his neighborhood, mostly one block of the neighborhood where he had his family, his home, his shop. Those were the things that mattered. Things he could touch and feel and love. Those were the things that he had to look out for, take care of, and protect.

And now there was this—something not abstract, but solid, material. Things he could hold in his hand that he had to confront head-on. Two boxes full of shoes that he'd have to slave over late into the night and all the next day to finish, if even then. Two boxes of betrayal that two thugs had brought into his world. And all the other betrayals that haunted Harry seemed to be packed inside them as well. Like the evils in Libby's Pandora's Box. And Harry had no choice. He opened the first box and went to work.

4

Lucille seemed to be an authority on organized crime in St. Louis and she gave Harry the lowdown over a cup of coffee and the clicks, clacks, and clatter of the pinball machine the hoods had shoved into a corner of her burger joint. It drove her nuts. She glared at the high school boys banging at the flipper buttons and shook her head, her grilled-onion locks slithering to life like Medusa's snakes.

She told Harry how Benny Killer B Apicella —"Apicella means little bee in I-talian," she said, "Ya know that?"—aka Benny the B, aka The B, clawed his way up the ranks of the organization and took over as boss in 1950. His ascension was steeped in blood.

"He's what ya'd expect of a guy like that—ya better not cross him, is all I can say."

He was brutal, ruthless, cunning, and loyal. Until he had to rub you out for his own advancement. When he got to the point where he no longer had to do his own dirty work, he put one of his soldiers on it.

"That's what he's got guys like Tony Allocco for— Tony the Pipe. But only if someone crosses the line. Or breaks the rules. Or pisses him off. There can only be one boss with guys like the B, Harry."

According to Lucille, Benny the B had a lineage in organized crime going back to his grandfather and he followed it into the family business. He was a made soldier in the crew run by a guy named Gino Barnini, a man he looked up to and who gave him every chance to prove himself when he was just starting out in the 30's. A bond developed between them that went beyond that of merely mentor and mentee. They became friends. As much as sociopathic killers can be friends.

But Gino Barnini was an early casualty of a turf war between the St. Louis mob and Marco Ziti's boys in Springfield, Illinois. He left behind a wife, three daughters, and a twelve-year-old son named Carlo, the baby of the family. Benny promised himself he'd always keep an eye on the kid and make sure he got the same opportunities that the boy's father had given him.

"This kid Carlo, might be his godson, I think. Whatever, he's under Benny's wing, that's for sure."

The area around O'Fallon Park had been off the radar of the St. Louis mob, but Apicella saw it as a little flower filled with pollen just waiting for him to dip his hairy hands into, and he decided to move in. Carlo Barnini had just turned twenty-one, and, as a birthday gift to his fallen friend's son, Benny the B teamed him up with Tony the Pipe who would show him the ropes. He also gave them their own small piece of turf to make of what they could—the neighborhood that Harry and Lucille called home.

Harry didn't tell Lena one word about any of this, or his new predicament. What was the point? There was nothing she could do about it anyway, he told himself. And then another concern presented itself: What if she did try to do something about it? Lena was not one to be pushed around. She had a certain strength about her that Harry admired but didn't share: a don't-tread-on-me way of folding her arms across her chest and standing her ground. He couldn't let her take a risk like that. This wasn't women's work. It was better to keep her in the dark.

Harry did, however, talk to Goldstein, in whispers over a beer at Dependahl's, a place that lent itself well to conspiratorial colloquy, with its dark corners, windows that let little light in or out, and an atmosphere that favored quietude over conviviality. It also reeked of must and stale beer. To its clientele of men, many of them drinking alone, it managed to be both dismal and homey at the same time.

Harry and Goldstein sat across from each other on wooden benches on either side of a worn wooden table. Harry leaned across it so he could keep his voice low, even though no one could understand him anyway—they were both speaking Yiddish. At first, Goldstein didn't seem to take him seriously. This talk of an extortion racket in the neighborhood was news to him.

"You're pulling my leg, no?"

"I wouldn't joke about such a thing, Meyer. This is

emmes."

When Goldstein was convinced, his reaction stunned Harry. Oddly, his friend felt a little left out.

"Why didn't they come to me? I make as much you, Harry. Don't I?"

"What are you complaining?"

"I'm not complaining, I'm asking."

"Who knows? They still might. And if they do, then what? What would you do?"

"I don't know. What will you do?"

Harry sighed. "I could do nothing. Just be another sheep to the slaughter." Without a word, both men envisioned the same gruesome image elicited by that phrase. Their eyes flickered past each other's, like two cars going in opposite directions on an open road. They both just wanted to move on. "Or I could do something."

"But what? These are tough customers, no? Killers."

Yes. Goldstein was right. Everyone knew what men like this were capable of. But no one had the faintest idea how to stop them. They finished their one beer in subdued silence.

Lucille had told Harry this whole thing was "bigger than both of us." There was nothing they could do and no way to fight it. If Harry tried, he'd be going it alone. And that would be suicide. But he couldn't get it off his mind. It was eating him up inside to be so helpless. So he kept thinking, kept trying to come up with something he could do.

Finally, he did. His inspiration came from the most obvious source, and he embarked on his new mission with hope—hope again—and the enthusiasm of an innocent. He put pen to paper and wrote a document, a founding document of sorts.

We the People of the Neighborhood who own the shops and restaurants and stores on Florissant Avenue and the other streets around here, in Order to form a more perfect Union, establish Justice, insure domestic Tranquility, provide for the common Defense, promote the general Welfare, and secure the Blessings of Liberty to ourselves and our Posterity, do ordain and establish this Promise to Stand Together and to not pay any Money to anybody who says give it to me or else. Or do forced labor neither! This is America!

At the bottom of his document, Harry signed his John Hancock, as big and bold as its antecedent and with as much of a flourish as he could muster. He would now need to find it some company.

Harry had fixed the shoes the hoods had brought him, and they were ready just in time for pickup.

MICHAEL VINES

But he promised himself he wouldn't do it again. To keep that promise, he would need the support of his fellow victims, his neighboring shop owners.

There was no way Harry could convene them all in public to exercise their first amendment freedoms of assembly and speech. He had to do this sub rosa, one-to-one, face-to-face. Once they agreed to sign the petition, then they could speak up, loudly, together, with one voice. So Harry made the rounds. The only places he didn't go were Western Auto and the RCA store. These tough guys weren't so tough that they'd take on the big companies and big money behind them. The small-fry shop keepers that they could intimidate and push around were more their speed.

So Harry went to them, one by one, each on a first name basis with every other: Phil Chervitz at his dry goods store; Al Dependahl at the tavern; Irving Hersch who sold hats; Lucille who slung burgers; Otto Mueller the butcher; Ernie Howe who owned Ernie's Hardware store; Linda and Elmer Horne who owned the candy store; Dick and Gracie at the Circle Fountain; Frank Krieger at his second-hand clothing shop; Ben and Luann Freeze who owned the Laundromat; and all the rest—even Ed, the thin, scraggly man with the grey stubble and hollow eyes who owned the pool hall that bore his name.

With blackout windows to keep passersby from seeing inside, and single-bulb fixtures over its four pool tables providing its primary source of light, Ed's made Dependahl's Tavern look like an outdoor café high on a sundrenched cliff overlooking the Mediterranean. Harry had seen Ed around occasionally, but he was one of the few people in the neighborhood he didn't really know. Harry had never been inside the parlor, and if one of the grandkids asked what the forbidding place was, the nearest adult would say, "Someplace you never go into," which was exactly the wrong thing to say if you wanted to make sure they didn't.

The pool hall was empty but for Ed who was perched on a tall wooden stool next to a wall and holding an amber bottle of Falstaff at eleven in the morning. He wouldn't be open for business for an hour, but the front door was unlocked, so Harry strode in carrying his document. He extended his hand, which Ed shook like someone who didn't want to get shoe polish all over his own. Then Harry began his pitch. As soon as Ed got Harry's drift, he stepped off of his chair, turned his back on him, and walked away through a swinging door behind the bar without saying a word.

Harry waited a few minutes, not sure if Ed was coming back, or what. He didn't. But Harry pressed on, giving the same impassioned spiel to everyone he met with.

"We're all in the same boat. None of us can do anything by ourselves. We're small and weak. But if we band together, we're big and strong. E Pluribus Unum. United we stand. Divided we fall. Let's all stand together and say NO to these thugs."

MICHAEL VINES

Harry was indefatigable. He lectured, he admonished, he exhorted, he implored. And when all was said and done, the entire community stood together and said, "No." To Harry.

They were united in their position that they didn't want any trouble, that resistance was futile at best, fatal at worst, and that, considering the stakes, it was a small price to pay. There was also unanimity in their questioning of Harry's sanity. Lucille had been right from the start. No one was going to sign up with him to take on the hoods. After a dispiriting day, Harry was on his way home when Keegan approached him twirling his baton.

"What's up, Harry?"

"Not much."

"Yeah? I seen you been pretty busy today. Just dropping by to say hi to everyone, that it?

"That's it."

"Since when do you play pool, Harry? I never seen you go into Ed's before."

"You seen me go into Ed's?"

"I got eyes and ears everywhere."

"So then, what are you asking? You know what's what."

"That's right. And my advice is you better back off. Before ya get yourself in trouble."

"Me back off? How 'bout you backing *on*, huh? You're the law. You're supposed to do something about this. You're supposed to protect us." Harry was losing control and raising his voice, something no one in the neighborhood would have heard him do before.

"Take it easy, Harry."

"We're being threatened and robbed by these good-for-nothings. And you don't lift a finger."

"Come on now, Harry."

"I know what's the score, Officer Keegan. I got eyes and ears everywhere too. I know what team you're on."

"Watch out what you're sayin', Harry."

"You should be on our side. Not theirs."

"Look, Harry. You think I got a choice? You think I can just buck the system here? Go my own way? Well, I can't."

"Who then? Somebody can do something."

"Nobody can do nothing."

"Well, we'll see," Harry said, without having any idea what he thought he might see. He had no plan. No options. He started to walk away but Keegan put a hand on his shoulder to stop him.

"Look, Harry, I like you. Everybody likes you. We don't wanna see you get hurt."

"Then do your job. I pay taxes. I pay your salary. Do what you're paid to do."

Keegan didn't raise his voice. He didn't have to. He bent his big body down so he could put his face right into Harry's and he said through clenched teeth, "I'm warnin' you, Harry. You're playing with fire. Now cut it out."

That was unsettling. Keegan was such a shtarker.

MICHAEL VINES

And Harry was so small next to him. Now he felt smaller, next to everything. A mote of dust in the air. A breath in a whirlwind. Everything was bigger than he was. And he trudged home feeling smaller with every step.

❋ ❋ ❋

The next day on his way to his shop, before he crossed the street, Harry looked over at his Bel Air parked at the curb, as he routinely did first thing in the morning, just to admire it for a moment and take pride in everything it represented to him. But this time, its shine seemed to have faded. Harry's first thought was that maybe he should go to Western Auto, get some wax and a new chamois, polish her up. But he knew that the problem went deeper than that and he was tugged by a dull sense that something was slipping away, or had been lost altogether. *See the U.S.A. in your Chevrolet* didn't have quite the jaunty ring it had just a week before. Something dark and evil that dwelt in the underbelly of his adopted country had lurched into the light of day, grabbed him by the lapels, and shaken him silly. And it was eating his *kishkes* out.

And then he noticed something. On the windshield, tucked beneath the wiper. A note? Had someone left him a note? Was it a threat? Had it come to that? He yanked the paper from under the wiper and read it. Yes, it had come to that.

HARRY GETS WISE

Harry looked in every direction and spotted Keegan standing on the corner. He was twirling his baton, as he often did, but now, it didn't seem like the happy-go-lucky display that it always did before. Now, it carried with it an air of menace. Like Tony the Pipe's pipe. Harry was undaunted and marched towards him waving the paper.

"What is this?"

Keegan took the paper from him. "What's it look like? It's a citation from the St. Louis Police Department."

"What for?"

"Parking too close to a fire hydrant, Harry."

"I'm not parked close to any fire hydrant."

"Well, you were when I wrote out that ticket. You must'a moved your car."

"My car's been right there all night, in that exact spot. I never moved it."

"Well, I'm saying it was parked right next to a hydrant. You callin' me a liar?"

Harry was trembling, unable to speak. And just then, Keegan held the ticket up in front of Harry and calmly, slowly ripped it in half. Then he handed the two pieces back to him.

"There. All better now?" Harry was hardly all better now. "Consider it a warning. Now get smart."

Harry could have taken Keegan's gesture as a peace offering, but he didn't. It was as much a show of arbitrary power—and his own helplessness in the face of it—as getting the ticket in the first

MICHAEL VINES

place. As much as the hoods forcing him to fix their *ferkakta* footwear. Without forethought, but plenty of indignation, Harry took the two halves of the torn ticket and tore them again, into quarters, eighths, sixteenths, and then he dashed the pieces to the ground like he had spit them out of his mouth. They blew away like confetti, scraps so small not even Harry, the Lone Ranger of Litter, would have been able to corral them if he tried. Not that he had any intention of trying.

He was still seething when he got across the street and saw a discarded magazine writhing on the sidewalk with a broken spine. He picked it up and saw it was an old copy of *The Saturday Evening Post* with a Norman Rockwell cover of a disheveled young girl, about ten or eleven, seated on a bench outside the principal's office, while he and a woman —presumably her teacher—look out disapprovingly through the open door. The girl has a black eye, ruddy cheeks, her hair flies in every direction, the ribbon in one of her braided pigtails is undone, and she's wearing a self-satisfied smile. It appeared that she had been on the losing end of a fight, maybe one she started. Then why's she got that big shit-eating grin on her puss? Is it a you-should-see-the-other-guy kind of smirk?

It made Harry think of Marshall when he had run to him crying after he had gotten the daylights kicked out of him by Jack and Jill on his way back from Dependahl's. For what? For being a Jew. This girl was no Jew, that's for sure. She had gotten into a fight over something, something trivial, no doubt—a disagreement over a game of jacks maybe, or whether her playmate stepped on a line in hopscotch—but something, nonetheless. For a reason, not for no reason—other than being who she was. And she didn't look the least bit displeased about it either. She looked proud. Proud that she stood up for herself? Fought back against an injustice, maybe? Even though she lost, it was worth it. Was that the message here? Standing up and fighting back is its own reward?

This cover was different from the Norman Rockwell paintings that showed idealized images of Americans—proud, strong, steadfast, paragons of virtue in the face of adversity. But it shared with those the portrayal of an ordinary person—a young girl in this case—having the courage to stand up for herself. To be unbowed.

Harry recalled Rockwell's paintings of The Four Freedoms, enumerated by FDR himself—freedom of worship, freedom from want, freedom of speech, freedom from fear. After first appearing in *The Saturday Evening Post*, they were all over the place. Millions of posters were printed, including those exhorting people to buy War Bonds, and a set of prints was given to those who did. The images hung in schools, post offices, and government buildings all over America. They were on postage stamps affixed to letters and cards you got every day. You couldn't miss them. And how those images, with their muted tones expressing such lustrous ideals,

MICHAEL VINES

filled Harry with pride. To be living in the land of the free—one of the luckiest people on earth.

But now, as he gazed at the picture of that smug little snot, Harry felt only a rising rage. It made him sick—sick of her entitlement, sick of her self-satisfaction, sick of her certainty and security, unless it could be shared by everyone. Rather than taking the magazine inside and throwing it in the trash where it belonged, as was his custom, he threw it back on the sidewalk and gave the little brat a good swift kick in the kisser, ripping the pages completely apart, and sending her on her way.

* * *

Harry's one-week grace period—not counting the forced labor—had passed. Waiting for the two hoods to arrive for their tribute, he worked without focus. He hit his thumb with his hammer, blackening its nail—a rookie mistake. He cut out a new sole and then forgot which shoe he had cut it for. Then he cut himself. He toyed with his awl, absently punching holes in a scrap of leather the way his grandsons did when they came by to visit. He was a mess. He got nothing done.

It was late afternoon when they finally showed up. Harry was almost relieved when they did, the operative word being "almost," the way the Rosenbergs might have been *almost* relieved when they were finally escorted to the chair the year before. At least the wait was over.

Tony the Pipe was not one to stand on ceremony. He didn't even say hello. Just, "Let's have it, Harry."

Harry did his best to act calm, despite not having experienced one second of calm all day long. He held his head up and spoke firmly.

"Let me say something to you, sir. What you're doing is not right. It's not the way to live in the world." Tony squinted and turned to his junior partner. Harry continued. "We have laws in this country. And what you're doing, this shaking down, it's against the law."

"Where the fuck am I?" Tony said, as much to himself as anyone else. "What the fuck is this?"

It wasn't a rhetorical question. He seemed genuinely perplexed and even a bit disoriented by Harry's response. As if he literally wanted to know where the fuck he was.

"Against the law?" Tony said. "Against the law?" He thought about that for a second, and then he burst out laughing. "Jesus Christ. Can you believe this guy?" He was asking Carlo, who laughed along with him.

"He's kiddin', Tony. Aren't ya, Harry? You're kiddin', right?"

Harry picked up a pamphlet he had placed on his counter and held it up, as if it would ward off Tony the way a cross would Dracula. "Have you read this?" he asked, now with a quaver in his voice. "The Constitution of the United States. This is the law.

We're a nation of laws."

Tony couldn't have been expecting this. He seemed to have crashed into an alternative universe and needed some time to get his bearings. When he finally did, he swatted the Constitution out of Harry's hand.

"I'll tell ya the law. The law is right here." And with that he whipped his pipe out of its holster. "Say hello to the fuckin' law. Now give me my fuckin' money."

Harry clung to his counter with both hands for support—at the moment he'd take any kind of support he could get. But to Tony, it must have looked like he was standing firm. Holding his ground.

"What the fuck am I gonna do with this guy? Is he gonna make me break his ribs right here and now?"

"Give 'im the money, Harry. Come on." That was Carlo Barnini. "He doesn't get it, Tony. That's all."

"Shut the fuck up." Carlo did. Then Tony turned back to Harry. "Listen you Jew kike motherfucker. You love your money so much? How much you love your money? Huh? You better figure it out, right now. Fuckin' Jew bastards are all alike."

So he had to go there. He'd threaten everybody, sure, but only Jews like Harry would get the cherry on top. Carlo didn't have much sway with Tony, obviously, but he was green enough and well connected enough to take one more stab at putting off the inevitable.

"Tony, this is his first time. He'll pay. Right, Harry? You'll give us the money? Give us the money, Harry."

Tony didn't wait for an answer. He charged behind the counter with the unwieldy power of an unpenned rodeo bull and punched open the cash register. It had only a few singles in it.

"Are you fuckin' kiddin' me?"

Carlo raised his eyes to heaven and threw up his hands. Tony frisked Harry roughly and when he came up dry, he pushed him hard against his shoe repair finishing machine. Something clicked and its gears and belts started whirring. Carlo shouted over the din.

"Harry, you'll get the money? Right? You'll get it today?"

"Tomorrow," Harry said. "Bank's closed."

That was true. It was after four.

"Fuckin' little Jew. Have 'em open the fuckin' Jew bank."

"He'll have it tomorrow, Tony."

"Fuck you, Barnini."

"We'll come back tomorrow. He'll have it. Right, Harry?"

Harry knew that there were only two ways to confront brute force like this: flee or give it back in equal measure. And neither was an option.

"I'll have it," Harry said.

"Okay," said Carlo. "Tomorrow. You'll have the

dough. No fuckin' around, okay?"

"Okay," said Harry.

"I oughta slam this pipe right into your fuckin' ribs," Tony said to Harry, before pushing him against the counter. Then he turned to Carlo. "And yours too." Short of doing that, Tony had only one other play. "Tomorrow then," he said to Harry. "You give me the money tomorrow. And double it."

"That's fair, Harry," Carlo said. "Tomorrow. First thing. Bright and early. Well, not too early. Tomorrow. No fuckin' around."

Harry watched them walk out the door as the racket of wheels and gears and belts and sanders of the shoe repair machine kept grinding behind him. He turned it off and waited for the silence to bring him relief. But it never came.

❋ ❋ ❋

That night, Lena fried Harry a steak in a cast iron skillet till it was well done and burnt the way he liked it, but he didn't eat much. He poured himself a shot of whiskey, which he did every night. Just one. He called it a schnapps. Then he poured another.

"What is it, Harry?" Lena asked.

"I'm not feeling so good tonight. I'll go to bed early."

Harry went to bed early, but got up early too, woken by his parched mouth at 2:30 in the morning. He got some water, slept fitfully for a couple more hours, and was finally up for good at six. He turned on TV and watched *Romper Room*. He liked it better than *Ding Dong School*. *Romper Room* was more civic-minded. And how did it begin? With Miss Nancy leading the kids in the Pledge of Allegiance (what else?), "under God" and all.

Harry didn't pledge along with them, but he stayed tuned to watch Mr. Do Bee and Mr. Don't Bee, who taught kids right from wrong. "Do be a sidewalk player. Don't be a street player. Do be a play-safe. Don't be a match toucher." That sort of thing. If only there had been a show like that for Tony Allocco to watch when he was growing up. It might have taught him some basic life lessons, like "Do be a nice person. Don't be a shakedown artist."

When Harry got to the street, he checked out his Bel Air again. This time there was no ticket on the windshield. But there was no windshield either. Harry ran to his machine, and there, on the front seat, surrounded by spider webs of shattered glass, he saw Tony Allocco's calling card—his metal pipe. A definite Mr. Don't Bee kind of thing to do. Don't be a windshield smasher.

Harry didn't expect them till the afternoon. Unlike the day before, he was able to concentrate on his work, expertly cutting strips of leather, stitching them together straight and true, precisely punching holes with his awl. He plied his trade like the craftsman he was and took pride in a job well done.

When they arrived late in the day, Tony looked

MICHAEL VINES

like he had just been startled awake by a terrible dream, but he always looked like that. And, as usual, he still seemed to be processing some terrible news. He had only one word for Harry.

"Money."

Harry handed him the cash, which he had gotten out of the bank first thing that morning. Tony counted it and shoved it into the pocket inside his jacket.

"Oh, Harry," he said, perking up a bit for the first time. "I lost one of my pipes. Last night I guess it was. Must'a misplaced it. You didn't see it around anywhere, did ya? By any chance?"

Harry nodded and handed Tony the pipe he had used to smash his windshield. Tony's eyes opened wide and he let out a breathy whistle. Carlo leaned in for a better look. It was a work of art.

"Very nice," Carlo said, admiring the beautifully crafted holster Harry had spent the day making, using the best leather he had in the shop.

Tony wasted no time taking off his old holster, holding a spare pipe, and trying Harry's on for size. He slipped it on, easily adjusted the length of the strap, which had ample room for his girth, and buckled it in place. The pipe fit snugly into the bespoke leather pocket and came out swiftly. Tony drew it out a few times in a quick, fluid motion.

"Fastest pipe in the West," he said.

Tony was ready to go now. He never said thanks. But just before he left, he pulled his pipe out of his new holster one last time and brandished it at Harry like he was about to flatten him. His idea of a joke. Harry cringed. Tony got a big kick out of that.

"Come on, Harry. I'm just playing with ya. Ha ha ha." Tony laughed and looked at his partner like he expected him to laugh too. Carlo made a half-hearted effort.

"You're all right, Harry," Carlo said. Then to Tony, "Didn't I tell ya? I told ya he was all right, right? You're all right, Harry."

Harry didn't respond. He just stood there, standing his ground. After submitting. Choosing the path of appeasement, you might say. And hoping for peace.

5

From her earliest memories, reading fairy tales as a child, Libby would always have preferred Prince Charming to have been a princess. And in her imagination, he always was. She remembered reading *Sleeping Beauty* in her second grade class at the Bryan Hill school, imagining herself as the beauty and her teacher as Princess Charming. The teacher happened to be Mrs. Aschenschmidt—she of the ruby red lips, auburn hair, and Teutonic bosom that had stoked the carnal desires of Libby's newly arrived immigrant father who rented a room from her—making Libby the second generation and the second gender of Beckers to fantasize about the *zaftig* widow.

Nothing came of it, of course, any more than it did with her father. However, Libby did have a little fling with a girl who was in that class with her. But not till later, when they were both in the seventh grade.

She and Lammy Delaney spent a lot of time together in the playground, skipping rope, playing tag and hopscotch, shrieking as they chased after one another, and playing all the other games that allow kids to touch and be physically, yet innocently, close. By the time they were twelve, Lammy had shown herself to be as precocious in her development as she was curious about what to do about it. Who better to experiment with than her best and oldest friend?

On a grey afternoon in the fall after school, Lammy told Libby that she wanted to show her something. Something secret. Lammy didn't take her regular route home, but led Libby through the back alley behind her house and down cracked concrete steps to the dirty basement, a dark repository of the building's innards, the place the coal chute led, and where you'd have to come down to bank the furnace to keep it burning through the night, and to light the water heater before you took a bath upstairs. There was a dark grey metal washing tub down there too, and a ringer to squeeze the water out of the clothes before they were hung on the line outside to air dry. There was also a shower head attached to an exposed water pipe.

Libby found it creepy but exciting at the same time, like she was watching some Boris Karloff movie where she was scared and on edge but couldn't pull herself away from it, intrigued to see what was going to happen next. Whatever it was, it would come with a frisson of fear and make her scream, of that she was sure.

"What'd you want to show me?" Libby asked.

Lammy unbuttoned her blouse to reveal the brassiere she wore underneath it.

"Look," she said. "You have one of these?"

"No."

Then Lammy reached back and unsnapped the clips of her bra strap. Her brand new breasts needed nothing to prop them up.

"You have these?"

Libby didn't answer, she just stared at the young blossoms bursting with pink buds and she tingled.

"Let's take a shower," Lammy said. And without waiting for an answer, she turned on the spigot, stripped out of her clothes, and said, "Come on, Libby. Take 'em off."

Libby did as she was told and they both stood under the stream of barely warm water.

"Go ahead, touch 'em," Lammy said, and Libby did, placing her palm on one of Lammy's breasts and holding it there in a tentative, almost clinical way, like she was feeling for a pulse rather than trying to turn her on. Lammy handed Libby a bar of soap and, without further instruction, Libby was soon rubbing a lather into her best friend's breasts and the next thing she knew they were kissing and Lammy was running a hand below Libby's belly and trying to push a finger inside her.

It was the most confused jumble of emotions Libby had ever experienced, thrilling and terrifying at the same time. She wanted to flee and to stay forever, but desire won out and she felt she couldn't have pulled away even if the building collapsed on top of them. It took a lot less than that. All it took was a sudden rumble that almost sounded like the building was coming down, but Libby knew that it wasn't. She knew exactly what it was—the coal man had come. And with him, came a black avalanche of coal and soot tumbling down the chute. Without a word, both girls threw their clothes over their wet bodies and ran up the steps out of the basement as fast as they could. Libby didn't stop running till she got all the way home.

She could think of nothing else the rest of the day, and that night, looking back on it from the bed she still shared with Tillie—Goldie had her own now, in the same room—Libby thought it was fitting that Lammy led her through the back alley and down to a dark, dirty basement where black coal hurtled down the chute. Dark, dirty, black. Those were the words for it. She wanted to undo it all. Wash it away. Wash the shower away. Make it not have happened. She couldn't imagine how she could ever face Lammy again.

And yet...she couldn't stop thinking about it and how much she wanted to take another shower with her.

They met a few more times like that, until Lammy got bold enough to start chasing boys, which didn't take much chasing on her part, and was, Libby concluded, what she really wanted all along. Libby saw herself as just a trial run, an undress rehearsal, like doing previews out of town before the big opening on Broadway.

After that, Lammy paid no attention to Libby at all. So rather than the beginning of a new kind of friendship, it was the end of an old one. Libby was humiliated, embarrassed, and hurt by the whole thing. So she repressed it. Pretended it never happened. And would certainly never happen again. It was—what? What was it? It was nothing. That's all. She denied that it happened. Denied her feelings. Denied who she was.

In high school Libby attracted lots of boys and went out on dates with them to the O'Fallon Theater and then to the Circle Fountain for an ice cream soda. She went to dances at Beaumont High, including the prom where she was on the Queen's court, escorted by Buddy Collins, one of the most popular boys in the class, the best athlete and—it might, therefore, go without saying—not even a Jew. He was handsome and sweet—a real prince. But he'd never be her princess.

In the summer Libby sometimes went to the ballpark with her girlfriends to see a Cardinals game. Women, including Libby, got dolled up, and the boys wore ties and two-tone wingtips, and the men wore suits along with their ubiquitous snap-brim fedoras or straw boaters. There was a lot of seeing and being seen going on at Sportsman's Park, which, as its name suggests, was a great place to meet guys. There were enough of them out there, even on Ladies Day—especially on Ladies Day—the guys being at least as interested in the girls as the game.

Though it was hard to admit it, even to herself, Libby was aware that for her, too, the primary attraction of Ladies Day was the ladies. Sometimes a particular girl in the stands might catch her eye and she'd spend the rest of the game stealing glances at her as clandestinely as possible. Sometimes it could be quite an ordeal. If the girl was sitting behind her, for example, she might pretend to have a kink in her neck and have to twist her head around as far as possible and hold it there for a second in order to work it out. Once, one of the guys she knew tried to be helpful and offered to massage her neck, and she'd have to let him, the two working at cross purposes. She'd look forward to the seventh-inning stretch when she could stand and twist and turn to her heart's content to get a better view of the girl behind her, and nobody would be the wiser.

Libby wouldn't dare approach the girl or just happen to go to the concession stand at the same time she did and engage her in small talk, just to be friendly. Something like, "Oh, I like your bag. Where'd you get it?" And then sort of see where things would lead from there—if an unspoken connection might be made. She wouldn't dream of doing that. She was there to watch the game. And maybe meet a nice guy, she kept reminding herself, inning after inning.

High school was rough on Libby. She was different, but not in a way that anyone would have ever guessed. Not in a way that she could have shared with anyone, even her closest friends, or

MICHAEL VINES

accept in herself. So despite how pretty she was and the winsome personality she probably inherited from her father, she always felt like something of an outsider. She didn't know what difference it would make, but she couldn't wait to get out of there.

After graduation most of Libby's female classmates went on to Miss Hickey's School for Secretaries, or got jobs in the ladies' departments at Stix Baer and Fuller (as the Grand-Leader was then called) or its rival, Famous-Barr, or maybe married their high school sweethearts without giving the slightest thought to the dark cloud looming just beyond the horizon—a new war that would soon take the boys away. And the girls themselves replaced them at local plants suddenly roused out of their Depression desuetude and retooled to make small arms ammunition, TNT for artillery shells, bomber turrets, amtracs, and anything else that could contribute to our national, segregated war effort to defend our freedoms and our way of life against Nazi and Jap aggression.

Libby didn't follow the path of her classmates and, unusually—as was typical of her—enrolled at Washington University, one block past the city limits, west of Skinker. And a million miles away from home.

Lena was resistant to the whole idea, but Harry was firm in his belief that everyone should have every opportunity in America, including girls —especially if they happened to be one of his daughters—so he found a way to come up with

$125 per semester to cover Libby's tuition. When that price doubled in her second year, it looked like the end of her days as a coed. But when she told her father that there was a course she wanted to take in fashion design being taught by Robert Mayes, who had designed the inaugural gown for Eleanor Roosevelt, that was all he had to hear. He was going to come up with that money even if it meant getting everything else they needed with Eagle Green Stamps.

It cost a dime for Libby to take the streetcar to school. Most of her classmates did the same, unless their parents lived in U. City or Clayton, close enough to walk, or could afford to put them up in the one campus dorm for women or three for men. Those were mostly for the out-of-towners, who came primarily from far-flung places like Illinois, Kansas, and Indiana. The dorm kids all came from money. They were the ones who wore the high status saddle shoes made by Spalding, whose distinctively shaped vamp set them apart from the cheap knockoffs Harry got for Libby. Same with her penny loafers, which were a faux version of the highly prized Bass Weejuns. You didn't have to have Libby's footwear pedigree to recognize the real McCoys. Everyone did.

Shoes were just one more thing to make Libby feel like an outsider. As far as she knew, there was no one else on campus like her. No one who seemed as different, as out of the mainstream as she did. Until she met Shelley Klein, the first New York Jew Libby

MICHAEL VINES

had ever known.

Shelley grew up in Brooklyn, but her father—a second-generation American whose grandfather made a fortune in the garment industry—moved the family to Manhattan when she was fifteen so they could live closer to Spence, the private, all-girls high school she attended on the Upper East Side. Most wealthy girls from back East stayed there for college, many going to one of the fancy sister schools like Wellesley or Bryn Mawr, which, before she got to Washington U., Libby had never even heard of. Shelley had her heart set on Smith, but her parents had other ideas—even if she could have gotten past the restrictive Jewish quota, which she did not. For a girl with Shelley's far too independent and rebellious spirit, they felt a little Midwestern leavening was just what the doctor ordered. And so they shipped her off to St. Louis and enrolled her at Washington University.

There was something just a bit off about Shelley that attracted Libby right off the bat. The sense that any convention existed just to be overthrown; every comforting middle class value, only to be debunked. Shelley didn't wear the coveted Spaldings, Weejuns, or the authentic Shetland sweaters that Libby could identify at twenty paces purely by their unique knit, but she could have if she wanted to. Her family might well have manufactured them. But she was too original for that. She wore other things, things in a dark monochromatic palette that gave her a unique style. She could wear an ordinary scarf in ways that made it seem that no one had ever worn a scarf before. And her dark, wavy brown hair was longer than was the fashion. She was beautiful, but in an unconventional, exotic way—there was something of the gypsy about her.

They met in their life drawing class. Libby loved her first chance to study a live nude model. She was totally immersed when rendering the female form, sometimes feeling herself getting lost in it, her line flowing across her paper like a caress. She had always been attracted to women's bodies, way more than men's, which did nothing for her, especially if they were hairy like Lenny Goldstein's, the guy her parents were always trying to push her on, even though he was practically like a cousin to her—she called his parents Uncle Meyer and Aunt Faye, for God's sake.

But she had other preferences. And why not? On the purest, aesthetic level alone, the female body always had universal appeal. Everybody was obsessed with it, going all the way back to classical sculpture and Renaissance paintings—although Michelangelo did have a thing for men's buttocks, Libby realized in her Art History class.

Libby and Shelley always sat next to each other in drawing class, commenting on each other's work. Shelley was competitive at first, but it was soon obvious that there was no competition—Libby was by far the better draftsman. They started having lunch together frequently after class, during which Shelley complained about the impossibility of

MICHAEL VINES

finding a bagel on campus.

"I'll take you to Pratzel's," Libby told her. "It's not far. Just off Delmar. Near the Loop. The best bagels. You'll love them."

"It'd also be nice if I could find a decent hot dog within a hundred miles of here. In New York, they're on almost every corner."

"What are you talking about? Hot dogs were invented in St. Louis."

"I never heard that."

"At the 1904 World's Fair."

"The hot dog?"

"Yes, the hot *dawg*," Libby said, imitating the way Shelley pronounced "dog", like a Chinese diphthong. "I love the way you say that."

"Whattya mean?"

"Your accent."

"I don't have an accent. You're the one."

"Me? I don't have an accent."

"Of course you do."

"There. There it is again. The way you say 'of course,'" which Libby imitated by eliminating any trace of the letter "r."

"When do they say that life begins, Libby?" Shelley shot back.

"Huh?"

"At what age? Life begins at...what?"

"Oh. Forty," said Libby.

Shelley burst out laughing. "You said 'farty,'" she said, imitating Libby's St. Louis accent. "It's not

89

'farty,' it's 'forty,'" which got them nowhere because Shelley's pronunciation was hardly standard, again ignoring the letter "r" and making the word sound more like "fawty."

When Libby learned that one of Shelley's passions—along with art, hot *dawgs*, and the ridiculous St. Louis accent—was the Brooklyn Dodgers, they made plans to go to a ball game together. And get a hot dawg. The Dodgers were coming to town and they were in a "dawgfight" with the Cardinals for first place. Libby thought it might be hard to get tickets in the heat of a pennant race, unless they could get standing room. But it turned out not to be a problem. In a miraculous display of the power of money and the connections that come with it, Shelley made one phone call to her father and just like that box seats were waiting for them at will-call—courtesy of the Brown Shoe Company— even though the park was packed. Libby had never seen influence flexed like that, let alone on her behalf. Or seen a game in seats so close to the field.

It was Saturday, September 13, 1941, eighty-five days away from the "date which will live in infamy," as FDR would tell the nation. Like everyone else, the girls couldn't have imagined anything like an attack on Pearl Harbor was just around the corner, and the troubled world on the brink of war was the farthest thing from their minds. They were at a ballgame. The Dodgers were in first, holding a one-game lead over the Cards.

"But tied on the loss side," Shelley pointed out,

MICHAEL VINES

meaning the Cardinals still held their fate in their hands, and proving that she knew what was what when it came to baseball.

And what a game they saw. It was a scoreless pitching duel, with both pitchers in complete command and both girls sitting on *shpilkes*—a word either one of them might have used to describe their tense and anxious state—for two hours and thirty-seven minutes. In the fifth, when the pressure was really starting to mount, Shelley conceded, "St. Louie's tough. Always has been. I've been scared of these guys since the Gashouse Gang," thus further, but unnecessarily, establishing her baseball bona fides.

As exciting as the game was, as absorbed as she was in it, Libby still had a little room left in her mind, or her heart, for other things. Like Shelley. She got a kick out of the way she kept calling it St. Louie, a pronunciation the locals would never use. Of course, by this point, Libby was a getting a kick out of everything Shelley said or did.

"No sauerkraut?" Shelley said. "What's a hot dawg without sauerkraut? And the mustard in this town's a joke. You never heard of Gulden's Spicy Brown?"

Charming, thought Libby.

"You're gonna have to come visit in New York, Libby. We'll eat hot dawgs and potato knishes till we explode."

What a lovely image, Libby mused.

During the seventh-inning stretch, when they both stood and squeezed each other's hands to relieve some of the tension, Libby felt a sense of foreboding sweep over her. It wasn't a premonition that the Dodgers were going to score in their next at-bat—which they did, with back-to-back doubles for the game's only run—but a fear that she was becoming infatuated with Shelley. And she was helpless to stop it. She could only hope that she wasn't falling in love.

They were on opposite sides, but Libby felt she and Shelley were sharing something special that brought them together. Shelley must have felt it too, for when the game ended neither was ready to part company just yet. They both needed time to catch their breath and settle down. Even though Sportsman's Park wasn't far from Libby's home on Warne, she suggested they take a streetcar to Forest Park, where they could walk it off for a while. The park's western boundary was Skinker Boulevard, across the street from campus. They could head in that direction.

By dusk, as the last of the day's visitors were straggling out of the park, they found themselves at the World's Fair Pavilion, a grand Spanish style open-air colonnade at the top of Government Hill, with red tiles on the roof, and a tower on each end. They stood together beneath one of its arches, close enough that their shoulders touched, and gazed at the fountain and reflective pool below them in complete silence. Libby couldn't have said

MICHAEL VINES

precisely what she was thinking, but she was filled with warmth, joy, and contentment. Suddenly, the fountain's lights went on, illuminating its thrusts of water in a rainbow of colors. And as if that were a cue, out of nowhere, Libby found herself being swept into Shelley's arms and kissed on the lips. She pulled herself away in shock.

"What are you doing?"

"Kissing you. It's called kissing." Libby could not speak, so Shelley filled the space. "I'm attracted to you. Are you attracted to me?"

"But, out here? In the open?"

That was all Shelley had to hear. She grabbed Libby's hand and the two girls raced together to Shelley's dorm, walking fast when they couldn't run another step, then running again when they were able. Shelley didn't have to worry about her roommate. She knew she'd be out for the evening.

Normal couples, like Shelley's roommate and her boyfriend, typically went out on Saturday night dates. If there were no dances scheduled, they might go to a movie at the Tivoli or the Varsity in the Delmar Loop, then drive up the road to Garavelli's on DeBaliviere for an after-movie snack and then, if things were working out, drive to Art Hill, just a short hop from the Pavilion, where they'd park in front of the Art Museum for some necking and heavy petting under the stony gaze of an equestrian statue of Louis IX of France, the city's namesake.

Libby had learned so much so fast. She had

met an upperclassman majoring in history who, in a futile attempt to get her up to Art Hill to see the statue up close, informed her that Louis IX, considered a reformer for his time, would, nevertheless, pluck out the eyes of a Mohammedan as soon as look at one; was quick to cut out the tongues of blasphemers or otherwise mutilate them; and was a well-known burner of books, with a particular zeal reserved for the Talmud and other Jewish texts. For this, he was memorialized in stone in full Crusade regalia mounted upon his caparison-clad steed, his arm outstretched and his sword held aloft as if he were ready to smite the young couples in cars if they started going too far. God only knows what he would have done had he suddenly become flesh, galloped over to Shelley's dorm room, and there beheld her and Libby in flagrante delicto.

For Libby, Shelley was a revelation. Everything about her was as authentic as the Spaldings, Weejuns, and Shetlands she didn't own because she was that authentic. She was real, honest, direct, and best of all, different. And she didn't give a damn what anybody thought. Not that she went so far as to be open about her sexual preferences, widely agreed among her peers to be perverted. But she didn't repress them either. Or feel the least bit guilty. Libby was sure she had something to learn from her on that score. All the passion that had been lying dormant within her all these years suddenly came bursting out, like the multicolored spouts of water shooting out of the illuminated fountain that they

MICHAEL VINES

had been watching from the Pavilion not long ago.

As they lay together in Shelley's narrow lower bunk, Libby opened up to her about everything that mattered—her feelings; her first inkling of her hidden nature; Lammy and even Mrs. Aschenschmidt; and most of all, her guilt. How she had felt so completely alone in the world. So isolated.

Shelley stroked Libby's hair and said, "You're not alone." Then she curled into her and whispered into her ear. "I can tell you something, but it has to be a secret. You can't tell anyone else. Can you promise me that?"

"Uh-huh."

"Say it."

"I promise."

"Swear to God?"

"I swear."

"On your honor of being a Jew?" This was a vow that few people outside of the religion had ever heard of before. But most people within it had.

"On my honor of being a Jew, I'll never tell anybody."

"Okay, then. I have it on very good authority, from a friend in New York, who has a friend, whose mother knows someone, who knows someone, who knows for a *fact*—are you ready for this?"

Libby nodded.

"Eleanor...Roosevelt...is one of us."

"What?" Libby couldn't believe it. "That's

impossible. She's married to the president."

"So?"

"So? Why would a woman who—"

"It happens."

Libby was dumbfounded. She couldn't quite believe it, but Shelley guaranteed it. And she ought to know. She was from New York. She had connections. And she supplied just the kind of detail that added credibility.

"Ever hear of Lorena Hickok?"

"No."

"She's a reporter. That's her lover. She lives in the White House, for God's sake."

"How do you know this?"

"I told you. I have a friend, who has a friend…"

So Shelley had it on good authority. And Libby, who was all too willing to believe it, did. She was convinced. And comforted. She wasn't alone. There were others. There was Shelley. There was Eleanor Roosevelt. There was Lorena Hickok, God bless her, whoever she was. It was okay. Libby was okay. Just don't tell anyone about it. And she wouldn't. There was no need. Because if it were true about Eleanor Roosevelt, Libby had nothing to worry about. Something to hide, maybe, but nothing to worry about. Nothing to fear, except fear itself. Her mother may never understand her or accept her. But that was okay too. Because now she was sure of at least one thing—even if her mother wouldn't, her father would. He just might even encourage her.

MICHAEL VINES

What's good for Franklin Roosevelt's wife was good for Harry Becker's girl.

6

Sam Brown, Goldie's husband and father of Marshall and Sandy, owned his own business operating on the tried and true Wall Street principle of "buy low, sell high." His area of expertise, however, was not in the rarified world of stocks and bonds, but the humbler realm of used auto parts, which he bought and sold in a junkyard located just across the northwest city limit in the town of Wellston. A hard worker in a physical trade, he came home every night with grease-stained hands and clothes, ate dinner, and fell asleep snoring on the sofa.

Sam was getting by, but Tillie's husband was the one with the big future ahead of him. Sid Gorman was a college man, courtesy of the G.I. Bill, and had been a rising star in the cost accounting department at McDonnell Aircraft. But even after a big promotion that put him on a career track to become manager, he decided he'd gone as far as he cared to go with the company and, about six months ago, in late '53, he and a colleague opened their own firm in a small office downtown. The gold letters stenciled on the frosted glass window of their door proclaimed: Gorman and Mendelson, Certified

Public Accountants. The family's first professional.

Tillie was anxious. After years of trying and two miscarriages, she was, at the time of Sid's big move, eight months pregnant with their second son, whom they would name Joseph. Sid had a steady job and a good salary. If he just stayed where he was, they'd be able to live out the full portion of the American Dream—a house in U. City where the best schools were, college for both boys, money in the bank, and a secure future. Freedom from want. Freedom from fear. Her mother tried to mollify her, preaching the gospel of American entrepreneurialism.

"Don't worry about Sid," Lena told her. "He can always earn a living. This is smart what he's doing. If your father had listened to me years ago, we'd all be sitting in clover today." In spite of all they had, Lena never let go of what might have been.

The baby was four months old now, and the only nipple he'd ever suckled was the rubber one on his bottle of formula. Neither Tillie nor Goldie ever even attempted to breastfeed their children. It was so old-fashioned and mother's milk wasn't as hearty or nutritious as the modern formula, they all believed.

Marty, only six, had no understanding of what his father did or why it was such a bold step for him to strike out on his own like that. But he could tell by the way everyone made such a big deal about it that his father was a special man.

Libby, still alone and without children of her

own, was the only sister who had a job, and a pretty high-toned one at that. She had parlayed her art degree and natural sense of style and taste into a job as an interior decorating consultant with the Famous-Barr department store. She was earning more than enough to support herself and live on her own, but in her world respectable women simply did not move out of their parents' home until they were married. It was unlike Libby to adhere to a convention like that, but, much as she wanted to have a place—and a life—of her own, she was afraid her mother would never understand. Family still mattered to Libby most of all, so she decided to keep the status quo—at least for a little longer. Besides, she loved being the favorite aunt and surrogate mom of her niece and nephews and wanted to stay close to them. Her parents made it tolerable for her by restoring what had originally been two upstairs apartments. She took one and had a front entrance all her own. A door separating the two flats could be locked with a latch on either side, so they all had their privacy. This was particularly important when Harry and Lena had one of their not infrequent dates—the ones that began with bourbon and sweet talk. Plus lace, silk, and high heeled shoes. Lena called it her *nafka* look.

When Passover arrived, the women of the house swung into action. The Beckers and their closest friends, the Goldsteins, began celebrating the holiday together back in the early 20s when they were still relative greenhorns, and the tradition continued to this day—about thirty years, give or take. Lena, Goldie, Tillie, and Faye Goldstein spent days preparing for the annual Seder. Libby, who had to work, pitched in when she could.

Lenny Goldstein hadn't been a regular guest for over a decade, since his freshman year at the University of Chicago where he now taught, but this year he was in town and joined everyone at the Beckers' table. He had rejected the formal observance of his people's particular opiate, including the High Holidays—an observance not even the most reformed Jews could abandon—but he loved Passover. Forgiveness and atonement were not his thing, but give him the opportunity to celebrate workers rising up against their oppressors, which is what Passover was all about, and he'd be there. Most years he held his own Seders with fellow travelers in Hyde Park, short on ritual but long, very long, on railing against the exploitation of labor.

Lenny more or less hijacked the Seder, telling the story of the Exodus as recounted in the Haggadah—Moses leading the Hebrews out of bondage in Egypt—in a fiery rendition fueled by multiple glasses of Mogen David and loaded like a spitball with his own spin on events, which included plenty of modern-day parallels to workers oppressed by industrialists around the world and commentary on capitalist greed in our own backyard. Harry, robed in a royal purple silk smoking jacket that he wore only for Seders and which gave him an anomalous regal air, tolerated Lenny's usurpation with the noblesse oblige befitting his appearance.

The Haggadah has a much anticipated break in the action so the hungry celebrants can finally eat. The feast began with Faye Goldstein's homemade chicken soup with matzo balls so dense they seemed to anchor somewhere in the alimentary canal where they were more abraded than digested. This was followed by gefilte fish made of carp and pike that Lena had ground by hand and might contain a stray sliver of bone. The main course was Goldie's overcooked brisket served with Tillie's vegetables that had been boiled till the last nutrient died. To top it all off, there was Libby's extra dry Passover apple cake served with that post-war miracle of American ingenuity, Reddi-Wip. And coffee, much of which was required to wash it down.

Sid smoked straight through dinner, often lighting a new cigarette from the smoldering tip of the previous one, until Tillie said, "Sid, enough already. Wait till after."

"She's the boss," Sid said with a good-natured wink at Marty as he smashed his butt into an ashtray next to his plate.

Just because the Seder was finished didn't mean Lenny was. He could exhaust the hell out of anyone. Especially Lena. She rose from her chair with a palpable sense of relief and she, with the rest of the women, went about clearing the table and washing the dishes. The kids, having located the *afikomen* —a piece of matzo hidden for them to find—

MICHAEL VINES

and receiving a quarter each for their efforts, were left to amuse themselves. The men sat around the table smoking and doing nothing, except for Lenny who continued to expound, mercifully out of Lena's earshot.

It was not a relief for Lena, however, when, after all the work was done and she was ready to call it a night, she saw Libby and Lenny huddled together in the front room having a quiet tête-à-tête. It was even more troubling when, as all the guests were leaving, Libby went to her room to get a jacket—a stylish red swing coat with oversized buttons and pleats in the back that she bought with her employee discount at Famous. It was a perk that Libby, who always had an eye for fashion, took full advantage of. She was never flashy. Far from it. But when she left her flat on Warne Avenue on her way to work downtown, she looked like a bird of paradise blooming in the desert. Her sisters, who dressed plainly—what they'd call *heimische*—understood her professional needs and didn't harbor the slightest jealously or resentment. Besides, they had the children.

"Mama, Lenny and I are gonna go for a little walk."

"It's late. Where are you going?"

"Just around the block. I'll be right back."

"Stay out of the park," Lena warned.

"Of course, Mama."

"Lenny, you'll walk her to the door."

"Absolutely. And thanks for a terrific Seder, Aunt

Lena. Great discussion. Just great."

At least he thought so. After they left, and Lena was alone with her husband, she said in Yiddish, "So, *nu*? Harry? Libby and Lenny?"

"So, *nu*?"

"I'm asking you."

"They went for a walk."

"A walk. *Balt*. He's gonna get her into trouble, Harry. He'll get her pregnant and he'll take her off to some socialist commune or something. And everybody will raise everybody else's children."

"You mean like a kibbutz?"

"Lenny Goldstein is not going to Israel. And what are you comparing? Israel's different."

Lena gave Israel a wide berth. All Jews did. Whatever Israel did, no matter how radical, how odd and unconventional, how questionable or dubious, they accepted without question. Children raised communally on a kibbutz? When you're building a new nation from scratch, whatever works. Women drafted in the military? If they were going to survive over there, it was all hands on deck. You couldn't judge Israel or hold it to the same standard as every other nation. Israel was different. And it had unwavering support among Diaspora Jews in America. Like so many families, the Beckers had a *pushke*—a blue and white tin box with a slot in the top for the loose change they put in it every day. They kept it on the kitchen counter and when it was full the money would go to planting trees in Israel.

MICHAEL VINES

They were Americans, but Israel was their country too.

"So don't compare Israel," Lena continued. "And did you hear him talk? Is he even a Jew anymore? The way he observes Passover? By adding matzo to his diet, he says."

"We're not so strict."

"More than that. I don't know what he's saying half the time. They'll wind up like the Rosenbergs if she's not careful."

Lena had expressed that concern before. But she didn't have to worry about that. Had she been privy to their conversation, she might have had other things to worry about. But not that.

* * *

When they had been sitting together in the front room after the Seder, Lenny told Libby about why he had come to St. Louis in the first place. And it wasn't for Passover. He was there at the request of Bernice Fischer, a union organizer he had known since they were both undergrads at the University Chicago. While she was still in school, she cofounded an organization called CORE, the Congress of Racial Equality. Fischer had also helped set up a chapter in St. Louis. And there was work to be done. Libby listened with passing interest, which became more focused when Lenny told her about CORE's mission.

"The crux of it is to end segregation and bring about racial equality. But I'd go further. We need equality for all people. And I mean *all*. All races, all creeds. All religions, all ethnic groups. Everyone, regardless of age, sex, or sexual orientation."

Sexual orientation? Libby asked him to repeat that. She had never before heard the words "sexual" and "orientation" used sequentially, but she understood immediately what it meant, and who and what it referred to, without Lenny's helpful explanation. She'd have bought into the principles anyway. Being Harry Becker's daughter, equality for all was in her genes. But this one thing, sexual orientation, was a new one to her, and it caught her attention. As everyone was leaving, Libby decided she needed to hear more and that's when she went out with Lenny for their walk.

The fresh spring air contributed to Libby's sense of hope and possibility as Lenny told her about Irv and Maggie Dagen, whose apartment was the headquarters for a group of interracial activists who met there to talk, plan, and strategize about how to fight for social justice—and win. They had been leaders in the movement that worked to integrate Washington University, which they finally succeeded in doing in 1952. Libby had never heard anything about this. She was so naïve that it never occurred to her that there were no Negroes at Washington U. when she went there. It had never crossed her mind that they weren't even allowed to attend, no matter how brilliant they might have been. But if one had, Libby would have noticed that, all right. They'd have stuck out like the negative of a photo of a full moon in a clear night sky.

"We're meeting Monday night," Lenny told Libby as they walked. "You ought to come. They live in U. City, near the Loop."

Those words, "near the Loop," triggered a memory in Libby that helped her understand one of the reasons she had been so oblivious in college. She wasn't just naïve, she was self-absorbed, and hopelessly in love—obsessed almost—with Shelley Klein. She was all Libby thought about. And when Lenny mentioned the Loop, it brought back wondrous, warm, delicious memories of Libby taking Shelley to Pratzel's bakery, not far from there, for fresh bagels at midnight.

Only a select few got into Pratzel's at that hour. But Libby had an in. Her friend Margie Burjoski, whom she knew from the Bais Abraham Synagogue, had a brother who was buddies with Nate Pratzel, the owner's son. Both were members of a YMHA club of well-mannered, good Jewish boys who went by the aspirational misnomer, the Rough Riders. No less rowdy an adventurer than Libby's Uncle Sid, Yeshiva boy and future certified public accountant, had been a Rough Rider too, a few years before Nate.

Margie, whom Nate had something of a thing for at the time, got the VIP treatment at Pratzel's and she took Libby and her friend Shelley there in the wee hours when the ovens were fired up. She rapped on the back door to the rhythm of "Shave and a Hair Cut, Two Bits," and said, "Hey, Nate. It's me, Margie. Open up."

Nate responded with the alacrity of a rutting stag, and in no time Margie and her friends were inside, grabbing freshly baked bagels hot out of the oven. Shelley was now a believer. They were the best, perfect just as they were.

"They don't even need a schmear," Shelley squealed with delight. She then had to explain to the others what a schmear was. For some reason, St. Louis Jews didn't use that word to denote cream cheese spread on a bagel.

With Margie's introduction as their credential, Nate let Libby and Shelley in any time they wanted, even when it was just the two of them. Any friend of Margie's was a friend of his. On nice nights, Libby and Shelley would grab some bagels, slip into the park to a sheltered spot they'd found not too far from Skinker, and wolf them down before taking turns going down on each other with still warm lips. Social injustice was the farthest thing from Libby's mind. And who could blame her?

That relationship didn't last forever. Libby got a letter from Shelley in July saying she wasn't coming back to Washington U. in the fall. She was transferring to Smith, where someone had managed to pull a few strings and get her in, despite the quotas. She didn't have to say anything else, but she did. And it was even worse. She was seeing someone who went there. A friend from her fancy high school. They had gotten back together over the summer, and well, what else do you need to know? Oh, there was the pro forma, "I'll always remember you, Libby." "We had such great times together." "You really meant a lot to me." "I'll miss you more than Pratzel's even." And "Love always, Shelley."

So that was it, just like that. A snap of the fingers. The same fingers—and the first and only—to have penetrated Libby's vagina, other than her own. To circle her clitoris and bring her to orgasm. With a mouth and tongue warmed by freshly baked bagels. Shelley's letter was glib and flirtatious, and Libby thought, "Why didn't she just shut up already? Just say, 'I'm not coming back. Nice knowing ya, kid. Have a great life. Goodbye,' and leave out all the other bullshit? She had to tell me about the other girl? She had to bring up Pratzel's?" which was code, of course, for oral sex.

It was so easy for Shelley and so hard for Libby. Everything was. Someone pulled some strings and just like that she got into Smith, as effortlessly as she got box seats for the Cardinal-Dodger game at the last second. And now she was back with some girl she never stopped loving, even while she was seducing Libby and being intimate with her and having sex with her all over the place—in the dorm, in the park, in the last row of the balcony at the Tivoli where they spent the whole movie fingering each other—all the fucking time.

Libby wrote her a long letter that covered

all the bases from understanding to confused, from exonerating to accusatory, from accepting to beseeching, from composed to out of control, and the moment she dropped it into the mailbox, she regretted it. What had she done? What was the point? Shelley never wrote back. Libby wanted to kill herself.

For Shelley, it was just a fling. For Libby, it was everlasting love. And suddenly, it was the end of the world. She'd never meet anyone like Shelley again. She'd never meet anyone again. And though her heart wasn't in it, Libby told herself that that would be for the best. It was all so crazy. An experiment gone wrong, a mistake. It never happened. Or if it did, it never would again. It was out of her system now. She was going straight.

Libby and Margie Burjoski started to become close around this time, and Margie was sharp enough to suspect that Libby and Shelley were bonded by something besides warm bagels. Libby, desperate for someone she could talk to, took a chance and confided in Margie—the only person she ever had.

Margie diagnosed Libby as being confused, that's all, something that would pass with time—and the sure-fire elixir of finding the right guy. And who was every girl's Mr. Right? None other than her own brother Bobby, a pre-med student at the University of Missouri and the sweetest ex-Rough Rider—not even a little rough around the edges—ever to attend their weekly meetings at the Young Men's Hebrew

Association on Union Avenue.

Bobby Burjoski was extremely good looking, with dark wavy hair, a gentle smile, and soft, delicate features that made him almost pretty. Not that there was anything effeminate about him. But he was cut from a different cloth than most guys —a high-thread-count cotton suited for satin bed sheets compared to the rough burlap of someone like Lenny Goldstein, for instance.

When Margie set them up, Libby was determined to give him every chance to sweep her off her feet. So wholehearted was her effort that by the end of the summer, Bobby had been swept off of his. The night before he was to go back to Columbia to begin his senior year at Mizzou, they parked on Art Hill for some good-bye necking and light petting. Shielded by foggy windows from the stern eye of Louis IX mounted atop his warhorse, Bobby worked himself into a lather, aching at the thought of having to leave Libby the next day, mumbling through lips pressed against hers that he had no interest in dating anyone else at school, that he couldn't wait for her to come up so he could show her off to his ZBT fraternity brothers, and finally, confessing exactly how he felt about her—how much he loved her and couldn't bear the thought of being away from her for even one minute. And before either of them knew what was happening or what they were doing, Libby found herself in the back seat with him.

Of course she didn't just "find herself" there. She knew what she was doing, all right, and she did it intentionally, that intention being to try to put Bobby off her, to show him that she was not really the kind of girl he thought she was after all. That she wasn't marriage material. Not realizing at the time that simply saying, "No, this is not my thing," would have been the surest and most honest way to demonstrate that, she allowed him to pull her skirt up and her panties down, and she opened up her legs for him. How strange it was for Libby. How terribly unpleasant and unsexy to feel him inside of her. She couldn't imagine why any woman would want a thing like that penetrating her body, let alone find it at all pleasurable. As Bobby entered her, slowly and gently enough, she supposed, but forcefully all the same, she lay there inert, more a receptacle than an active participant.

If she had intended to put him off, it didn't work. It was another experiment gone wrong. And now it was her turn to break a heart. All through autumn, it was she who was getting long, lovelorn letters. Bobby apologized again and again for the terrible mistake he had made on Art Hill. His respect for her, he wrote, in his fine, somewhat feminine cursive, was as sincere and undying as his love, and he promised it would never happen again. At least not before they were married—and she could consider that letter a proposal, one he'd repeat in future letters. He implored her to take it as seriously as he intended it and begged her to give him a chance.

When he was home for Thanksgiving, she could hardly refuse to see him, and they met for coffee in the Loop. Before going there, she had rehearsed what she would say. Sure, she "liked him, maybe loved him even, but not in 'that way.'" Libby was peremptory. She simply had no interest in repeating the mistake she had made on the scratchy, cracked leather backseat of his old Ford—nor, even, on 600-thread-count sheets of Egyptian cotton in the bridal suite of the Chase Hotel. And if she had no interest in that, not even with the gorgeous pre-med heartthrob, Bobby Burjoski, what man could she ever have an interest in? That's what her mother wanted to know. And Libby had no answer.

So she resigned herself to spinsterhood. She embraced celibacy, knowing she had no desire for a man and not daring to risk another relationship with a woman, even if she could find one she was attracted to and interested in, which she couldn't, of course. Not like Shelley. Not in a million years.

But there was this young, rather beautiful woman whom she certainly found physically attractive, if not very interesting. She was a newlywed planning to redecorate the Ladue mansion of her much older husband in order to expunge any trace of his former wife. The client had all the money in the world but knew from nothing. She met Libby at Famous-Barr, liked her, and trusted her taste, which was impeccable—at least that much she could discern—and she decided to consult with Libby on a complete makeover of each of her home's fourteen rooms.

First on the list was the master bedroom. She

couldn't bring herself to lie in the same bed her husband had shared with his ex, and she didn't. She slept in one of five other bedrooms, which she could barely abide either. She made an appointment for Libby to come to her home, located in the most affluent section of St. Louis's most affluent suburb, to see the space and get some ideas of what she could do.

The bedroom was bright and airy with French doors opening on acres of rolling green grass fit for a fairway, a professionally tended garden, a gazebo, and a swimming pool with a pool house big and well-appointed enough to live in. Libby was enthralled by the possibilities. When she returned a second time with a layout, swatches, and binders full of furniture to choose from, she had not expected that one of the possibilities was that the two of them would wind up sprawled on the bed the newlywed had never even lain in, tearing at each other's clothes, ripping a button off Libby's smart suit jacket fitted at the waist, and groping each other like it was the first and last time either of them would ever feel anything approaching sexual desire.

But Libby's desire couldn't begin to compensate for the cavernous emptiness that followed. There wasn't an alley within miles and miles, but now, in Libby's mind, the gorgeous home was nothing but an upscale suburban version of Lammy Delaney's dark, sooty basement. She felt ashamed, dirty, and, despite being a willing, even eager participant, somehow used.

MICHAEL VINES

Landing the job was a coup for Libby. Fourteen rooms in Ladue could bring in a fortune. She'd be a star. But now she didn't want it. She dreaded seeing her client again and was always cautiously on the lookout for her when she stepped onto the floor at Famous, hoping to see her before she was seen so she could make herself scarce in a hurry. She hoped and prayed the newlywed wouldn't phone her again. But when she did, Libby apologized for being busy and referred her to another decorator. Even that dim dame got the message.

But now, here was Lenny Goldstein, of all people, to the rescue. Not in the role of Prince Charming, but in the role of...of what? Moses. A great liberator with a beard. Even though she missed the fight to integrate Washington U., Libby now realized that that fight was her fight. Take the story of Passover and replace Hebrews in Egypt with Negroes in America, the way Lenny did during the Seder, and it all fit. Now substitute Negroes with dykes, and it fit too. Negroes might now be accepted at the university, but if you were gay, you better keep your head down and your mouth shut about it. And that oppression had to end too. And all of a sudden, along comes Lenny Goldstein offering something she had never even imagined possible. Liberation. The freedom to be who she was. To be accepted, not just by others, but by herself.

It had been a long time before Libby could look at a Pratzel's bagel without thinking of Shelley, and even if she still sometimes did, at least it no longer

HARRY GETS WISE

hurt. She remembered Shelley teasing her about her accent.

"When do they say life begins, Libby? At what age? Life begins at...what?"

At farty. Life begins at farty. Although now Libby pronounced it the proper way. Forty. She had practiced. Along with all those other "o-r" words that were pronounced "ar" in St. Louis. She must have said "Farty shart harses" a million times till she got it right. Forty short horses. She had to train those facial muscles. It required a lot of concentration. Especially when an "o-r" word was followed by an "a-r" word, or vice versa. That could be tricky. To this day she could overcompensate and was as likely to say "narth store" as "north star," or "carner bore" as "corner bar," if she wasn't careful.

If what they say is true—that life begins at forty—Libby still had a way to go. But maybe she wouldn't have to wait that long anymore. Maybe her life could start sooner. Maybe it could start now.

7

Tony the Pipe and Carlo Barnini were reliable, at least—you'd have to give them credit for that. They dropped in on the Liberty Shoe Doctor every Thursday without fail, always in the late afternoon just before closing time. And Harry, equally reliable, always gave them the money they had come to collect.

After a few months, Harry was relieved to see that Carlo started coming alone. The kid had a little experience by then and, because it was such a routine job—with no chance of resistance—the boss thought that sending The Pipe was a waste of good plumbing supplies. The last thing Tony did, though, before turning things over to Carlo, was to raise the amount Harry had to pay. Not by a lot, but enough to squeeze him that much harder.

Benny the B was true to the promise he had made to himself to give the kid every opportunity. Carlo now had the territory to himself, including the B's blessing to run the numbers racket there, and a chance to prove himself.

Like everybody else, Carlo grew fond of Harry and sometimes he'd drop by just to shoot the breeze. This was highly unprofessional, of course, and if

Benny the B got wind of it, he'd probably take Carlo aside, slap him in the back of the head, and say something like, "What the fuck, Carlo? What are you, a fuckin' *gavone*? Whatsamatta with you?"

But he never found out. He was more of a big-picture guy and was pretty laissez-faire when it came to small potatoes like the North Side. Just do what had to be done and bring in the dough. He didn't much care about the details. In fact, sometimes the less he knew, the better he liked it.

There was something about Carlo Barnini that appealed to Harry, in spite of himself. Maybe it was because Carlo still displayed a surprising air of innocence. Perhaps it was that, by comparison to his former partner, anyway, who'd threaten you with his *ferkakta* pipe before you knew what hit you, Carlo, despite his bravado, had a gentle quality to him—even a certain kindness. Harry could see it in his soft blue eyes. There was a human behind them, not a brute. Carlo did his best to hide it, play the tough guy, but he didn't fool Harry. He saw how Carlo rolled his eyes at his aggressive partner behind his back. He saw how Carlo tried to rein Tony in after he went berserk when Harry waved the Constitution at him and explained the rule of law. Carlo was definitely not a hardened killer. At least not yet. Despite their vast differences in age, background, and anything else that Harry could observe and measure, Carlo seemed almost like a kindred spirit.

One afternoon—not a collection day—Carlo came by, stretched out his long legs and made

MICHAEL VINES

himself as comfortable as he could on the hard wooden chairs on the customers' side of Harry's counter while Harry worked on a new sole. They talked a little about the Cardinals who, despite having a couple of standout players, like Musial and Red Schoendienst, and having just won six out of their last seven, didn't seem to Carlo like they were going anywhere. 1954 wasn't going to be their year. Harry wasn't so sure. It was so early yet. And they had this rookie named Wally Moon who everyone agreed had a lot of promise.

"Their pitchin's garbage, Harry. After Haddix they got nothin'. Can't win with those arms," Carlo said.

It was hard to argue with that, but the season had just begun and Harry wasn't ready to throw in the towel so soon. He held out hope. Carlo then changed the subject to something that he had clearly been thinking about for a while.

"You know what I need, Harry? A nickname."

"What, like Tony the Pipe?"

"Well, yeah. That's a pretty good one. For him. I mean his pipe and all. But I need one that works for me. Got any ideas?"

"Me? I don't know from nicknames."

"Yeah, well, whaddya think of this." He paused dramatically and struck a Hollywood-leading-man pose. "Handsome Carlo?'"

Harry took a good look at Carlo's face, then raised his eyebrows and cocked his head as he considered it. "Well, you are handsome, Carlo."

"Ya think?" Carlo clearly knew he was, and was proud of it, but was obviously just feigning modesty. "Yeah, I guess I'm easy enough on the eyes. I could mention a few ladies that think so too. One of 'em, I was asking her about it, she came up with this. Pretty Boy Barnini."

"Pretty Boy?"

"Got a nice ring to it, don't ya think. The way it sounds. Boy and Barnini. Pretty Boy Barnini?"

"Eh. Pretty is for a girl. Men are handsome, not pretty."

"Well, there was Pretty Boy Floyd."

"So, it's been used."

"Yeah. And I sure wouldn't wanna wind up like him."

It went on like this for a while, with consideration given to Carlo the Face Barnini, or just Face Barnini. Then simply The Face. He threw Gorgeous Carlo out there, but there was a wrestler who called himself Gorgeous George who grew his hair long, dyed it platinum blonde, wore it in curls, and adopted a feminine persona anomalous for the hyper-macho world of wrestling. He was, as they said, on the flamboyant side, meaning he carried on like a *faygala*. There was no room for that in Carlo's line, so he dropped it on the spot. He put Baby Blue Eyes Barnini up for consideration, but it was too long so he shortened it to Blue Eyes Barnini, before he circled back to just Baby Blue, which morphed

MICHAEL VINES

into Baby Barnini, but what percentage was there in being a baby? But baby led naturally to Bambino. And Carlo liked that one. The Bambino, like Babe Ruth. The Sultan of Swat. Which gave Carlo a new idea.

"How 'bout this? Bats Barnini. I love that."

He explained to Harry why it appealed to him. First, he seemed to be partial to alliteration, a word neither of them would have known, but he liked the sound of repeating consonants. But even more, Bats implied the potential for violence—using bats as a tool of enforcement, the way Tony used pipes. Plus it conveyed the sense that maybe Carlo was a little nuts, a little batty, and, therefore, frighteningly unpredictable. Someone you'd have to watch out for at all times.

"You use bats?" Harry asked.

"I could start. Keep one in the back seat. Walk around with it. Why not?"

Carlo was selling himself on the idea, but Harry shrugged. "You don't seem like that guy to me."

"Well, maybe I should be," Carlo said, becoming defensive and frustrated. He turned to the side table next to his chair and picked up the magazine Harry had placed there.

"Hey, how 'bout this? Huh? Right in front of my nose. This could be it."

He held up the current issue of *The Saturday Evening Post*, dated May 1, 1954, featuring none other than Stan Musial on the cover. It wasn't by

121

Rockwell, but it was rendered in a similar style by an artist named John Falter. Harry didn't subscribe to the magazine and never read it, but a woman in the neighborhood did, and she regularly brought back issues to Harry's shop for his customers to glance at while they waited. But Harry didn't wait for her to deliver this edition. As soon as he saw Stan on the cover at the newsstand, he eagerly shelled out the fifteen cents it cost to buy it for himself. Along with about everybody else in town.

There was Musial in his snappy Cardinal home whites with red trim standing on the steps of the dugout signing autographs for a group of adoring all white, all-American kids who were reaching out to him with pens, pads, and a baseball. Stan had a reputation of being not just one of the greatest players—the day after the magazine's publication date he became the first ever to hit five homers in a double header, as if to prove he belonged on the cover—but hands down the nicest guy in baseball. So the portrait captured his character perfectly. Here was a good man who cared about the fans, especially the kids. You got a sense that he'd be signing autographs till they had to physically pull him away to start the game. He was indeed Stan the Mensch.

"Carlo The Man," Carlo said. "Now that's a nickname. The Man." He took it out for a test drive. "Hey, where's the Man? Uh-oh, here comes the Man. This is a job for the Man."

"Carlo," Harry said, putting down the knife he was using to cut a sole and leaning toward Carlo

MICHAEL VINES

to get his full attention. "First, it's taken. Second, you can't give yourself your own nickname. Other people have to give it to you. It has to be something that's real about who you are. Something true. On the inside. And if it's good, it sticks. You have no say so in this."

"Well, I could sorta plant the idea in someone's head. Ya know? Like you. You start calling me the Man. Like you see Lucille, you say, 'Seen the Man around?' She'll say, 'Who's the Man?' You tell her that's what they call me. Right? You call me the Man, other people would too. They respect you, Harry. It'll catch on."

"It won't work, Carlo. You're too young to be the Man."

"I'm twenty-fuckin'-one years old."

"That's what I'm saying. Carlo the Kid, maybe. That would work." Harry was thinking Carlo the *Pisher*, the Yiddish word used with condescension for a little punk who was still wet behind the ears and maybe too big for his britches, but he didn't say it.

"I'm not gonna be Carlo the Kid, okay? Forget about it. I'm not a kid. I'm twenty-one. I got my own territory. So don't call me kid."

"Fine, fine. But you can't be the Man. Not at your age."

"Bullshit."

"People would laugh."

"They better not. I start carrying around a

baseball bat, they'll call me Bats. That's how you get a reputation."

"I don't know, Carlo. You don't seem like someone who goes around klopping people over the head with bats."

"Oh yeah? Well, you'll see, Harry. You don't know who I am. You don't know what I can do. One day, you'll find out. And you better hope you're not sorry."

Carlo returned to the magazine and began turning the pages with a vengeance, almost ripping them out as he went. Suddenly, he stopped on a page that caught his attention and said, "What a bunch of crap."

"What?"

Carlo turned the magazine towards Harry so he could see what he was reacting to—an ad for Timex featuring World Heavyweight Champion Rocky Marciano punching a heavy bag while wearing a Timex watch. The headline read, "The Watch 'The Rock' Couldn't Stop!"

"The Champ's punchin' a body bag wearin' a fuckin' Timex. You know why? 'Cause he couldn't care less about that worthless piece o' shit."

"'It takes a lickin' and keeps on tickin'.' That's what they're saying."

"Yeah, I get it. I wouldn't be caught dead in that fuckin' thing."

"What do you want? It keeps good time."

"You think I give a shit what time it is? You

MICHAEL VINES

don't wear a watch 'cause you wanna know what time it is, Harry. You wear a watch 'cause it's got class. Like that Rolex Tony wears. Betcha a hundred bucks, Harry, my paisan here, the Rock, he took that money they paid him to wear the Timex and bought a Rolex with it. Like Tony's. I'm gettin' one of those, definitely. That's fuckin' class."

"Why? 'Cause it costs a lot of money?"

Carlo was exasperated. "Yeah, Harry. 'Cause it costs a lotta money. Whaddya think, I'm gonna wear some twelve-dollar piece o' crap? 'Course, I wouldn't be paying full price for a Rolex. I know a guy, if you know what I mean."

"What d'ya mean?"

"Don't you know nothin', Harry? He can get it for me wholesale. Very wholesale."

"So, good. Go, get the watch if it makes you happy."

"Why wouldn't it? Every time I looked at it I'd be happy."

"Then *gezunterheyt*."

"Excuse me, Harry, did I sneeze?"

"It means in good health. Go with the watch in good health."

"Ge-what? Say that again."

"*Gezunterheyt*."

"*Gezunterheyt*. I like that."

* * *

A few days later Harry had just locked up the shop with his usual vigor and was on his way home to have lunch and tickle his baby grandson's belly, which they both got a kick out of—Harry at least as much as little Joey—when he saw Carlo hustling towards him like something was up.

"Harry, come with me."

"Where?"

"Don't worry where. Come on."

"I'm going home for lunch."

"I'll buy you lunch. This way."

Carlo grabbed Harry's arm and pulled him in the opposite direction from home and straight to Ed's Pool Hall. As they walked in, Carlo called out, "Hey, Ed. Two beers," and then he commandeered one of three open tables. Ed crept over with a spectral gait and handed two bottles to Carlo, who handed one to Harry with the single word, "Lunch."

"I drink Budweiser," Harry said with a Falstaff in hand.

"Next one. Rack 'em, Ed. Nine-ball."

And while Ed was sorting the balls in the diamond-shaped rack with the nine-ball in the middle, Carlo asked, "You play pool, Harry?"

"Never."

"Well, I'm gonna show ya how."

Carlo wasn't a bad teacher. He had to show him everything in reverse because Carlo was a lefty, but he taught Harry how to chalk up the tip of his cue, form a bridge with his left hand, grip the cue handle lightly in his right hand, line up his shot, and hit the cue ball with a firm, steady stroke. Then he taught him the rules of Nine-ball.

"Nickel a ball, Harry, whaddya say?"

"What nickel?"

"I give you a nickel for every shot you sink, you give me a nickel for every one I do."

"You think I'm some kind of schlemiel, Carlo?"

"Come on, Harry. It'll be fun."

"Fun, fine. But not for money."

"Fuckin' killjoy. Okay, start off, we'll play for fun. But once you get the hang, you gotta put some skin in the game."

Harry didn't commit, but he went ahead anyway, just to humor Carlo and get it over with. Once he started playing, however, Harry realized that not only was it fun, but he had something of a knack for it. When he called a shot and sank it, Carlo said it was beginner's luck. Sure, there was some luck involved, but it was more than that. Because Harry, a skilled craftsman, had an artist's eye and touch. He also had the hand-eye coordination of an athlete, which, never having played any sports, came as a surprise to him. Carlo was not so gifted, but he was able to handle Harry easily enough. For now, anyway.

It was only the second time Harry had been inside Ed's, the first since his failed attempt to get him to sign his petition. But it wasn't the last. Harry got the bug. He started going to Ed's so often he became something of a regular—enough so that Ed snapped the cap off a Budweiser as soon as Harry walked in and said, "Rack 'em, Ed," just like any other pool-hall rat. Nine-ball, Harry's game of choice, went without saying.

He started getting better, and the better he got, the more he wanted to play—had to play. He thought about the game all the time and soon everything was an angle he was measuring as if he were lining up a shot. The glass of seltzer on his kitchen table in relationship to the bottle. Where would he hit the glass, and how hard so that it struck the bottle at the precise point with the exact force to send it just over the edge of the table? Seltzer bottle, side pocket, Harry said to himself. When he was on the felt, Harry practiced not only sinking his called shots, but perfecting techniques he picked up from fellow players, like putting draw and English on the cue ball to leave himself in good position for the next shot. Before long, Harry was thinking two and three shots ahead.

Soon he got good enough to hold his own against Carlo and he was playing for a nickel a ball. He generally broke even. But one night, Harry was really on his game and ran the table on him.

"You been sandbaggin' me, Harry?"

"What's sandbaggin'?"

"It's pretendin' you can't play pool when you can. You're a fuckin' shark, Harry." Carlo threw his cue across the table and called Ed for another beer.

MICHAEL VINES

Another time, in a tight game, Carlo inadvertently kissed the cue ball with his stick while he was still setting up his shot. Harry called him on it.

"Nice shot, Carlo. Move over."

"What?"

"You hit the cue ball. My shot."

"Bullshit. I didn't hit the fuckin' cue ball."

"You think I can't see with mine own eyes?"

"That wasn't a shot. I barely touched it."

"But you touched it. My turn."

"That didn't count."

"It's the rules. It counts."

"Well, fuck the rules. Don't be such a little old lady, Harry. Get outta the way, I'm shootin'."

"Okay, then. Game over."

"Harry, gimme a break, will ya?"

But Harry wouldn't give him a break. He refused to play with Carlo if he was going to cheat. Carlo caught up with Harry as he was walking out of Ed's and, when they were back outside, he picked up where he left off.

"Man, you're one fuckin' hard-ass, Harry."

"You gotta play by the rules, Carlo. You can't just make 'em up as you go along."

They were about to cross the street when a brand new Cadillac, its horn blaring, came speeding by and forced them back onto the curb.

"Hey, fuck you," Carlo shouted and gestured at the driver as he passed. "See that, Caddy,

Harry. That's the car for me. A great big Cadillac convertible. Baby blue to match my eyes. Boy, the dames will really go for that."

"So get a Cadillac. *Gezunterheyt.*"

"I will. As soon as I get the scratch."

"What is 'the scratch?'"

"Money, honey."

"Then go make money."

"Oh, excuse me, Harry. You got a problem with money? Like it's the root of all evil or somethin'?"

"I don't say that. We all need money. Being selfish —that's the root of all evil. So go make money. Just don't be selfish. And play by the rules." Harry wasn't about to let that go.

"Playin' by the rules is a chump's game, Harry. You gotta look out for number one."

"That's no way to live. We look out for each other. We all have the same rules."

"Yeah? And what if someone doesn't give a shit about the fuckin' rules? Even one person, Harry. He'll take over is what'll happen. Only saps play by the rules. Like you. And where's it got ya?"

"I'm doin' fine, thank you."

"You drive a fuckin' Chevy."

"What's wrong with a Chevy?"

"It ain't a Cadillac is what's wrong with it."

"Where can I go in a Cadillac that I can't go in Chevy."

"You don't get it, do ya? It's not where you go. It's how you get there? Know what I'm sayin'?"

"Sure. That's what I'm saying too. And you gotta get there fair and square."

"That'll get you nowhere, Harry. Believe me."

"If everybody thought the way you do, Carlo, where would we be?"

Carlo threw his hands up in the air. "We'd be right here. 'Cause that's the way everybody thinks. Everybody looks out for number one. That's the only rule that counts. Look, you're a good man, Harry. That's why everybody likes you. But you wouldn't scare a flea. Guys like you—the boss eats guys like you alive. You're sheep to the slaughter."

Carlo lit up his last Chesterfield and deliberately threw the empty pack on the sidewalk right in front of Harry who, of course, picked it up.

"What's the matter with you, Carlo? You don't do that."

"You see. That's exactly what I'm talkin' about. Who goes around pickin' up other people's trash? Only you, Harry."

"Don't litter. That's a rule. You follow the rules. That's what means being a good citizen."

"Yeah, well, citizens are suckers."

"Maybe in your world, not in mine."

"What world you livin' in, Harry?"

"In America. Where we have rules. We have laws."

"And who makes 'em, Harry?"

"The people. The people make the laws."

"Oh, for fuck's sake. The bosses make the laws.

The guys with dough and muscle. We'd all be bosses if we could. And one day I'm gonna be."

"Be a boss then."

"Don't worry, I will. Bosses rule the world. That's the way it works. And if you cross 'em, good luck, 'cause you're gonna need it."

"I don't know people like that."

"You know me. And there's a lot more like me than you. You know, sometimes I worry about you, Harry."

* * *

Harry never forgot that conversation. He thought about it often, played it over in his head and tried to come to terms with Carlo's worldview. It was a creed of selfishness. The root of all evil. And Carlo wasn't alone. Everything was about power and money and looking out for number one. To Harry's way of thinking, that's why the world was and always had been such a mess, so unjust. People wanted what they wanted, and if they got that, they wanted more. And they'd do anything to get it. Maybe Carlo was right. They'd all be bosses if they could.

If that were the case, how could there be a just society? Life, liberty, and the pursuit of happiness. Everybody remembered that phrase from the Declaration of Independence and repeated it all the time. But if you could peel the words away

MICHAEL VINES

from the parchment and read them apart from the sacred trappings, couldn't liberty and the pursuit of happiness be considered a creed of selfishness too?

Harry needed to think this through. And he did so aloud, using his old friend Goldstein as his sounding board. They were at the Florissant Lanes, lacing up their bowling shoes when Harry broached the subject with him.

"You know the Declaration of Independence, Meyer. It says we have the right to life, liberty, and the pursuit of happiness."

"Yeah."

"Well, what do you think?"

"What do I think?"

"Yeah, what do you think?"

Goldstein had obviously never given it a moment's thought in his life. "I think that's right. That's America."

"Okay, now let me ask you. What if what makes me happy is being selfish. Only thinking of myself? Looking out for number one, that's what they call it. You know what I'm saying?"

"No," said Goldstein, who generally didn't delve too deeply into such matters.

"What I'm asking you is, what if what makes me happy is being a selfish good-for-nothing. What if to me liberty means the liberty to take everything for myself and the hell with everybody else? To make my own rules? Not follow the law."

"You can't do that. Not here. You go to jail."

133

"Ha!" said Harry, using the tone Lena sometimes used on him.

Harry dropped the subject, but he chewed on it as he bowled. In the fifth frame, with their score tied at forty-three—Harry was much better than that but he wasn't concentrating on bowling—he sprung another surprise question on Goldstein.

"What about the Preamble to the Constitution? You remember what it says?"

"Remind me."

"Exactly. Nobody talks about that. It says that the Constitution is to promote the general welfare. That they don't remember. But it should count for something too, no? It's more important if you ask me. 'Cause if you promote the general welfare, you can't look out only for number one. You can't be a selfish son of a bitch."

"Harry, what are you making such a spiel? We're here to bowl. To relax."

Goldstein bought Harry a Budweiser and a Falstaff for himself, and Harry dropped the subject. But he kept thinking about this moral dilemma, trying to come to terms with human nature and what it meant for the promise of America.

He remembered what Lena had said to him when he was agonizing over Joe McCarthy and the hearings he watched on TV. She said that America was a young country. It was still learning. But it would grow out of it. It was America, after all. Harry latched onto that and wrapped himself in the

MICHAEL VINES

comforting mantle of hope. Perhaps America was still just a promising rookie, like Wally Moon. But to live up to its potential, to earn its place in the Hall of Fame, everyone, all its citizens, had to be onboard and do their part. To play by the rules and promote the general welfare.

And what were the chances of that, he wondered? Zero. If all we cared about were ourselves, our own individual liberty to be as selfish and greedy as we pleased, it wouldn't take much to pull down the nation by its very foundation. Just a few of the basest, most venal, most corrupt, and most selfish would suffice. Maybe it would take only one, if he were the right one—meaning the wrong one. Make him the boss and what would happen then? Harry had seen it before. But in other places. Not here.

As Harry considered this, it reminded him of something that the Hassidim believed, only in reverse. The Hassidim—the fanatic followers of the Baal Shem Tov, an eighteenth century Jewish mystic who lived variously in the Ukraine, Galicia, what was Poland one day, Russia the next (Harry's original stomping grounds), all within the Pale of Settlement, the sole area in Eastern Europe where Jews were permitted to reside, though hardly unmolested. The Hassidim were *meshugganas* all, in Harry's estimation, but they meant well. They weren't looking out for number one. In fact, quite the opposite. They were looking out for everybody, for all mankind, and they believed in the power of collective action to achieve their greatest dream.

Among their beliefs was this doozy: if all Jews, every last one of them all over the world, observed the Shabbos properly, together, on the same day, just once, it would usher in the arrival of the Messiah, who, though currently existing only in the divine realm, was said to be on a first-name basis with the Baal Shem Tov—the Besht, to his friends— with whom he had regular conversations. Just one universal observance of the Shabbos, and the world would be redeemed, suffering would end, Paradise would be restored.

Of course, what was the likelihood of getting all Jews to agree to do that? Getting a bunch of Jews to agree on anything, on where to eat lunch, even, would be a tall enough order. But observing Shabbos? And if it were required that all Jews participate, that would have to include not just the selectively observant Harry Beckers of the world, but the recalcitrant refuseniks like Lenny Goldstein too. And that was about as likely to happen as getting every American to be just, honorable, and selflessly upholding the nation's founding ideals. Both are fabulous. Both impossible. Maybe that was their point. Like a little Hassidic inside joke. They set the bar unachievably high. Jews were never all going to observe Shabbos. So the Messiah was never going to arrive. Get it? But then again, maybe they actually believed it.

It took a special kind of person to believe something like that. It took a person capable of faith.

MICHAEL VINES

Unalterable, unwavering, no matter how dilatory the Messiah. Harry marveled at the Hassidim, the Christians, and all the other religionists who believe the things they do—without so much as a scintilla of evidence, and even less of doubt. And if they believed those things, what else were they capable of believing? It made Harry worry about how easily they could be duped, conned, sold a bill of goods, fall under the spell of a strongman, a charismatic tyrant who'd play upon their greatest fears, like death, for instance, tell them all would be well in the end if they just followed him. They'd do whatever he said, even go so far as to give up their freedom —without realizing that's what they were doing— for the chimera of something better beyond. They might even, paradoxically, give up their cherished lives for it. They'd surely go to war.

Although Harry was never a man of faith, he sometimes envied those who were. It was easier. Comforting. Everything would take care of itself. In fact, everything was already taken care of. All you needed was a little patience. Or a lot. But if Harry was incapable of faith, then he could never have had faith in America either. Hope was as far as he could go. Too bad, because if he had faith, he wouldn't need hope. He'd have certainty, and if you're certain about something, you don't have to hope for it.

Since faith was out, Harry had to settle for hope and belief in America. But unlike faith, hopes can be raised or dashed, and beliefs can turn to doubts in the face of new evidence. And now Harry had to confront the possibility that his belief in the promise and possibilities of America might need to be reassessed. That his hope for America was false hope. And that this American Dream was nothing more than a dream. Nothing but a chump's game after all.

8

Aside from their proximity to Pratzel's bakery, the apartments north of the Delmar Loop had little in common with the spacious, luxurious high-rises with doormen on Skinker Avenue facing Forest Park near Washington University or the elegant homes just south of Delmar. Maggie and Irv Dagan lived on the top floor of a cramped three-story walk-up that Libby would have felt perfectly at home in were it not for all the people crammed into it for the weekly CORE meeting. The first night Lenny took her there, a multi-colored conglomeration numbering at least thirty and ranging in age from teens to seniors occupied every square inch of the place, its hive-like atmosphere buzzing with energy to put the world to rights.

Lenny was planning to spend the whole summer in town as CORE's lead organizer, working to integrate lunch counters and cafeterias in the city. High on the target list were the soda fountains at Stix Baer and Fuller and Famous-Barr, large department stores that welcomed people of all races as shoppers, but not as diners.

What was the difference? Libby wondered. It didn't make sense as a business decision. Revenues were revenues and the only color that should matter to a business was green. After thinking it over for a while, she finally concluded that the root of their animus might have something to do with the physiology of eating, its visceral physicality. It was so basic, the primary directive of the survival instinct: eat or be eaten. Was it a reminder that we were all animals, Whites no less than Blacks, and in that sense, all the same? Was this recognition too hard for some people to take?

Once Libby landed there, on the basic instinct for self-preservation, it was a short step to preservation of the species. Which meant sex. One minute they're taking their lunch with you, the next minute they're taking your women from you. The ultimate taboo. Is that what they were thinking? Better not let them eat with you in the first place, lest they get any ideas. Before you know it, they'd be dancing together. After that, well, copulation was sure to follow.

The tactic CORE adopted—what they referred to as non-violent direct action, inspired by Mahatma Gandhi—was simply to have Negroes, sometimes accompanied by a white person, sit at the counter or a table and wait to be served. The goal was to get the community used to the idea of people of different races eating together. In time, the reasoning went, it would seem as natural as the act of eating itself. No harm would result—mixed-race dancing wouldn't suddenly break out—and proprietors would integrate voluntarily.

CORE wasn't trying to start a ruckus, publicly

shame anyone, or even seek media attention, which was just as well because they weren't going to get it from the *Post* or the morning *Globe* anyway. The newspapers knew which side their bread was buttered on and who was doing the buttering. The department stores were one of their cash cows, as sacred to them as those of flesh and blood to the Hindus of India, and the editors were no more likely to report stories that might put their big spenders in a bad light than Gandhi was to eat one of Lucille's hamburgers.

For the first time it sank into Libby's oblivious head that not just the soda fountain, but her entire workplace was as segregated today as her school was when she was a student at Washington University over a decade ago. Famous-Barr hired Negro women for certain jobs—maintenance workers and others on the invisible lower echelon, of course, but also some who interacted with the clientele, like elevator operators. Those working on the floor all had at least this in common: they were light skinned, very good looking, and very well built.

Libby could excuse that to a certain extent. Looks were a consideration in the hiring of all the women who represented the company's public face. But not only were the colored girls prohibited from enhancing theirs in the beauty parlor that the white employees were encouraged to use, they weren't permitted to eat in the employee cafeteria that Libby ate in either. There was a separate cafeteria on a different floor for them. Libby had no idea what it was like, or what kind of food they served, but she could imagine. Like the jobs they held, the food they were served was certainly humbler and less desirable. She couldn't think of going down there to see for herself. It would have been unheard of. She'd have drawn as many confused and confounded looks as Negroes would have had they come up to the white-only employee cafeteria. And not just confusion, but also resentment. How could they not resent her? They had every right. But they wouldn't have had the contempt that whites would have had for them.

Libby couldn't risk being involved in anything like a sit-in at Famous, or anywhere else. She'd be putting her job in jeopardy. But there was another item on Lenny's to-do list, an extracurricular pet project of his own concerning housing discrimination. And he made Libby hip—to use his own words—to restrictive covenants that were rampant in St. Louis.

"They work like this," Lenny explained to her as he drove her back home to Warne. "What they do is all the property owners in a neighborhood get together and agree not to sell or rent to Negroes. It's like a gentlemen's agreement—some gentlemen, huh? What they say, what they actually put down in writing, is that they won't rent or sell housing to, and I quote, 'people of the Negro or Mongolian race.' Can you believe that? Well, I guess they discouraged all those Mongolians from settling in St. Louis, anyway. So the colored working man and woman are locked out of a lot of neighborhoods, ones near the jobs, with good schools, ones these 'gentlemen' would prefer to keep lily white. Can you get any more racist than that? You can imagine how devastating that is for these people, the descendants of slaves, Libby. People who were forced to come here. Not like our parents. I mean, if they can't get *to* a job, they can't *get* the job."

Libby had never imagined it before, but now she had to. What if she tried to rent an apartment and they wouldn't let her because she was—what? The daughter of an immigrant? A Jew? A woman? A woman of a certain sexual orientation? She had been hoping to work in that area, for people like herself, but that unusual combination of words hadn't come up and didn't appear to be on the agenda at the moment. Still, there were lots of other worthy causes to fight for. And this was one of them.

"That's just not right at all. But what can we do about it?"

"Sue 'em. 'Cause they're breaking the law. There was this case called Shelley v. Kraemer that started right here in St. Louis and went all the way to Supreme Court. You know Thurgood Marshall, right?"

"No. I'm afraid not," said Libby. She had never heard of him, but there was that name Shelley again. Was it a coincidence or was there a deeper meaning behind it, an acknowledgement from some unknowable place that she was now part of this group for a reason. She took just a moment to consider this, then let it pass.

"You gotta get hip, Libby. You gotta read the papers. Marshall's arguing a big case before the Supreme Court right now challenging segregation of public schools in Kansas. If he wins that, it'll change everything. All over the country. He also argued Shelley v. Kraemer and won it in '48 on the grounds that these restrictive covenants violate the Fourteenth Amendment of the Constitution, the equal protection clause."

Libby was doing her best to keep up with all this. All the names, all the cases, clauses and amendments were new to her.

"So here's what we're gonna do. First we send a Negro couple to try to rent a place. They'll tell 'em sorry, no vacancies. We'd love to have ya, but there just aren't any apartments available right now. Come back another time. Like never. Then you and a white guy, say me, I'll go with ya, we go to the same place and see what happens. And I'll tell ya what'll happen. They'll say, 'Well, what are you interested in? A one-bedroom, two, or three? Take your pick. You have kids? No? Well, you're probably thinking of having some, so make sure you have enough room for the whole family. I'd recommend the three-bedroom. You'll grow into it.' Then we got a case. We can sue 'em."

Lenny turned on his wipers as rain began to fall and recounted some of the injustices that had occurred right under Libby's nose. Now she could smell how deeply drenched in discrimination her city was. The wipers squeaked, punctuating each as he ticked them off, one by one. There were the swimming pools, including the one at Fairground Park where she learned to swim, which had been briefly integrated in 1949 after Negroes protested.

"Those were CORE members who led that protest," Lenny said with a touch of pride.

And it was a pack of white racists who answered it with a protest of their own, a riot actually, using bricks and bats on the interlopers. Soon the authorities shut down the pool entirely.

Libby remembered that, at least—the Fairground Park riot. It was big news at the time, and her father was incensed. So was she. But even though it was shameful and happened in her own backyard, more or less, other things took precedence in Libby's life. Like her job at Famous-Barr. That was her primary concern.

There were also the segregated schools and colleges—including Washington U., of course, when she was a student. There were all the neighborhoods where Negroes were not allowed to live. And then Lenny hit her with this:

"Sportsman's Park? Great place to watch a game, right? Unless you happen to have the same skin color as Jackie Robinson. Remember when he came up, how everybody wanted to see him, Libby?"

"They still do."

"Right. But back then, it was history being made. We all wanted to be a part of it, but they wanted it the most. A Negro in the big leagues. One of their own. They couldn't believe it. But the closest they could get to him when he came to town was the right field Pavilion, where they set seats aside. Just for them. How thoughtful, right? Ever sit out there? By the rivers of Babylon?"

Libby had to know all this, but somehow it never seemed to have much to do with her. Now, she realized how much it did. How much she empathized and identified with the oppressed minority. How their struggle was her struggle. And how embarrassed she was, again, at how blind she had been to it all.

Lenny was right—she had to start reading the newspapers more, or more of the newspapers. Right now her reading was limited mostly to the style section, articles on fashion, movie reviews, and, during the baseball season, the sports section. She perused interior design publications at work and indulged in the guilty pleasures of Hollywood gossip and stargazing in *Photoplay* and *Silver Screen* while she sat under the dryer at the beauty salon on the ninth floor at Famous, tended to by colored women who couldn't use it themselves. It was time she went beyond those frivolous interests and started reading hard news to keep abreast of the things that really mattered. It was time she started getting hip to the moral outrages that were happening right under her nose and to which her complacency was

MICHAEL VINES

inadvertently contributing.

Once Lenny had planted the seeds of awareness in her brain, they began to sprout shoots and tendrils that spread unpredictably into areas she was surprised to see them go, but helpless to prevent. Maybe it was a moral failing on her part, but she found her mind wander, from the general back to the specific—specifically herself—and she imagined not merely pretending to be interested in renting an apartment, but actually renting one. Moving out of her family's flat and starting a new life on her own.

Despite her mother's common sense, her *sechel*, and ready adaptation to the enterprising ways of life in America, she had never entirely shaken the dust of Sokolova from her feet. Something of the shtetl remained and, like galoshes over a pair of new leather shoes on a snowy day, perhaps served a protective purpose. Perhaps, even in America, she found nourishment in her roots, roots so deep it was impossible for her to imagine Libby moving out as a single woman. That modern, Lena was not. Nevertheless, Libby couldn't help thinking that the time had come.

And this thought led Libby to another that shocked her even more. She imagined going to a realtor under the pretense of wanting to rent an apartment and then, when he handed her the lease, signing it—with Lenny Goldstein. Together. And how many kids were they planning to have? Two, she'd say. That sounded about right. A boy and a girl.

Or two boys. Or two girls. What difference would it make? She'd take what she got. Two kids. Or maybe three. No, two would be plenty. Oh, who knows? They'd take the three bedroom.

It was now clear to Libby that she had had the wrong idea about Lenny all along. She had made a judgment about him based on the fact that he was a man, and a hairy one at that. Two things he could do nothing about. Was that any less prejudiced than the opinions racists formed about people based on the color of their skin, something they could do nothing about? Once Libby got beyond Lenny's hirsute maleness, she saw the good, generous human being within. His wealth of knowledge, his passion for what is right, his uncompromising sense of justice, his moral commitment, his energy coiled inside him like a fully cranked windup toy ready to spring into action—non-violent direct action—at any moment. These were his strengths, strengths she had not seen before, that now revealed something attractive about him. They could get on your nerves, these strengths, she'd grant that, any one of them by itself could drive you crazy after a while, and taken all together, look out. But he had so much to offer. There was a lot she could learn from him.

Maybe she could get Lenny to shave. She could watch the Friday Night Fights with him on *The Gillette Cavalcade of Sports*, something she instinctively recoiled from—those sweaty brutes beating each other to a pulp were far too primitive

MICHAEL VINES

for her refined tastes—though her father, as mild mannered a man as ever there was, without a pugilistic impulse in him as far as she knew (and who would know better?) never missed a bout. She watched a few rounds with him on occasion, and when one of the boxers struck a hard blow into the breadbasket of the other, Harry would groan as if he took the hit himself, and grunt, "*Oy*, right in the *kishkes. A Yid kin gehrget vern.*" A Jew could get killed.

But Libby could force herself to watch the fights with Lenny, just a few times, and when the catchy jingle for Gillette came on (probably written by Jews) exhorting men to "Look Sharp, Feel Sharp, Be Sharp," maybe he'd get the idea. She'd buy him a razor—and make sure he was always fixed for blades, "Gillette Blue Blades, we mean," as they sang so often and ubiquitously that even she knew every word. They made three Super-Speed Razors—light, regular, and heavy, the last one, no doubt, with men like Lenny in mind. And a tube of Barbasol, she'd get him that too. Picturing Lenny's clean, smooth face, she was almost able to imagine having a family with him. Lenny Goldstein, of all people.

But why not, Libby asked herself? Crazier things had happened in this world. Why not that? And once her mother got to know Lenny as Libby did now, she'd realize what a catch he really was. A good and decent man, a college professor, and a Jew. Sure, you might want him to pipe down once in a while, but his heart was in the right place. And he could earn a living. What more could a mother ask for? If Libby let this fantasy play out, maybe there was a fairy-tale ending waiting for her on the last page. Living happily ever after with Lenny Goldstein. Her Prince Charming with a five-o'clock shadow, a left-wing stubble to rival Richard Nixon's on the right, a man for whom her father, as well as Lenny, harbored a visceral hatred the first time they laid eyes on him.

Libby and Lenny did go through the motions of trying to rent an apartment from a landlord who was a party to a restrictive covenant, and, although they were offered a lease which had been denied to a Negro couple the day before, they didn't sign it. Libby had done her part to get evidence of a legal violation, but in the end, she was right back where she started. With one difference: now the idea of moving out of her parents' place was locked into her brain. Though she had no idea how to pull it off, she thought about it all the time.

In a way it was too bad that Margie Burjoski was now Margie Fine and had been for years—happy though Libby was for her. Their closeness and mutual affection would have been obvious to anyone who saw them on one of their frequent walks on nice Sunday afternoons, sometimes arm in arm. Had Margie still been Burjoski, they might have moved in together, as roommates only, and perhaps Lena would have given her blessing. But it was too late for that. Moving out was one thing, but living alone was another, and Libby had no interest in doing that.

"I just think you have to accept things for the way

MICHAEL VINES

they are and get on with it, Libby," Margie told her as they walked in the gardens of the Jewel Box, the aptly named greenhouse in Forest Park constructed in the thirties with money from the WPA, as Libby's father proudly reminded everyone. "You've gotta live your life. It'd be way worse for you in the long run if you don't. It'd be like taking one of these beautiful flowers and depriving it of water and light. What would happen to it? It would wither and die, Libby. Don't let that happen to you. Choose life. Right? Who said that? Somebody. I don't remember."

"It's in the Torah. I think."

"Okay. There you go. So choose life. You've got so much to offer. Get out there and start offering."

After her experiences with Lenny, or capers as Libby thought of them, she was feeling more comfortable with him, but she was still uncertain about how candid she could be. How much could she reveal about herself? So she began to explore the boundaries. She asked him again about what he had said about CORE and his own principles on the night of the Seder, a subject on which Lenny needed no urging to expatiate. She steered him surreptitiously, she hoped, back to the part that captured her from the start.

"Equality for everyone, you said. Every race, every creed, religion...what was the rest?"

"Sexual orientation? That what you mean?"

"Yeah, that's it," Libby said, trying to give Lenny the impression that she was thinking about it

HARRY GETS WISE

deeply.

"And?"

"Well...it's good. It's right. The whole thing." That was about as far as Libby was prepared to go.

"I agree," he said.

Libby waited for Lenny to go on, to get into specifics, but he never did. So it was up to her to get to her point.

"It seems like most people would agree with most of that. But not everything, maybe."

"Like what? Sexual orientation?"

"Well, I never heard it put that way before, but yeah. I guess."

"I thought so."

Libby wasn't ready for how fast and direct Lenny was. "Thought what?"

"That you were particularly interested in that. I sort of assumed."

"What did you assume?"

"That you'd be interested in that."

"Why?"

"You're single, Libby. Alone."

"So are you."

"I'm impossible to live with. Ask one of my ex-girlfriends. But you, there are a million guys who'd scoop you up in a second if you'd let 'em. Including me, if you don't mind my saying. Besides, on Passover, at your place, as soon as I said, 'sexual orientation,' you perked up a little. And you came to the meetings."

152

"Is it so obvious? Do you think my parents—"

"They haven't got a clue."

"You sure."

"Absolutely."

"Oh, Lenny, I've just got to get out of there. I've got to get a place of my own and—oh my god, what can I do?"

"Move out."

"Easy for you to say. My mom. She'd never understand."

"She'll get over it."

And here's where Lenny made his proposal. He had just rented a room for the summer from a woman he had met through CORE named Sophie Kahn, a widow in her sixties. She lived all alone in one of those huge houses on Waterman Avenue, just south and a few blocks west of the Loop. Her kids were grown, married, and had kids of their own.

"The place has five bedrooms and she's looking to rent out another one. It's a short walk to the streetcars and you could be at work in no time. It'd be perfect for you. And you'd be perfect for her."

"What's she like?"

"She's one of us, Libby. An activist and a good person. And a Jewish *bubbe*. Your mother would like her."

He made it sound so easy, but Libby was hesitant. It wasn't easy at all. It was complicated. But it was also thrilling. Libby would have to give this some serious thought. But already it was beginning to sound almost doable to her.

"Tell your parents it's just for the summer. Ease 'em into the idea. It's like jumping into cold water—bracing at first, but once you're in, you're in. You get used to it. So will your mom. And once you're out, you're out. There's no going back."

Lenny was so wise, so thoughtful, so convincing. And so right. And here he was offering her a way out. What did she have to lose but her chains? she imagined him asking. He was leading her to the Promised Land, but it was up to her to jump into the bracing waters. If only they could be miraculously parted. But Libby couldn't wait for miracles. She had to find it within herself to take the leap.

9

It wasn't easy to keep things from Lena Becker. She had an ability to size people up with a single look. She may not always know exactly what was cooking, but she usually knew when something was. Even though her instincts and intuition may not provide the facts, they put her on high alert, and she kept a sharp eye and keen ear open for clues. One way or another, she always seemed to get to the bottom of things.

She had been on one such alert for about a month over Harry's uncharacteristic comings and goings. He didn't come home for lunch as frequently and often asked her to make a *vursht* sandwich for him to take to the shop because he was so busy. Sometimes, he came home a little later in the evenings, telling her he and Meyer Goldstein bowled a quick game and had a beer just to relax. He'd disappear for an hour on weekend afternoons, just taking a walk in O'Fallon Park, he'd say. And his profits seemed to be down a little, too. Was business off? If not, where was the money going? Something was fishy, that much was obvious. What, she couldn't say. But she'd find out. She always did.

Summer hadn't yet arrived, but the crushing

heat and humidity of the Central Mississippi Valley didn't wait for it, plopping down upon the region like a big drooling St. Bernard who had arrived early for the dog days and suffocated everyone trapped under its thick wet coat. It was on one of these stifling late spring days slouching towards the solstice, that Harry, in a halo of sweat and a little late for dinner, walked into his still, airless flat and got busted.

"Where have you been?" Lena demanded in Yiddish, which they still spoke exclusively when they were alone together.

"Me? A walk. I needed a little fresh air."

"What air? It's 100 degrees outside, you're soaking wet. There's no air."

"Yes, it's hot. You're right."

"Tell me something and don't lie to me. You have a girlfriend, Harry?"

"A girlfriend? What? Where'd you get such an idea?"

"Where do you go then, for your walks? Your air? There's something you're not telling me and I want to know what it is."

"There's no girlfriend, Lena. Don't talk such nonsense."

"No? You don't have a little *nafka* over at the pool hall?"

"Pool hall?"

"Don't give me that. You think I don't live in the neighborhood? I don't know where you go? Not the bowling alley, Harry."

"I bowl. Sometimes."

"What's with the pool hall? They got private rooms in back where you *shtup* your little *nafka*? It wouldn't surprise me one bit. Is that what you spend your money on? You're not bringing in as much, Harry. You think I don't know? I keep the books."

Now Harry had to fess up. She was already on to him, up to a point, anyway, so there was no use denying that he'd been hanging out at Ed's, a disreputable joint if ever there was one. Why else would it have its windows blackened if not to prevent people from seeing what was going on inside? And what was going on inside, besides a little pool? Was it a front for some kind of who-knows-what? A brothel, maybe?

Ed's might have been on the sketchy side of the street, but it was a pool hall, not a whorehouse, and Harry wasn't having illicit liaisons and wouldn't in a million years. Lena should know better. He proved to her regularly that even after all these years she was the only woman he ever wanted, the only *girl*, he might fairly say, because when he looked at her today, in her fullness and maturity, he saw still the teenage shtetl girl carrying a basket of eggs to the market who, despite being clothed in *schmattas*, had about her an alluring sensuality—and she knew it.

She didn't wear *schmattas* anymore, least of all in bed, they both saw to that, using Libby's Famous-Barr employee discount to shop in the lingerie and shoe departments and to splurge on an intoxicating perfume by Chanel that Harry gave Lena—and himself—every year on their anniversary. Harry was willing to go along with Lena's ban on German mustard but, despite Coco Chanel's well known collaboration with the Boche and her cohabitation at the Hôtel Ritz with a Nazi intelligence officer during the occupation, Harry gave her perfume a pass, and Lena acquiesced. Harry's rationale, as he conveyed to Lena, was that they were doing their part to support Coco's former partner, Pierre Wertheimer, a Jew who had fled France for the U.S. during the war but returned after to resume control of the company. There was truth in that, but it wasn't the real reason. The real reason was that while Harry did indeed love German mustard, Chanel N° 5 was no mere vinegar-based condiment —it was the very scent of desire. As such, it was one of life's necessities.

Their intimate hour would begin with bourbon whiskey for Harry and, for Lena, his special mix of bourbon and sweet talk. And it would end with the two of them limp on the mattress, simultaneously catching their post-coital breaths and uttering in unison, "*Oy*." Neither of them ever took this for granted. The next morning Lena would wake up feeling renewed, rejuvenated, grateful for a good man's love and all that they had together. Harry might be honing his straight razor on a leather strop or whipping soap from a solid bar into a lather with the badger-hair bristles of his shaving brush when

MICHAEL VINES

he would spot Lena's camisole hanging on a hook reflected in the mirror of the medicine cabinet. He'd turn around, press his face into it, inhale, and be transported, as if its fragrance were a drug. It is said that in every relationship there is the lover and the loved. If so, then perhaps Harry was the lover, and that would be fine with him. For while the loved one may receive the gift of forever love, the lover is blessed with the even rarer gift of forever desire. A fair trade in Harry's mind. Even-steven.

Lena had Harry dead to rights about Ed's, and he might as well admit that he was playing a little pool once in a while—a far lesser offense than infidelity, in fact, not really an offense at all. There were no victims here. Nobody was getting hurt. But simply admitting to playing pool wouldn't be the end of it. Lena would want to know more. She'd noticed his income had been down. Why? He'd have to offer an explanation.

Since no story is better or easier to tell than the true story, that's what he told her—the truth, the whole truth, and nothing but the truth, as they say in American courts of law for which Harry had so much reverence. And the whole truth included not only telling Lena about his newfound passion for nine-ball—and his surprising natural talent for it— but how he was introduced to the game in the first place. Which meant he had to tell Lena about Tony the Pipe and Carlo the Man, a moniker the kid was trying to make stick, to no avail.

He told Lena, for the first time, that he was being

shaken down, forced to hand over hard-earned dough to the mob every week. He wasn't sure how Lena would react to this, and he was a little afraid she might want to take matters into her own hands with the help of a rolling pin. She could be so naïve, he thought. What did she really know about the world? If she had gone to the gangster movies with him once in a while, she might have learned a thing or two.

"Did you go to the police?" she asked.

"Yeah. It's no good."

"No good? What do you mean no good? This is America. There are laws," she said, as if she were telling Harry something he didn't know. He hated to be the one to break it to her, but he had to tell her the way things were. How they were squeezing every small business in the neighborhood, and how Officer Keegan was in on it, on the take like the rest of the cops all over town. The so-called long arm of the law wouldn't lift a finger.

"There's an underworld out there, Lena. Even in America, not everything is the way it seems."

Lena responded swiftly, not waiting for logic to catch up with her. "You'd rather go back to Sokolova?" she said. "We'd all be dead by now. None of us would be here. No children, no grandchildren. Nothing. All up in flames. Poof."

"Of course not. That's not what I'm saying, Lena."

"And what's this got to do with the pool playing? This *pisher* forces you to play pool with him?"

160

"He doesn't force me. He just showed me how. And I like it. I'm good at it. I win."

"Win? What do you win?"

"Money, honey," Harry said. This Lena understood.

"How much?"

"Enough to pay off the little *pisher*."

And that was true. In a remarkably short time, six weeks tops, Harry had gotten to the point where he could spot Carlo two balls and still beat his pants off. Despite Carlo's jones for gambling, he stopped playing Harry for money. There was no point. He might just as well have handed the cash over to him and get it over with. But Carlo, always looking for an angle, figured if you can't beat him, join him, and he began promoting Harry, setting up games for him with workaday players who came from other parts of town just to see what this new guy had, certain that whatever it was, he'd be no match for them. They were wrong. Harry cleaned the tables with them. He began to get something of a reputation in pool circles, started playing for higher stakes, and even got a nickname that stuck better than Carlo's.

"Anybody gets a nickname without even trying, it's a compliment," Carlo told him with more than a smidgen of envy while they were shooting around at Ed's just for fun late one afternoon.

"It's not a compliment. A compliment would be Shooter Harry. Harry Hustle. Something like that. Or Doc. Why not Doc? I'm the Shoe Doctor. That would be a compliment. Not Harry the Yid. I don't like it."

"Whatsamatta with it? It's what you are. Isn't that what ya told me? A nickname's gotta be somethin' that's true to who you are. And you are a Yid, Harry. A big one. No offense, swear to god on my father's grave," he crossed himself with that. "Nothin' you can do about that. And nothin' you can do about them callin' you that, either. It stuck."

"It's not nice."

"Aw come on, gimme a break already. 'Not nice'? You walk into a joint, people take notice. They say, 'Look out, it's the Yid. Hide your money.' Heh heh. And I don't mean that in a bad way, Harry. Like the Jew's gonna jew ya outta your money. Which is what a lot of 'em think anyway, let's face it, but I don't mean it like that. I mean it in a good way—that you're gonna clean 'em out. Beat 'em at their own game. Fair and square, right? That's respect. It could be a lot worse, Harry. You and me, we both know that. What they *coulda* called ya? Am I right?"

"Them, I can't stop. But I don't want you should call me that."

"No, never Harry, never. Not to your face, anyway. But if I'm setting up a game, that's another story. 'Harry the Yid,' pardon the expression, is a draw."

So Carlo set up games at night—after Harry's grandkids were asleep—booked bets, and took a little vig off the top of Harry's winnings, which

MICHAEL VINES

Harry had no objection to. He was still making more than enough to pay Carlo his weekly tribute, which Carlo let slide more often than not. Harry's pool playing had become a profit center. And now that Lena knew what was up, she didn't mind Harry hanging out at Ed's to hone his skills and get a little action, as she had taken to calling it. She would have liked to see him play, but she didn't dare. No woman had ever set foot in Ed's—not even a *nafka*. As for Harry, he may not have liked his nickname, but he loved to play and he wouldn't be getting all this action without Carlo.

Harry didn't think of it this way, but he and Carlo were now in business together. And Carlo, trying to figure out how he could parlay their new partnership into a really big score, came up with an idea: he and Harry could take over the Florissant Lanes and put tables in there. Make it Florissant Bowling and Billiards. He took Harry there to scout the place and sell him on his vision.

"What do you mean, 'take over'?" Harry asked.

"I mean we take it over."

"You mean we buy it?"

"Yeah, sure, why not? We buy it, whatever you want."

"Where we gonna get the money?"

"Don't worry 'bout the money."

"It costs money to buy the bowling alley."

"We get a loan, Harry. Okay? Make you happy?"

"With what collateral?"

HARRY GETS WISE

"We don't need collateral. I know guys. I can always get a loan, don't worry about it. We just get the place, okay? We could call the pool room Harry's. Or Doc's. Whatever the hell ya want. Put tables in right over there. Cut the bar in half. All those tables and chairs, nobody uses 'em. It's wastin' valuable real estate. Then, instead of fixin' stinkin' old shoes all day long, you'll be playin' pool. Bowlin' a little when you feel like it. Havin' the time of your life. We could really build something here, Harry. It could be *the* spot. People comin' from all over town —across the river too. The whole Midwest. Hustlin' Harry's. We could call it that. How's that sound to you? We'll put it up in a neon sign." Carlo waved his hand across the air imagining the letters in glowing script. "Hustlin' Harry's," he intoned. He always did have a weak spot for alliteration.

"What about Ed?"

"What about 'im?"

"What's gonna happen to him?"

"We put 'im outta business is what."

"How's he gonna make a living?"

"Jesus, Harry, are you kiddin' me? What d'you care? You gotta worry about everybody? We'll give 'im a fuckin' job, okay? He can serve beers—although I wouldn't mind getting some sweet little cocktail waitresses in there. Good for business, if you know what I mean. Ed can rack balls, sweep floors, clean the johns, who gives a fuck?"

As tantalizing as the prospect of playing pool

all day sounded to Harry, he didn't give Carlo's proposition even a moment's thought. Going into a new business he knew nothing about with an entry-level mobster; putting his trust in a guy who, by his own admission, was looking out only for number one, who thinks playing by the rules is for chumps, and who had all the early earmarks of being a compulsive gambler; walking away from a steady business he had spent his entire life building just so he could do nothing but hang around and play pool; and, on top of all that, having to tell Lena the great news—*mi daf zeyn meshugga*. He'd have to be crazy. It was so preposterous Harry actually looked forward to telling Lena about it. They'd share a good laugh.

"Maybe we keep the shop too. Hire a shoemaker to work for us." Lena always had an enterprising spirit.

"What?"

"Why not? There are other shoemakers. We could have two businesses. People do. It could be an opportunity, Harry."

"What are we talking? You can't go into business with people like this. These guys, they're two-faced guys, Lena. What if they don't want to sell the bowling alley? That's a good business, Lena. They got Budweiser and Falstaff playing there."

At the time, St. Louis was the undisputed bowling capital of America. The big breweries sponsored teams and the best players came from there, or went there to face the stiffest competition,

HARRY GETS WISE

among them, Dick Weber, Ray Bluth, and the king of them all, the Stan Musial of bowling, Don Carter, all of whom played for Budweiser at the Florissant Lanes, often against the Falstaff team who, though formidable in its own right, was no match for them.

"You think that would stop them? They'd strong-arm them, Lena. That's what they'd do. They'd drop bowling balls on their heads." Harry didn't really believe Carlo had that in him, but he was sure Tony the Pipe did, and one way or another, it might come to that. "No, no. What are you even talking?"

"Nobody says strong-arm. You do it your way. The right way. Stick to your guns."

"They're the ones with the guns, Lena. No. This is completely *meshugga*."

So Harry's partnership with Carlo would stay just as it was and go no further. Carlo would book matches. That's it. And when he got wind that a guy he'd heard of from Chicago called Donny Deuce was in town on family business, Carlo went to work. The Deuce—a nickname Carlo would have found enviable were it not a reference to Donny's waist line (you could just about fit two guys into a pair of his pants)—was just the kind of mark Carlo was always on the lookout for. Someone who thought he was a shark, but wasn't. When Carlo told him about this pushover called Harry the Yid, the Deuce was eager to empty they guy's pockets, and a match was set up at the Mecca of billiards in St. Louis, Arata's on Olive just off Grand Boulevard.

The neighborhood was an eclectic energetic hub of nightlife attracting people from all over the area, so many that on weekend nights a cop stood in the middle of the brightly lit intersection of Grand and Olive directing pedestrian and motor traffic. The Continental Building, a magnificent multi-tiered Art Deco tower evoking a truncated version of the contemporaneously built Empire State Building, soared above it. The Fox Theater, a cathedral to the cinematic arts built in the late twenties in a wildly ornate architectural style dubbed Siamese-Byzantine—but more humbly described by Lena as *ungepatchket*—was just around the corner on Grand, a few blocks south of the St. Louis Theater, the venue for vaudeville, in its day, and live stage plays. Elements of the demimonde could be found at the seedier haunts just a block to the east on Olive and, of course, your pool hall habitués of every class found their way to Arata's.

Harry was still in Sokolova as a shoemaker's apprentice, learning his trade and a little English, when Frank Arata opened his parlor in 1913. No one would have called it a joint. The men who played there at the time did so sporting their finest threads, sometimes even tuxedos. Pictures of old greats who played there over the years, like Willie Hoppe, Kansas City's Bennie Allen, and John the Greek, adorned the walls. Below those, theater seats were hung to give spectators a comfortable, unobstructed view of the best players Arata's still attracted.

Like Ed's, Harry's home hall of dark shadows, it

was illuminated only by drop-lights hanging over the tables. But unlike Ed's, it had the kind of tables they didn't make anymore. There were about twenty-five of them for both billiards and pocket pool, some over seventy-five years old, when they still used thick four-piece slabs of Vermont slate, assuring a straight and even plane, covered with green baize. When balls hit their mark, they dropped into the leather webbing adorning each pocket, some sinking almost silently as if into a drift of snow, others with a resounding thwack that could rattle the darkened windows.

Arata's shared a street level entrance with Garavelli's, a restaurant owned by the same Garavellis who had the place on DeBaliviere that attracted the Washington University crowd on date night. This one had a history behind it, including murals depicting scenes of the Old West, and a 1905 bill of fare still hanging on the wall—roast beef sandwich 5 cents. A balcony wrapped above the main floor for additional seating. Harry met Carlo there for a quick bite, early enough to give himself plenty of time to go upstairs and get a feel for the table he was going to play the Deuce on—the texture and speed of the baize cloth, the firmness of the rails, the chiaroscuro of light and shadow.

They sat in the balcony at one of the booths made of a darkly stained wood—so utilitarian it could have been designed by the Shakers or the people who made the Rosenbergs' electric chair—and ordered roast beef sandwiches au jus that cost about half

MICHAEL VINES

a buck by then, courtesy of Carlo. The waiters in their black coats had a well-earned reputation for doling out heaping helpings of insults with a side of abuse to their customers, but they knew what was what and who was who and they paid the highest deference to Carlo and his guest, serving them promptly and courteously. When they finished their sandwiches, Carlo raised the sleeve of his jacket over his wrist to show Harry his new watch—a Rolex.

"Hey, whaddya think, huh? Ain't she a beaut?"

"Very nice." Harry wasn't impressed.

"This is thanks to you, Harry. A little present for myself. And, uh, I got a little somethin' for you too."

Carlo snapped his fingers and motioned one of the waiters over to the table. He came bearing the gift that Carlo had asked him to set aside in a safe place until he called for it.

"Here you go, Champ," he said, handing Harry a long narrow leather case.

Harry knew what it was on sight and he paused to admire the craftsmanship of the leather case —pigskin, he could tell, not kosher, but all right. Then he slowly unzipped it to reveal the treasure inside. There, resting upon a red plush inner lining, was a gorgeous two-piece Brunswick Willie Hoppe Signature Professional cue, the number 19 —stamped on the forearm just below the ring— indicating its weight in ounces, exactly the same as the ones Harry always chose off the rack at Ed's. But that's where the similarity ended. He screwed the

HARRY GETS WISE

two parts together, cocked his head over the base of shaft, and stared down its length. Never before had he seen a cue as straight and true as this one, without so much as the slightest warp detectable even to Harry's keen eye. Never before had he held a cue as finely tapered and balanced.

"It's a beauty, Carlo."

"It's yours, pal. You deserve it."

"You got this for me?"

"Yeah. *Gezunterheyt.* Hey, don't get all teary eyed on me, Harry. It's an investment, okay. A business expense. And I expect it to pay off."

Harry examined every detail of his new cue: the midnight-black leather wrap where his right hand would grip the handle; the ebony and scarlet arrows running up the birdseye maple forearm pointing straight to Willie Hoppe's signature; the intricate mother-of-pearl inlay below the wrap; just above the ivory butt, a decal of the Brunswick logo, which included "Reg. U.S. Pat. Off.," meaning—the magic words, Harry's can of spinach—Made in the USA; the …wait a minute, what was this? On the opposite side of the logo—the engraved initials "EJE."

"What is this EJE?" Harry held the initials right up to Carlo's face.

"I don't know, the model I guess."

"It's a Willie Hoppe model. What is EJE?"

"How am I supposed to know?"

"I'll tell you what it is. It's somebody's initials. Where'd you get this, Carlo?"

170

MICHAEL VINES

"I got it, that's all. From a friend. Gave me a good price."

"I'll bet he did. This cue is hot, isn't it?"

"You said it, Harry. And it's gonna make you hot too. You never played with anything like this."

"And I'm not gonna. I don't want no stolen cue."

"Okay, here we go. Look, Harry, EJE, you know what it stands for? I'll tell you. It stands for...Every Jew..." Carlo thought for a second. "Enjoy. Okay? Every Jew Enjoy. I had it put there myself. Just for you."

"Don't give me that bunk. You think I'm some kinda greenhorn? I don't know shit from Shinola? Who you think you're talking to, Carlo? You little *pisher*."

"Whoa, whoa, Harry. Watch out, now. Don't you call me that. That ever sticks, you're in deep shit, Harry. Up to here."

Harry slashed a hand through the air like he was swatting an annoying little pest buzzing around his head. "Ah. Take your *ferkakta* cue and *shtuffen tuchas*. I'll use what they got on the rack."

"Harry, I don't need this *tsuris* from you, right now, okay? Don't be a fool. Use the stick. You can beat this guy."

But Harry wouldn't listen. He wouldn't be reasoned with and he wouldn't be strong-armed and he wouldn't be sweet-talked. If he was going to play Donny Deuce, he'd do it his way, on his own terms. Fair and square. Even-steven. He lurched

171

from the booth in the balcony, stomped down the stairs, then up the other stairs leading to Arata's with Carlo following close behind, holding the pool cue that they both knew would give Harry an edge, but that he refused to use. As a matter of principle. Because to use it would have violated everything Harry believed in. It would be wrong, dishonest, dishonorable. It would have been un-*menschlichkite* and worse—it would have been downright un-American.

10

Where better to be alone with her father than at a ballgame? Just the two of them, the only real fans in the family, although Tillie's six-year-old, Marty, looked to be a precocious prospect. It was the one place where Libby could have him all to herself for a few hours and, as they watched the game, let their conversation roam from the action on the field to a range of topics as wide and open as the Great Plains.

St. Louis had been a primary jumping off point for the nation's westward expansion across those plains, and Sportsman's Park, newly renovated and newly named Busch Stadium, would be Libby's jumping off point for her own westward expansion. It was there she could talk to her father about her dream of heading west—to Sophie Kahn's house in University City.

In an impulsive move that surprised her, she bought two box seats to a Tuesday night game against—as fate would have it—the Brooklyn Dodgers. As she checked the tickets before leaving the counter, she'd have to admit that the high-stakes nail-biter between the two clubs that she attended all those years ago with Shelley Klein did cross her mind. The neural pathways were so deeply etched into her brain she could never pave over them. They persisted just below the surface, like indelible glyphs on an ancient palimpsest. But she was well over Shelley by now and she didn't dwell on it. She simply acknowledged the memory and skipped right over it, like a crack in the sidewalk.

The Dodgers were much better than the Cardinals in 1954, but not that night. Wally Moon fortified his case for rookie of the year going 3 for 5 with 4 RBIs, and Stan Musial, who needed no further proof that he was one of the most dangerous hitters in baseball, went 2 for 5, adding 4 RBIs of his own, a triple, and his twentieth homer of the season with over two-thirds of its games still to be played. He was on a pace for sixty, with a chance to eclipse the Babe himself. The Cards were up eight-zip after five on their way to a 10-3 rout, so it was a relaxing game for the fans, giving them plenty of breathing room and space to talk about anything on their minds.

Libby was always able to talk to her father as effortlessly as drifting downstream on the lazy current of the Mississippi River, Huck Finn-style. But when it came to the subject of moving out, she got bogged down, stuck in muddy shallows from which she was helpless to break free. For some reason, probably because the topics were all bound together in her brain, she turned to Eleanor Roosevelt to help tug her out.

"I admire her so much, Papa. She's a real role model for me."

"You couldn't pick a better one."

"She's such a humanitarian."

"The biggest," Harry concurred.

"Always standing up for the little guy. And such a strong voice for civil rights and racial equality."

She didn't have to tell her father. She learned that at his knee. Well before Eleanor got to the White House, she was outspoken in her support of trade unions and women's rights. As First Lady, she dared to speak out even against New Deal programs that discriminated against Negroes. She quit the Daughters of the American Revolution because they refused to let the internationally acclaimed Black opera singer, Marian Anderson, perform for an integrated audience at their Constitution Hall. To right that wrong, she arranged to have her sing instead at the hallowed steps of the Lincoln Memorial before a multi-hued crowd of over 75,000 packed onto the National Mall, and millions more over the radio.

"If she were from St. Louis, she'd have told the Veiled Prophet where to get off," Libby said.

"Yeah. In *drerd*," Harry said.

Eleanor Roosevelt may have been a daughter of privilege, coming out as a debutante at the Waldorf-Astoria in New York when she was seventeen, but could there be any doubt that, had she debuted in St. Louis, she would have wanted no part of that city's premier social event of the year, The Veiled Prophet Ball? A private gala thrown exclusively for the city's white Christian swells and their debutantes, it celebrated the brutal and fatal quelling of the Great Railroad Strike of 1877. As this strike included many Negroes, it caused the powers that were (and always are) even greater alarm, fearing, as they did, nothing more than labor united across racial lines.

"That outfit he wore pretty much says it all," Libby said.

"*Mit* the robe, noch!" said Harry.

In case anyone missed the point, the eponymous prophet was, as his name implies, veiled, and in his earliest incarnation wore a long flowing robe that bore more than a little resemblance to those worn by his kinsman in the Klan.

"She'd have run for the hills to get away from that guy. And the nearest hills are pretty far away. Mmm, let's get some peanuts."

"Peanuts!" Harry called to the vendor.

The former First Lady got Libby going. From there, it was a short step for her to tell her father all about her activities with CORE, which he approved of wholeheartedly. Then, circling back, "Speaking of Eleanor, have you ever heard of Lorena Hickok, Papa?"

"No, I don't think so. Who is she?"

"A very close friend of Eleanor's."

"I don't know her."

"She's a reporter. A journalist. Did you know Eleanor invited her to live in the White House? And she did for a while."

MICHAEL VINES

"Really. Why'd she do that?"

"I don't know. I guess just 'cause they were such close friends. They were *extremely* close, Papa."

Libby wasn't sure how far she could take this. She couldn't just let it rip and tell her father that Eleanor was a lesbian. She had no proof—just gossip from Shelley Klein—and even if she had, it's not really the kind of thing you talked about at a ball game with your dad. She wondered where she thought she was going with this, what made her bring up Eleanor Roosevelt at all, let alone Lorena Hickok. It was all beside the point. What Eleanor Roosevelt was or wasn't had nothing to do with Libby wanting to move out. Or what Libby herself was. And she wasn't about to tell her father about that. Not there. Not then. Not ever. No one could ever know. Except Margie Burjoski and Lenny Goldstein, to whom she had already spilled her guts and trusted to keep her confidence.

It was hard enough for Libby to endure the insidious asides and routine insults—not even directed at her—from otherwise polite people that she knew and worked with. Even the other designers, whom you'd think would be more enlightened.

There was a young interior decorator named Jack Brandt who, with his outré taste and flamboyant personal and design style, had opened his own store in U. City and was making a name for himself. He was about the same age as Libby and even attended

Washington U. for a couple of semesters when she did, also studying art, though she knew him only in passing.

One day Libby was getting her hair done at the Famous salon, idly chatting with a few of her colleagues when Jack Brandt's name came up. One of these supposedly sophisticated and respectable women heard his name and said of him—a man who had served in the Pacific for three-and-half years during World War II—"Well, I guess every fruit has his day."

It wasn't simple jealousy. It was bigotry and malice. The woman had a pretty face, beautiful almost. But when she spoke those words, the forty-three muscles that gave it shape and expression contorted it into something ugly, and Libby saw in that moment what the pretty young woman would look like in twenty years, after her face had been hewn by character, chiseled by streams of spite and bile the way torrents of water carved through earth and rock to form the rifts and ridges of a canyon. But unlike the geological wonders left in the water's wake, her once-pretty face would have been disfigured into something repellent.

Libby's other colleagues seemed to get a big kick out of the little joke. But it struck Libby as a blow aimed directly at her. She didn't say a word, though. Worse, coward that she was, she forced herself to laugh along. How she hated herself for doing that. How ashamed she was of herself—another thing to be ashamed about.

MICHAEL VINES

It happened at home too. From her own brother-in-law, Goldie's husband, Sam, who blustered crudely on almost any subject, right in front of everyone. Most of the family said *shvartzer* when referring to a Black person, but not necessarily out of animus. *Schvartz*, after all, is the Yiddish word for "black." But when Sam used it, you knew it was with something other than benign intent. He also used coon, shine, and nigger synonymously. Sid never talked like that. He was more refined and too kind for that sort of thing. But Sam was another story. He came from nothing, quit school after the eighth grade to go to work, and had to find people to feel superior to, Libby supposed. Blacks, homosexuals, women, anyone in a position of weakness and unlikely to fight back would fill that role nicely. At a family picnic by the water fountain below the Pavilion in Forest Park, Sam was not the least bit shy about telling this story:

"So this *faygala* comes in looking for a tailpipe for a '48 Buick. I tell him I don't have one, and he says,"—and here Sam does his most flaming impression—"'Darn. I really need that tailpipe.' So I said to him, 'I'll bet you do. I'll bet you need all the tailpipe you can get.'" Sam punctuated his story with a self-satisfied chortle, a meme which his son Marshall, a sweet eight-year-old who wouldn't have had the slightest idea what his father was talking about, picked up on, and copied.

Whether Sam had actually had the nerve or the presence of mind to say that to the man, Libby wasn't sure, but she doubted it. Sam wasn't that quick. It was probably just a joke circulating in the auto parts trade he was retelling and taking credit for. But did anybody object? Not really. Even her father seemed to think nothing of it. Her mother admonished, "*Shah. Der kinder, der kinder,*" to which Sam replied, "Bullshhhh—" not finishing the word. But Libby felt her mother's concern was only that the children shouldn't be contaminated by any talk of homosexuals, not the malicious nature of the talk itself.

Libby could have said something. It was just Sam. She could have told him it wasn't right to talk to or about people that way. No matter who or what they were. But if she did, she might have left herself an open target for Sam's scorn and cutting comments. She was the only single woman in the family and could well imagine how he might retort if he felt threatened by her. Why take the chance? So Libby did what she always did. She willed herself to ignore it. Pretended it didn't happen. So much of Libby's life was pretending.

As she sat in her box seat, she wondered what would happen if she just stopped pretending. How would her father react if she just stated the facts, simply and directly. Matter-of-factly, while the pitcher was checking the sign before going into his windup.

"Oh, Papa, here's something I never told you before. I like pussy. How 'bout that? Funny world, huh? Ha ha ha. Takes all kinds. Ball?! Come on, ump!

That was right over the plate!"

But no, she couldn't say that. That would never do.

Despite all the scoring, it was a quickly played game, less than two-and-a-half hours from first pitch to last. The bottom of the eighth snuck up on her before she knew it and, as the Cardinals came up for what would surely be their final at-bat, Libby let it out.

"Papa, what would you think...look, Papa, you know I love you and Mama and I'd never do anything to hurt you or upset you in any way, but what would you think if I moved out and got a place of my own? Not of my own, exactly. I'd be living with another woman. An older woman. She's a *bubbe*."

"You want to move out?"

Libby studied her father's eyes carefully to get a sense of what was going on behind them. She saw nothing beyond their natural softness. At least they revealed no resistance. Maybe he was even saying to himself, "It's about time."

"I've been thinking about it. I'm a big girl, Papa. You understand."

She wasn't sure he did, but she said it in the declarative hoping to make it so. In the restless clamor of the crowd, Harry seemed to be the only person sitting still, in complete silence. And then he said, "Sure. Sure, I understand."

Libby felt like she had been lifted from her seat, floating lighter than air above the ballpark, like the Goodyear Blimp. How she loved her father. So understanding. So tolerant and accepting. Libby didn't know how he got that way, but he always had been. Some things, you're just born with. You bring them into the world with you. Libby knew that as well as anyone, she supposed.

"Really, Papa? You do?"

"Sure. Of course." And then he added, "But I don't know," and Libby settled back down to earth.

"What don't you know?"

"I don't know. It's a big step, Libby. You don't want to rush into anything. We should think about it a little, no? Talk it over together?"

"I have thought about it, Papa. For a long time. I've thought about it a lot. This is what I need. What's best for me."

"I know, but the family, Libby. We're all together. You want to move from the family?"

"It's not like I'd be moving to Timbuktu. I'd be in U. City."

"It's nice there. Who is this *bubbe*?"

Libby felt like he'd just signaled his consent. "Her name's Sophie Kahn. She's a widow and lives alone in a huge house. Right near the loop. She goes to B'nai Amoona."

B'nai Amoona was the Conservative synagogue in an enclave that included Tpheris Israel, Orthodox; and Shaare Emeth, Reformed; all three clustered on or around a street called Trinity Boulevard, an ironic coincidence, considering. University City was so

MICHAEL VINES

christened because of its proximity to Washington University and, to extend the theme of higher education, many of its streets were named after universities. Besides Washington and Trinity, there was Harvard, Yale, Princeton, Columbia, Cornell, Stanford, Amherst, Dartmouth to name a few—aspirational colleges that the Jews who moved to the suburb and generously funded its school district hoped their sons would eventually attend. They had no such expectations for their daughters.

Harry didn't know the neighborhood well, but University City had cachet. His friends, the Shermans, moved there early on, but not in the tony, premium-priced neighborhood that Libby was talking about. They bought a house on the other side of the tracks, north of the redundantly named Olive Street Road, on a block called Colby, which was nice enough, but not in the same league as the near mansions south of Delmar. Sid and Tillie planned to move to U. City themselves, as soon as they could find something they liked and could afford, so Marty and Joey could go to what were among the best public schools in the state, arguably, the entire country.

"Look at it this way, Papa. You could rent out my space. Take off the door and put up dry wall. Fix it up a little. I'll pay for all the work. And you'll have money coming in." Libby was overplaying her hand. When you win, you're supposed to stop talking.

"Does everybody think everything's always about the money? This is not about money,

Libby. I'm surprised by you. Money doesn't solve everything."

Libby knew that all too well. If only it could. No price would be too great to relieve herself of the burden she carried every day. Just for being who she was.

"I know, but...I just want to make this as easy for everyone as I can. Come on, Papa. You said you understand."

"I do understand. But it's not all up to me."

"Then you'll talk to Mama?"

"Me? I thought you were a big girl."

"But you can make her understand. Will you tell her it's okay with you?"

"Did I say it's okay by me?"

"Well, is it?"

Harry didn't reply. Libby knew it would be hard for him not to have his daughter living under the same roof as the rest of the family. And he had to be wondering how Lena would react. He let his eyelids fall, as if dozing off for a second, until Libby roused him by saying softly, "Papa."

"All right. All right. We'll talk to your mama. *You'll* talk to her. I'll sit there and nod, all right, *meydeleh*?"

He smiled at her through those soft eyes of his, placed his hand on her forearm, and squeezed gently, the way he'd check the ripeness of a peach. Libby could ask for no more. She threw her arms around his neck and gave him a big fat kiss on his

MICHAEL VINES

scratchy cheek. He could use a shave, she thought.

"Thank you, Papa. Thank you. I knew you'd understand."

11

There was a driveway behind Harry's shop that trucks could use to make deliveries and that also had space for a few cars to park. That's where Carlo wheeled in with his '51 De Soto—a car he couldn't wait to replace with one more fitting a man of his station. He jumped out of the driver's seat, strode to the back entrance, and banged on the door.

"Harry. Harry. It's me. Get out here."

When Harry came out, Carlo was standing beside his car's open trunk, which was glutted with shoe boxes, and tapping his left foot fast. He pulled one of the boxes out and opened it for Harry to see what was inside.

"Look at these babies, will ya? Whaddya think, huh?

It was another marvel of the advances in physics and engineering made by scientists during World War II, applied in a way guaranteed to grab Harry's attention—a pair of women's shoes. Designed for Dior by Roger Vivier, their towering slender heels— made possible by the same high-tensile steel used in skyscrapers—soared over three inches high while tapering down, where the rubber hit the road, to the width of a few strands of fettuccine. Yet they were still strong enough to support a woman's weight. What Reddi-Wip heralded for the future of processed foods, Vivier signaled for the future of women's shoes. They would perfectly complement the aerodynamic tail fins soon to adorn the cars rolling out of Detroit, making it the preferred footwear for the fashionable woman as she stepped into her husband's new Cadillac.

Harry let out a low whistle. "Those are really somethin."

"What'd I tell ya? Come on, let's unload 'em."

"Where to?"

"Your shop."

"What for?"

"So you can sell 'em."

"My customers can't afford shoes like this."

"Don't worry. I'll give you a good price. They'll walk outta here all by themself."

"Not so fast, Carlo. Where'd you get 'em?"

"They fell off a truck, whaddya think?"

"You stole 'em."

"I didn't steal anything. I'm just a middleman. I bought 'em. You'll sell 'em. We'll both make a profit."

"I'm not selling these shoes."

"Why not?"

"I'm not a thief."

"Nobody says you are, Harry. You'd didn't steal 'em, so what's the problem?"

"I don't sell stolen goods."

"Oh, here you go again. Gettin' all high and

mighty. Like with the pool cue."

"*Genug* with the pool cue already."

"You shoulda used it."

Carlo still hadn't gotten over Harry's refusal to use the Willie Hoppe cue he had procured for him to play the Deuce at Arata's. Would it have made a difference? There's no way to know. Whatever benefit it offered might have been offset by the guilt Harry would have felt using it. So he chose a cue right off the rack, just as he said he would. And he was running the Deuce right off the table. It was quite a sight to watch that plus-sized paisan plant himself upon the table like a beached whale, his blubber spilling across the baize, the tip of one toe touching the floor as he stretched for the cue ball that was just barely within his reach. Harry didn't need any fancy-schmancy cue to beat this guy. A crooked branch he could have picked up in O'Fallon Park would have done the trick.

"Now you're cookin' with Crisco," Harry said to himself after he ran the table in the first two games without the Deuce getting even a shot. Harry was on a roll. Until—who knows why?—he lost his touch. Maybe the table wasn't as straight and level as advertised. Maybe all the goombahs in shiny suits with bulges in their jackets barking out bets gave him the jitters. Whatever it was, Harry suddenly went cold. His shots didn't fall. It was one near-miss after another. And just as suddenly, the Deuce got hot.

"You coulda beat that fat fuck, Harry."

"I had a bad night."

"Yeah, 'cause you were too fuckin' stubborn to use the cue."

"Maybe the cue is what jinxed me. Maybe it was giving me the Evil Eye."

"A fuckin' cue can't give the Evil Eye, Harry. It doesn't have an eye. You woulda eaten that fatso's lunch with that cue. We both of us know it. And it woulda been a big fuckin' lunch."

"Yeah, well, I didn't take your *ferkakta* cue and I'm not taking your *ferkakta* shoes."

"Aw fuck, Harry. I'm doin' ya a favor here."

"I don't need no favors."

"You know, you got a lot to learn, Harry. You don't sell stolen goods? You live on stolen goods, how 'bout that? Your nice little flat across the street. Your shop right here. They're both fuckin' sittin' on stolen goods."

"What are you talkin'?"

"I'll tell you what I'm talkin'. You know Chippewa Avenue, Harry. Route fuckin' 66? Why do you think it's called Chippewa Avenue? Huh? I'll tell you why. 'Cause way back in the Wild West it was a fuckin' Indian trail or somethin'. Chippewa Indians. That's why they called it Chippewa Avenue. Did ya know that, Harry? That's right. All the settlers come in, the white man, and they say to the red man, 'Nice little trail you got here. We'll take it. And all the rest of your fuckin' land too. Now get the fuck outta here before we break your fuckin' legs.' And they took it. Including the land we're standin' on right now. It was all Chippewa territory, Harry, till we stole it and made it ours. Now it's my territory."

"I never stole nothin'. I had stuff stolen from me. Plenty."

"Everybody steals from everybody, Harry. It's the American Way. Ever since Christopher Columbus discovered the place. A paisan, by the way. You knew that, right? That's why we got Columbus Day. Now Columbus, he was a standup guy. But after him, it was one fuckin' *goniff* after another, Harry. Look, maybe I didn't do too much school, but I remember one thing. Manhattan? New York fuckin' City? They bought it from the fuckin' Indians for twenty-four bucks in beads or some shit. If that ain't the biggest shakedown of all time, I don't know what is."

"They gave something for it. That's not stealing. They bought it."

"It was a con, Harry. A big fuckin' con. They said, 'Here are some beautiful worthless fuckin' beads. Maybe they got magic powers or somethin', who knows? You take these. We'll take the land.' Sound fair to you, Harry?"

"They made a deal."

"Some deal. They took advantage of a bunch o' wild savages that didn't know shit. And they kept making the same deal all over the fuckin' place. 'We get this, you get nothin'.' That was the deal. Cowboys and Indians, Harry. You go to the movies. What

MICHAEL VINES

happens? The fuckin' cowboys come in and kill the fuckin' Indians. Every time. And the fuckin' cavalry too. Go see *Sitting Bull*. It's at the O'Fallon right now. Come on, Harry, wise up. There wouldn't be any America if we didn't steal it. Now don't make the same mistake twice, and help me unload this shit. Hey, Stan Musial's place is on Chippewa. Musial and Biggies. Ever been there, Harry? I didn't think so. But you play ball with me, we'll go there together. Eat steaks this thick. My treat, Harry. How's that sound?"

Carlo took as many boxes as he could stack into his arms at one time and carried them into the storage area in the back of Harry's shop. Harry followed him in, stacked the same boxes into his arms, and brought them right back to the trunk of Carlo's De Soto, a Sisyphean pas de deux that Carlo could do nothing to stop.

"Hey, hey, Harry! Whaddya doin'? I'm tryin' to help you here."

Carlo piled up yet another stack of boxes, but as he carried them into the shop, they toppled out of his arms, their contents spilling all over the pavement. And that did it. He'd had enough. He bent over and grabbed the shoes willy-nilly, not even trying to match pairs as he shoved them into the nearest box.

"Fuck you, Harry," he said as Harry bent down to help him pick up the shoes. "Have it your way. Your fuckin' loss. Just like with the Deuce. Fine. I got somebody else I can sell 'em to. He won't give me a fuckin' hard time about it neither, and he'll make a good fuckin' buck, too. Jeez. Try to do a guy a favor."

It's true that Carlo worried about Harry, about how naïve he was about the world and its ways. But Harry worried about Carlo too. Doesn't the poor schmuck know how coercion works? Harry wondered. Doesn't he know he can't take no for an answer. A real enforcer would rough Harry up at the first sign of resistance, before he could turn around. And if that wasn't enough, he'd burn down his shop and let that be a lesson to him—and everyone else.

If Carlo didn't know that already, then he simply didn't get it. And if he didn't get it, he wasn't cut out for this line of work. Unless he did get it, but was just making an exception for Harry, his friend. Which was just as bad, if not worse. Even Harry knew that. If Carlo were to get anywhere in his chosen field, he should know it too. He shouldn't have to be taught, it should be in his nature. How's he gonna make it in this world—his world, Harry asked himself. How will a kid like him end up? In the trunk of a car, probably. And the thought of that hit Harry hard.

Carlo had told him a little about how he had gotten mixed up with these hoods. How he had just gone into the family business, as if that were the only thing he could do. But he didn't seem cut out for it. He wasn't a tough guy. He was no Tony the Pipe Allocco, that's for sure. He wasn't a killer. He was a misfit, like someone with the soul of an artist who became an actuary because his father sold life

MICHAEL VINES

insurance.

Carlo's father was an immigrant too, just like Harry. Maybe that's one of the reasons Harry felt a connection with the kid from the beginning. And he couldn't help wonder if Carlo had been his son, how different he would have turned out. The boy had a good heart, deep down inside. Harry could see it, and had he been the one to guide and nurture him, to teach him right from wrong, enlighten him about the rule of law and the three branches of government, it would have been a different story. He surely would have taken a different path.

Carlo was no dummy and, given the opportunity, he could have made something of himself. For starters, Harry would have made sure he stayed in school and got an education. And a bar mitzvah, too. Even if the minute it was over he turned his back on the religion and never read another word of Hebrew in his life, he would still have been inculcated with the ethics and morals of its teachings and the comforts of its traditions and culture.

Maybe today he'd be in his senior year at Washington U., or the University of Missouri, studying American history, getting his facts straight about Christopher Columbus. He might have specialized in the nation's westward expansion, gone on to graduate school, written his thesis on Manifest Destiny, and become so radicalized he'd make Lenny Goldstein look like a Chamber of Commerce Republican. But whatever he became, he would also have become a mensch.

Harry picked up the last shoe from the ground and placed it in a box with its mirror-image match. These were a particularly graceful pair of pumps known as the Roger Vivier Aiguille Stiletto, a masterpiece of midnight blue satin bursting into a rosette atop the vamp and balanced on a vertigo-inducing three-inch heel. Harry was a connoisseur of shoes, not a fetishist, but these nearly took his breath away. He knew how much Lena would love them and how she would look in them, how she would stand so proud and so tall, even taller than he, towering like a statue inviting him to the Promised Land. As he handed the still-open box to Carlo, he felt a covetous pang in his heart and was helpless to prevent himself from asking, "You got these maybe in a 7?"

That was desire speaking and, right or wrong, desire desired what desire desired. There was no talking sense to it. It was out of its mind. Carlo thought he must have misheard him.

"What? What'd you say?"

"A size 7. You got like this in a 7?"

"What, for Lena?"

"Who else?"

A grin, far more triumphant than lascivious—but there was a hint of that too—spread across Carlo's face.

"Harry, you fuckin' horndog," he said. Then, turning to the mess of boxes crammed into his trunk, "Well, let's see. Let's just see what we got

MICHAEL VINES

here."

And Carlo carefully examined every one, checking joyously for a size 7.

"Harry the Horndog Becker. That should be your nickname. Horndog Harry. I like that."

12

At least a week went by and Harry hadn't seen Carlo around at all, which was unusual. He kept an eye open for him when he went on his daily litter collection walks and dropped into Ed's a few times, not to shoot pool, but to see if maybe he was hanging out there. He wasn't. It wasn't like Carlo to keep a low profile. He had become a ubiquitous and loquacious presence in the neighborhood, even more so in Harry's life.

Whatever his faults and despite the foul business he was engaged in, Carlo was also a breath of fresh air—his youth, his energy, his exuberance all brought life, not to mention a little action, into Harry's contented but otherwise staid and settled domesticity. Carlo could be exasperating, but he could also be fun and could make Harry laugh. If Harry were to be completely honest with himself, he'd have to admit that he missed the kid—missed his enthusiastic extortionist.

Lena had never met Carlo, but Harry knew she would have found his enterprising spirit, his eye for a good scheme, and his relentless search for an angle admirable. They could have been a good team. Better than he and Harry, whose high principles and lofty values could only cramp Carlo's style. He wondered if Carlo had decided he'd had enough with a guy who would look a gift horse in the mouth the way he had with the pool cue and the designer shoes. Maybe he decided Harry wasn't worth the effort. There were plenty of far more fertile fields to plow.

But beyond all that, Harry was also beginning to worry. Carlo was involved with some rough customers, and who knows what trouble he could find himself in? It went against Harry's own best interest, but he was glad that today was collection day, and he looked forward to Carlo showing up in the afternoon.

But Carlo never showed up. Instead, it was Tony the Pipe, someone Harry had hoped he'd seen the last of. He looked liked he wasn't too thrilled to see Harry either, like he'd fallen asleep in his suit and been dragged out of bed just in time to keep his appointment at Harry's shop. He wasn't one to make small talk and he greeted Harry with one word: "Money."

It was no longer business as usual for Harry.

"Where's Carlo?"

"What d'you care?"

"He usually collects."

"Not anymore. He's out."

"What's this mean, 'out'?"

"It means gimme the fuckin' money."

Harry opened his cash register and took out some bills.

"This is it?"

"That's what I pay. Every week."

Tony, a man of as few words as Carlo was of many, barged to the other side of the counter, stuck his pudgy fingers into the open drawer, and yanked out a handful bills. He held them up for Harry to count. "Every week. *Capiche*?"

Harry nodded. He didn't at all *capiche*, however, what it meant that Carlo was out, but he knew better than to ask Tony again. It could have been all the incentive he needed to jam his pipe into Harry's ribs and say, "It means he's out." So Harry held his peace.

The next day, still worried about Carlo, Harry went to Lucille's for lunch, mostly to grill her for anything she knew about what might have happened with him.

"Yeah, he came back to me too, the pussycat with the pipe. Don't look too happy about it, does he?"

"That guy happy? Never seen it." Harry hadn't forgotten about the smile he had put on Tony's face when he gave him the holster, but it wasn't a happy smile. "He says Carlo's out? What's that mean?"

"Probably means he's been a bad boy. Got in trouble with the boss or somethin'. Not earnin'. Still wet behind the ears, you know. So they demoted him."

"You think he's all right? I hate to think. You know, Lucille, between you and me, I worry about Carlo."

"Don't. Ain't none of your business, for one. Mine

MICHAEL VINES

neither. And two, ain't nothin' you can do about it. He'll be okay. He's tight with The B, ya know. Family goes back. Still, the kid's gotta make his bones."

"What's that, make his bones?"

"You don't want to know, Harry."

Perhaps not, so he let it slide. And she was right that there was nothing he could to help Carlo. It's not like he could pay a little visit to Benny the B and inquire about him. Put in a good word.

"Hello, Mr. Apicella, I should like to introduce myself. My name is Harry Becker. You might know me as Hustlin' Harry? No? Horndog Harry? Well, maybe Harry the Yid? Yes, that's me. I'm the guy, yeah. Sure, you can call me that. Go right ahead. Just Yid? Of course, that's good too. Whatever you like. Anyway, I don't want I should take too much of your time, but I just want you should know that Carlo Barnini, that's one fine *boychik* you got there. You can always count on him. Smart as a whip. Always thinking a step ahead. And he shakes down like a real professional."

No, a client testimonial wouldn't do. He could do only what he always did. He could hope. His option of last resort. So he hoped for the best. He hoped Carlo would show up soon, good as new. At the very least, he hoped he would get word that he was all right.

A few nights later Harry was coming out of Ed's where he'd spent about an hour playing nine ball for a nickel a ball with the locals. He broke even against players he usually mopped the floor with but he was having a hard time concentrating on the game and never really had his heart in it. Every time the door opened and someone walked in—which wasn't all that often—Harry looked up, even in the middle of lining up a shot, hoping it was Carlo. If only there were some way he could get in touch with the kid, be sure he was all right, then he could at least have a little peace of mind.

It was just after dark when Harry headed home and was stopped by a loud whisper calling out his name.

"Harry. Harry. Over here."

Harry followed the voice to an alley beyond the reach of a dull streetlamp adorned with an acorn-shaped, frosted-glass globe perched atop a concrete post. He could hear a staccato rhythm striking the pavement—a dead giveaway. He took a step forward and saw Carlo, cloaked in shadow, his left toe tapping like a tremor he couldn't control, his eyes visibly darting from side to side. Picking up on Carlo's whisper, Harry spoke in one too.

"Carlo. Where you been?" Harry slapped the side of his arm and gripped it in a gesture of more than mere camaraderie. It was a comfort, a relief for Harry to feel him in the flesh. To make sure he was really there and still in one piece.

"Been workin'. Got a few things goin', Harry. Big things."

"You're okay?"

MICHAEL VINES

"Yeah, yeah. It's good. It's good."

"It's not good. The *mamzer* with the pipe is back."

"Yeah, well, don't worry 'bout him."

"He's squeezin' me hard, Carlo. Makin' me fork over more than I can pay."

"Yeah, well, things change, what can I tell you?"

"He says you're out. What's that mean?"

"That's bullshit. I got put on another thing, that's all. It's big. It's gonna be good, Harry. You'll see."

"You're not in trouble with the boss?"

"No, no way. Tight as a five-dollar whore. But, listen, Harry I need you to do me a little favor."

"What favor?"

"I need a little cash. Just for a few days."

"What happened to your dough? We were winning?"

"Yeah, *were* winnin'. Till you…never mind, I ain't gonna say it."

"*Noch amol* with the cue?"

"*Noch amol*? What's that? Like, *genug*? It's not shut up."

"It means 'again.' Again with the cue."

"*Noch amol*. Got it. Look, Harry, a few days, that's all I need it."

"Are you in Dutch with some Shylock?"

"Me? No. No. Where'd ya get that?"

"You think I'm born yesterday?"

"Look, it's just that I owe a guy. And I gotta pay. Now."

HARRY GETS WISE

"How much?"

"Two-fifty."

"Two hundred and fifty dollars? You lost that much?"

"With interest, yeah. Adds up fast, Harry. It's a good fuckin' business if you got the stomach for it. You know, we get a stake together, one day you and me, we could make a killin'. I mean, you're a natural at pool, Harry, but that don't figure. But Shylockin', I mean, your people invented it, right? Hell, that's in your blood. You could do that standin' on your head. And we'd make a good team, me and you. You do the numbers part, I'll flex the muscle. 'Course, you could never be family, but that's okay. There's a place for outsiders with talent. You could do book too. I'll bet you could do book real good. Jews are the best at that."

"*Zey shtil*, Carlo. No Shylocking, no booking, no nothin'. *Gornisht*. Capiche?"

"Yeah, yeah, *capisco*, okay. I'm just saying, you'd be great at it. But look, Harry, you gotta help me out here. I'll pay you back. In a few days."

"You don't have it now, how you're gonna get it in a few days?"

"I gotta deal goin' down. I just need you to float me for a little, that's all."

"What deal? Somethin' else fell from off a truck?"

"Harry, quit bustin' my balls, will you? I'm beggin' you, okay?"

"Don't beg, Carlo. Never beg. You need money,

why don't sell your *ferkakta* watch, huh? The fancy shmancy Rolex. That's so important to you?"

Carlo snorted. "'Cause it's fake, Harry. Okay? It ain't real. I could get more for a fuckin' Timex than this *shtick drek*. And you wanna hear the best part? It doesn't take a lickin' too good neither, Harry. Got a glass jaw."

Carlo held up the fake Rolex he was still wearing on his right wrist. Harry couldn't see it clearly in the dark, but he could tell it had the wrong time and the second hand was frozen in place.

"It's just for show, Harry. That's all. Worthless piece o' shit."

"Did you know it was a fake when you bought it?"

"What? Yeah. Sure I did. I knew it. Whaddya think?"

"I think you're lying to me, Carlo. I think you got conned. You took all the *gelt* we won and you bought a fake Rolex."

"Get out, Harry."

"*You* get out. Don't lie to me, Carlo. I don't want no two-faced guy."

By this time they were both speaking above a whisper.

"What the fuck difference does it make anyway, Harry? Huh? The watch is fake, that's all. But you know what's real? What's real is I need two-and-half bills. That's what's real. As real as this fuckin' stink."

Carlo kicked over a grey metal garbage can and its reeking contents spilled into the alley with a rattle and roll. A light went on in a window on the second floor. They both froze till it went out again. Only then did Carlo dare to speak, this time in an even lower whisper than he started with.

"Harry, you gotta help me. Please."

"You think I got two-and-half bills hanging around. Growing from trees?"

"You can get it though, right? You got credit at the bank. You got collateral."

"And I should give it to you? So you can throw it away? You say I got a lot to learn. *You* got a lot to learn, you little *pisher*."

"That's a low blow, Harry."

"That's what you are."

"Okay, fine. I'm a *pisher*. Spread it around. Carlo the *Pisher*, if it makes you happy. And I'll break your fuckin' neck, okay?" Carlo squeezed his fists and stomped his foot on the ground. "Look, I'm in trouble, Harry. I admit it. But I need dough and, fuck! I got no one else to go to."

Harry was furious. Furious on more levels than he could count. Furious with Carlo for getting himself into this mess, for getting involved in the rackets in the first place, and furious with himself for giving a damn one way or another. He knew he wasn't responsible for Carlo, but he couldn't just leave him swinging in the wind. If anything happened to him and Harry hadn't helped him when he could, that would be on him, and he'd never forgive himself.

MICHAEL VINES

Carlo was still young. Maybe he could turn himself around. All he needed was a second chance, his birthright as an American. And maybe, he could get one with Harry's help. He'd still be a long shot, but Harry was a long shot too at one time. Who'd have put their money on him? And look at him today. He got his second chance and he made it. Maybe the same could happen with Carlo. But first, he had to get out of the jam he was in and if Harry didn't help now, he might not get the chance to help later. Second chances don't keep coming forever. Not even in America. Harry agreed to meet him the next morning at the back door of the shop, first thing, at 9:15 sharp, hours before Carlo usually rolled out of bed.

* * *

Just minutes after Harry got there, straight from the bank, he heard Carlo's knock and answered it. Carlo wasn't his usual dapper self. His hair was dry and mussed and he hadn't shaved. The coil inside of him that was always so tightly wound had gone slack. He had a little of Tony the Pipe's weariness about him.

"You're one stand-up guy, Harry. Thanks a million. Really."

Carlo had jumped the gun a little, because before Harry handed him the money, there was something he wanted in return.

"Collateral? I don't got no collateral. What the fuck, Harry."

"Yes you do. You have your word, Carlo. I want you should give me your word that you'll pay me back every penny. Will you do that?"

"Sure, Harry, you got my word."

"On your honor of being a mensch."

"Yeah, sure, sure, honor of bein' a mensch. You got it, Harry."

"One more thing, Carlo. A *bissel* advice. And I want you should think about it. Get out of this racket. It's not for you. You're a smart boy. You can do better than this."

"Me? What?"

"You could go to school. Night school."

"Are you fuckin' kiddin' me?"

"I did it. Lena did it. Why not?"

"I work nights, Harry. Besides, me, I can't do school. I couldn't sit still in school five minutes at a time. Drove me nuts. I did tenth grade, Harry. And didn't finish that."

"You could try. You could at least try."

"N-O spells no, Harry. No school."

"Okay, you don't want school. Then learn a trade."

"Excuse me, Harry, you fall on your head or somethin'? You know who you're talkin' to here?"

"You could be my apprentice. Be a shoemaker. Make something of yourself. I'll teach you. I'm not gonna be around forever. It could be your shop one day."

"Harry, come on. You *gotta* be shittin' me. Can you see me slappin' soles on some slob's old shoes 'cause he can't afford new ones? Then shinin' 'em up like some fuckin' *mulignan*? No offense, Harry. But get the fuck outta here. That just ain't me, Harry. Not in a million years. This is the job for me. I'm outside, I make my own hours, I'm doin' different things every day, I'm part of a crew, meetin' interesting people. This is what I'm cut out for. Forget it, Harry. I'll pay you back the two-and-a-half yards. You got my word as a mensch, but that's it."

From the moment he came up with it, Harry knew his offer was as preposterous as Carlo was saying it was. But it couldn't hurt to try. And now that he had made the effort, he was quick to drop it. He handed Carlo the money.

"You won't be sorry, Harry. I'll make it up to you. Swear on my father's grave." Again with his father's grave. Carlo crossed himself, as he always did when he made that oath. "I'll pay you back Shylock rates."

"I don't want no Shylock rates. I'm not a Shylock. Principal only."

"You're a real mensch, Harry. And you'll get it. Every penny. And don't worry. I'll make it up to you. You'll get your vig one way or the other."

Harry watched Carlo drive off, then went back inside. But he wasn't ready to start work. Instead, he sat on a bench in his stock room and took stock. Personal stock. He asked himself how he got here, where here even was, and who he was as well. Who had he become?

Just the week before, along with the usual mix of bourbon and sweet talk, he surprised Lena with the Dior Roger Vivier stiletto pumps that he bought from Carlo for pennies on the dollar. When she rose to show them off, as unabashedly as a runway model, she became to Harry a statuesque figure of ineffable beauty, even as she stood on the far side of middle age. And despite the shoes' dubious provenance, he had no regrets. How could he? He was in a realm beyond reason, helplessly stuck in the sticky web of his own desire, where regret was given no quarter.

But the light of day was harsh and unforgiving, and he hated himself in the morning. Not even the siren's scent of Lena's camisole, visible in the mirror hanging on the hook behind him as he shaved, could bring him solace. Instead he began to wonder, what was the real price he had paid for those shoes? The total price when he factored in aiding and abetting a *goniff*? As surely as Carlo, the self-described middleman, was a thief, so was he. And now, he had compounded that guilt by allowing himself to be dragged into Carlo's latest *mishegas*, paying off a Shylock charging usurious interest. He was in the middle of it all now, oiling the wheels of corruption in which he himself was a cog.

But then again, maybe he was being too hard on himself. Perhaps a case could be made that his actions were more noble than corrupt. Helping his

MICHAEL VINES

fellow man in a time of need, even sacrificing for him—what could be a greater mitzvah than that? Maybe he deserved a little *rachmones*.

Harry had gotten to the bank that morning as soon as it opened. He didn't have to take out a loan to get the money Carlo needed. He simply withdrew it from his savings account. Nothing could be easier. A walk in the park. Yet, as he handed the teller his passbook, he tingled with a sense of foreboding. His entire body was a mass of latent energy waiting to be released, like the colorful balls racked on a pool table just before the white one smashes into them and sends them careening in all directions as dictated by laws of physics. Or like an atom just before it's split, setting off the chain reaction that unleashes its terrible energy.

What did he think he was doing? Two-hundred-and-fifty dollars was a lot of dough. It had power. And because it belonged to Harry, the power was his. The thought of tapping into it so cavalierly was both nerve-racking and exhilarating. If someone had told him as he sailed on the crowded crate that brought him across the Atlantic that the day would come when he would have a savings account from which he could withdraw that much cash to loan to a friend in need and still have money left in it, you could have knocked him over with one of the *schmattas* he had stuck in a sack that he used for a pillow. If he were still able to maintain his capacity to speak, he would have said only one word: America.

But the promise of America wasn't just a promise, it was a deal, and it had to go both ways. For it to be fulfilled, for the promise to be realized, every citizen had to do their part to prove themselves worthy of that promise by their acts. If not, they betrayed it. And now Harry had to face the possibility—no, the fact—that that's what he had done. Maybe he wasn't a thief, not in the strictest sense, anyway, and he certainly wasn't a Shylock, but he was living in a grey area now and he could no longer say he was keeping his end of the bargain. He wasn't even living up to his own ideals, unattainable though they may have been. But then again, neither had America. Harry had come to understand that by now.

When he came out of his reverie, he caught sight of the shipment he had received the day before. The items were stacked on a roughly hewn wooden shelf —soles and heels from Cat's Paw, taps, glue, polish, some new tools, and a new apron that was still folded and wrapped in plastic. He left that apron where it was and put on instead the old soiled one that he had been wearing for nearly a year, so stained with polish, dye, and glue it looked as if his grandchildren had finger-painted all over it. He didn't feel like putting on something pristine.

13

When Libby felt her breast in the shower, she remembered the first time she had touched one other than her own—Lammy's, beneath the water streaming from the showerhead in the dirty basement. The memory was indelible, but contradictory. She remembered it as an exciting, frightening exploration of their sexual awakening, but she also recalled there being something clinical about it, like she was feeling for a pulse, or a lump, which she had never heard of at the time, but thought of now. Because that's what she was doing. Feeling for a lump in her breast. She performed her self-examination thoroughly, careful to cover every inch of each bosom, sensitive to the slightest anomaly, the tiniest nodule, but found nothing. The same could not be said for Goldie.

Libby hated thinking of herself, but the news couldn't have come at a worse possible time. She had just moved out and now her family might need her more than ever. Not that this was about her. It was Goldie she should be thinking about. And she was. But no matter what else was on her mind and how selfless she may be, there was still room left to consider her own interests. Though she was connected to a larger whole—her family—she was also independent of them. Tethered but on her own. Together, they were like a mobile made of unique, delicately balanced constituent parts—touch one of them and it affects every other. And as Goldie now brought home to them, they were all hanging by a thread.

Libby's move a few miles away to U. City was not the jolt to the system she expected it to be—certainly not compared to the few centimeters of fibrous mass that was discovered in her sister's left breast. Had Libby's move caused real distress, a serious rift, Goldie's lump would have put things in perspective. But it never came to that.

Lena's reaction to the move surprised both Libby and Harry, as did so many of her reactions. Always a practical woman, she felt that Libby having a place of her own might serve a larger purpose—helping her to finally find a suitable man. Libby would be able to entertain a gentleman caller in complete privacy, whet his appetite with a little nosh—a nibble on her ear, maybe, a squeeze of the *pulke*—and get him coming back for more. It was a tried-and-true strategy by which more than one man had met his match.

But it was the secondary benefit Libby mentioned to her mother—having another apartment to rent out—that proved dispositive. Lena hoped that Libby's summer trial would be successful. The sooner they could get to work re-dividing the top floor—the cost of which she'd be

MICHAEL VINES

happy to take Libby up on her offer to pay—the better. So without the slightest Sturm und Drang, they loaded Libby's possessions into the Chevy Bel-Air and drove together to the green pastures of the city's closest western suburb—University City: safe, clean, and loaded with Jews besides their friends the Shermans.

It would be hard not to be impressed by the civic structures erected in the planned city's center. On either side of Delmar, where it intersects with Trinity, stand the Lion Gates, originally called the Gates of Opportunity. Atop each limestone pedestal soaring 40-feet high, prowls a lion cast in concrete, though the one on the north side, thought of as a lioness, is actually a tiger. Both bare their teeth identifying themselves not as a welcoming party but as fierce defenders of their territory.

On the northwest corner of the intersection, right next to the putative female lion, a Masonic temple topped by a ziggurat emerges, as if decreed in one of Coleridge's drug-induced dream visions. Just east of there is the City Hall, an equally fantastic 135-foot octagonal tower with a verdigris dome and a carbon-arc searchlight mounted on its apex. What were they searching for? Who knows, but it appeared to be a well-guarded community, and something splendid to all their eyes.

The house that Libby was moving into fit right in —a stately dwelling set off from the street by a rising double-tiered knoll of green lawn, two bay windows on the second story, a single large gable on the third, an entrance portico, and a Mission-style roof similar to the one on the Pavilion in Forest Park.

On the day of the move Lenny Goldstein made himself scarce. Sophie Kahn baked mandelbrot to welcome the Beckers, suffusing her entire home with a warm, welcoming aroma. She served it with hot tea in short water glasses, accompanied by sugar cubes for her guests to place in their mouths and suck as they sipped, Ashkenazi style. What was not to like? It was a smooth transition.

Lena was right in her expectation that having her own place might help her daughter get laid. Libby met a woman named Rosie through CORE who was also gay. There was no attraction there, but Rosie invited her to go with her to a place such as Libby did not even know existed—a lesbian bar. As if the forces of the universe were playing a little joke on her, it was called Shelley's.

Located on the 3500 block of Olive, the center of gay and lesbian nightlife in St. Louis, it was about a block from the Fox, hard in the middle of the entertainment district around Grand Boulevard, which included Arata's and Garavelli's. Shelley's was for the ladies, the Golden Gate exclusively male. There were other hospitable haunts besides, including the Onyx Room and the Act IV Coffee House, and there was plenty of bar-hopping going on between them.

Although the Missouri General Assembly had passed a law that prohibited purveyors of liquor

MICHAEL VINES

—under threat of revoking their licenses—from serving what they were not reticent to refer to in writing as "degenerates," the cops looked the other way, motivated not by some prevailing open-minded sentiment among them, but by the same incentive that made Officer Keegan and his cohort so cooperative with the crews running the city's rackets.

Like a kid with a new toy, Libby couldn't wait to get out there and experiment with her new freedom, so on her first Saturday night in her new place, she and Rosie made the scene. It was beyond anything Libby had experienced. The habitués of the clubs were obviously gay and didn't seem to care who knew it. The women were of two types—or three, if you include Libby: brazen hardcore butches wearing black leather or men's suits and jackets, either with neckties or turned-up collars, and projecting an attitude that one cross look was all they'd need to put a shiv in your gut; or très femme types dressed to kill in spangles and glitter, black cocktail dresses, the latest designer fashions, and heels that could have literally been put to lethal purpose, like, as the name implies, the Roger Vivier Aiguille Stilettos that Libby would have been shocked to learn her mother also owned.

The third type was Libby. She wanted to look attractive—and she always did, so that was easy —but not attract attention to herself. She dressed casually in a flared calf-length black swing skirt cinched at the waist with a two-inch-wide red plastic belt, a cream cotton blouse with a keyhole neckline, and low-heeled pumps. She could only hope she wouldn't be seen by anybody who knew her.

But what if she were? Just going to a place like this was a huge risk. What if she were spotted by a friend, an acquaintance, a co-worker? Would it be one of those moments of mutual revelation where the person would say, "Libby, what are *you* doing here?" and she could respond by asking the same question with the same emphasis? She'd probably get away with that, but it would still expand the small circle of people in town—two, now three counting Rosie, and Sophie Kahn was nobody's fool, so make it four, at least, and growing—who knew her secret. So before she came down, she had a cover story all worked out.

"Oh, I'm supposed to meet Jack Brandt. You know we went to college together? Well, he wanted to talk over a few things, strictly professional, and he asked me to meet him here. You haven't seen him, have you? Interesting place, this, isn't it?"

Despite all the belles mademoiselles floating in and out, Shelley's was, in Libby's mind, appropriately dark, rank, and seedy. She knew she didn't belong there, but also knew she belonged nowhere else. She was timid, anxious, and well aware that if she were to get even a little less uncomfortable, which was the most she could hope for, she'd have to get plenty *schickered*. So she got down to business working her way through whiskey

MICHAEL VINES

sours, which went down pretty easily, especially after the first. After her third, she had lost all inhibitions as well as all ability to walk without staggering and speak without slurring. And that was all the excuse Libby needed to exonerate herself when she wound up bringing a stranger home with her to U. City.

She couldn't remember many details, including the name of the gum-chewing gal with the dark close-cropped hair and turned-up collar who wasn't there when she woke up. But she would never forget how heavily hungover she was and sick to her stomach—the latter not just from drink. She couldn't even remember if the sex had been consensual. Yes, she had invited the woman to her house. At least, she thought she had. She was so plastered, she couldn't say for sure. But she must have. Why else would she have been there? Unless the woman had offered to take her home under the pretense that Libby was in no condition to get there on her own, and then decided to make herself at home while she was at it. But whatever happened to Rosie? She had no idea.

Libby wasn't so sure she had wanted to go down on this gal or that she had done so of her own volition. As it came back to her in dribs and drabs, Libby stitched together her recollection of the events. She remembered the woman, a bona fide butch, clutching her head and pushing it down. Forcing it down. She was strong. Libby felt that if she resisted, the woman could break her neck, maybe not inadvertently. Had she actually felt that way at the time, or was that what she felt the morning after when she struggled to comprehend how the whole sordid incident could have come to pass? To exempt herself from any responsibility in the matter.

She couldn't blame it on drink, though she tried at first. But that was too easy. For even now, cold sober, Libby couldn't say for sure if she had wanted to have sex or not. And even if she had wanted to, would she have to have been coerced into it? Could she possibly have both wanted to go down on her and to be forced to? Would she have to have been raped? Or have allowed herself to be raped? There were no easy answers. There were too many grey areas, too many things Libby couldn't be sure of. When push came to shove, it was more or less a push. It could have gone either way. Or both.

This couldn't be the life she was embarking on, Libby said to herself as she lay in bed aching, catching through the corner of her eye a wad of dried-up chewing gum and a Juicy Fruit wrapper —Juicy Fruit, of course—that had been discarded on her bedside table. Something to remember the bitch by. Evidence, if she needed it, that it hadn't been merely a bad dream. This wasn't the life for which she had left the bosom of her All-American immigrant family. It made her fling with the rich newlywed in Ladue seem respectable. Something to be proud of. Someone to bring home to her parents.

"Mama, Papa, I'd like you to meet my new friend.

MICHAEL VINES

She's also my lover, but don't worry. She's married."

This was not who she was. She was a responsible woman with an enviable job. She was a beloved and loving aunt. Rather than to suffer even one more empty, anonymous liaison—or worse, become the victim in a lurid newspaper headline—she'd happily babysit for her nephews and niece every night of the week and change Joey's diapers five times a day —something she actually enjoyed, providing, as it did, vicarious fulfillment for her natural maternal instincts.

It was just a week after that night, which began at Shelley's (Really? It had be called Shelley's?)—a week Libby spent contemplating a life of resigned celibacy—that Goldie discovered the lump in her breast. And Libby found herself in the shower examining herself for one of her own. Better it should be in her breast than in Goldie's, Libby thought. She'd have taken it from her if she could. Goldie had the children.

❊ ❊ ❊

Nobody knew if Goldie had cancer, a word that could never be uttered above a whisper, if uttered at all, in the Becker household. All they knew is that Goldie said she felt "something fishy" while she was bathing herself and, when Lena told Faye Goldstein about it, Faye insisted that Goldie see a doctor immediately. So Lena made an appointment for her with a Jewish doctor at the Jewish Hospital, which was one of the city's best, but even if it weren't, where else would they go? St. Luke's?

As far as Goldie was concerned, St. Luke's would have been fine. She believed in nothing and she believed in everything. Rabbit's feet, a found penny, wishbones, a charm fished out of a box of Crackerjack—all were potential portents of good luck, especially if their acquisition coincided with a winning streak. Goldie was a card-crazy gambler, the wildly popular game of canasta being her current favorite. But she'd play anything: poker, gin, hearts, casino, kalooki, mahjong, or any other game of chance that offered a payoff. She was quick to get in on the action when she heard that some handsome small-time hood—just a fast-talking *pisher*, really—had recently shown up in the neighborhood selling numbers for as little as a two-cents a pop. She never played the losing ones twice, but if she ever won, she'd stick with it. Those would be her lucky numbers. Until, over time, they proved not to be.

Goldie had little idea about what lay ahead for her, but she'd heard, in hushed tones, the words biopsy, radiation, mastectomy, and they all terrified her. It was a good thing she was ignorant of a common procedure known as the extended radical mastectomy—removal not just of the breast, but also of the breastbone, ribs, chest wall muscles, and lymph nodes under the arm. The whole ball of wax. Biopsy was bad enough.

She accepted that she had to see a doctor, but Lena had scheduled the appointment on the day of Goldie's regular poker game with her girlfriends held in a private room at a restaurant on Delmar with the peculiar name of Golden Fried Chicken Loaf. Goldie liked playing there. She considered its odd name, the first word of which echoed her own, to be good luck. Sometimes it was, sometimes it wasn't.

Goldie was partial to gold and the color became her signature. She wasn't originally a blonde but she became one—a golden blonde—and she accessorized with gold costume jewelry, always to excess, ignoring Libby's advice that she scale back.

"Before you go out," Libby said, "look in the mirror and remove one piece of jewelry."

Or two or three, Libby might have added, but she started small. Goldie did the opposite. She was equally lavish in her application of bright red lipstick, as bright as Mrs. Aschenschmidt's. When all decked out, her ensemble recalled Carl Sandburg's painted women under the gas lamps luring the farm boys, though that was not her intent.

Goldie wanted to reschedule the appointment, but Lena would have none of it. She promised her that Harry would drive her to the hospital and then, after the appointment, drop her off at her game, or what was left of it.

The morning of her appointment, Goldie decided to hedge her bets. On East Warne Avenue near the far end of O'Fallon Park, walking distance toward the river from her home, was the Mount Grace Convent and Chapel, a cloister of contemplative nuns known as the Pink Sisters owing to their signature pink habits that complemented some of the palest pink faces known to the terrestrial world, which faces were framed like cameos by white wimples topped by long white veils that fell down their backs to their waists. There she met Sister Michaela who, upon hearing why Goldie had come, offered to intercede before the Lord on her behalf.

"Lord Jesus alone can save you," Sister Michaela said, speaking in the broadest sense that Jesus alone can save her immortal soul, but which Goldie took in the narrowest—that Jesus alone could save her from cancer. Though she didn't buy one word of what she called "that whole *goyische* megillah," she was as inclined toward supernatural intervention in the material world as were the true believers, so she figured why not give the Sister a shot? Maybe it worked. Anyway, it couldn't hurt. So Goldie prayed with Sister Michaela and, on her way back home, she detoured down Florissant Avenue to Chervitz's and bought herself a pink silk scarf. Despite the heat and humidity, she wrapped it over her head and wore it like a babushka.

Dr. Ephraim Weinberg was not one to take a wait-and-see approach—perhaps because he didn't appear to have a lot of time himself. With beclouded eyes and skin tissue-paper thin—so transparent the sand in his hourglass could almost be seen trickling

MICHAEL VINES

down to its last grains—he didn't look like he had long to go. Goldie recoiled from him at sight. He looked too much like death, maybe because that was so much on her mind. But then again, his senescence could be seen as a good sign. He was experienced, had seen it all and, after examining her, feeling her breasts and the lymph nodes of her armpits, he offered his diagnosis.

"The lump has palpated," he said.

"What's that mean?"

"It means it's large enough that I can feel it."

"I can feel it too and I didn't finish medical school. Why else would I be here?"

"Very good," Dr. Weinberg said.

Weinberg recommended they take X-rays immediately to see if anything else untoward showed up on either breast. Directly after that, he would perform a biopsy on the known lump and any other nodule revealed by the X-ray. He would then have the pathologist freeze and stain the specimen or specimens to highlight the cells and determine if they were malignant. They'd have the results in a couple of hours. Goldie then heard for the first time the words extended radical mastectomy.

"You mean you'd put me under and I'd wake up with everything gone?"

"That's right. Then you'd undergo radiation therapy. You'd lose your hair."

"My hair?"

"It'll grow back."

"How about my breast? Will it grow back?"

"Of course not."

When Dr. Weinberg met with Harry and Lena to repeat what he had told Goldie, Lena covered her face with her hands and sobbed. Goldie stared blankly into the distance. Harry tried to comfort them both, but to no avail. Goldie wasn't ready to go under a knife, even for just the biopsy. Besides, as she muttered to herself in her state of shock, she still had time to catch the last games at Golden Fried Chicken Loaf.

"Forget about your *farshtunkene* game, Goldie. Please. This is no game," Harry said to her. Then, to the doctor, "There's nothing else she can do?"

"She could pray and hope and for the best."

Goldie and her parents exchanged looks, signaling their offense at Weinberg's arrogance and condescension. But he was the doctor. What did they know about medicine, about cancer? Nothing, of course. Still, Goldie would put her money on prayer and good luck charms any day of the week before she let this harbinger of death lay a hand on her. And her parents knew it.

"Excuse me, Doctor," Harry said, "but can Goldie have some time. To let all this sink in? To get ready."

"I wouldn't wait too long."

"But she can wait. She can have a few days."

"I wouldn't, but it's up to her."

After they climbed into the car and before he started it, Harry said, "I don't like this doctor. I don't

MICHAEL VINES

like the way he talks down."

No one had the strength to utter their agreement aloud.

Harry didn't drop Goldie off at Golden Fried Chicken Loaf and she didn't notice. If she had, she wouldn't have cared. In her condition, she wouldn't have known a jack from a king anyway.

They sat in silence as Harry drove home, accelerating at the right times, stopping at lights when they turned red, making the correct turns, avoiding running into other vehicles, all automatically without thinking. He was surprised to find himself approaching his neighborhood, as if it happened without his agency, without his being conscious of it. Because he wasn't. He was conscious of nothing, not even the thought process that led him to abruptly announce, "This doctor has an opinion. In America, everybody's entitled to an opinion. And my opinion is we get another opinion."

* * *

That night, Lena instructed all the woman in the family to examine themselves every day. And though daily prayer was not a family ritual, it became one. Goldie's prayers were pantheistic.

The following day, Lena sought comfort and counsel from Faye Goldstein.

"She shouldn't wait to see another doctor," Faye said. "You can't play around with cancer."

225

"Sha."

Faye rephrased her last sentence without the final forbidden word, but still reverting to the requisite whisper. "This is no fooling around. I know of another doctor. The best."

Dr. Marvin Ehrlich, also at the Jewish Hospital, whose father was a doctor and whose grandfather had been one too, was the second cousin of an acquaintance of Faye Goldstein's. He was the one to see, Faye assured Lena. He had medicine in his blood. And unlike this *alte kaker* Weinberg who was too old to be up to date, Ehrlich was young and would know all about the latest treatments. He wouldn't be so quick to cut women to pieces because of a tiny little lump. Faye lit a cigarette and offered the pack to Lena, who waved it away.

"Feh."

"Go ahead. It's good for the nerves."

Lena was a nonsmoker, as were all the Becker women save Goldie, who had picked up the habit from her card-playing friends who lit up as frequently as they anted. But this once, Lena took Faye up on the offer and took a puff without inhaling. Then she squashed the cigarette into the ashtray.

"Feh," she said again. She rubbed her hand across her face and was repulsed by the smell of tobacco on her fingertips. Seeking to distract herself, she turned the conversation away from her own worries. "So what's with your Lenny?"

MICHAEL VINES

"Lenny? You know. He's organizing, he calls it. To integrate for the *shvartzers*. He lives in U. City. A big house over by the Loop. On the fancy side, my Bolshevik."

Lena paused. For the first time in days, she actually thought about someone and something other than Goldie and her lump. But these new thoughts did not bring her comfort.

"The fancy side? Where?"

"You know a street Waterman?"

Lena calculated the infinitesimally low odds of this being just a coincidence. "How'd he find such a place over there?"

"A woman, a widow. She rents him a room."

Now the odds were zero. But Lena pressed on. "What's her name, the widow?"

"Her name? Kahn. Her husband left her a big empty mansion."

"*Oy gevalt.*"

"You know her?"

"I gotta go."

"What, Lena? Where are you rushing?"

"I have to call the Ehrlich doctor."

"Yes. Right away. He's at the Jewish."

"I have to call. Now."

"Let me know," Faye called after Lena as she hurried out the door.

And Lena raced out to make a call. But not to Dr. Ehrlich.

14

It was a good thing that Harry was the master craftsman he was, for he plied his trade with the same level of consciousness with which he had driven home from hospital the day before—none—going through the motions automatically, without thinking. He cut a sole with one of his new knives, so sharply honed that in less skillful hands it might have presented a danger. One careless slip could have cost him.

He may not have been thinking about his work, but he was thinking, deeply, about other things: breasts and lumps, Goldie and Lena, Tillie and Libby. He had personally examined Lena the night before in the most clinical fashion. If one of his girls had it, the others might too. If not now, eventually. It was the same curse that had taken his mother so many years ago. She had gone quickly, but painfully. And he couldn't escape the feeling that as far as his daughters were concerned, he was somehow responsible. Perhaps he was the carrier and had passed on the disease—which generally exempted men—through his own blood line.

Harry was skiving the edge of a newly applied sole when Carlo showed up. It was earlier in the morning than Carlo's usual business hours and he looked as bleary and tousled as he did the last time Harry saw him the day he lent him the money. Seeing Carlo brought Harry some relief, or at least a respite. He could turn his attention elsewhere.

"A little early for you, Carlo, no? You don't look so hot. What, you don't sleep?"

"I got a lot on my mind, Harry. That's all."

"You and everybody else in the world."

"You don't look so hot yourself. What's eatin' you?"

"Don't ask. So, you got the money you owe me?"

"You really saved me there with that, Harry. I'd have a lot more *tsuris* if you didn't give me that dough."

"I didn't give, Carlo. I lent."

"I know, I know."

"So where is it?"

"Listen to you. You sound like a real Shylock already, ya know that?"

"Stop with the Shylock. I did you a favor."

"And I thanked you."

"Don't thank. Pay."

"Jeez, Harry, you'll get it."

"But not now. Now you don't have, right?"

"I'll have, I'll have. Just cut me a little slack, will ya?"

"So nobody broke your legs at least."

"It wasn't my legs I was worried about. This guy, he's a guy in Martinelli's crew I owed."

"Who's Martinelli?"

"Frank Martinelli. Big fuckin' capo."

"He's got a nickname, this Martinelli?"

"Fingers."

"Fingers Martinelli?"

"Frankie Fingers."

"Ah. Frankie Fingers. I bet you like that, Carlo. Yeah?"

"Well, yeah, sounds good, I gotta admit, but it's pretty fuckin' sick, Harry. It's on account o' you get on his wrong side, he'll take a fuckin' finger off ya."

"What are you talkin'?"

"I'm tellin' you. A pinky. He'll cut it off. Or a guy in his crew does, anyway, and Martinelli gets it. Sick, am I right? It's like a savage. Like the Indians with the scalps. He keeps 'em in these little jars with formaldehyde. Lined up on a friggin' shelf."

"*Gay avek.*"

"*Emmes*, Harry. You saved my fuckin' finger. I owe you."

"You owe me two-and-a-half yards is what you owe me."

"*Noch amol*? I said you'll get it. I'm just a little tapped out right now's all. Look, I'm gonna level with you. I had to pay Martinelli first. That's fixed. Now I just gotta get square with Benny, and I'm back in business. Then you'll get your dough. Real soon. Even Steven."

"Benny too you owe?"

"Not money. I just gotta do somethin' for him,

MICHAEL VINES

that's all."

"So, go do."

"I will. Don't worry about it."

"You're the one looks worried, Carlo."

"I'm not worried. I just...I gotta take care o' somethin' is all."

"So *gay*, *gezunterheyt*."

"Yeah, you too, Harry. But, Harry. Here's the thing."

Carlo stopped, his face slackened. Suddenly he looked paler, smaller, depleted, like he was shrinking right in front of Harry's eyes. He sank into a chair and pushed back the long forelock that fell from his forehead. His left foot was tapping, but not at its usual tempo—it was keeping time more to a dirge than a jitterbug. Harry stopped trimming the sole he was working on and waited for Carlo to continue. But he didn't. It was as if he had uttered some magical incantation and put himself in a trance.

"What? What's the thing?"

Finally Carlo managed to speak, his voice hoarse and hollow. "It's a big fuckin' job."

"What is it?"

"It's nothin'. That's all. It's fuckin' nothin'. Don't worry 'bout it."

Carlo looked out the window. The sidewalk was empty. He got up and closed the front door, blocking off whatever whisper of air was being drawn into the shop on this hot, still, St. Louis summer day. Then he stepped up to the counter and spoke to

Harry in a low voice.

"Can I talk to you, Harry?"

"Yeah, sure."

"On the QT. Between you and me. Nobody else."

"I don't gossip, Carlo. I mind my business."

"Yeah. Well. Listen. You know, Benny. Benny the B, right? Killer B?"

"Yeah."

"Well, you know, like I said, he wants me to do him a little favor."

"So? Do."

"I don't know, Harry. I don't know if I can."

"Maybe I can help."

Carlo sniggered, then whispered, too low for Harry to understand.

"Speak up. Who can hear when you talk like that?"

Carlo leaned closer to Harry. "He wants me whack somebody."

"What means, 'whack somebody'?"

"*Shah. Zey shtil*, will ya, Harry? He wants me to bump a guy off. You know what that means, don'cha?"

Harry had seen enough gangster movies to know. "No, Carlo. No. 'Whack' you call it? No. No whacking. No bumping off. That you cannot do."

"I mean, the guy would deserve it, Harry. He wouldn't be just a regular citizen. Like you, Harry. He'd be a criminal type. Like me. He's got it comin', Harry, believe me."

MICHAEL VINES

"I don't care who it is. No whacking, Carlo. Never. Is this the way you make your bones?"

"Well, yeah. But it's not like I got a choice here, Harry."

"You always have a choice."

"Yeah, well, here's my fuckin' choice. Whack or be whacked. Law of the fuckin' jungle, Harry. That's how the world works."

"What world? Get outta that world, Carlo. I told you."

Carlo spoke above a whisper for the first time, with a trace of indignation. "It's your world, too, Harry. You live in the same fuckin' world. I told *you*."

"In my world we don't go around whackin' people. We don't go bumpin' off. It's forbidden!"

"Oh, yeah? You make me laugh, Harry, you really do. You bump off plenty people in your world. You just have someone else do it for you. Just like Martinelli and Benny the B. Only difference, in my world, it's guys like me do the dirty work."

"In my world we bump off? What are you, *gansa meshugga*?"

"Yeah, I'm *meshugga* all right. Come on, already. Sometimes...you got a short memory, Harry. What about the fuckin' war? Ever hear of that, or did you forget already?"

"What are you comparing? We had to fight. To fight for America. For freedom. For everything decent in the world. To fight for innocent people."

"Gimme a fuckin' break, Harry. The atomic

233

HARRY GETS WISE

bomb? Hiroshima? Those were innocent people too, except for being Japs. And we killed 'em all."

"It was war, Carlo. They started it, the Japs, the Nazis. Hitler. Hitler would kill everybody. We're supposed to sit back and let him? All the Jews, he killed. Old men and women. Children. Little boys and girls. Babies. They could hurt him? Everyone, he killed. Burned to ashes. Innocent people. We had to fight Hitler. For that you had no choice."

"Well, there's lots o' little Hitlers in the world, Harry. They're all over the place. And I don't have no choice either. Let's see you try to fight 'em."

"Listen to me, Carlo. You think you kill someone and that's the end of it? No. It's the beginning. That you can't undo. It stays with you forever. Every time you turn around, it's there. Every time you look in the mirror. You end someone's life, you end your own too. I'm telling you. You kill one person, you kill the whole world. You kill yourself."

"You don't get it, Harry. You think this is what I want? This is my idea of a good time? It ain't. Not by a long shot. What I want is to drive down the street in a big fat baby blue Cadillac convertible and toot my fuckin' horn at every babe I see waggin' her sweet ass down the street. And when I pull over, some of 'em'll just put their head down and walk the other way. Most of 'em will. But some of 'em, not a lot, but all you need is one, she'll say, 'Nice car, sailor.' And when I ask her if she wants to go for a little ride, she'll say 'Sure, why not?' And then we take a short

MICHAEL VINES

sweet ride to fifteen minutes of paradise. You know what I'm talkin' about, Harry. I know you do, you ol' horndog. Well, that's what I want. But you don't get the one without the other. You just don't get it, Harry. You just don't."

"I get it. I get it all right. You're the one who doesn't get it. You think like a little *pisher*, and the way you're goin' you're gonna end up a little *pisher*. You'll die a little *pisher* if you're not careful."

"Look, Harry. I like you. We're friends, right. You help me, I help you. But this is the way it is. This is what I gotta do."

"No. No, Carlo. You do this, I'm not your friend no more. That's it. Now go. Get outta my shop. And if you do this thing, don't come back. I wash my hands of you."

Carlo balled his right hand into a fist, brought it to his mouth, and bit his index finger, grunting like a cornered animal. Then he stomped out the door and slammed it shut.

Harry came around the counter and opened it back up. The air was so thick and heavy, he could hardly breathe. He couldn't work. He had too much on his mind.

❊ ❊ ❊

It wasn't long before Lena showed up at the shop in a huff, coming directly from Faye Goldstein's.

"We have to go down to Libby tonight. Right after

HARRY GETS WISE

you close up. She's home at six."

"Why? There's a problem?"

Lena knew better than to tell Harry everything she'd heard from Faye and—having a head for numbers and the ability to add one plus one— everything she had surmised. If she had barged in and told Harry that Libby was living with Lenny Goldstein and they had to do something about it immediately, Harry would have taken a more temperate approach, tried to calm her down and talk sense to her. He would never have agreed to show up at Libby's unannounced, search for evidence on the premises to prove Lena's suspicions—like they were some kind of secret police—and confront their daughter head on. He would have tried to reason with her. But Lena was in no mood for reason. She needed to get to the bottom of things and she needed to do something about it quickly, that evening, before it was too late, if it wasn't already. So she lied.

"I have to bring her some things she forgot to take. That's all."

"Tonight she needs them?"

"Yes. Tonight. You'll take me there in the machine."

Lena didn't pose that as a question or suggestion. And after making her demand, she changed the subject before Harry had a chance to object or ask any more questions.

"There's a new doctor I got from Faye. Ehrlich his name is. He's at the Jewish too. I have to call

236

MICHAEL VINES

him, right away. You leave it to Goldie, she'd wait till Purim."

That part was true, and the first thing Lena did when she got home was to look up the phone number of Dr. Marvin Ehrlich in the enormous St. Louis phone book—the kind a strongman would use to prove his mettle by somehow, impossibly tearing in half—and call his office. The soonest available appointment was the following week, five days away. Five days of nonstop anxiety. After that, Lena grabbed some clothes that Libby had left behind in her closet and waited impatiently for Harry to close up shop and drive her to U. City.

* * *

When they got in the car, Harry saw what Lena was bringing for Libby—an overcoat and a woolen suit.

"This Libby needs tonight? It's a hundred degrees."

"It's supposed to cool off."

Harry had no idea what Lena was up to and he didn't bother to inquire. It would have been futile anyway. She was on a mission and they were already on their way. As he pulled out of his parking space, Lena told him that she had made an appointment for Goldie with this Dr. Ehrlich. They would all be sitting on *shpilkes* for the next five days.

On the drive out, the air hung over them

HARRY GETS WISE

heavy as Libby's winter overcoat, and they kept to themselves, too hot and too wrapped up in their own thoughts to talk about them. Some of the things couldn't be talked about anyway. Harry wasn't about to tell Lena that Carlo had to whack to somebody, and Lena wasn't about to tell Harry that Libby was living with Lenny. He'd find out soon enough. With Libby, Harry could have made small talk about the Cardinals, just to distract themselves. But Lena followed the team only through osmosis and didn't really care about them one way or another. Harry would have liked to turn on the radio and listen to the soothing sounds of the summer game as he drove, but it wouldn't start for over an hour. He and Lena could have talked about Goldie, but what was there to say that they hadn't said already? They were helpless as newborns, but crying and kvetching would bring them no succor, no warm relief such as a baby would receive from a mother's breast. They could cry their *kishkes* out and it wouldn't do any good. So they drove all the way to U. City gazing out the window in silence, seeing and saying nothing.

* * *

Libby hadn't been home long and when they arrived she was surprised to see them. When she asked why they had paid the unexpected, unannounced visit, Lena handed her the winter

238

clothes she had brought.

"I don't need these now, Mama."

"You never know. Better you should be prepared."

Harry hugged Libby, then, holding both her hands in his, stepped back and spread her arms, taking his measure of her, making sure she was healthy and whole, as if he hadn't seen her in years. It was he who missed her most of all.

"How's my *meydeleh*?"

"I'm fine, Papa. This is a surprise."

"We wanted to see you. How you're doing. It's okay, no?"

"Of course. But next time, call first, okay? I could have been out and you'd have come all this way for nothing."

"So where's Sophie," Lena asked.

"Out somewhere, I guess. I don't know."

"And your other roommate?"

"Other roommate?"

"You have another roommate? Yes?"

Libby paused and thought for a second. "Sophie rented out another room. Yes. Why do you ask?"

"I'd like to meet this other roommate. She's a nice girl? You like her?"

"I like my roommate fine, Mama."

Lena had already grown impatient with her charade and suddenly dropped all pretenses.

"So what's going on with you and Lenny Goldstein?"

"Lenny Goldstein?" Harry asked. "Lena, what are

you talking?"

"She knows what I'm talking. He lives here. With Libby. In this house. Am I right?"

"No, Mama. You're not. It's not like that."

"Lena, *vus machs da*?"

Lena answered him in Yiddish. "I'm finding out what's going on."

"Nothing's going on, Mama."

"No? Is he upstairs? Your roommate, Lenny Goldstein? Let's go to your room, Libby."

"Mama, no."

Just then Lenny, who had heard everything that had been said, came walking down the stairs.

"Yes, Aunt Lena. I'm upstairs. Or I was. You're right. I live here too."

"You've got some chutzpa, Lenny Goldstein. Let me tell you. Living together like this. Are you married and you maybe forgot to tell us about it?"

"No, Mama. We're not married."

"You're getting married then? At least?"

"We're friends, Mama."

"Friends you call it? Living together you call friends?"

"Mama, we're not—"

"You think I'm blind? I can't see what's going on right in front of my face? You live here, he lives here."

"How'd you find out?" Libby asked.

"What, you think you can pull the sweater over my eyes? You can't Libby. I'm not born yesterday. So, Mr. Bolshevik, you're gonna marry my daughter?"

MICHAEL VINES

"Marriage is something of a bourgeois construct, Aunt Lena."

"Don't talk all high and mighty with me, mister. I know more than you think I do. You're gonna make an honest woman out of her?"

"Mama—"

"Libby, let me handle this. Uncle Harry, Aunt Lena, Libby and I have been spending a lot of time together. And in that time, we've gotten very close. We've found that we have a lot in common. And why not? We pretty much grew up together, right? Anyway, when I came here for the summer, I needed a place to live. Libby wanted one too. So we both wound up here. And now, well, we're just going to see how things develop."

This came as a shock to Libby. She had no idea that Lenny had thought that way, or even if he really did. He couldn't. He knew better. Then again, maybe he knew even better than she. Maybe he had a sense of things—of her—that she herself did not. In any case, he had thrown her a lifeline, again. A way out. He was taking control, and Libby, relieved that at least somebody had an inkling as to how to handle the situation, stood back and watched. To see how things would develop.

"You'll be relieved to know that we have separate rooms. Across the hall from each other. We're not living together any more than that. We're neighbors."

"You have separate bathrooms?" Lena asked.

"No. We share a bathroom."

"Mm-mm. And what else? What else do you share?"

"We share a lot of things. A lot of ideas and values. We've been working together on things that we both believe in. Integration, equal rights, social justice."

"So Libby, you're a Bolshevik now too?"

"No, Mama. But we do have a lot in common. Our values. They're the same ones I got from you and Papa, and Lenny got from Aunt Fay and Uncle Meyer."

"That's right," Lenny said. "And maybe...well, we're seeing how we are together. Right now, nothing's going on between us. Not the way you think. But, well, we'll see."

"This is way too modern for me." Lena said to Harry in Yiddish, and Harry answered her the same way.

"What do you expect? We're in America, Lena. The Old Country is over. It's gone. Kaput. It's not even there any more. Here, it's different. The kids are different. They have different ideas. They're free. The old way didn't work out so good, Lena. Maybe they have a better way. It couldn't be much worse."

"*Oy*," Lena sighed. "I don't know. I don't know from nothing anymore."

Both Lenny and Libby understood every word they said, and when Lena hesitated, when she said, "*Ich vais nicht*," "I don't know," as if admitting

MICHAEL VINES

that the new world and its ways were beyond her comprehension, that perhaps there was another way of looking at things, even a better way, Libby grabbed the opening.

Knowing that nothing could bring her family together like food, she said, "Mama, come. Let's relax. Stay for dinner. I roasted a chicken yesterday. All I ate was a *pulke*."

"Sounds good to me," Harry said.

"I don't feel like food right now."

Harry took Lena's hand. "Come, Lena. Eat. You'll feel better. Libby made a chicken."

Lena acquiesced. Just to give herself something to do, she searched the refrigerator, found some broccoli and carrots, and cooked them in her customary fashion—within an inch of their lives. Throughout the meal Lena said nothing, but kept one eye on Lenny as he pulled a *fliegel* from the carcass—like a caveman with that beard—and ate with such gusto that she couldn't help imagine him taking her daughter with the same ravenous zeal. She should only be so lucky, Lena thought.

Harry talked baseball, asking the others if they thought Wally Moon would be named rookie of the year. Only Libby had an informed opinion, which was that this kid Aaron on the Braves would give him a run for his money. Lenny said he'd heard something in Chicago about the Cubs having a terrific rookie, but he couldn't recall his name.

"Ernie Banks," Libby said. "And he's nothin' to

sneeze at either."

"A shortstop," Harry said. "With power. Go find one for us."

Lena aside, it was just the kind of small talk the rest of them needed. And so went dinner. Casual, superficial, and, thanks to Lena's unresponsiveness, a little awkward. She never got comfortable, and it was obvious to everyone that she couldn't wait to get out of there. Harry accommodated her. They ate and ran.

As soon as they got in the car, Harry put on the radio and was happy to hear the voices of Harry Carry and Jack Buck—in their first year of calling Cardinal games together—crackling across airwaves as he drove back to Warne. Even if he hadn't understood the language or known the first thing about the game, he would have been calmed by the comforting sounds of baseball seeping through the speakers. They didn't have the same effect on Lena. She didn't even appear to be listening as she stared out the window, lost in her disquieting thoughts.

"They're no good," she said.

"No, you're wrong, Lena. They're good kids. They'll be fine."

"I mean your Cardinals. This isn't their year."

"No. You're right about that," Harry said, even though Stan Musial had just hit another homerun.

* * *

MICHAEL VINES

Back at the house on Waterman, as they washed and dried the dishes together, Libby allowed herself to imagine a life of idealized domesticity with Lenny. If it could somehow be possible, it would make everything so easy. Of course, she had no interest in him sexually, but maybe sex wasn't as important as everybody made it out to be. It could hardly be less satisfying than her most recent sexual encounters, few and far between though they had been.

Perhaps, over time, she could grow to love Lenny, and her tender feelings could evolve into sexual desire. If not, she could still perform her connubial duty once in a while. At least enough to have a couple of kids. And kids were something that appealed to her. She enjoyed being an aunt, but she'd love to be a mom. Other women like her had done it. Since time immemorial, she was sure. Besides, didn't the passion burn out for most married couples once children entered the picture? Didn't most of them lose interest after a few years regardless? Her father was kind, loving, and affectionate, but she couldn't imagine him and her mother having much physical passion in their relationship. Not anymore, anyway. Marital bliss, sexual fulfillment, they were as much a fairy tale as Prince Charming stumbling upon his lady love, making her his princess, and living happily ever after. If Lenny became frustrated, he could always have an affair with another woman. She wouldn't object. They could live separate lives in that regard.

HARRY GETS WISE

Have an open marriage. Like any Bolsheviks worth their salt. Lenny was a free thinker and so was she—or so she thought—so why not?

"Lenny, what you said to my parents. Do you really think this might be some sort of a trial run for us?"

"No. I know better, Libby. I'm not that lucky."

"Then why'd you say that? You could have just told the truth."

"Well, I'll tell you. I'm thinking a little ahead here. You might want to have a cover, Libby. Know what I mean?"

"What, a pretend boyfriend?"

"Right. They call it a beard."

"I know."

Lenny wasn't deceiving himself, even if she was. But deep down she knew better too. No matter how close they became, no matter how much she came to love him, she knew she'd never desire him. Or any other man. She had a choice to make. To be upfront and honest about who she was or to continue living a lie. And when she put it that way, she realized she had no choice at all. If she flouted convention, defied biblical injunction, violated every taboo, and lived openly and freely as a lesbian, she'd lose everything that mattered to her. She'd be ostracized, banished, the most horrible punishment the ancients could imagine. Few things are worse than living a lie, but that would be one of them.

Lenny was a good man. A good friend. And it

246

MICHAEL VINES

was nice to know he was there for her. For that, she should be grateful, even though she wasn't. When they had finished drying the last of the dishes and wiping down the counters, Lenny headed into the living room to watch TV.

"Guess you won't be interested, Libby. Friday Night Fights."

"I'll watch a little."

They sat beside each other on the sofa, and after the first Gillette commercial, Libby asked, "Ever think about shaving your beard, Lenny?"

"Me? No. It's mandatory for us Bolsheviks."

"I'll bet you'd look good without it."

"You mean I don't now?"

"I didn't say that."

"There was the implication."

"Well, it's not what I meant. You look just fine."

"'Just fine.' Let's not go overboard, Libby."

Libby punched him playfully on the arm and stayed for the first two rounds but she didn't feel much like watching two men beat each other up for sport, so she excused herself to go up to her room and read. When she reached the stairs, Lenny called out to her.

"Hey, Libby, don't forget. You ever need a beard, I just happen to have one."

Libby smiled at him and continued on her way. She waited till she was alone in her room, with the door closed, to allow herself to cry a little.

15

Tony the Pipe Allocco was a small-time hood with small-time dreams. When he closed his eyes at night, before tumbling into his typical thrashing, unsettled slumber, what danced in his head were visions of nickels. The old Buffalo nickel, which had been minted until 1938 was still in wide circulation. With the profile of an American Indian on the "heads" side and a bison on the "tails," it captured the imagination of the people and held a special a place in their hearts. But to Tony, a man without an ounce of aesthetic or scintilla of sentiment, a nickel was a nickel—coin of the realm. Buffalo or Jefferson, all that mattered to him was how many he could collect from the pinball machines that Benny the B had shoved into bars, bowling alleys, diners and the like all over St. Louis. In Harry's neighborhood alone there were over half a dozen—three at the Florissant Lanes and one each in Dependahl's, Ed's, the Circle Fountain, and Lucille's. Along with the cacophony of thousands of others scattered throughout the rest of the city, those nickels added up. They were also small and easy to skim a little off the top.

Tony had been leaning hard on Harry and, on the most recent collection day, he told him, "This place

MICHAEL VINES

could use a little livenin' up. Might be a good spot for a pinball. Draw some of the foot traffic."

"I don't have room for that," Harry said.

"We'll make room. Turn the storage area into a little—whaddyacallit?—arcade. Yeah, that's right. Got room for a couple back there. Maybe three."

That was something Harry wanted nothing to do with. Neither he nor his clientele wanted kids traipsing into the shop and making a racket on those machines, raucous with bells and buzzers and clacks and clangs. He could only hope that Tony was just thinking out loud. That he'd never go through with it, or would forget about it. Now it was all the more important that Harry keep him appeased and not do anything to upset the status quo. As much of a burden as it was for Harry to meet his current payments, he couldn't afford to come up even one cent short. He didn't dare, even if he had to dip into his savings to cover it.

For this he came to America? For another czar to boss and push him around, a Little Caesar like Edward G. Robinson in the movie? It wasn't much different, the Czar or the boss. Nicholas or Benny the B, take your pick. They both had an imperial hierarchy. They both had soldiers. The B had capos, too, a word smoldering with associations that Harry struggled to avoid.

Extortion, pinballs. That was just money. Money and things. And those can always be replaced. People can't. Considering what Goldie was facing, how could Harry fail to keep that in mind? Putting things in perspective was one of the consolations of adversity. Compared to Goldie, what else could possibly matter? How could another threat from a thug like Tony the Pipe be anything more than minor nuisance?

* * *

Goldie was so afraid of receiving the dreaded diagnosis that she pretended to be too sick to go to her early morning appointment with Dr. Ehrlich. But Harry and Lena would have none of that and they insisted that she keep it. Once they met the doctor, they knew their daughter would be in good hands.

Dr. Ehrlich was nothing like Dr. Weinberg. He was young, but not too young, with a high forehead rising like a monument to his towering intellect— a feature that might have been intimating had it not been for the kind eyes set just below it and the natural warmth he radiated.

Unlike Dr. Weinberg, who was cavalier about extended radical mastectomies, Dr. Ehrlich would perform one only as a last resort. However much he differed from his colleague, though, he was in complete agreement with him about the need for a biopsy. Right away. Right then and there, if possible.

Goldie again said that she wasn't ready, that she needed a few days to prepare herself. But Dr. Ehrlich

MICHAEL VINES

emphasized the urgency with such sincere, heartfelt empathy that he was able to convince her that she had no choice. She needed no convincing that, if it had to be done, he was the man to do it. The whole family was relieved that Goldie was listening to reason. That they were at least doing something. But the relief evaporated as soon as they started doing it.

The biopsy was routine and not what she could call painful, but Goldie milked it for all it was worth. Once it was over, she needed rest and relaxation. And a little recreation. So the next day, while they awaited the results of the biopsy, Lena took care of her kids, Marshall and Sandy, and Harry put up the sign on his door that said, "Back in 20 minutes," then drove Goldie to Golden Fried Chicken Loaf for a card game—about twenty minutes there and twenty minutes back. She'd call if she needed a ride a home, which she did.

Knowing that the results of the test could come in at any moment, the ride home was excruciating. She had hardly won a hand that day and her luck looked to have run out. To put off the inevitable and help steel herself against what she feared was sure to be the severe decree, Goldie insisted that they stop for an ice cream soda, the family's time-honored palliative. Harry suggested they pick one up at the Circle Fountain, but for Goldie, that was too close to home for comfort. She wanted to keep as far from the neighborhood as she could for as long as possible. So Harry drove out of his way on Natural Bridge Road and pulled into the Goody Goody diner,

HARRY GETS WISE

where he knew they had a first-rate fountain.

Together they lingered at the counter, where Goldie sipped and slurped so slowly the ice cream all but melted before she could spoon it out. Harry understood her delay tactic and made no attempt to rush her. He took his time too. And why not? What was done was done, what was written was written, and there was nothing they could do about it anyway. They might as well relax, find comfort where they could—if they could. Take time to stop and sip the sodas.

While Goldie dawdled, Harry let his mind drift —anywhere but in the direction of what was at the very top of it. He considered the diner's clean and simple décor, the red and black motif of the tables and booths, the diamond-shaped pattern embossed on the stainless steel splashboard behind the counter. Red and black recalled the preferred color scheme of the Führer—the *capo di tutti capi*—and his clean, simple, frighteningly powerful graphic designs. The diamonds made him think of baseball and the Cardinals, but there wasn't much hope for them—even Lena knew that. Not wanting to feel frightened or hopeless, Harry let his thoughts move on.

The hum of the crowd penetrated his consciousness, and he wondered why this popular place, packed with people in the late afternoon, didn't have a pinball machine in it. Or two or three. It had room enough for them. Benny the B and Tony the Pipe couldn't possibly be unaware of this

252

MICHAEL VINES

potential goldmine. Was Goody Goody being shaken down too? Or did the owners somehow dodge that bullet? Did they have an in or an angle of some kind? So much happened beneath the surface. So much Harry knew nothing about. How did things really work? he asked himself. One was selected. Another was spared. Why? Was it just plain old luck, pure and simple? Like the few who somehow survived the camps in Europe? And when he found his thoughts had drifted in that direction, he had to call it quits.

"Goldie, so *nu*, already? Time to go."

"I'm not finished, Papa. Let me finish. Who knows how many more chocolate sodas I'll have?"

Goldie could certainly milk it.

* * *

The call from Dr. Ehrlich came shortly after Goldie got home, where Harry and Lena waited with her on pins and needles—*shpilkes*, they would say. Goldie answered, and when she heard the news she shrieked in anguish and broke into tears.

"Negative! The results are negative!" she sobbed to Lena as she handed her the phone.

Lena was as shaken as Goldie, but when she was finally able to process what Dr. Ehrlich explained to her—the counterintuitive fact that a negative result was positive news—she too began to shriek, but with joy and relief. The lump in Goldie's breast was not malignant. It was benign. She had averted the

253

HARRY GETS WISE

severe decree. She had been spared. Overjoyed, Lena handed the phone to Harry and began explaining the good news to Goldie.

When Harry took the phone, he heard the word "But..." There was a but. Yes, the lump was benign *but* it had to be continually and scrupulously monitored. If it grew, it could yet become malignant. There was also the possibility that other fibrotic regions contained nodules too small to be detected by the X-ray, so Goldie would have to conduct frequent self-examinations and see Dr. Ehrlich for regular checkups.

Dr. Ehrlich next mentioned groundbreaking research by a man named Raul Leborgne in Uruguay that employed breast compression to improve the image quality of the X-rays and could, in certain cases, detect radiographically visible microcalcifications. Dr. Ehrlich thought this technique was promising and, though still in its nascent stages, something that should be considered as they went forward. The earlier the detection, the better the patient's chances, so Ehrlich was eager to help pioneer the process in the States.

Harry couldn't understand all that medical mumbo jumbo, but one thing stuck out for him: Uruguay. Uruguay? He'd heard of it, but he certainly didn't associate it with state-of-the-art medical research. How could some small, backwater South American country like Uruguay be more scientifically advanced than the U.S.? Ahead of

MICHAEL VINES

America in anything? Was it even a democracy? Did it have three branches of government? Every day, it seemed, Harry was confounded with new evidence of his ignorance.

But that conundrum could be considered another time. The good news was that medical science was advancing from every corner of the world, and what difference did it make where it came from? As long as it augured well for Goldie, for all Harry's girls, for all women everywhere, that's all that mattered. Leborgne wasn't a German name, so at least he wasn't likely to be one of those Nazis who escaped to South America, though it wouldn't have surprised Harry if he had been. Those Germans produced some damn fine scientists, he had to give them credit for that. And if Leborgne were a German, an escaped Nazi even, and had discovered a cure for cancer, would anyone turn their back on it? No, nobody, not for one second.

But then Harry asked himself a more difficult question: what if this imagined cure had been discovered inadvertently, through so-called medical experiments in which innocents were tortured by sadistic German doctors at Auschwitz and Dachau and Ravensbrück? They had been put on trial at Nuremberg and found guilty. But what if their research, despite their best—that is to say, worst—intentions, had yielded life-saving benefits for all mankind? What would be the right thing to do then? Could good come out of evil? Would the ends, unintended though they were, justify the means?

That would be a moral dilemma so profound that few people in the world were prepared to ponder it. And Harry was not one of them. He couldn't say if it would be right or wrong—he'd leave that to the philosophers and ethicists—but his first reaction, the reaction of a helpless father was, "I'm sorry for those who suffered. But I can do nothing for them. What's done is done. But at least their suffering shouldn't be in vain. Give me the cure. Save my Goldie."

For now it was enough to know that Goldie did not have cancer, a word they still didn't dare say aloud. "Benign" became the word of the day, one they could shout from the rooftops if they felt like it. But...

The "but" gave Harry pause. It meant that Goldie didn't get a clean bill of health—not completely. The lump could still grow. Could still turn malignant. Not only that, there could be others, still in their infancy, invisible now to the instruments and methods available to modern science, except for one guy in Montevideo, of all the unlikely places. And Harry knew all too well that where there was one, there were others. Anybody ever see just one cockroach? A solitary little insect who shared with Garbo a disposition for solitude? Or one Cossack? One storm trooper?

The forces of evil liked company. They roamed in packs like the dogs they were. Harry knew them. They weren't brave enough to go it alone. And they'd never be gone for good. They'd show up one day out

MICHAEL VINES

of the blue, do their damage, then might go away as suddenly as they came, and it would all be over. For a while. But they'd come back. They always did. You had to be vigilant. As Goldie would with her lump. It could come back, bigger, more virulent than before, and this time unstoppably lethal. And it wouldn't be alone. Harry knew better than to bring this up with his family. He knew to keep these apprehensions to himself.

* * *

And who did Goldie have to thank for her happy result, her new peace of mind? Surely her parents deserved some credit. Were it not for their persistence, insistence, and support, she might never have gotten around to seeing a doctor in the first place, or would have hemmed and hawed until it was too late.

Faye Goldstein had to be in line for honorable mention, at least. Faye was not only the prime mover, the one who told her parents that lumps were nothing to fool around with and had to be looked into immediately, she also happened to know about this brilliant doctor with the prominent forehead that announced his intellect like a giant billboard that read, "GENIUS AHEAD."

And he was young too. Not too young, but a lot younger than Dr. Weinberg, whom Goldie would never have had anything to do with in a million years. Young enough to keep abreast of the latest methods, treatments, and breakthroughs in his field. So thanks, Faye, for recommending Dr. Ehrlich.

And of course, there was Dr. Ehrlich himself. Had he not had such a soothing bedside manner, been so genuinely concerned and understanding, Goldie might not have felt comfortable or confident enough in him to put herself in his hands. What did he say specifically that put her so at ease and earned her trust? She couldn't remember a single word. It didn't matter anyway. His eyes did most of the talking.

Then there were the wonders of medical science in their own right, without which a tiny tumor might never have been radiographically observed and diagnosed, and left instead to metastasize, spread silently and insidiously throughout her entire body, ravaging her slowly and so painfully that she would have considered an extended radical mastectomy to be a blessing.

A blessing indeed. And in Goldie's mind, that's where the real credit lay. Not in the people who loved her, the doctor who cared for her, or the science that allowed the medical professionals to work their miracles, but in real miracles—supernatural intervention. Dr. Ehrlich may have performed the biopsy, but he had nothing to do with the outcome. For that, she credited Sister Michaela of the Mount Grace Convent and Chapel. And she thanked a god she didn't believe in for the Pink Sisters.

The next morning she returned to the convent and told Sister Michaela the good news. Sister Michaela was not reluctant to give credit where she knew it was due. Together they prayed, thanking Jesus for making the tumor benign, for sending them Dr. Ehrlich and blessing him with the forehead behind which was seated the brains and judgment that permitted him to do Jesus's work on earth, even though, he himself was destined to burn in hell for all eternity. Or so it was written.

Before she left, Sister Michaela presented Goldie with a gift, which was hers to keep for a small donation. It was a silver chain strung with white beads and had a crucifix attached.

"It's called a rosary," Sister Michael said.

"It's very nice," said Goldie. "Do you have something in gold?"

Sister Michaela rummaged through cabinets and drawers until she found a rosary made of some cheap gold-colored metal chain, golden beads, and a golden crucifix. It was just Goldie's style, and hers for a slightly larger donation.

Sister Michaela explained to Goldie what a rosary was, what it meant, and how to use it for devotional purposes. She recited for her the Apostle's Creed, Our Father, Hail Mary, Glory Be, and all the rest. She enumerated the twenty mysteries to be reflected upon, five in each classification: Joyful, Sorrowful, Glorious, or Luminous. When Sister Michaela had gone through all that, she handed Goldie an illustrated pamphlet that had in writing everything she had just articulated. It was something Goldie could study and refer to daily until she had memorized every word.

It all went in one ear and out the other. As far as Goldie's was concerned, this holy devotional object was nothing more than a nice addition to her collection of baubles and costume jewelry. And her newest good luck charm. It may not have been kosher, but Goldie wore the rosary as a necklace, the crucifix hidden inside her top. On the way home, she walked a few blocks out of her way down Florissant to Woolworth's where she picked up a tube of lipstick. Rather than her usual bright red, she chose a more subdued shade—shocking pink. As garlic is said to ward off vampires—which Goldie, despite never having met one personally, was prepared to believe—pink might ward off cancer. It was paying off so far and she was going to ride out her streak as long as it lasted.

16

The third generation of Beckers that began with Harry as patriarch—the first first-generation Americans, not counting Libby—faced dangers that the previous ones had never imagined. And they imagined plenty. More than imagined. But there lurked in this new land another kind of threat, an indigenous breed of monster that seemed to rise exclusively from American soil.

The first example was the kidnapping of the Lindbergh baby—whose family name Harry (and surely FDR, as well) had been unable to utter without affixing the epithet "the son of a bitch" ever since the infant's father revealed his fascist sympathies before the war. But that abduction and murder was a distant nightmare. And the target —an international celebrity and the apotheosis of American individualism for flying solo across the Atlantic on a plane he dubbed The Spirit of St. Louis —was even more remote. Both he and his tragedy were unique, something that couldn't happen to regular people like the Beckers.

But another kidnapping had occurred less than one year ago, much closer to home, and neither Harry's family nor any other with children escaped

HARRY GETS WISE

the grip of fear and panic it inspired. The panic abated in time, but the fear persisted.

A six-year-old named Bobby Greenlease was in class at his Catholic school in Kansas City, Missouri when a woman named Bonnie Emily Brown Heady came by and told one of the nuns that she was Bobby's aunt, which she wasn't. Her next lie was that Bobby's mother had suffered a heart attack, and they had to go to her immediately, before it was too late. Everyone believed her, even the far-too-trusting Bobby, who'd never seen the woman before in his life.

Harry followed the story closely in the papers and on TV, along with everyone else in the nation. He was riveted, shaken, shocked, unable to sleep. As horrified as he was, he couldn't shake an odd concern.

"Bonnie Emily Brown Heady?" he'd say. "How many names does the *chaleria* need?"

Bonnie Emily Brown Heady brought the boy to her lover and accomplice, a morphine addict named Carl Austin Hall, who sent ransom notes to Bobby's family demanding $600,000 for his safe return. The Greenleases held up their end of the deal, but Hall was about as trustworthy as most drug addicts. He had already put a bullet into Bobby's head before sending the first ransom note, then buried him in a shallow grave outside Bonnie Emily Brown Heady's home.

The couple were caught and, less than three

262

MICHAEL VINES

months after their conviction, received the same punishment as Julius and Ethel Rosenberg (just five months before them), by way of the gas chamber instead of the chair.

Though the entire nation was horrified by this story, nowhere was the horror experienced more acutely than in St. Louis where Hall and his paramour were arrested, she after a world-class drinking binge at the seedy apartment on the South Side where Hall had abandoned her, and he at a motel on Route 66 where he was no doubt getting his fix.

When Harry drove the kids to Ted Drewes for frozen custard, he took Route 66, and he imagined Carl Austin Hall stopping there to get some for himself. Harry sized up the other customers waiting in line, upstanding citizens all on the surface, and wondered if one of them could be a monster too. When he passed a motel on his way, he wondered if that was the one Hall had holed up in. Everything looked so normal, so benign, but unspeakable peril could be lurking anywhere. It gave Harry the heebie-jeebies, and he feared that maybe he had strayed too far from home, beyond the Pale, into unfamiliar and dangerous territory. But even when he was back home with the family, all of them safe and sound, the fear stayed with him.

"Never talk to strangers," he told his grandchildren. "Never take candy from strangers. Never get into a car with a stranger. Never. Never. A stranger comes up to you and offers you candy, you run away as fast as you can. Run into the hardware store. A restaurant. Even the pool hall if you have to. But run."

The oldest cousin, Marshall, seven years old by this time, took it upon himself to lecture his juniors and with greater specificity. "If some strange guy comes up and says your mom's sick and she's in the hospital and you have to go with him, don't go. He's lying. Even if he says your mom's dying and you're the only who can save her life, they're lying. Don't go."

His cousin Marty was just two years younger, but the scenario Marshall described was so vivid and terrifying to him that he burst into tears.

"My mommy's not dying," he wailed. He was inconsolable until Tillie, having heard her son from the other room, rushed in and swept him into her arms.

"You're not dying, you're not dying," he cried.

"No, no, darling. Mommy's right here. I'm all right."

"And you're never going to die."

Tillie hesitated for just a second before she answered. "No. Never. Mommy will always be here."

There was still another threat to the children, this one universal and it targeted them all, high or low born, Black or White, Jew or gentile, American or European, African or Asian. And this one didn't come with candy and a smile. This one was inhuman, invisible, and thrived in the same streets and playgrounds as the children it preyed upon. Children were unlikely to get cancer, but they were the primary target of the polio virus.

Harry closely followed the polio epidemics that broke out during the summer months of the forties and fifties, and made sure the children strictly followed all the orders issued by the health authorities to protect them. They were to keep away from pools of water, known to be breeding grounds for the virus. They were to stay out of alleys where puddles formed in depressions of their cracked, potholed pavement. They were prohibited from using public water fountains and swimming pools, for reasons that had nothing to do with racial animus. The sprinklers in O'Fallon Park that kids could run through to cool off were shut down. Water, the source of life and the one thing that could offer relief from the city's unbearable heat, was off limits.

The world was so dangerous and unpredictable, the threat to kids from man or microbe so immediate and palpable, it was easy to forget that everyone else was living on the edge too. Until Goldie came along and reminded them. The grandchildren were shielded from her ordeal, but adults had now to stare it in the face: the possibility of sudden unexpected death.

* * *

Marty was a happy child by nature and it didn't take him long to put Marshall's horror stories out of his mind. He was too focused on something else to let that bother him for long. All he talked about was getting a bike and learning how to ride it. And Sid and Tillie were planning to get him one as soon as they could. Sid had been working such long hours —even on weekends to get his new accounting firm off the ground—that time was at a premium. He confided to Tillie that he was afraid that the kids would grow up behind his back, that he'd put so much into building a future for them that he'd miss out on the present, miss their childhood, miss being a father.

"Not enough hours in the day," he'd tell Tillie when he came home after the kids were asleep. "I need more time."

And he made a promise to himself that he would get it. He would make time. He also promised Marty that on the coming Saturday the two of them would go to Sears together where Marty could pick out the bike of his dreams.

"A red one," Marty said, which was his only criterion.

Sid kept his word and on Saturday morning he and Marty drove off together. Tillie, holding the baby, and Harry and Lena all waited for them outside, fanning themselves as they sat on the concrete steps that led up to their doorways. When a cooling breeze picked up, but only for a second, Lena

MICHAEL VINES

said, "Ah, a *mechaiyeh*."

Sid's car finally pulled up, and the family greeted the father and son like they had just returned from a great adventure, bringing with them some rare and fabulous find. Sid popped open the trunk and pulled it out: Marty's first bike, a bright red J.C. Higgins model with white fenders and training wheels. Marty couldn't wait to ride it, and the whole family stayed outside to watch him take his first spin. It was a day none of them would ever forget.

Sid had never taught anyone how to ride a bike before, though he knew how to ride one himself. Marty followed his dad's instructions. He sat on the black leather seat, took hold of the red rubber grips on handle bars, put his feet on the white pedals, and pedaled away while his father ran alongside him, holding the rear fender to help Marty keep his balance. They went up and down Warne Avenue, Marty getting faster and more gleeful as he gained confidence. And each time they got back to home base, his mother and grandparents greeted him with a round of applause.

"Okay, let's take a little break, Marty," Sid said. "It's hot today."

"Again, Daddy."

"Again? Well, okay, one more time."

And after they rode up and down the block one more time, Marty repeated himself.

"Again, Daddy."

"Whoa, hold your horses. Let's go inside and get a

drink of water first. Whaddya say?"

"One more time first."

"Daddy's thirsty, Marty," Tillie said. "And so's the baby. Come on, let's all get something to drink now."

"Then maybe later we'll try it without the training wheels," Sid said, offering him an incentive as he wiped the sweat off his brow. "Whaddya think of that?"

It must have seemed like a good deal to Marty because he hopped off his bike like a cowboy off his horse and followed his family inside.

Sid took his glass of water into his bedroom and plopped down on the mattress. He was a little short of breath and perspiring heavily after exerting himself like that on such a hot day. He drained his water glass in one sip then lit a cigarette.

The rest of the family was in the kitchen, drinking their own glasses of water while Tillie fed the baby a bottle of formula. Marty wandered off for a moment, then came running back into the kitchen.

"Mommy, Daddy fell asleep."

"Fell asleep?"

"On the floor."

They all rushed into the bedroom and found Sid collapsed on the floor, a cigarette smoldering on the bed. Harry grabbed the butt, slapped his hand against the blanket before it could catch fire, and crushed the cigarette into the ashtray on the side table. Then he bent down and tried to rouse Sid, who

MICHAEL VINES

lay there limp, unmoving.

"Call a doctor," Harry said.

"The police," Lena said.

"No police. A doctor. An ambulance."

When Lena called the family doctor she was connected to his answering service and told the operator what was happening. The operator took over from there.

Tillie placed the baby in his crib and helped Harry lift Sid onto the bed. Her short, slight husband seemed to weigh two-hundred pounds.

"Sid, Sid, can you hear me?" she said, shaking him as she spoke. But he didn't respond. "Oh my God."

Harry went into the kitchen to get another glass of water for Sid. To throw it on his face if he couldn't get him to drink it, as he had seen done in the movies to bring someone back to consciousness. The others paced back and forth, going in and out of the bedroom, helpless to do anything but wait, cry, and call out in desperation. Marty started crying too. Then the baby.

"What's happening, Mommy?" Marty cried.

Lena grabbed Marty's hand and said, "Come, come with me," as she led him into the front room and sat him on the sofa. "Sit now. Just sit," she said in Yiddish, and Marty understood.

"What's happening, Grandma?"

"The doctor is coming. Just sit now." The first sentence in English. The second back to Yiddish.

Then she turned on the TV.

"Is Daddy okay? Can we ride the bike some more?"

"Not now. Just sit. Watch the television." The tube had warmed up by then and a baseball game illuminated the screen. Lena turned down the sound. "Baseball. Watch the baseball."

Lena went back into the bedroom and stood over the bed. She reached out and touched Sid's hand. She placed her fingers on his neck, then held his wrist.

"Tillie," she said. "He's dead." Her tone was without affect, matter-of-fact. She, like the rest of them, was in shock.

"No! What are you saying, Mama? No! It's the heat. He passed out from the heat." Then Tillie reached out to Sid, held his hand, and fell onto her knees beside the bed, sobbing, heaving, and gasping for breath.

The doctor arrived in about twenty-five minutes, followed shortly by two police officers, whom he or the answering service must have notified. None of the family had ever seen them before. The doctor pronounced Sid dead at 1:47 in the afternoon. An ambulance arrived. Sid was lifted onto a gurney, loaded into the emergency vehicle through the tailgate, and driven away. Harry went with him. Tillie stayed behind. She couldn't leave the kids.

※ ※ ※

MICHAEL VINES

Harry's attitude towards life was that it could always be worse. Even this, he said to himself, could have been worse. The blanket could have caught fire from that *ferkakta* cigarette that Sid had to light up, as he always did. Then the mattress. The fire could have spread through the apartment, the whole building—the whole thing could have burned to the ground. They could have been trapped, all them, the whole family, all the *kinder*, Faye's too, every one of them could have been lost. The entire family wiped out. Gone up in flames. Like all the rest before them.

But the worst had not happened. They were still here. Stumbling around like zombies, but still here. Spared the worst. What would happen now? What would Tillie and the children do now, without Sid? A good man. A devoted husband and father. A real mensch. What now?

What now? They would do what they had always done. The family would come together. They would bury their dead. Their dead husband and father. Their dead son. Their dead brother. Their dead brother in-law. They would put him in the ground and they would shovel dirt over his casket. They would rend their garments and they would cover the mirrors and they would mourn. They would sit shiva, contort themselves onto stools as low to the ground as they felt in their hearts. And they would say Kaddish, as had generations before them. And they would eat. They would eat from shiva platters sent to them from friends and delivered by Sol and Eli's delicatessen—lox and bagels and white

HARRY GETS WISE

fish in the mornings and brisket and chicken in the evenings. They would eat the burgers and fries that Lucille sent over from the Warne Grill and gallons of ice cream sent from the Circle Fountain. They would eat because life goes on.

When Harry worried, he worried about his grandchildren, about their vulnerability. What horrors could befall them. They, who were helpless in the world. It was up to the adults to protect them. He didn't worry about their parents. They were grown men and women, they could take care of themselves. He never worried about Goldie, not since she had become an adult with children of her own to worry about. He certainly never worried about Sid. The college man with the big future ahead of him. He didn't have to. Besides, who could think the unthinkable?

It was time now to think ahead. But none of them was ready to. Tillie would have to go to work. Sid's accounting firm was over as far as she was concerned. His partner, Benny Mendelson, would have to reassess things, see if he could make a go of it on his own, without Sid who was the prime mover and had all the personality. But that no longer had anything to do with Tillie. She'd have to find a job. Leave her children at home and go back out into the world. But what could she do?

During the war, like a lot of the girls she had grown up with, she had worked at the Grand-Leader, as she still called it, years after it had changed its name to Stix Baer and Fuller. She met Sid before

MICHAEL VINES

he went overseas through mutual friends who were dating former Rough Riders, the high school club at the YMHA of which Sid was also a member. They dated casually, but it was obvious to everyone who knew them that Sid was falling head over heels. When he got called up, he dared to ask Tillie to marry him, but she said she wasn't ready for that. It wasn't the right time. Without committing, she said they should wait till it was all over and think about it then. It wouldn't be long, they assured each other. After Sid shipped out, they became pen pals and, through the power of the written word, the romantic spell of distance, and the ultimate stakes of war, Tillie fell in love with him.

One night during the shiva period, after friends and family had left, Tillie pulled out the letters Sid had sent her from overseas and re-read them. One was dated August 5, 1945, from "Somewhere in the Philippines" as he designated under the date. It was the day before Hiroshima as it turned out, but Sid certainly had no inkling of that, and the letter betrayed no hint of the carnage and slaughter that had occurred everywhere around him, or the cataclysm that was about to change the world forever. It was light and airy, idle chitchat really, but his warmth, kindness, and humor came through.

> *This evening I saw a film*
> *but I just couldn't digest*
> *this one. "Delightfully*
> *Dangerous." What a*
> *stinkeroo! If you haven't*

*seen it, be sure to miss it.
Don't worry about me in
that picture I sent. I may
not look my best, but I've
never felt better. I have lost
a considerable amount of
weight, but that's due to
the extreme heat and not
because of overwork. (Hope
my C.O. won't note that
statement). The heat here
is really something. Makes
summer in St. Louis seem
like spring on the Riviera.
We'll have to go there
some time—maybe our
honeymoon?*

He closed by saying that he loved her and always would, and signed off with, "My regards to your family and friends. Love, Sid." Even over there, he remembered her family. What a mensch.

After the war, they got married, but they never made it to the Riviera. Maybe some other time when they could afford it. Sid took a clerk's job at Ralston Purina for a couple of years while he finished his degree in accounting at night at St. Louis University. When she got pregnant with Marty, Tillie, like every other mother she knew, took on the role of fulltime housewife. Now that role was over. No one could expect her to think about what her next one would be. Not yet. But she'd have to deal with that

MICHAEL VINES

sometime, sooner rather than later.

The apartment was filled with family, friends, neighbors, and neighborhood shopkeepers for the entire seven days of shiva, and the consequent hubbub helped to keep such worries at bay. Lenny had driven Libby over right away, as soon as she got the call the day it happened. Lenny had always seemed to be a part of the family, if a distant one, like a second or third cousin, but now he seemed much closer. And not just because of the way death has of bringing people together, united in their loss, confronted by their common destiny, which they otherwise necessarily ignore. He was so attentive to Libby, they seemed like a couple. And the family knew they were living under the same roof together. But at the end of the day, Libby didn't return to University City with Lenny. She stayed on Warne in her vacant apartment upstairs and helped take care of the kids. After a couple of days, however, she'd have to go back to work. She had her own life to live.

On the second evening of shiva, the apartment was so packed with condolence callers there hardly seemed room for one more, let alone one who brought with him an enormous arrangement of flowers that barely fit through the door—a wreath of white carnations, mostly, with a few white roses, draped with a black ribbon that read R.I.P. Flowers are customarily not sent to Jews sitting shiva, so a small vase would have stood out. By that standard, these looked like they belonged in the Rose Bowl Parade.

HARRY GETS WISE

Carlo drew stares when he entered. He didn't know what to do with himself or the flowers he had brought, but he found a place for them by moving a table in the corner and tucking the wreath behind it. Then he found a place for himself, against the wall and out of the way, where he was standing when he spotted Harry sitting on the sofa next to Lena. Carlo nodded gravely in their direction. Harry hadn't seen him since the day Carlo confided to him about what he had to do for Benny the B, and Lena had seen him from afar, but never met him.

"Give a kick. What's he doing here?" Lena asked Harry in Yiddish.

"What do you think? Like everybody else."

Harry felt sorry for Carlo, a man so clearly out of his element, an outsider unsure of how to conduct himself in a setting he knew nothing about. Harry could relate all too well. Wanting to put him at ease, Harry got up and walked over to Carlo, who took his hand.

"I'm sorry, Harry. My heart goes out."

"This is life, Carlo."

"I'm sorry, Harry."

Harry nodded. "Go eat. There's food."

Harry pointed to the dining room table where the spread was arranged, and Carlo helped himself to a serving of brisket. He regarded the exotic item on a serving plate beside it—stuffed derma, or *kishke*, as the Jews called it—with mild trepidation. He forked a sample onto his plate, sniffed it,

276

MICHAEL VINES

shrugged, and gave it a try. Same with a stuffed cabbage. Then he spritzed himself a glass of seltzer and ate by himself, standing up, tapping his toe as he chewed.

He had just finished when a rabbi in attendance called for the evening service to begin. Carlo may not have been much for social graces, but he knew better than to eat and run—it would have been disrespectful to Harry. So, following the lead of the other men, he took a yarmulke from a wicker basket and placed it on his head; he took a tallis from a pile crumpled on the table like dirty laundry, and, copying the others, draped it over his shoulders. A man with a beard handed him a book. Carlo opened it to a random page as the men began reciting. In Hebrew. He had no idea what they were babbling and didn't try to mimic their words, but he hummed along as they davened. Swept up in the communal sway of more than the minimum of ten Jewish men required to form a minyan, he swayed along with them.

Out of the corner of his eye, Harry watched him bobbing and rocking with all the Jews. Carlo was completely out of place—too tall, too handsome, too slender, too graceful—and yet, somehow, he almost fit in. At least to Harry. The yarmulke and tallis were like a costume on him, but he wore them well and nearly pulled it off. A little education and some proper guidance from a caring father were all he needed. Look at that *punim*. The strong jawline, the symmetrical features, the Roman nose. It wasn't a

Jewish face, but it wasn't a criminal's either. There was a kindness there. A stronger spin of the wheel, a different roll of the dice, Harry thought, and who knows what might have been?

The proper guidance from a caring father, Harry thought again. Where would Marty and baby Joe get that? Only one place. He'd have to be a father again, he realized, as well as a grandfather.

After the Kaddish ended, Carlo put his yarmulke and tallis back where he got them and headed for the front door, but Harry stopped him before he got there.

"Carlo. You daven like a real Jew."

"Daven? That's a new one."

"Pray, it means."

"Okay. Daven. Got it."

"You see, Carlo, what life is? Life is short. We have to make the most of the time we got."

"That's right, Harry. You're right about that."

"Don't take it for granted. Be a good boy. Be a good man."

"I will, Harry."

"Life is precious, Carlo. Every life. I don't care who it is. Life is precious. You hear me?"

"Yeah, Harry. I hear you."

Harry fixed his gaze on Carlo until their eyes locked. "Every life. Capiche?"

"Yeah, Harry. *Capisco.*"

They shook hands, a gesture of understanding and agreement, Harry thought. Or at least he hoped.

MICHAEL VINES

Even now, when he was hard pressed to find even the faintest glimmer, he could hope.

* * *

On the final day of the mourning period, a Sunday, Lenny dropped Libby off early in the morning. She entered the apartment carrying in one hand her blue hard-shell vanity case with a mirror attached inside the lid and, in the other, a small overnight case. Lenny carried two others. The large ones. She had bought the matching set with her discount at Famous, certain she would travel someday, imagining someplace more exotic than University City. Paris, for sure. Maybe Rome or the Riviera. Libby hadn't moved out for long, but now she was back. She had to be. Her family needed her.

17

By sundown on the seventh day that brought the ritual mourning period to a close, Harry needed to get out of the house, to be alone for the first time all week, and get back in touch with himself. He needed desperately to be part of the world again and thought that taking a little walk alone would be a good first step. He might stop by the shop—which he'd reopen for business the next morning—just to feel his body inside it, stand behind his counter, and inhale its familiar, life-affirming aromas. It was a portal back to the material world, the land of the living.

Before he went out, he told Lena he was going. Maybe he'd stop by Ed's and play a little nine-ball, he said. It had been a long time and that could be just the thing he needed—an activity, unlike mourning and saying Kaddish, that allowed him to focus on something trivial, something that didn't matter a hoot. He said he might be a while and told her not to worry. She understood.

The heat had broken at last and when he stepped onto the porch and felt the breeze, he said to himself what they all always said: a *mechaiyeh*. Perhaps it would help clear his head of its heavy burdens as

MICHAEL VINES

it had the air of its heavy humidity. As he crossed Warne and smelled the first wafts of fresh air, his step lightened, and he made up his mind to hit Ed's after a visit to his shop. He'd play for only pennies, but he could use the action.

When he got to the front door beneath the awning that read Liberty Shoe Doctor, he saw the sign he had put up when he last locked up: "Back in 20 minutes." Give or take a week, he thought to himself. Then, as he reached for his keys, he saw something that should not have been. A light was on in the storage area. It was very unlike him to have left it on, but he must have. And it had been burning all week. Good thing Lena didn't know that. But she was sure to find out. There'd be a spike in this month's electric bill, which Lena was responsible for paying, and Harry would have to explain. She wouldn't be happy about it.

Harry entered and walked to the back of the shop where he saw that not only was the light on, but most of his inventory of the cheap shoes he sold was gone. The back door was ajar. He'd been robbed, he thought. But in a moment, he saw that wasn't it. Tony the Pipe trundled in carrying an armful of fur coats, each wrapped in its own clear plastic bag. Harry's appearance startled him, but just for a moment.

"Good timing. I could use a hand with these."

"What are you doing?"

"There's more in the trunk."

"Where's my stock?"

"New stock, Harry. Go grab some and bring 'em in."

"You think I can sell those here?"

"Not sell. Store. I'll take care of the selling."

Tony hung the coats he was carrying onto a rack he had also brought in. This, Harry did not need. But if it was the world he wanted to get back to, he just did. Sid's death and the shiva that followed had been a respite from it. His grief and concern for his family's uncertain future—Goldie and her lump, Tillie and her boys—had forced everything else out of his mind. Tony Allocco, the squeeze he was putting on Harry, his talk of pinball machines, and everything he represented—authoritarian rule and the threat of violence, the things Harry had fled from in the first place—had taken a back seat to his family's well-being. And now there was this. His inventory cleaned out to make room for stolen furs. Well, at least they were better than pinball machines. They didn't make any noise. But just because furs were in didn't mean pinballs were out. It was just a matter of time.

In the moments it took Harry to consider those things, Tony had already lost his patience, if he had any to begin with, and suddenly it was no more Mr. Nice Guy. He barked out his order like his next move would be biting Harry's head off.

"Go on, I said. I ain't got all night."

Harry just stood there, giving no indication that

MICHAEL VINES

he was going to do what Tony said. He found himself clenching his fist, an uncharacteristic reflex that he had no familiarity with, and it frightened him almost as much as Tony did.

"You fuckin' deaf or somethin'? You hear what I said?"

Harry heard him, but he was still processing this latest intrusion. It wasn't that he was going to do anything about it. He wasn't even going to say anything, but he would at least take a moment to think.

It must have appeared to Tony that he was resisting, and, to forestall even the remote possibility of that, Tony smacked him hard across his face, a blow that spun Harry around and hurled him against the wooden shelves that stood behind him. A cardboard box of nails fell off, sending its contents scattering across the concrete floor like skittering roaches, clattering as they went. But Tony wasn't done yet. He grabbed Harry under his armpits, pulled him away from the shelves, and slammed him back into them, crashing Harry's back against the hard wood. Harry crumpled to the floor with a groan, the wind knocked out of him.

"You listen to me, you fuckin' Hebe. When I tell you to do somethin', you fuckin' do it. Now get the fuck up and unload that trunk."

Harry grabbed a low shelf and started pulling himself up slowly. With one hand, Tony pulled a pack of Luckies out of his jacket pocket, shook it so a cigarette popped up, and grabbed it between his lips. With his other hand he pulled out his Zippo and, using just his thumb, flipped it open, flicked its hard metal wheel against its flint to spark a flame, held it up to his Lucky, and inhaled, blowing smoke out of his nostrils. As Harry struggled to his feet, Tony watched disinterestedly, as if he were waiting for an egg to boil.

Harry reached for the next higher shelf to give himself a boost. When he placed his hand on it, he saw, inches away, an awl, one of the new tools in the shipment he had received a couple of weeks ago. Thoughts of reprisal raced through his mind, but a rational man would know better than to even consider doing anything so foolhardy. Harry, however, was not thinking rationally. He wasn't even thinking. He was all emotion, indignation, and raw fury born of injustice—the injustice of this two-bit thug holding a position of power over him; the injustice of the lousy hand Goldie had been dealt; the injustice of Sid's sudden, inconceivable death; the injustice to his widowed daughter and his fatherless grandchildren. The injustice of a God that allowed these things to happen, if such an omnipotent God even existed. And the injustice of an implacable, arbitrary universe if he did not. Thinking about none of those things, but feeling every one of them in his deepest, darkest places, Harry grabbed the awl, turned, and in one swift gesture, plunged it into Tony's stomach.

Harry breathed hard as he watched Tony stagger

back and look down at his paunch. Tony was breathing hard too, and Harry wouldn't be able to say which of them was more surprised by what he had just done. Right in the *kishkes*, just like in the Friday Night Fights. *A yid kin gerhghet vern*, Harry thought. A Jew could get killed. An *italyenish* too? Apparently not. Blood had begun to trickle out of Tony's wound, but aside from his astonishment, he seemed otherwise unfazed, and he yanked the awl out of his belly with a grunt.

"Fuck!" He examined the awl and dropped it onto the floor. "Oh, you're a dead man now, you little kike."

Tony pulled his suit jacket to one side and reached into the holster that made him the fastest pipe in the West. He drew it out smoothly and swiftly, befitting its design and craftsmanship. He was fast, but Harry was faster, and before Tony could raise his weapon, Harry had grabbed a hammer from the shelf next to where the awl had been, and with it struck Tony on the forehead. He didn't give it everything he had. He pulled it back a bit just as he made contact, fearful of doing serious damage. Tony reeled but he wasn't out. Like one of those palookas Harry had seen on TV—the ones who took a licking but kept on ticking—Tony took the punch but kept coming, slouching towards him in a crouch. And when he got close enough, Harry struck him again, not taking any chances this time, not tentatively, but with all his might, delivering a sidearm blow to the left side of Tony's head just in front of his ear—the vulnerable temporal region of his skull.

It was a direct hit, and Harry watched Tony drop like the sack of shit he was. He lay on the floor like a piece of trash that Harry would pick up off the street and throw away; like bird dropping on the fender of Harry's shiny Chevrolet that had to be cleaned up with a *schmatta*; like a stain on the gleaming idea of America that had to be rubbed out.

Such were Harry's thoughts, and he could have gone on. But he was too exhausted. Too stunned. So instead, he collapsed onto a wooden bench in a state of shock, looking at Tony and wondering who had done this thing that he had just done. He didn't think he could possibly have been the one. But there was this body, a man unconscious at his feet, dead he assumed, blood spilling from the laceration in his scalp like the river when it flooded the plain, and pooling under his head. And that body didn't get there by itself. Harry now wondered what he would do next. Nine-ball was out. He had some wet work to do. He also had some time. He told Lena he'd be out awhile.

But first, he had to collect himself, pick up the shards of his shattered, splintered self, hoping he could find them all and that they still fit together to make a whole. He remembered what he had told Carlo.

"You think you kill someone and that's the end of it? No. It's the beginning. That you can't undo. It

MICHAEL VINES

stays with you forever. Every time you turn around, it's there. Every time you look in the mirror. You end someone's life, you end your own too. You kill one person, you kill the whole world. You kill yourself."

But this was different. Wasn't it? This wasn't murder. It was self-defense. Wasn't it? That was a tricky question. He had to be sure, so he reconstructed the sequence of events as best he could. Tony was a threat, always had been. Not a threat only to his property and livelihood, but to his person—a lethal threat. He was the one who started this. He smacked Harry, slammed him hard into the shelves, and left him lying on the floor gasping for breath while he stood over him smoking a cigarette. No *rachmones* from that guy.

Then again, Harry had to admit that it was he himself who had escalated things. He was the first to use a weapon—the awl. But the awl wasn't a weapon, certainly not by design. It was a tool of his trade. If it was a weapon, it was a lousy one. And it wasn't lethal. Tony Allocco plucked it out of his stomach like it was a splinter.

There was also the question of intent. Did he intend to kill Allocco when he shoved the awl into that butterball belly of his? What was he thinking? As far as Harry could recall, he wasn't thinking anything. He was reacting to brute force. And then Tony pulled his pipe on him. The pipe— that technically was not a weapon either. It was a plumbing supply. But Tony Allocco wasn't planning on repairing any sinks. There was no question of intent where he was concerned. Once he went for his pipe, it was, like Carlo said, whack or be whacked. Law of the fuckin' jungle.

Another question: who drew their lethal weapon first? Did Allocco grab his pipe before Harry grabbed his hammer? Harry couldn't say for sure. But Allocco was certain to go for it, Harry could assume that much. Therefore, he had no choice. It was self-defense.

Then again, things didn't have to happen as they did. Harry could have just done what Tony told him to do. Unload the trunk, bring the furs into his shop. But he didn't. He had a choice and he chose not to. Or that choice was made for him when Tony assaulted him. And before he knew it, Harry did what he did. He may have had a choice at first, but he didn't later on. Besides, if a choice presupposes rational thought, Harry couldn't have made one. He wasn't rational and he wasn't thinking.

A case could certainly be made for self-defense. Justifiable homicide. Harry could clear himself on those grounds. And so would the law, here in the land where the law prevailed. The law of men, not the law of the jungle. But no matter what the law had to say about it, the fact remained that Harry had just bludgeoned a man to death. A made man. And those who made him would not take the law of men into account when they came to even the score. The law of the jungle had been around a lot longer and, for those guys, took precedence. Any way Harry looked at it, he was in trouble.

MICHAEL VINES

He couldn't say how long he sat there, with Tony on the floor beside him, thinking these things over. It could have been two minutes or twenty. He had no idea. But he was finally stirred out of his catatonic musings by the sound of footsteps creeping outside, approaching the back door. He almost wished it was Officer Keegan. He could surrender to the hands of the law, place himself at the mercy of the courts —one of the three branches of government—and put his trust in the American judicial system. That would solve a lot of problems. For the time being, anyway, and right now he welcomed a quick fix. He didn't have the strength or wherewithal to figure out what to do by himself, let alone what the right thing to do was. He didn't have the energy to clean up his mess by himself either. He needed help. Let it be Keegan, he said to himself. He'd deal with Benny the B another time. For now, let it be Keegan.

It wasn't. Harry looked up for the first time since he plopped on the bench and saw standing before him, glaring at him, another man. Holding a gun.

It was Carlo. His forehead rippled like a washboard as he darted his eyes from Harry to Tony back to Harry and back to Tony again. Harry could almost hear the mechanism whirring in Carlo's head, the racks and drive pins and slots tumbling into place as he tried to add things up. But the look on his face revealed that the sums he arrived at were always irrational numbers.

"Harry, what the...? You? You did this?"

"I can't say I didn't."

Tony Allocco. One of the most violent and brutal men anyone ever knew, felled by one of the gentlest and kindest. If this could be, what couldn't? Harry knew now that he had a breaking point. If he were pushed far enough, here in America, he wouldn't run, he'd fight back. With a *gezunta klop* in the *kopf*, he said to himself. And a moment later he thought, "Tony Allocco. Clobbered by a cobbler." Harry wasn't capable of smiling yet, but if he were, he might have cracked one when he considered how Carlo would love the lyrical consonance produced by the combination of those words.

"Jesus Christ. Jesus fuckin' Christ," Carlo kept repeating.

"And you. What are you doing here?"

Carlo didn't answer. He just stared down at Tony. Breathing hard and fast, Carlo bent his long legs and knelt over the body. He lifted Tony's left hand, stripped the Rolex off his wrist, and slid it over his own. The band was a couple of links too big for him, but he could get that taken care of. Carlo next tried to tug the sapphire ring off Tony's fat pinkie. He pulled and yanked, but couldn't get it to budge, so he gave up, breathing even more heavily now as he regarded the bulk before him.

"What now, Carlo? They'll come after me, won't they?"

"What? No. Listen to me, Harry. Tony was no good. He was stealin'."

"What stealing? You all steal. That's what you do."

"Not from the boss we don't."

Carlo then patted Tony down, reached into Tony's inside jacket pocket and pulled out a wad of bills. Then he reached into his pants pockets and pulled out another, even larger.

"See? This is Benny's money. Fuckin' Tony's been holdin' out on him. These furs, Tony's doin' this on his own. A little side business. And Benny's onto him. That's why he put a fuckin' contract out. For me to whack. He's the fuckin' guy, Harry. Tony's the guy I was supposed to clip. And believe me, his fuckin' life ain't precious."

Carlo stood up, unable to take his eyes off his former partner. "I was waitin' outside for 'im. Thought he'd never come out. Guess I was right." Carlo then started counting out bills he fished out of Tony's pockets, lots of C-notes, with a few tens and twenties, thrown in. "Here Harry, five hundred. We're even."

"You only owe me two and half."

"Plus the shy, Harry. Shylock rates. Take it."

"I don't want no Shylock rates. Just the two-fifty."

"You don't want—what's wrong with you? You earned it, Harry."

"It's blood money."

"Take it, Harry." Carlo peeled off more bills, all hundreds, added them to the stack, and held it in front of Harry. "Take it. For Tillie. And her kids. They need it. Take."

Harry didn't have to think about it for long to know that Tony was right—Tillie did need it. And a lot more. Still, he didn't want to take it. But he didn't have to. Carlo stuffed the cash into his shirt pocket. Another time, Harry might have pulled it out and thrown it back at him. But not now.

"And we got the furs too. These'll bring in a few grand, easy."

"What? You'd steal from the boss? No, Carlo."

"He'll get his cut, don't worry 'bout it. And so will you."

"Count me out."

Carlo bent down again and took a closer look at Tony. "Boy, you really did a number on this *mamzer*, Harry."

"I killed a man."

"This wasn't a man. This guy was fuckin' scum, Harry. Vermin."

"Vermin? That's what they say about everybody. Everybody they want to exterminate. Vermin. Roaches. Rats. Not human. You can't say that, Carlo. He's a man. I killed a man."

"Yeah, well, he had it comin'."

And Harry had to consider that, yes, maybe he did. This Tony Allocco was indeed a *mamzer*, a bastard son of a bitch, a parasite if there ever was one. If a word like vermin could be applied to any human being, it was that guy. Harry couldn't have killed a man. He could only have killed vermin.

MICHAEL VINES

"We gotta get rid of the body," Carlo said. "And your little ice pick, too."

"It's an awl. Brand new. So's the hammer."

"Yeah? They look used to me. Get new ones. Got any *schmattas*?"

Harry stood up and grabbed the new apron still wrapped in plastic that was stored on the shelf. There were other rags lying around, and he handed those to Carlo, too, who wrapped them tightly around Tony's head to stanch the wound. Then he covered them with the apron's plastic wrapper.

"Get me some of that plastic, off the coats."

Harry ripped off the plastic and Carlo wrapped it around Tony's head. Together they rolled the body and wrapped plastic around the stomach. Carlo was in control. He seemed to know what he was doing.

"Now, help me get 'im into the trunk of his car. You drive it and follow me."

"Where? Follow you where?"

"The river. We dump 'im there."

"What if somebody sees?"

"Nobody's gonna see."

"But what if?"

"We kill him too, Harry? Okay?"

"What are you talkin', Carlo. No."

"I'm just messin' with you, Harry. Look, it's dark. And where we're goin', deserted. Nobody's gonna see nothin'."

Again, Harry didn't have much of a choice, so he helped Carlo lift Tony. It wasn't easy.

HARRY GETS WISE

"Fuckin' guy must weigh a deuce and a half," Carlo said.

They dragged him more than carried him to the door. Before they went outside, Carlo turned off the light in the storage room. But there was enough moonlight that Harry could see his inventory dumped in the alley.

"All my shoes. Look what he did."

"Later. I'll take care of it. Don't worry. Just do what I tell you now. I've got it all planned."

At least someone had a plan. Someone was thinking, knew what to do. And since Harry wasn't and didn't, he followed Carlo's lead. First they emptied Tony's car of the rest of the fur coats and brought them inside. Then they managed to lift his body, in stages, head first, into the trunk of his own car, then shove the rest of his dead weight in behind him, like they were stuffing spiced meat into a cow's intestine to make *kishke*. Tony's arm hung out, but Carlo tucked it back in before he closed the trunk, as quietly as he could. Then, the two-car caravan pulled out of the back alley and headed to the river.

❊ ❊ ❊

They drove to an unpopulated area south of the city, turned left off the road, and headed east over wild pampas grass, maiden silvergrass, shrubs, and reeds growing in the dirt and mud on the banks of the Mississippi, and in the river itself. Carlo was

294

MICHAEL VINES

right. It was dark and deserted. They drove as close to the river as they could, then stopped, got the body out of the trunk, and dragged it the rest of the way.

The clouds played peekaboo with the moon, allowing it to briefly show its face before scudding back to cover it, drawing a dark curtain over the sky and the land below. Harry felt like he was watching himself from outside of his own body, as if he were a character in one of those Warner Brothers film noirs he always liked, on the wrong side of the law, conducting nefarious business in the shadows.

When they reached the water's edge, Carlo told Harry to wait while he ran back to his car to get something. Alone in the dark, Harry was left to struggle with the enormity of what he had done and what he was doing, but he couldn't quite process it. He had killed a man. And he said so out loud. Carlo got back just in time to hear him.

"Shut up with that, Harry. It's done. Now help me out here."

Carlo had retrieved a cinderblock and a chain from the trunk of his car. Harry was impressed. The kid came prepared. Good for him. His faith in the boy was rewarded. Carlo looped the chain through a cavity in the cinderblock, then lay the chain at a right angle, perpendicular to Tony's waist.

"Roll him," Carlo said.

Harry helped Carlo roll Tony's huge body over the chain, then Carlo wrapped it around him and locked it in place.

295

"Just barely long enough, the fuckin' pig. Okay, time for a swim now," Carlo said, addressing Tony. Neither he nor Harry responded.

And then Carlo had a worrisome thought. "What if this thing don't hold him down? What if he floats away and comes up down river, in Natchez or somewhere, wherever the hell that is? If they find him, they'll see he got his head smashed in. He wasn't shot."

"What difference does it make?"

"It's not professional." Carlo thought some more. "I could say I used his pipe on him. 'Cause I'm so vicious. Gave him a taste of his own medicine."

"But you didn't. I killed him. With the hammer. Not you." When Harry articulated that, something broke through to him for the first time. Suddenly, this whole nightmare became real to him. And he repeated, "I killed him. Me. I killed a man. Not you. Me."

And as the fact of the matter sunk in just as he was preparing to throw his victim into the river, Harry gasped for air in a way that sounded like his own death rattle, and he began to whimper.

"Harry, stop. Let it go." And then Carlo had another thought. "Wait a minute. He might not even be dead." Carlo bent over the body and put his ear against Tony's chest. "Quiet, Harry. *Shah.*" Carlo listened and then felt for a pulse. "It's still beatin', Harry."

"What?"

MICHAEL VINES

"He ain't dead."

"You're sure?"

"He's got a pulse."

"Let's get him to a hospital."

"Are you crazy? That ain't gonna happen."

"But he's alive. We can save a life."

"Jesus, Harry. I got the contract on him. I can't save his fuckin' life. He's gotta go. Don't you get that?"

Carlo didn't wait for him to respond because it wasn't really a question and whatever Harry might say didn't matter. Instead, he went straight for his gun and placed the barrel against Tony's head. And then he paused, breathing like he had just sprinted a hundred yards. He waited a moment longer, turned his head away, closed his eyes, and squeezed the trigger. The ambient silence amplified the sound of the shot.

"There. You see? You didn't do it. I killed him, not you."

"You killed a dead man."

"He wasn't dead. His heart was still beatin', I tell you. I heard it. I felt his pulse. You didn't do it, Harry, I did. You saw me."

"I don't believe you, Carlo."

"Believe whatever you want. He's dead now. Let's get him in the fuckin' river already."

And the two men, partners for sure now, dragged the body from the where it lay, and waded into the water. The dead weight was lighter now, at least. But

297

it wasn't sinking. The water was too shallow, only up to their thighs.

"I thought the river was supposed to be deep," Carlo said.

"Farther out."

They waded farther out, trudging through the water, and pulling the body behind them, but the waterline hardly rose.

"What the fuck?"

"Farther," Harry said.

Harry took a few more heavy steps and then, a final one, which sent him plunging into a sudden, precipitous drop in the river bed. He gasped for air and flailed his arms wildly trying to stay afloat, but to no avail. Unlike his children, he had never learned to swim at the Fairground Park pool. Not that he had anticipated the necessity for something like this.

Is this how he would meet his end? Harry wondered as the river began to swallow him alive. If so, he had it coming for what he had done: taking the life of a fellow human being, lowlife *mamzer* that Tony Allocco objectively was. How fitting that Harry would share a watery grave with his victim.

Harry was not only sinking, but being pulled downstream by the suddenly swift current of the unpredictable river. Who would tell his family? That would fall to Carlo, he guessed. And what would he say? Live by the sword, die by the sword? What an unfitting and ignominious end for a man who had always tried to do what is right. To do what is fair

MICHAEL VINES

and just.

But Carlo wouldn't have to tell Harry's family anything. Because he had learned how to swim, at the YMCA, and apparently had some basic lifesaving lessons, too. He swam to Harry, placed the crook of his arm under Harry's chin, and tugged him about five yards or so out of the depths and back to where they could both stand up on their own.

Harry and Carlo watched Tony's body, still afloat in the water, bobbing like it was attached to a fishing line. Then, at last, the cinder block and gravity took over, pulling him slowly, but inexorably, beneath the surface.

Harry and Carlo lay soaking on the bank, catching their breath, and watching the moon pierce the clouds to show its face again. Carlo had killed one man and saved another. Or maybe Carlo had simply saved the life of a killer. Harry would never know for sure. But however he felt about everything that happened that night, however it would affect him, at that moment, he was just glad to be alive. He could go back to taking care of his family.

But first Harry had one more job to do— to get behind the wheel of Tony's car again and follow Carlo to a chop shop under Benny the B's management where a guy was waiting for them. The man let them through the gate and they dropped off the car. Some of the parts could wind up in Sam's junkyard for all Harry knew. His own son-in-law.

When Harry got home, he told Lena everything.

HARRY GETS WISE

Every last detail. It was ghastly, but she wasn't about to shed a tear for Tony the Pipe. Besides, she was a practical woman and she focused on the here and now. Harry had been gone for far longer than she expected, and she was just glad to have him back, safe and whole. Whether he was whole or not was another matter.

"The electric bill will be higher this month," Harry told her, being in a confessional state of mind, and then he remembered that he hadn't left the light on in the shop the whole week after all, so no, it wouldn't be, and he told her that too.

Lena hung up his wet clothes in the bathroom. She'd wait till they dried, then burn them. She put a bag of frozen peas over Harry's eye where a shiner was forming from Tony's blow. She poured him a schnapps, and one for herself, and prepared a plate of food for her husband. Leftovers from Sid's shiva.

18

After Libby moved back home, Lenny would sometimes pick her up and they'd go out for the evening together. They both played it down, but only a little, saying they were just going to a CORE meeting at Irv and Maggie Dagan's place, which was only sometimes true, and everybody knew it. There was a relationship between them; anyone would have to have been blind to miss it. What they really missed, however, was what the young couple was actually up to.

Libby had met a woman named Paula O'Neill through Maggie Dagen, both of whom taught social studies at Clayton High School in the suburb just south of University City. Paula was a St. Louis girl herself, from Holly Hills, a leafy community on the south side that Libby knew nothing about. She'd never even heard of Carondelet Park, the city's third largest, which marks the neighborhood's southern border and has a swimming pool, ball fields, tennis courts, a lake, and a boathouse with a colonnaded pavilion all its own. There was a whole *goyische* world out there within a few miles of Warne Avenue that might as well have been on Mars, for all Libby knew. She was still learning how sheltered her life in

St. Louis had been.

But as different as their backgrounds were, they overlapped along the way. Though Paula attended Mary Institute, a private school for girls where families of means sent their daughters, she went on to Washington University a couple of years after Libby had graduated. Paula was also a thoughtful young woman, politically aware, with a keenly developed social conscience, making her a ready recruit for Maggie Dagen, whose efforts to integrate the university Paula had participated in as a student. She didn't have much of a fashion sense, but Libby thought that was something, by its absence, that might ultimately connect them. She felt a sense of commonality with her. Silent signals passed between them, readable only by people who shared something intrinsic, like members of the same tribe, which, in a way, they were.

"Famous is having a sale," Libby told her over coffee in the Loop. "There'll be great discounts."

"Oh, I'm useless at clothes. If you haven't noticed."

"Maybe I can help you pick things out, if you want."

Paula took her up on the offer and came down to Famous just as Libby was getting off work. It wasn't a first date, but there was an undercurrent of possibility about it, an intimacy springing from the natural emphasis on the body as they modeled outfits for each other. Libby gave her opinion on what flattered Paula, which, in Libby's mind, was nearly everything.

"With your figure, you can really wear anything," Libby told her.

Libby took the liberty of adjusting a scarf around Paula's neck, cocking it at a rakish angle. With her strawberry blonde hair and pale rosy complexion, she looked so pretty it was all Libby could do to keep from kissing her. But she didn't dare. She took full advantage, however, of the freedom to straighten her collar and feel the fabric of a blouse she was trying on. The dressing room fashion show gave them both license to touch one another or let a hand linger a little too long, followed by a blush and sheepish smile on both their faces.

The three them, Libby, Paula, and Lenny, would sometimes go to The Parkmoor, a local favorite famous for its fried onion rings just a short drive from the high school on Clayton Road. Sometimes others would join them and they'd go as a pack to a movie or bowling alley. Other times Lenny, Libby, and Paula would just pick up a pizza at Pagliacci's, bring it back to the house on Waterman, and watch TV. After a while, Lenny would excuse himself, and the women would stay up, talk, and eventually bare their souls. Paula told Libby about a difficult breakup she had not too long ago, and Libby told Paula about her own, very long ago. They were both taking it slowly. Especially Paula. And Libby gave her all the space she needed.

At one of the CORE meetings at the Dagens' home, a straight Black woman told the story of how the manager at Shelley's had a fit when she entered the club with a white lesbian friend of hers and refused to serve her. He was afraid that if he did, his all-white clientele might just pick up and leave. Even out-groups had their out-groups. But his biggest fear was that if the cops got wind of it, they'd close him down and he'd wind up losing his liquor license. Everyone at the Dagens' was outraged by this unbridled display of racism, but no one more than Paula O'Neill.

"Oh, so the cops look the other way when it comes to serving lesbians—people they themselves and the city council call degenerates—but they draw the line at Blacks? So the straightest, most upright, church-going Negro is worse in their eyes than a degenerate dyke? Just because she's Black. That is just too fucking sick, excuse my French."

Those redheads could be fiery, and Libby admired her spunk. She even felt a secret, unwarranted pride in the way she spoke up, took a stand, and rallied the troops. But Paula wasn't finished. She had one last declaration to make.

"I say we go there and integrate that place."

Paula first looked at the Black woman who had told the story, in a show of solidarity, then she turned her gaze directly at Libby, as if seeking her approval, wanting to be sure she was onboard. Libby was all for it, of course. In theory, anyway. But after

MICHAEL VINES

her first and only experience at Shelley's, she didn't look forward to going back to the place where her shameful episode and possible sexual assault by the woman she picked up, or was picked up by, began. The memories disgusted and frightened her. But with Paula imploring her and leading the charge, how could she refuse? So Libby cheered her assent along with everyone else.

* * *

Even though he hadn't slept much and dreaded returning to the scene of the crime, Harry got to his shop early the morning after, prepared to have a lot of cleaning up to do. But to his surprise, everything had been taken care of. The shoes were out of the alley and back on the shelves where they belonged. The furs were gone, as was the coat rack, and the murder weapons—the awl and hammer. Everything was just as it had been, just as it should be, all cleaned up spic and span—literally Spic and Span as attested by a half-empty box of the cleaner that had been left behind.

Everything, that is, but for the dull brownish red blotch of blood on the concrete floor—close to the color of cordovan shoes in need of a shine, Harry thought—that no less wonders than Spic and Span or Ajax or Clorox or any other extra-strength household cleaner conjured up by the wizards of American enterprise could bleach away, even with the help of the hardest-bristle scrub brush carried at Howe's little mom-and-pop hardware store across the street, or even the vast selection of industrial-strength models on offer at the enormous emporium known as Central Hardware, founded by Jewish immigrants from Poland at the beginning of the century as a single shop selling tools, and now grown into a chain of retail stores throughout the city selling "everything from scoop to nuts," according to their motto. Harry would come to realize how indelible that stain was when he put his own elbow grease into the job, over and over again, for weeks and months to come, to no avail. It had seeped in too deeply and would be there forever.

Harry had often wondered how people could do some of the horrible things they did. What did it mean to be human when humanity itself had so much blood on its hands, was dripping with it since the beginning of time? How could the same species that had minds capable of pure reason; the intuition to unravel the mysterious workings of the universe; the intelligence to develop the scientific and medical miracles that saved so many lives, then turn around and use that same genius, those same tools, those same discoveries to destroy each other on such a massive scale? The more they achieved and the greater the heights they scaled, the lower they sank and the freer and faster the blood flowed. It was inexplicable.

Harry was not the only person baffled by such questions. So too had been the most brilliant human minds since history began. But Harry hadn't studied these things or spent a lifetime ruminating on them. He wasn't schooled in philosophy or logic or psychology or ethics. His understanding was innate because he was human and, therefore, possessed a human brain and the ability to think and to reason. Were those very gifts what would doom us, after all? Were we destined to destroy ourselves and take everything else along with us just because we could?

Though Harry would never have an answer, he continued to ponder what man was capable of. And on that first morning, as he regarded the irregular, ineradicable stain on his concrete floor, he understood that we are all capable of anything. If anything encapsulated the sum of human experience, it was that.

And then there was Carlo. His ally. He had come back in the middle of the night and taken care of everything, just as he said he would. He helped Harry when he was alone and desperate and had no idea what to do. He saved Harry's life. He wasn't pure, he wasn't perfect; he was a criminal, a thief, a killer, perhaps, but somehow, in spite of it all, he was also good, emblematic of both our hopelessness and our hope. That, too, was inexplicable.

Carlo showed up in the afternoon of the day after, fresh faced and Brylcreemed, to check up on his friend. When he first arrived, they said nothing, but just looked deeply into one another's eyes, sizing each other up, reading each other on a level far beyond anything they could express in mere language. But language finally intervened—perhaps for corroboration of what they already understood.

"You doin' okay, Harry?"

"Eh."

"That's quite a shiner you got there. Hurt?"

"Only when I blink."

"Well, I seen worse. So have you."

Harry knew that Carlo was trying to commiserate with him, make him feel better, but he wasn't comforted by the remark.

"It's okay, Harry. Everything's good. Don't worry, all right?"

"You cleaned up good back there," Harry said, canting his head in the direction of the storage room.

"I told you I'd take care of it, didn't I?"

Harry nodded. Carlo was eager to move on, to escape the ineffable and return to the mundane.

"Cards still got a shot, you think?"

"Sixteen, seventeen back. I don't see it."

"Well, you never know. Anything's possible."

"That's for sure."

"Yeah. Well, don't lose hope, Harry."

"Maybe next year."

"Sure. That's right. Hey, you need anything, let me know. Okay? I'll be around."

Harry didn't respond.

"You take care now," Carlo said. "You hear me?"

Again Harry didn't respond. He just watched

MICHAEL VINES

Carlo go.

* * *

Harry spent almost all his free time with Tillie and her kids now, devoting an especially large share of it to Marty. Joey was just a baby, unconscious of the tragedy that had befallen him. He'd be okay, Harry assumed, not realizing that the infant's loss, oblivious to it though he may be, was like a landmine that lay buried underground, only to be stumbled upon years later to exact its devastating toll.

Marty was another story. He was old enough to know that his father was gone for good, never coming back, but too young to understand or even begin to cope with it. Seeing him so brokenhearted and bewildered, Harry did his best to reach him, but he cursed his helplessness to do so.

He tried bringing Marty around by telling him for the hundredth time the tried-and-true story of the *cozzella*, the little goat that Harry's family kept when he himself was just a kid in Poland. There wasn't much to the story, but the grandchildren never tired of hearing it. As Harry told it, a bowl of *lokshun* had been left outside, for reasons never explained, and when Harry and his mother went back out to get it, it was all gone. The *cozzella* ate the *lokshun*. That was the whole story, beginning, middle, and end.

309

But Harry elaborated on it. He knew how to tell a story, and he set it up by first explaining how his mother had made the *lokshun* in a big pot of water that took forever to boil; how she was going to use it to make a delicious *lokshun kugel*, her signature noodle pudding that his whole family loved; and how much care and love she put into the preparation. But none of those details, or Harry's abundant skills as a storyteller, accounted for the magic that sent all the grandchildren into fits of laughter over it. He supposed it was that concluding line, the words themselves, that explained the story's enduring appeal: the *cozzella* ate the *lokshun*. Those words packed the punch. *Cozzella* and *lokshun*. Carlo would love them too, Harry was sure, though he had never shared them with him, nor ever would.

But now, Marty wasn't in the mood for the story. He told his grandpa that he didn't like the *cozzella* and didn't want to hear about it. So Harry tried a different tack. The bike. He suggested that he and Marty go out and grandpa would teach him to ride his new bike.

It was the worst idea Harry could have come up with. The mere suggestion sent Marty into hysterics.

"I hate that bike. I never want to ride it. Never," he gulped through his tears, and ran away.

It was easy enough to understand, of course. But impossible to do anything about. The way Marty must have seen it, if he hadn't insisted on getting that bike and making his father run up and down

MICHAEL VINES

the block with him in the heat, he'd be alive today. It was his fault his father was dead. He had killed him.

How could Harry talk sense to him? Explain to the boy that he had it all wrong? He wasn't responsible for his father's death. He was innocent. Were there words that were up to the task in any language? Or would this patricidal guilt be something that Marty would carry with him for the rest of his life, something that would come to define him? Something that he would always remember, of course, but also something he would regret and recriminate himself for even when he had reached Harry's age, and had grandchildren of his own, god willing. Harry was helpless to bring the boy relief. Not even with the good old reliable *cozzella*.

* * *

Carlo was back the following week, this time on business. He was bright and chipper, a new man in Harry's opinion. Though Harry still carried the burden of his experience, Carlo seemed to have shed it entirely. Harry's black eye had healed by then, but Carlo didn't even mention it. He acted as if none of what had happened ever had. The past had been washed away with the flow of the river.

"Mornin', Harry," he said at three in the afternoon. He sat down in one of the shop's wooden seats and lifted his left foot to show Harry the sole of his shoe. "Look at this."

311

HARRY GETS WISE

There was a hole beginning to form in the ball of his foot.

"Take it off," Harry said. "Both of them."

Carlo did and handed his shoes to Harry, then sat back down.

"I don't get it. How come I'm all the time wearin' out my shoe in the same spot."

"You don't know?"

"No."

"You're always tapping your foot, Carlo."

"I am?"

"Yeah. All the time."

Harry nodded in the direction of Carlo's shoeless left foot and Carlo followed his eye line to find it tapping away on the floor.

"Yeah? Really? Who knew?"

"Everybody knew."

"Hunh. Is that a bad thing, Harry?"

"Doesn't bother me."

"Doesn't bother me either. Guess it bothers the shoe."

"I'll fix. I'll put a tap on it too."

"'Service while U wait.'" Carlo drew the letter "U" in the air as he said the word. "Just like it says on your sign. 'U.'" He drew it again. "I like that."

While Carlo waited, he made himself comfortable. Stretching out, he grabbed a magazine Harry had for his customers on a side table and flipped through the pages looking at the pictures and ads. They talked baseball mostly—the Cardinals

312

MICHAEL VINES

were sinking fast—while Harry did his job. When he finished, Carlo inspected his new soles, now with shiny taps on the toes.

"Be-a-u-tiful, Harry. Like new. How much do I owe you?"

"You don't owe me nothin'."

"I know. I'm just messin' with you. Put it on my tab," Carlo said, laughing as he laced up his shoes. When he finished, he stood up and said, "Come on, Harry. Let's see a little smile, huh? You got nothin' to worry about. You got me?" Then he leaned over and whispered, "I'm in, Harry."

"What in? You're made?"

"In the shade. Ain't nobody's gonna be collectin' from you anymore, neither. That's all over. You done good, Harry. We're a good team. Didn't I tell you that?"

"We're not a team, Carlo."

"We're friends. You're a friend of mine. You could never be part of the family, okay, but consider yourself an associate."

"No, thanks."

"And you know what else? The boss, he likes you too."

"The boss? What's he know?"

"Nothin', he don't know nothin', don't worry 'bout it, but he likes you, Harry. I let him know you're a standup guy. And one tough Jew. He likes tough Jews. Like this guy, Lansky in New York. Meyer Lansky his name is. You know him? Got a genius

313

head for numbers. Books like nobody's business. Collects vig from casinos all over the world. London, Havana, everywhere. The boss is a big fan. You could be like that, Harry. If you put your mind to it. You could be the Meyer Lansky of St. Louis if you wanted to."

"I don't."

Harry knew plenty about Meyer Lansky, his landsman, another Polish Jew who came here for the same reasons as all the rest. And he admired him too, but not for the same reasons the Boss did. Harry knew that Lansky may have been a crooked thug, and worse, but he was their crooked thug. Lansky and his gang had broken up German American Bund (aka Nazi) rallies in New York before the war and, during it, he worked with U.S. Intelligence fingering German infiltrators, busting up their plans to sabotage American ships being built in New York Harbor, and busting up plenty of deserving heads while he was at it. This sort of thing wasn't widely known among the general public, but Jews knew it, a lot of them anyway, through that same collective consciousness that informed them which show biz celebrities were among their paltry but somehow ubiquitous number. Harry knew also that he was no Meyer Lansky. Not in a million years. Even if he wanted to be, he didn't have the brains or the guts. Lena, maybe, if she were ruthless, but not he.

"Your choice, Harry. But cheer up, will you? It's a new day. You need anything, let me know. I got your back."

MICHAEL VINES

Carlo improvised a little dance, clicking his new taps as loudly as he could.

"The fifth Step Brother, huh?" Carlo said.

"Maybe the fourth Ritz Brother."

"Yeah. They're White. Jews too, right?"

"Yeah."

"What's with you Jews? You're all over the place. TV, the movies. Not to mention the banks. Harry, you're a member of one talented race, I gotta give you that."

Carlo started dancing again, improvising his own version of Shuffle Off to Buffalo out of the shop. When he was gone, Harry stepped to the other side of the counter, sat in the seat Carlo had occupied, and picked up the magazine he'd been flipping through and left open on the chair beside him. Harry closed the issue and saw the cover for the first time. When he did, he felt a coldness rising to the surface of his skin from his vital organs, suffusing him with an eerie sense of dread that caused the hair follicles on his forearms and neck to rise and tingle.

It was a *Saturday Evening Post* from earlier in the summer, dated June 12, 1954. The title of the cover art was "Bike Riding Lesson," illustrated by a man called George Hughes in the style of Norman Rockwell. As the title suggests, it depicted a man, about Sid's age, teaching a boy, a little older than Marty, maybe, and presumably his son, to ride a bike on the sidewalk of an all-American suburban neighborhood of two-story clapboard homes with white porches set atop manicured lawns.

Behind the father and son is the mayhem they have left in their wake. An older man, about Harry's age, perhaps—it was difficult to tell—bends over to pick up not litter, as Harry might, but a newspaper that had been knocked out of his hands when the boy nearly hit him as he careened down the block. Behind that man, a woman covers her mouth with her hands to show concern or disapproval, or both. The boy on the bike has his legs spread apart in a "V" shape, his feet nowhere near the pedals, his eyes and mouth wide open in an expression of joy and reckless exhilaration, secure that his father is at his side to keep him safe from harm.

And the father...the father is open to interpretation. But the way Harry saw him, judging by the man's posture and expression, he was on the verge of collapse, falling backward, his eyes frozen with panic, and his tongue lolling uncontrollably as if he were about to have, or was having, a heart attack.

Harry ripped off the cover and crushed it into a ball with both hands. One thing for sure, Marty must never see this. Never. He'd experienced enough trauma already for a six-year-old. For a sixty-year-old. Harry was about to throw the wad of glossy paper in the trash, then thought better of it. Instead he carried it back to his storage area, dropped it in a metal bucket—the one Marshall sometimes used to bring him beer from Dependahl's—and set a match to it, just as Lena had done to the clothes Harry

MICHAEL VINES

had worn the night he left the indelible stain on the floor, the stain he was standing on as he watched the flame burn the cover to ashes.

19

As soon as Libby got home from work, she changed quickly into a lightweight sun dress—it was August in St. Louis—with a spaghetti-strap halter top and neckline just low enough to allow a peak of her flattering décolletage, and waited for Lenny to pick her up. She didn't have to wait long. Lenny made of point of saying hello and goodbye to Harry and Lena before he and Libby drove together for another of their more and more frequent dates.

After they left, Lena said, "Did you see that dress."

"Very nice."

"Nice? Sexy. That's what they call a dress like that. She's going after him, Harry. I told you."

"They make a nice couple."

"He's going back to Chicago. What's she gonna do then? Go with him? Quit her job?"

"It's not far. He can visit."

"The way she looks in that dress, he's gonna want more than a visit. If you know what I mean."

"They're adults, Lena. And Libby's a good girl."

"Do you know where they're going tonight?"

"Out to dinner somewhere."

MICHAEL VINES

"Dinner, *balt*. I'll tell you where they're going. Straight to that house in U. City, that's where. I'll bet anything."

If Lena had placed that bet, she would have lost. Lenny drove Libby not west to U. City, but south to Holly Hills where she was meeting Paula who wanted to show her where she grew up and take a walk through Carondelet Park before it got dark and they went out for dinner. Paula was waiting for her on a bench at the southwest corner of the park where Lenny dropped her off, and Libby arranged for him to pick her at the same spot at ten o'clock sharp.

"Wow, you look great," Paula said.

Paula's shoulder-length hair was naturally abundant and lustrous, if not exactly styled, but Libby could detect she felt a little dowdy in her old skirt and blouse, which she was. She tried to put Paula at ease.

"Well, I wanted to. Is it okay?"

"Yeah. You're beautiful. Maybe I should have put on one of the things you picked out for me. I almost did. But I didn't want to seem, oh, I don't know, trying too hard."

"No, you look great, Paula. Really. Maybe I'm the one who's trying too hard."

"No, not at all. And if you did, it worked."

They both smiled self-consciously and then Paula gave Libby a walking tour of the neighborhood, ending at the house she was raised in. It wasn't anything grand, like some of the houses around there, which rivaled those in the nicest sections of U. City, but it was lovely—a red brick gingerbread bungalow with limestone trim just a block west of the park. Paula's parents didn't own it anymore, having retired to Florida after she graduated college.

"It's even nicer inside. It's got stained glass windows and this big beautiful limestone fireplace in the living room. We always used to have a big Christmas tree on the other side, away from the fire, of course. Christmas was like a fairy tale when I was a little girl, especially when it snowed and the fireplace was roaring."

Of all the ways their experience of growing up in St. Louis diverged, Christmas said it all. Libby's family wouldn't have had a tree in a million years and never missed it. The rest of the city was aglow in Christmas lights and decorations, but they never appealed to Libby. They were too garish for her taste. Famous-Barr and Stix competed to create the most elaborate Christmas displays, drawing mobs downtown—including the Becker family—to see their windows dressed in holiday style. Libby had to admit that the mechanical Santa and toy-making elves, and the miniature kids sleighing down a cotton-covered slope were ingenious. But the far subtler Chanukah menorah, adding illumination to the year's shortest days with candlelight, was all she'd ever need. It was far more tasteful, she thought. Libby wondered if Paula's family had a nativity scene on their front lawn, and hoped they

MICHAEL VINES

hadn't. Those things always gave Libby the creeps.

"I'd love to buy it back one of these days, but on a teacher's salary, I don't think so."

On my salary, Libby thought, we could do it, maybe. We could surely do it together.

"Oh, well, you know what they say," Paula continued. "You can't go home again."

"That's not true. I did."

"That's different. You did the right thing, Libby. I admire that. And it won't be forever. You'll get a place of your own again."

"Yeah, one day," Libby said, allowing herself to imagine the two of them getting a place of their own together. Two respectable women with good, responsible jobs who just haven't been able to find the right men, and would keep each other company until they did.

What would they do on Christmas? Libby wondered. Could she live with a Christmas tree? Maybe she could talk Paula out of it. Not likely. She knew full well how gentiles were with Christmas and their trees. But a crèche was out of the question. That she would definitely not have.

It probably wouldn't have bothered Goldie, her nonsectarian sister who wore so much pink these days—her lucky color and homage to the Pink Sisters—that their mother once asked her, "So, *nu*, Goldie, who are you, Pinky Lee now?" referring to the zany television entertainer, born Pincus Leff, a Jew who wore a trademark "checkered hat and

321

HARRY GETS WISE

checkered coat," as he sang in his show's opening, and also a shirt to match, the whole ensemble presumably pink gingham. It wasn't, but it was impossible to tell on black and white TV, so it was fair to assume.

One day, Goldie bent over to pick up a pack of cigarettes she dropped on the floor, and out from the top of her pink blouse tumbled the cross attached to the rosary she wore around her neck.

"Goldie, *vas iz das*?" Lena asked.

"It's nothing, Mama. Just jewelry?"

"A cross by you is jewelry? Why are you wearing a cross?"

"Good luck, Mama, that's all."

"Wear a mezuzah, then. Not a cross. What, you're a *shiksa* now?"

"I do wear a mezuzah. See?" She pulled on a thin gold chain hanging beneath her blouse and reeled it up to show her mama.

"*Oy a broch*. I don't know anymore. *Ich vais nicht*."

But Libby was different from Goldie, so much so, it was sometimes hard to believe they were sisters. Libby could never be seduced by Christian iconography.

Paula would probably want stockings hanging over the mantel of the fireplace too, Libby thought. Those could actually be kind of cute. Maybe they could compromise. Something from Christmas for Paula, something from Chanukah for her. But nothing freighted with religious symbolism. Libby

322

MICHAEL VINES

imagined a row of secular stockings, alternately red and green, perhaps some with red and green stripes in the mix too. And stuffed inside each, miscegenating, there'd be candy canes and Chanukah *gelt*—milk chocolate wrapped in gold foil so they looked like coins.

Libby found herself cringing at the thought of Chanukah *gelt*, though she never had before. But now, in the context of Christians and Christmas, of Paula viewing it as an outsider, it seemed to play into the stereotype of Jews being obsessed with money. But if anyone was obsessed with money— at least in terms of the things that it could buy— it was the Christians. They spent way more money on Christmas presents for each other than Jews ever did on Chanukah gifts, even those who gave their children a gift on each of its eight nights. Those were small tokens. And they only gave gifts to the children, not to everyone they knew, including the mailman. And come to think of it, whose founding myth glorified not just frankincense and myrrh, but gold for the newborn king? Real gold, not chocolate candy in gold colored wrappers.

Libby was hopeful that they could work out their religious and cultural differences. They could meet halfway. No tree, no menorah, just stockings hung by the chimney with care. Libby knew the poem, the first lines of which she could recite by heart, as could just about every other American. She read it every Christmas in grade school. When Libby was in first or second grade, she remembered one of her teachers—not Mrs. Aschenschmidt, so maybe it was third grade—having the class sing "Jesus Loves Me." Libby refused to sing along. She just moved her lips without emitting a sound. The same teacher sometimes led the class in prayer—Christian prayer, naturally. All the children bowed their heads and prayed, except Libby, but no one would ever know. They were all looking down, so she got away with it.

Putting on Christmas plays; saying Merry Christmas to all the gentiles and having them say the same thing back to you even though you don't celebrate the birth of their Lord; praying to Jesus in school; reciting Christmas poems and singing Christmas carols—Libby was fine with "White Christmas," written by Irving Berlin (Jew), but not with "Noel" or "Joy to the World"—this was the price of entry for Jews in America.

As they strolled through the park, Libby wondered if maybe she should look for a Jewish girl. But she knew she was kidding herself. It was hard enough just finding a girl—any girl she was attracted to, could relate to, and had so many important things in common with, let alone one she could fall for. On top of that, add another limiting criterion? The odds were low enough already.

The Boathouse in Carondelet Park reminded Libby somewhat of the Pavilion in Forest Park, on a much a smaller scale. They were both topped with roofs covered in orange-red mission style tiles and featured a colonnade overlooking a lake. Libby and Paula stood beneath an arch of the colonnade looking out at Horseshoe Lake with its spout of spraying water. It was fine, but just an oversized lawn sprinkler compared to the fountain at Forest Park. All these things triggered memories in Libby, and it was impossible for her not to recall her first kiss with Shelley Klein. Recall, but not dwell.

Paula and Libby stood side by side and leaned over the parapet.

"Ready for Shelley's next week?" Paula asked.

"I guess."

"You ever been there before?"

"No," Libby said, then corrected herself immediately. What was she lying about? "Yes. I was there. Once."

"What's it like."

"Pretty awful."

And then Libby began to explain what was awful about Shelley's. And she didn't stop there. She went on to tell of the far more awful incident that followed. She might as well have been in a confessional booth the way she let it all out and somehow felt better for having someone she could share it with.

"Oh, Libby, I'm so sorry."

Paula let her hand slide over Libby's as a gesture of sympathy and comfort. Then, maybe because she realized where she was—in her old neighborhood—and there were other people around, some of whom might recognize her, she pulled her hand back, but not entirely. She let it lie close enough so their

HARRY GETS WISE

pinkies kissed. Libby took the initiative to wrap her pinky around Paula's, interlocking them and squeezing and pulling the way kids might do if they were making a bet. In a sense that's what Libby was doing. Placing a bet on Paula.

"It'll be different this time. We'll be together," Paula said. "And we're on a mission."

They didn't kiss goodnight that evening. But they let their arms sway into each other's as they walked side by side, and sometimes they allowed their hips to brush against each other, and, as they sat on the designated park bench waiting for Lenny to come back and pick Libby up, there wasn't room between them to slide a tissue.

After Lenny walked Libby to her door on Warne, she went upstairs and lay in bed replaying the entire evening in her head. They wound up not having dinner, just walking, talking, and stopping for an ice cream cone. Libby got vanilla and Paula strawberry, like her hair and complexion. They each held out their cones for the other to taste their flavors. It was while visualizing that moment that Libby finally fell asleep. And maybe also fell in love.

20

The *cozzella* was a bust, the bike-riding idea a disaster, so Harry played the last cards in his deck. Hamburgers and fries at Lucille's followed by an ice cream soda at the Circle Fountain. Just the two of them. It seemed to work. For the first time since they buried his father almost four weeks ago, Marty seemed to be enjoying himself. Sitting in one of the green banquets at the Circle, Harry invented a new game on the spot: who could make the loudest noises sucking the last sips of their sodas through their straws. Marty loved the idea and was eager to play. He perched himself on his knees in his seat to give himself an advantageous angle, called out the ready-set-go! countdown so they started at the same time, and began slurping with all the strength in his little lungs. He made a lot of noise, and as he burst into laughter, the soda took an alimentary detour and spurted out of his nose.

"I win," he said.

"You win," Harry conceded, wiping the boy's face with a napkin. He wiped with exaggerated vigor, making cartoon animal grunts as he did, which tickled Marty all the more.

Marty held his grandpa's hand as they walked

back home down Florissant Avenue. From behind them they heard the staccato blast of a car horn getting louder as it got closer, and they turned around to see what was up. It was Carlo, tooting the horn of his new baby blue Cadillac convertible. He swerved toward the curve and pulled up in a screech.

"Come on, hop in. Both o' youse."

"What, where to?" Harry asked.

"Ballgame. Let's go."

Harry pulled out his pocket watch and checked the time. "It's too late."

"Cincy tied it in the ninth. They're goin' into extras. Come on, you're wastin' time."

"Let's go, Grandpa," Marty said. And Harry, who could never say no to him, was not about to start now.

"How d'ya like the new wheels, Harry?"

"You like, I like."

"Aw come on, Harry, you can do better 'an that. Get a load o' this horsepower."

Carlo put the car in neutral, floored the accelerator, and let it roar. Marty, sitting in the backseat, didn't say anything and probably wouldn't have been heard over the revving engine if he had, but the look in his eyes said, "Wow."

"V-8, Harry. That's muscle." Carlo then slipped the transmission back into drive, pulled out, and maneuvered the car through the traffic. "That's not all. Power steering, power brakes, power everything. Watch this. Electric windows. You just press a

MICHAEL VINES

button."

Carlo demonstrated, and the front and rear windows went up and down at the touch of a fingertip. Marty's face froze in silent astonishment, his jaw dropped and his mouth opened as if to say, "Wow."

"How 'bout that, Harry? Is that class or is that class? And look at the space. It's like a living room on wheels."

"Very comfortable."

Carlo leaned over to Harry and said in a whisper, "Or a bedroom. Huh?"

"*Zey shtil. Di kind.*" Marty understood he was talking about him. So did Carlo.

"Wanna hear the game?" Carlo turned on the car radio and Harry Carry's voice boomed through the speakers. "Signal not clear enough for ya, Harry?" It was, but that didn't stop Carlo. "No problem. Watch this."

Carlo pressed another button on the dashboard and, as if by magic, the outside antenna began to rise. "Look at that? See it goin' up?

This time Marty actually uttered the word, "Wow," and asked "How'd you do that?"

"That's a Caddy for ya, kid. I can get Pittsburgh sometimes. Picked up a Pirates game the other night." Carlo lowered the volume so he could take center stage again. "I hate these Redlegs. Always have. But that Kluszewski, he's got some *gezunta* arms on him, doesn't he, Harry."

HARRY GETS WISE

"Like telephone poles."

"And the way he shows 'em off in those sleeveless shirts they wear. Like we're supposed to be scared of 'im."

"He is pretty scary, Carlo. Shtarker like that."

"Eh, he ain't so much. Ain't no Musial, that's for sure."

Harry couldn't argue with him there. By the time they made the right turn on Grand Boulevard heading toward Dodier Street and Sportsman's Park, the game was in the bottom of eleventh, still tied. When they got there, Carlo didn't bother looking for a parking place, but drove right up to the private lot reserved for the players and VIPs. A city police officer was on duty securing the entrance and when he saw Carlo, he nodded and waved him in.

"Thanks, Tommy," Carlo said to him.

"What's this?"

"Pull, Harry. I got pull. You'll see."

Carlo parked and they all got out of the car. He didn't lead them to an entrance gate but to the clubhouse door—the players' entrance. There, a beefy security guard blocked them.

"You can't come in here," he said.

"I'm Carlo Barnini. Benny sent me," he said. And that changed everything.

"Oh, sorry, Mr. Barnini. Sure. Right this way." The security guard unlocked the door and held it open for all three of them to enter. Carlo didn't bother saying thanks. He just turned to Harry with a self-

MICHAEL VINES

satisfied smile, proud to show him what a big man he was.

As they entered the clubhouse, the Cardinals were just bouncing in after scoring the winning run in the bottom of the eleventh. They were in good spirits but, seeing as they were still eighteen games out of first, they weren't exactly whooping it up. They went to their lockers and started stripping down for their showers.

"Hey, Marty, look," said Carlo. "There's Red Schoendienst. See 'im?"

"Yeah."

Red was one of the easier Cardinals to identify, given his nickname. And in a minute, it was plain to see that it applied to every inch of him. Marty's eyes grew wider as he gazed in awe at these giants whom he had never seen up close before, and were now right there before him in the flesh. Almost entirely.

Wally Moon—easy to spot because of the dark unibrow brooding over his squinty eyes—headed to the showers, his hairy body concealed by only a towel wrapped around his waist. Harry and Carlo were familiar with the names of the other players in various stages of undress, like Rip Repulski, Joe Cunningham, Alex Grammas, Vic Raschi, but they would have had a hard time putting a face to them. Harry felt proudly exhilarated at his sudden realization that the families of these young men had come from all over the world to this wide open country where they learned to play and excel at

HARRY GETS WISE

baseball. America's national pastime could hardly be more international.

One player stood out from the others and would have not because he was a sky-scraping six-foot-five, but because he possessed a quality that was unique in the clubhouse: black skin. Seven years after Jackie Robinson came up with the Dodgers in 1947, Tom Alston became the first Negro ever to play for the Cardinals and was the only one on the team. Marty was so transfixed at the sight of him that Harry had to snap the boy out of it with a gentle shake of his shoulder and tell him it wasn't nice to stare.

Then all their eyes turned in the direction of a jocular laugh that echoed joy off the hard walls of the clubhouse. There he stood, still wearing his baseball pants but no jersey, taut, lean, strong, brimming with life and all that was good in the world—Stan the Man Musial himself.

"Come on, follow me," Carlo said to Harry and Harry did, taking Marty by the hand along with him. Carlo's swagger flagged just a little as he approached the Man.

"Hey, Stan, how are you?"

"Good, thanks. We met?"

"No. I'm Carlo Barnini. I'm a friend of Benny Apicella's."

Stan gave Carlo an oblique glance. "Is that right? Well, that's just fine."

Stan knew the name—everybody in town did— and he had even met The B himself when he came to his restaurant.

"Yeah, and this here's Harry and his grandson, Marty."

Stan nodded to Harry, but when he saw Marty looking up at him, he bent down on one knee to shake his hand, as if he were genuinely happy to meet him, which he probably was.

"Hey, Marty, whaddya say, whaddya say, whaddya say?"

"Hi."

"You play baseball?"

"I play catch."

"Well, that's the way to start. Keep playing and I'll tell you what. I'll keep a seat warm for you. One day you might play for the Cardinals too, how's that sound?"

"Good."

"Hey, Butch," Stan called out to Butch Yatkeman, the equipment manager who'd been with the team since about the time Libby was born, and whom Harry knew to be a Jew. "Get me a ball, please, will you? New one."

In a moment, Butch tossed Stan a brand new baseball, fresh out of the box, and Stan reached into his locker for a pen.

"'At's a fine name you got there, Marty," he said as he signed the ball. "I got a good friend with the same one. Marty Marion, ever heard of him?"

"No."

"He was a great Cardinal."

"A great shortstop," Harry said, keeping to himself his recollection that Marion had also been a mediocre one-term manager for the Cardinals in '51, as well as a complete bust for his once-beloved Browns the two seasons after that, their last in St. Louis.

"Sure was," Stan said smiling up at Harry. "And great guy."

Musial's rounded cursive autograph stretched between the stitches of the ball, and above it, he wrote a personal message: "To Marty, see you in the Big Leagues." Stan handed it to him.

"Wow," Marty said as he held it in his hands.

"What do you say, Marty?" Harry asked.

"Thank you."

"Yes, thank you, Mr. Musial," Harry said. "It's such an honor. We're big fans, Marty and me. Very big fans."

"Well, that's nice to hear. Where you from Harry?"

"Poland."

"Yeah? So's my dad. Call me Stash," he said, offering Harry his hand.

"Stash," Harry said as he shook it.

"We're pretty lucky we wound up here, right?"

"You betcha."

"Make sure Marty can hit the high hard one."

"I'll try, Stash." Harry said.

"Now, you be good, Marty. Eat your vegetables and do your homework. Can't go wrong like that."

MICHAEL VINES

"I will."

"Say, Stash," Carlo said, "uh, you think I could get one o' those? A ball? For my kid brother."

"Butch," Stan called. "One more, please."

"It might interest you to know that, uh, they call me the Man too," Carlo said. Harry turned toward Carlo and, with pursed lips, shook his head from side to side.

"Is that right?" Stan said.

"Yeah. Carlo the Man."

Stan thrust up his right arm and, as quick and natural as a frog snatching a mosquito out of the air with its long sticky tongue, snared the ball that Butch had tossed him.

"You could write that on there. To the Man, from the Man."

"I thought you said it was for your kid brother," Musial said as he signed the ball.

"Yeah, well, you know, I'm gonna give it to 'im."

Musial handed Carlo the ball and said, "Okay, gotta get goin'. See you at a game sometime, Marty."

And off Stan went, leaving Carlo to stare at his ball in disappointment when he saw that Stan had written his signature and nothing else.

Back in the car, Carlo said, "He coulda wrote what I asked him."

"Nobody calls you the Man, Carlo. You're not the Man."

"Yeah, well I could be if he'd a' wrote that. I mean, if Stan says I'm the Man, I'm the Man."

335

HARRY GETS WISE

"Be happy you got the ball. That's enough."

Carlo blared his horn at the car in front of him for no reason whatsoever and drove back to Warne.

✻ ✻ ✻

A couple of days later, Harry looked out his shop window and saw Marty pedaling his bike down the sidewalk across the street all by himself. Harry was even more surprised when he realized that he was riding without the training wheels. Marty was a little unsteady—he held the handlebars like he was steering a giant ship in choppy seas, and the front wheel wobbled a bit—but he kept his balance well enough and didn't fall off. Harry ran out the door to get a better look, and when he did, he saw Carlo trotting behind his grandson, calling out to him. Harry was so eager to get across the street and see all this close up, that he locked his front door with a only single turn of the key and, for the first time ever, didn't bother to shake and pull at it for about five minutes to make sure it was secure. He didn't even put up his sign, "Back in 20 minutes."

"Look, Grandpa. Did you see?"

"I see, that's wonderful, Marty."

"Carlo taught me. Watch."

Marty started pedaling again showing off his new skills to his grandpa. He tried to turn around, but he had not yet perfected that maneuver, and the bike toppled over, taking its rider along with it.

MICHAEL VINES

Harry ran down to him.

"You okay, *bubeleh*?"

"Yep. Watch."

And Marty hopped right back on his bike. He had a hard time getting started so Harry helped him get straightened out, gave him a little push, and watched him pedal back to where Carlo was standing in front of the Beckers' flat.

When Harry caught up with him he wrapped his arms around the boy and said, "*Mazel tov*, Marty. You ride a bike now. Just like a big boy. I'm so proud."

"Carlo taught me," he said again.

"Eh, you taught yourself, kid. You're a natural," Carlo said.

"Carlo says he's gonna take me to a ball game, Grandpa. From the beginning."

"Yeah?"

"And he's gonna take me to Ed's too."

"Ed's?"

"To shoot around a little."

Harry turned a stern gaze to Carlo. "What?"

"He says it's fun."

"Might as well start the kid early, Harry. If he takes after you, he'll be the next Willie Hoppe."

"I'm gonna show Mommy," Marty said, and he raced inside to get her, leaving the two men on the sidewalk alone.

"*Vas iz das*?" Harry demanded. "What do you think you're doing?"

"I taught him to ride a bike, that's all."

HARRY GETS WISE

"That's all? What's this about a ballgame? And Ed's? You think you're gonna take him to Ed's? Are you *meshugga*."

"Why not? Let the kid have a little fun."

"He's not setting one foot in Ed's, okay, Carlo? You hear me?"

"Awright, awright. Probably not big enough to reach the table anyway. But Harry, a baseball game? What's wrong with that?"

"Not with you Carlo. You're not taking him to no ballgame. You're not taking him to Ed's, you're not taking him nowhere."

"Man, oh man. Talk about an ingrate, Harry."

"I'm not messing with you, Carlo. You stay away from him, you hear me? Stay away from my grandchildren. From my family."

"After all we been through, Harry? Really? This is the thanks I get? I thought we were friends."

"Friends, maybe. But you listen to me. I can never be part of your family. You can never be part of mine. *Capische*?"

For the first time since he had known him, Harry saw what Carlo looked like when his feelings were hurt. It hurt him too, to see that expression on his face, to know it was he who caused it, caused him to feel this pain of rejection. And Harry knew from the muscle memory of his own face that if he looked in the mirror at that moment, the look on his face might not be a whole lot different.

Just then, Marty came running out with Tillie

behind him, holding the baby. She looked at Carlo with a sign of recognition. He'd been at the shiva. She nodded to him and smiled.

"You're Carlo?"

"Yeah. How you doin'?" he said with a shallow bow.

"Watch, Mommy, watch."

Carlo stood back. He let Harry help Marty get on the bike and give him the first push he needed to send him on his way. And down the sidewalk he rode, getting more confident and steady as he went. He even turned around at the end of the block, slowly, but without faltering.

Tillie's eyes revealed a jumble of conflicting emotions. So happy that her son was moving on, that he was so full of possibility and life. And so heartbroken that Sid wasn't there to see it. Either feeling might have yielded the same result, but together they were an unstoppable force, combining to produce a flow of tears as she cheered her boy on.

"That's it, Marty. Ride, sweetie. That's so good!"

While all eyes were on Marty, Carlo slipped away unnoticed. He didn't hang around to watch Marty reach home base or join in the joyous family celebration that followed. That was something he could never be a part of.

21

Tillie had never aspired to be anything but a mother and housewife, just like every other woman she knew who had kids. She had been perfectly happy in that role and expected it to last the rest of her life. But life had changed. It had been thirty-two days since Sid had died—she knew the precise number because she was counting—and not for the purpose of observing the ritual thirty-day mourning period. She'd mourn a lot longer. She also knew, along with everyone else in the family, the unspoken reality that she would have to get a job. Sooner rather than later.

A lawyer who had done work for Sid and to whom Sid had referred clients, consulted with Tillie as a courtesy. The good news was that she was the beneficiary of a small life insurance policy, and she and the kids were each eligible to collect death benefits from Social Security. The bad news was that it wouldn't be nearly enough to raise a family. But something was better than nothing.

"Thank god for FDR," Harry said, as he had so many times before about so many other things.

Tillie's options were limited. Even if Sid's former partner, Benny Mendelson, had a job he could offer

MICHAEL VINES

her, which he didn't, she knew she'd fail miserably in an office. She had a high school diploma, but was a lousy typist and ill-suited for clerical work. Her organizational skills and attention to detail skewed to the lower end of the spectrum.

She didn't want to go back to the Grand-Leader where she had worked as a salesgirl in the cosmetics department during the war. It had been fine at the time—all the girls were working—but even though she had a natural rapport with customers and knew how to sell, she sure as hell wasn't up for it now. Other than waitressing, which she had never done and, therefore, underestimated its own organizational demands, she could think of nothing else she was qualified to do.

One way or another she'd have to put herself back out in the world again, even though she wasn't that kind of woman. She was, by nature, a homebody, a housewife, a mother. Not a career woman, like Libby, though Tillie had no expectation of a career. She'd inevitably wind up standing on her feet all day, developing varicose veins, and coming home exhausted just in time to make the kids dinner and give them their baths before bed. At least her mother would do the grocery shopping for her so there'd be something in the Frigidaire when she got home from work. Lena would also take care of the kids while Tillie was at work. Tillie would be glad to delegate the grocery shopping, but she wanted desperately to maintain her role as the mother of her children, to cook for them and to feed them, to comfort and nurture them, to read them a story and tuck them into bed at night, to be there for them. Even though it meant she'd in effect have two jobs, the one as mother was the only one she valued. The one she'd never surrender.

Libby used her connections at Famous-Barr to help get Tillie a job there. Not that it took much influence. The economy was booming and they were always looking for girls to work the floor. But thanks to Libby's reputation and value to the company, management made the unheard-of concession that Tillie wouldn't have to start right away. They'd hold a place for her till she felt ready to begin. And she wasn't quite ready yet.

Tillie's gratitude was marbled with resentment. True, Libby had pulled some strings to ease her way, but ease her way to a physically demanding job she didn't want to begin with. It was like giving a ditch digger a brand new spade. How excited was he supposed to be about that? What's more, she had to accept that her baby sister was the big girl now, and, on a certain level, their relationship had subtly shifted. Despite her seniority, despite Libby's selfless intentions simply to help in any way she could, Tillie couldn't help feel she had come down a notch in the pecking order.

✺ ✺ ✺

The night that Libby had been anticipating with

trepidation had finally arrived. Lenny picked her up, made his customary special point of saying hello to her parents, and then drove off with her, presumably for an evening together. It would be a short evening for them as a couple. They drove to Olive Street, about a ten-minute ride from Warne Avenue, where they met the rest of their comrades from CORE—including six colored women—for dinner at a welcoming place called, somewhat ironically, Dixie's Hamburgers. Lenny and a few other men stuck around for burgers and a final strategy session-cum-pep talk. But after that, the women would go it alone. That's the way they wanted it.

They were all overdressed for Dixie's. Paula was wearing a charcoal grey pencil skirt suit and blouse that Libby had picked out for her when she came to the sale at Famous. Libby, as well as all the other female CORE members, were dressed in similarly respectable, conservative fashion—what might have been considered appropriate business attire, which was all the more appropriate because these ladies meant business. The Black women were wearing what they'd call their Sunday-go-to-meeting clothes.

They entered Shelley's en masse, in numbers so overwhelming that the manager—a guy named Gus —was helpless to turn them away. They took seats at tables for two, three, or four, each including at least one Black woman, and waited politely and respectfully, as they had been trained to do, no

HARRY GETS WISE

matter how much they were provoked. They wanted service, not trouble, but they were committed and prepared for it if it came their way.

Paula had been right, but only partially. It was different this time for Libby. They were together and they were on a mission. But even though Libby took some comfort in the broader fight for equal rights and social justice, she couldn't quell her narrower, personal anxieties aroused by memories of the Juicy Fruit-chewing bitch she had met there last time, nor could she help keeping one eye open for her. She kept reminding herself that she was doing something that mattered with someone who mattered to her, but it brought her little solace. She felt like she needed a drink and couldn't wait to order one—just one this time, that would be her limit—but she knew she'd have to wait. She also knew she'd most likely have to order more than one. Maybe a lot more. That was part of their strategy.

It was the same approach they took at the lunch counters where Whites and Negroes would sit together and wait to place their orders. And wait, sometimes for an hour or more. Eventually, the White person might get served, but not the Negro. When he was, he would pass his order to his snubbed companion. The reaction from the manager and wait staff was often belligerent. They expected as much tonight.

Shelley's was beginning to fill up and they still hadn't been served. Gus couldn't let all his regular customers stand around and wait forever, so he sent his waitresses to the mixed-race tables to take orders—from the White patrons only. One of the waitresses came to Libby's table, clearly conflicted, and asked her what she would like.

"A whiskey sour, please," she said.

"And you," the waitress asked Paula.

"I'll have the same."

The waitress stopped there, as if Esther, the dark-skinned woman sitting at the table with them were invisible, and headed towards the bar to get the two drinks.

"Excuse me," Paula called as she walked away. "You forgot somebody."

But the waitress hadn't forgotten anyone, and they all knew it. When she came back with the drinks, Libby slid hers over to Esther and said, "I'll have another, please."

"Look," the waitress said, "I got no quarrel with you or anybody else, but you want me to get fired?"

Libby hadn't thought about that. She hadn't considered the position she'd be putting the waitress in, forcing her to put her own neck on the line if she defied her boss. She didn't want that. All she wanted was for everyone to be treated fairly. Libby demurred, but Paula didn't seem to take that into account and pressed the issue.

"No," said Paula, "we just want you to do your job and serve your customers. That is your job, isn't it?"

"My job is to follow the boss's orders."

The waitress then looked over at Gus, who

stared back fuming. He marched over to the table and grabbed the drink from Esther, spilling half of it over her dress. She didn't flinch, but sat there with perfect equanimity. Libby was nowhere near as stoical. She was a novice at this.

"How dare you?" Libby shouted, rising to her feet.

"This glass is dirty," Gus said. "We can't serve dirty glasses."

"Or dirty people," someone said nearby.

Behind her, Libby heard a gaggle of women arguing among themselves.

"Why should we leave?" one of them said. "They're the ones who don't belong here. They should go."

"They got as much right here as we do," another said.

"What, a bunch o' niggers? And nigger-lovin' Jews?"

Paula must not have heard that because she didn't respond. She slid her drink over to Esther and said to Gus, "This glass is perfectly clean. And I'd like another, please."

"You want to get us closed down? Is that what you want? Why don't you just leave and let everybody go about their business?"

"This is our business," Libby said, surprised to hear herself say anything at all, let alone so vehemently. Paula must have emboldened her.

"We all have a right to be served," Paula said.

MICHAEL VINES

Just then, someone pushed Libby, or was pushed into her. Then Paula got up and shoved that woman, and the dominoes began to fall. It seemed like everybody was pushing everybody else, but it was impossible to know who was on whose side. Some of the tougher butches were using their fists, throwing actual punches and shouting hoarsely while the femmes squealed and screeched and, being girls, fought like girls, mostly pulling each other's hair, and kicking and scratching. Good thing none of these women were wearing Dior Roger Vivier stilettos. Those could have been lethal. Still, there were plenty of long, brightly painted fingernails among them, more than adequate to at least draw a little blood.

Given the choice between fight or flight, Libby would always choose the latter. Must run in the family, she assumed. But as she turned to flee, she found herself face to unforgettable face with a tough-looking, short-haired butch wearing a black jacket with the collar turned up and chewing what had to be at least three sticks of gum. There was a brief moment of mutual recognition, and, though Libby didn't know where Miss Juicy Fruit's sympathies lay, she didn't much care. For Libby, this was no longer about fighting for a noble cause. This was about getting even. She found herself reflexively clenching her fists, then, with unmitigated malice, delivering a powerful left uppercut, right to the *kishkes*. Watching the Friday Night Fights with her father finally paid off. The woman fell back—both the wind and the chewing gum knocked out of her—and was out for the count.

All around Libby glass shattered, bottles broke, chairs fell, and though it never escalated into the complete mayhem of a barroom brawl typically seen in Westerns, that's what it felt like to her. There was no sheriff to burst through swinging doors to restore order with a single reckless shot fired into the ceiling, but there were cops who charged through the front door, blowing whistles, swinging billy clubs indiscriminately, pulling women apart, lining them up against the wall, and making them wait there until a paddy wagon arrived.

By the time it did, the cops, with Gus's help, had figured out who the troublemakers were, and their selection process was heavily biased against the colored girls and their CORE cohort. They were hauled down to the precinct and placed under arrest on charges of disturbing the peace, assault and battery, destruction of private property, public drunkenness, and, just for good measure, lewd and lascivious behavior.

It was past 11:30 p.m. before Libby was finally processed. She was told she could make one phone call.

The obvious person to call was Lenny. And that was what she fully intended to do. Not only was he a charter member of CORE and the one who recruited her, he was also by now her best friend—her beard—reliable, discreet, and always there for her. She loved

MICHAEL VINES

him dearly, but was not in love with him, of course, nor could she ever be. He'd be down to bail her out in a heartbeat. He was the one to call. No question about it.

But as she inserted her index finger into the number seven slot of the rotary dial, aligned with the letters "P, Q, R, S," the "P" being the first initial in University City's Parkview exchange, she hesitated. Surrounded by grey walls, grey desks, and large pink-faced men in blue with black guns strapped onto their hips, she could hardly believe where she was. In jail. And for what? For being who she was. A fighter for social justice, for equality, yes, but even more fundamentally, a woman of a particular sexual orientation. That was her primary identifier, and it took precedence over all others. Without it, she might never have gotten involved with CORE in the first place, let alone been arrested. She was who she was and, though she had at least reached a point where she could be honest about it with herself and a couple of her closest friends, that was not enough.

Not that she wanted to tell the whole world— that she would never do—but she was sick of lying about it to everyone else she cared about. Everyone she loved. Especially the person she loved so deeply and most uniquely, loved in a way she could never love anyone else. The person who was and always had been there for her, way before she had ever heard of Lenny Goldstein.

Libby pulled her trembling finger out of the dial's seven slot and let it wander and fidget around till

it found the number three slot, which corresponded
to the letters "D, E, F," E for the city's Evergreen
exchange. She dialed and waited with shallow,
uneven breaths for an answer.

When she got it, she said in a quavering voice,
"Papa. It's Libby. I'm in trouble."

❊ ❊ ❊

Harry picked her up by himself. All the charges
against Libby had been read to him, including lewd
and lascivious behavior, and, though she honestly
denied that she had engaged in any such conduct,
she denied nothing else. By the time they got home,
Harry knew everything. Everything. Nothing
had to be spoken. It was all implicit and mutually
understood. But Libby confirmed it all the same.
She volunteered it. And, truth be told—to himself—
it didn't come as the complete surprise that Libby
assumed it would. That he himself might have
assumed it would before Libby made it official.

It was so foreign to Harry, so out of his
experience that it wasn't easy for him to accept. But
Harry had always been an accepting man, and he
had it in his heart to accept this too. What choice
did he have? So he accepted it without judgment,
but not without bafflement. The truth now revealed,
the certainty of it, left him not reeling, but a bit off
balance, all the more so because he wasn't sure what
to do about Lena. If it were just he, he and Libby

could go on with their lives as always, with Harry minding his own business. But Lena was another story. How would he talk about it with her. Libby asked him not to do so at all.

"It would be too hard for her, Papa. She's not like you. She won't understand."

"You think it's better to go on, then. Without her knowing? We're a family. She's your mother. My wife, Libby. It would be very hard on me to live like that."

Libby sat beside him in the front seat and considered his words. "Not now," she said at last. "Not tonight."

"Sometimes, she can surprise you, you know."

"I don't think so. Not about this."

Harry acquiesced and drove on, each of them silently absorbed in their own thoughts. The short ride to Warne seemed to take hours. When they got home and sat around the kitchen table under a harsh light drinking glasses of seltzer, Lena didn't waste any time asking for an explanation.

"What, Libby? What did you do?"

"Nothing, Mama. I was just in the wrong place at the wrong time."

"Since when do you go to bars? And with such roughnecks?"

"I don't, Mama. It was a civil rights thing. We were there to integrate the bar."

"Restaurants is one thing, but bars too? At this time of night, *noch*?

"That's when they're open."

"Who knows what kind of characters you run into at a place like that? At all hours. Drunks. Bums. They could have knives. Guns. You could get hurt, Libby."

"I'm fine, Mama."

"Hmph. What kind of woman goes to bars like that? Loose women. Floozies. Picking up drunks. That's who."

"It wasn't that kind of bar, Mama."

"No? What kind of bar was it? A nice bar at this time of night? The men were there studying Torah?"

Lena was behaving according to form. Emotional, irrational, a bit aggressive. Her reaction didn't surprise Harry one bit. But Libby's response to her did. After sitting at the Formica table listening with clenched teeth to her mother go on like a broken record about bars and the kind of men they attract so late at night, Libby couldn't take it any more. Not for another second. She wanted to stop her, just make her shut up already. What could she say that could do that?

"It was a lesbian bar," Libby blurted out.

And Lena stopped. Silence struck the room like a wrecking ball, bringing down a wall of deception and propriety with swift and stunning force. It might not have lasted more than a few seconds, but it seemed much, much longer.

"A what?"

Libby waited, preparing herself, and then she

repeated, "A lesbian bar, Mama." And then, in the weakest little trembling voice that ever came out of her mouth, she added, "I'm a lesbian."

Even though he was already aware, Harry was as shocked as both women to hear Libby say this. The very words. The very word. It was said out loud. Lena ran her fingers through her hair like she was trying to pull it out.

"What? What are you saying, Libby? I don't understand you."

"Yes, Mama. You do."

"No."

"There's a reason I never found a guy, Mama. I'm not interested in men. Not in that way."

"Libby, what are you saying, Libby?"

"Can I make it any clearer? Don't you get it?"

"*Oy, oy, oy*. No, Libby. What are you telling me?" Libby didn't answer. Why would she have to? "What about Lenny. You're not with Lenny?"

"No, Mama."

"He's a nice boy, Libby. You make a good couple. Harry, you're hearing this?"

Harry had already poured three shot glasses of bourbon, kept one for himself, and placed the two others on the table in front of the women.

"No, thanks, Papa."

"Go ahead."

Lena grabbed hers and slammed it back in one gulp. Then she got up and poured herself another.

"I don't understand," she said. And she said it

again. "It's America, that's what it is. Too much freedom. Too much. People don't know what to do with themselves. Libby, you don't have the freedom to do this. Not this. You go with Lenny. Get married. Have children. That's all. Forget all this other *mishegas*."

"It doesn't work like that, Mama."

"Don't tell me, I know a thing or two. Don't tell me how it works."

"Lena, *genug*."

"Mama, I can't make myself something I'm not."

"Oh yeah? Who says? In America, you can make of yourself anything you want."

"I can't make myself want Lenny Goldstein. Or anybody else."

"Why not? He's a good boy. From a good family. The finest. You don't have to be so in love. Who was ever in love? Who ever wanted someone?"

"We did," Harry said. "I wanted you."

"That was different. Lightning out of nowhere. For most, it was arranged. You learn to live with someone. You learn to love. You can learn, Libby. You can learn to want Lenny Goldstein."

"I want someone else, Mama."

"Yeah? Go ahead. Want all you want. Want a man."

"It's a woman."

After a frustrated pause where their breathing was the loudest sound in the room, Lena said, "What, you have a lady friend?"

MICHAEL VINES

"I don't know."

"You don't know? You have or you don't have."

"Or you might," Libby said.

"Yeah? And what do you do with this lady friend you might have? The two of you?"

"What do you mean?"

"You kiss?"

"Oh, Mama, for God's sake."

"Tell me. I want to know,"

"We hold hands. A little."

"That's it?"

"We're just getting to know each other."

"You can get to know Lenny Goldstein just as much. You can hold hands with him."

"Mama, listen to me. I feel things for this woman I could never feel for Lenny."

"You're in love?"

"I might be. I think. Maybe. "

"Then you can think you're in love with Lenny Goldstein, too."

"*Oy a broch*," said Harry.

"And when you know each other, you and this woman, then what? What will you do?"

"Lena, *shah!*" Harry said. "You want she should draw you a picture? Use your imagination. Be happy for her, Lena. Libby, be happy for yourself. You're young and in love. Is there a better combination?"

Libby was doing her best to hold back her tears, but they were beginning to get the better of her.

"Lena," Harry said, "look at us. We have a nice experience together. Don't we? We have love and affection. We have desire. Yes, Lena?" Libby cocked her head and arched an eyebrow as her father continued. "You would trade that for anything? Tell me. Don't you want Libby should have that too?"

Lena plopped into the kitchen chair and rubbed her hands into both cheeks like she was kneading dough to make a challah.

"I have three daughters," Lena said. "One's a widow, one's a goy with a cross, and now this. *Oy. Meyn leben iz a leben nisht.*"

"Your *leben*," Libby said, angry now. "It's my life, Mama. *Meyn leben.* My life is no life."

With those words, Harry lost all sympathy for both of them. He had had enough.

"*A leben nisht. A leben nisht*, you say? Listen to me. Look. Look at this."

And with that Harry strode to the sink and did something that each of them did every day. Without giving it a second thought. He turned on the spigot and a stream of water came rushing out of the faucet.

"Look. See? Look, Lena. Look, Libby. Water. Fresh. Clean. You can drink it, it won't make you sick. And it's right here. As much as you want."

The women both stared at him, bewildered, and watched the water gushing from the faucet.

"Too much freedom in America, Lena? Too much freedom that you should have good water coming out whenever you want? You had this in the Old Country? No. Remember, Lena? Remember what it was like before? And you don't want to drink water, drink seltzer, then. Drink Coca-Cola. Have a schnapps." He poured himself another shot and slugged it down. "And no one will stop you. Listen to me. I don't say everything is perfect here, Lena. America is not perfect. I know. It's not everything we dreamed. It's not everything it promised. I don't say it is. But here's what I do say. What's most important is to remember and not to forget. To be grateful and not take for granted."

Harry took a long pause and considered what he had just said. He'd never realized it before, and never articulated it, but if he had acquired any wisdom in his life, that was it. To remember and not to forget. To be grateful and not take for granted.

"You too, Libby. *A leben nisht*? No. We have everything. Everything that matters we have here, in America. Under this roof. We have fresh water. We have family. We can live and be left alone. That's why we came here. And you, too, Libby. You have that, too."

Harry then had another sudden realization. For the first time he understood that Libby's life experience, here in America, was, perhaps, in some ways not all that different from his own. She too was an outsider, the other in a land that was less open, less welcoming to her than America had been to him. And if welcoming was asking too much, then how about just being left alone? At heart, isn't that what they both wanted? To be left alone. To live a life unbothered? Un-hounded? Did she have to be a refugee, too? To run, not from her country, but from her life? From herself?

"That's all Libby wants, Lena. To live and be left alone. Let her live, Lena. *Lozn zayn*."

Lena slouched in her chair, a chastened expression on her face. It seemed that Harry had said the last words that any of them were going to say. And she had no answer for them. She had no argument to make. Anything else was expressed in sniffles, tears, small gasps, and silence. But even though she knew there was nothing left to say, that didn't stop her from saying it.

"Tell me, Libby, this maybe lady friend of yours, this woman. She's Jewish?"

"No, Mama."

"Ach," Lena said. And the silence took hold again, until Lena said at last, "Well, you can't have everything."

22

The *St. Louis Post-Dispatch* didn't waste much ink on the raid at Shelley's, "a squalid club patronized primarily by a clientele of dubious moral character," as the paper reported in a short article placed towards the back of Section A, with no mention of the high moral purpose of the patrons who sparked the confrontation. At least they weren't referred to as degenerates. Also on the plus side, the story didn't name names or have pictures accompanying it. Still, the proceedings were a matter of public record. The names of those arrested were listed in police files, available to anyone who cared to look for them or happened inadvertently to stumble upon them. Libby knew that, and for years after she lived with the underlying fear that one day she would be found out.

The three of them, Harry, Lena, and Libby, saw each other differently after that night. The stereotypes of father, mother, and daughter fell away. They each caught a glimpse of the other's inner life and hidden desires, the way a flash of lightning in a storm at midnight illuminates for a moment an otherwise dark and invisible landscape. And they all came away with a fuller understanding of each other as human beings, in all their complexity and contradiction.

The Cardinals were still playing out the string but their season was over. Less than a week after Libby's bust, they were mathematically eliminated from contention after losing to the Phillies 5-4 and falling twenty-three games behind the Giants with just twenty-two left to play. Their end came as no surprise to anyone who had been paying even a little attention, so no hearts were broken. It was just a matter of time and the time had come. Like losing a loved one who had been suffering too long with a terminal condition, difficult as it was to let go, it came with some relief. Their demise, however, didn't stop Harry from continuing to follow them every day, reading the box scores, and listening to games on the radio. Though it made no sense, after a win—even when all was lost—he'd sometimes find himself lying in bed with a smile on his face as he fell asleep.

One night, stripped to just his boxers and a sleeveless white T-shirt, Harry heard the Cardinals score three in the top of the ninth to nip the Dodgers 6-5 at Brooklyn. As he always did after wins— and only wins—he stuck around for the post-game wrap-up, the happy totals, as Harry Carry called them. Following that, he stayed tuned to hear the nightly news while he got ready for bed. On this night, the announcer all but interrupted himself with a dramatic breaking story.

"This just in. Moments ago, Benny "Killer Bee"

MICHAEL VINES

Apicella, also known as Benny the B, boss of the St. Louis crime family, was brutally murdered in a gangland-style killing, gunned down as he was leaving Angelo's, a popular Italian restaurant in the 5200 block of Shaw Avenue on the Hill. Also killed was his bodyguard who has not yet been identified. We'll provide further details as they come in."

Lena was already asleep, but there was no way Harry was going to join her. Sleep was impossible now. He set the volume low on the clock radio in the kitchen, poured himself a schnapps, and stayed up waiting to hear the latest as it came in, waiting to hear the only thing he cared about: the name of the bodyguard who was killed with Benny the B.

Harry imagined the worst. And he blamed himself. If he had done the right thing—taken responsibility for killing Tony the Pipe, called the cops, turned himself in, confessed, and faced the music—Carlo couldn't have taken credit for the hit and wouldn't have made his bones. He wouldn't have become a made man and been so close to Benny the B.

Of course, if Harry had done that, the music he would have had to face would come not just from the law, but from Benny the B himself, echoing the strains of the bloody climax of a tragic Italian opera. Regular citizens didn't get away with knocking off made guys, no matter what the circumstances. Harry would have been committing suicide. Carlo saved his life in that way too, before they even got to the river.

But just as much as Carlo saved Harry's life, Harry had put Carlo's at risk. He knew Carlo wasn't cut out for this line of work—Carlo had confessed as much when he told Harry he didn't know if he had it in him to do the job he had to do for the boss. To whack a guy. Thanks to Harry, he didn't have to find out. Harry did it for him, inadvertently, yes, but he did it all the same. And that's how Carlo got square with Benny. Harry always feared that sooner or later Carlo would get on somebody's wrong side and wind up like Tony the Pipe. He never thought he would be a link in that chain of events. And he ached at the thought that Carlo's blood, too, was now on his hands.

The news on the radio came in bit by bit. Harry learned that Benny the B's last meal was linguini with clam sauce, that there was some sort of family rivalry going on between him and Frankie Fingers Martinelli. Part of the bad blood may have had something to do with a soldier named Tony the Pipe Allocco—thought to be in cahoots with Martinelli —who had disappeared about a month ago without a trace. And Martinelli made his move to settle the score that night. More violence was expected. Maybe even a full-blown gang war. They reported all that, but they never mentioned the name of the bodyguard who went down with Benny Apicella. Maybe the guy was such small potatoes, he wasn't worth talking about.

Harry resisted pouring himself a second shot. He had to work the next day, so he settled for a glass

MICHAEL VINES

of seltzer and felt the bubbles tingle on his tongue and tickle the back of his throat while he waited for more news. Exhaustion was overtaking him, and not the physical kind. He was just sitting down drinking seltzer. How exhausting was that? But he was completely spent.

Just as he was about ready to call it a night, Harry heard a few drops of rain pelting his kitchen window. When he heard it again, he got up to close it. As he approached the window, he saw that it was dry. It wasn't raining. Just then, he heard the sound again—his window being struck by a third salvo of pebbles. Harry looked outside and saw, standing in his backyard near the children's swing set, Carlo holding a paper bag in his right hand and getting ready to hurl more pebbles with his left. He stopped when he saw Harry, and waved at him to come down. Harry wasted no time. He threw on a pair of pants and raced out the door.

"You gotta help me, Harry."

"You're okay, Carlo. Thanks god, you're okay."

"Yeah, I'm okay, but I'm in deep shit. I need you, Harry. You're the only guy can help me."

Carlo talked fast and told him everything, including the name of the boss's dead bodyguard, just because Harry asked, even though it didn't matter anymore, the name meant nothing to him, and he couldn't care less. Then Carlo explained exactly what he needed Harry to do and why. Harry was so happy to see him alive he'd have done anything to keep him that way. Horrible as the favor was that Carlo asked of him, when Harry thought it through, he knew he had no choice.

"Wait here," Harry said. "I'll be right down."

Harry climbed the stairs up to his apartment two at a time, his feet so swift and light they might have been the cat's paws on the decal he displayed in his shop window. Harry grabbed what he needed and ran right back down, just as quietly and quickly. Without another word, they dashed across the street, two figures in silhouette against the dull street lamps. They turned into the back alley behind Harry's shop and entered through the rear door. Before Harry turned on the light, he made sure the door leading to the front of the shop was closed so nothing could be seen through the front window.

"You're ready for this?" Harry asked.

"Now or never."

The first thing Harry did was uncork the new bottle of bourbon he had grabbed from his kitchen cabinet and hand it to Carlo. Carlo took a healthy swig. Then another.

"More," Harry said.

Carlo took another slug from the bottle. It was just as Harry remembered doing himself so many years ago—not fine Kentucky bourbon, in his case, but a bottle of rotgut grain alcohol distilled in a metal tub by the shoemaker he was apprenticing with in Sokolova. Harry was only sixteen at the time, and the only other alcohol he'd ever consumed

MICHAEL VINES

was a sip of wine after saying the blessing over it on Shabbos—which he was permitted to do since his bar mitzvah—and, at his family's last three Passover Seders, a full glass, which went straight to his head. The shoemaker's homemade poison would have come in at about 190 proof, so it didn't take much. Harry was drunk in no time, numb to the pain he was about to have voluntarily inflicted on himself. An act of violence to help him escape far worse violence.

When young Harry was sloshed near the point of unconsciousness, the shoemaker put his foot in a vise. Harry wondered how the memory could be so vivid when he was all but passed out at the time. Perhaps he had imagined it after the fact. But imagined or not, in Harry's memory the pain was real—fierce and savage—as the shoemaker wielded the same skiving knife he used to cut leather on the sole of a boot to carve through the joint of the big toe on Harry's right foot, slice through sinews, and saw through bone until he had finally lopped the bloody thing off and dropped it into a bucket. The shoemaker stanched the bleeding with *schmattas* that Harry and had washed with soap and bleach himself for that very purpose, wrapped them as tightly as possible, and let Harry lie there till he came to. That's when he felt the pain, searing like lava flowing over his butchered foot. Harry remembered now. It wasn't just his imagination.

And now Harry would practice what he had learned and experienced firsthand as an apprentice in Poland. On Carlo. Not on his toe, but his finger. His pinky. Again, an act of violence to help his friend escape far worse violence.

As Carlo had just explained to Harry in his backyard, to the counterpoint of the swing set squeaking in the wind, Frankie Fingers was the boss now and had a contract out on him for whacking Tony. It seems that Frankie and Tony had been silent partners, doing deals behind Benny's back, and plotting to move in on him when the time was right. Once they bumped Benny off, Frankie would be boss, and Tony would rise from just another soldier to underboss in the new regime. But Carlo had gotten in the way and screwed up their plans. Frankie Martinelli regrouped, bided his time, and finally struck. Now that Benny had been taken care of, Carlo was number one on Martinelli's hit list.

"Here's what you gotta do," Carlo told Harry, the rusty swing chirping over his whisper. "You gotta cut off my little finger. I seen you cut a sole, Harry. You got skill at that. Now, do the same thing to me and get it to Martinelli. That's what he wants most, if you ask me. The guy's sick. And it'll be proof that you whacked me and took this little prize after. A tribute to him for his fuckin' collection."

"How's he gonna know it's your finger?"

"He'll know. Cops got my prints. He's got the cops."

Harry thought for a moment, then said, "This is crazy, Carlo? He'll never believe I whacked you."

MICHAEL VINES

"You got a reputation, Harry. A hustler, a standup guy, and one tough Jew. Here's what you tell him. I came to you and wanted help. But you knew he whacked Benny—it's all over the news—and it was nothin' doin'. If you was gonna help anybody, it was the new boss. Him, Martinelli. You didn't wanna be on his bad side.

"Just tell it exactly the way it's happening, Harry. I come to you for help. Only you don't help me. You whack me, got it? And take my finger. Keep it simple. Just tell the truth about what we did with Tony. Only this time, I'm Tony. And you did it all yourself. You smashed me in head with your hammer and dumped me in the river. Simple as that."

Carlo was always thinking, always working an angle. He was one smart *boychik*, that's for sure. Oh, what he could have been. Harry didn't have much time to think it over, but he was worried. It seemed so farfetched. And he didn't want to get involved with any of these people. As of now, he couldn't have picked Frankie Fingers Martinelli out in a lineup and he wanted to keep it that way. He didn't want to have to see him face to face and tell him anything, let alone give him Carlo's finger. As what? A tribute, Carlo said. *A shtick* tribute. He'd be taking a terrible risk. It was too much to ask. But as he continued to think about it in the few seconds he spent doing so, he could come up with no alternative. Carlo's life was at stake, and Harry would do anything to save it.

And now, in the back of his shop, Harry was about to do what had to be done. Carlo took another slug from the bottle.

"One more," Harry told him. And Carlo took it.

"Okay, let's go. Let's get this over with already."

Harry gazed deeply in Carlo's bloodshot eyes. "One more."

"No more. I gotta drive after."

Harry nodded. The kid was always thinking, and more prudent than he gave him credit for.

"Okay. We're gonna need the vice. One second."

Harry turned off the light in back, and opened the door to the front of his shop. He knew every inch of it so well, he probably could have made his way blindfolded, but a streetlamp cast its dim light inside, just enough for him to see what he was doing. He picked up the vice and came right back to Carlo, who was pacing in the dark. Harry turned the light back on and centered the vice on a wooden table. Carlo sat on a bench next to it, his left foot tapping a beat fit for a hopped-up bebop quartet. Harry chose his newest, sharpest skiving knife from the shelf holding his latest shipment of tools. He examined its finely honed edge, then lifted Carlo's left hand.

"Other one, Harry. I'm a lefty."

Harry nodded and positioned Carlo's right hand into the vice instead, tightening it not one turn more than was necessary to prevent him from yanking it out. Carlo was far too sober for this to be painless, so Harry selected a brand new thick leather sole from his shelf.

MICHAEL VINES

"Say 'Ahh.'"

As Carlo did, Harry stuck the sole into his mouth and told him to bite down hard. Then he felt for the knuckle nearest Carlo's palm. It was a messy business, this business of dismembering the human body. But it was easier than Harry thought it would be. Surprisingly so. Much easier than severing a toe, at least as he remembered it.

Harry placed his blade along the line of the joint and slashed into it with one clean, powerful stroke. Blood splattered and flowed like wine in the land of milk and honey. It was a good start, but he wasn't done. With surgical precision, Harry guided his blade back into the gash he opened and, with about as much carving, twisting, and tugging as it would take to get the *pulke* off a Thanksgiving turkey, he yanked off Carlo's finger. Carlo grunted and bit hard on the strip of leather between his teeth. All things considered, it went pretty well. Fast, simple, done. Harry was indeed a skilled craftsman. He pulled the leather sole out of Carlo's mouth.

"That's it?" Carlo asked. "I don't hardly feel nothin'. You're a genius, Harry. Doctor is right."

Carlo, always thinking, had prepared for the aftermath, too. In the bag he'd brought with him were a half-dozen rolls of sterile gauze, a roll of adhesive tape, and a Johnson and Johnson First Aid Kit that contained more gauze, surgical tape, sutures, and sterile wound dressings. Harry used the supplies as best as he could figure and finally wrapped Carlo's hand as tightly as he could in gauze and tape.

"Wrap the finger too," Carlo said. "And get it straight into your freezer. Put it in ice before you take it to Martinelli."

"Yeah, yeah. Sure. You okay to drive, Carlo?"

"Yeah, fine. Thing's startin' to sting a little, but I'm good. Oh, one more thing. I'm takin' your car."

"What?"

"It's a good deal for you, Harry. You get the Caddy. That thing kinda sticks out on the road. No one's gonna be looking for me driving a Chevy, that's for sure. If the finger ain't enough proof for Martinelli, the Caddy will be. Everybody knows I'd die for that car. Title's in the glove compartment. Signed over to you. It's yours, Harry. *Gezunterheyt.*"

Once again, Carlo had been thinking ahead. It made perfect sense. Harry nodded, and they exchanged car keys.

"Where you're gonna go, Carlo?"

"Somewhere they'll never find me. Someplace I can live my fuckin' life in peace, away from all this shit."

"But where? Where is such a place?"

"I dunno. Far away. Other side of the world, maybe. I dunno."

Harry locked the back door, not tarrying to make sure it was good and locked in his customary manner, and together he and Carlo made a beeline to his Chevy. Before Carlo got in, Harry reached out for

MICHAEL VINES

a parting handshake, but when he realized Carlo's hand was covered in bandages like a giant blood-soaked mitten, he instead opened his arms to give him a hug.

"Whoa, whoa, Harry, whaddya think I am, a fuckin' *faygala*?"

"I don't care if you are. Don't be that way, Carlo. Leave people alone. *Capiche*?"

"Yeah, fine." Carlo allowed himself a halfhearted hug. "Look, Harry, thanks. I owe you everything. I'll never pay you back. I couldn't in a million years."

"We're even, Carlo."

"Yeah, maybe so. Even Steven. You take care, now, Harry. And take care of business, yeah? Give Martinelli the finger. Ha! That's right. Give 'im the fuckin' finger for me." Carlo gestured with the middle finger of his left hand to make sure Harry got the message.

"I will, Carlo."

"See you in the funny papers, pal."

Harry stood at the curb and watched Carlo drive off in his Chevy Bel-Air for a new world, leaving him behind in this one, alone, to do what he had to do. He waited till the taillights disappeared before heading for home.

Exhausted, he trudged up the steps to his flat as quietly as he did before so he wouldn't wake Lena. But he didn't have to worry about it. She was up and pacing around the living room when Harry walked in carrying the bag that held the finger.

"Where have you been? I'm a nervous wreck worrying—"

She stopped abruptly in the middle of her sentence and Harry realized immediately why she did. His sleeveless T-shirt and bare shoulders were splattered with blood. He should have worn an apron, though that wouldn't have been enough. His face, too, was spotted with bloody freckles.

"Harry, you're all right?"

"Fine, Lena."

She hesitated a few seconds, a shadow of dread crossing her face, her eyes reflecting the enormity of her next question, "Harry...did you kill somebody again?"

❋ ❋ ❋

The next morning Harry got up early, retrieved from his freezer the bandaged finger he had placed in a plastic bag, and opened his shop. But not for long. He picked up his multi-purpose bucket—the one Marshall had filled with beer at Dependahl's; the one Harry used to set fire to the bike-lesson cover of *The Saturday Evening Post*. Then he put the "Back in 20 minutes" sign on his door, locked it to within an inch of its life, and hied over to Lucille's where the morning breakfast crowd was keeping her busy. He asked her to fill the bucket with ice. After she did, he went outside, ducked into an alley, and buried the plastic bag that held the finger deep into bucket.

MICHAEL VINES

Then he drove his new Caddy for the first time.

He couldn't believe it. He loved his Chevy, always had, but this was a revelation. If the Chevy could be called a car, an automobile, or, as Harry customarily said, a machine, then it hardly seemed fair to use the same words to describe this Cadillac. He decided the only thing to call it was a *mechaiyeh*. As much a pleasure as a cooling breeze on hot summer day.

It took some getting used to. There were so many buttons that did so many different things when he pressed them, he had to learn which did what by trial and error. Trying to lock the doors, his seat slid back. Trying to turn on the radio, he raised the outside antenna. Trying to open the window, he lowered the canvass convertible top. That was fine with him. He was hoping he could figure out how to do that anyway, to make sure he could be easily identified behind the wheel. No one would mistake his old Jewish *punim* for handsome Carlo's.

Harry drove to the Hill and turned onto Daggett Avenue, the street Carlo had told him Martinelli's social club was on—the place where he conducted business. It was not as welcoming as its moniker might imply. Security was tight, and gunsels were out in force up and down the block. A phalanx of them descended on Harry, some with pistols drawn, and trotted alongside him as he looked for a place to park the *Mechaiyeh*. They recognized the car, but not the guy driving it.

"Hey, who the fuck are you? Where'd you get the

car? That's Barnini's car," they called out over one another.

Harry stopped dead in front of an open space, then he said, "Not anymore."

That shut them up. It even seemed to earn him a little respect. But they kept their leery, puzzled eyes glued to him as he began to park.

Maneuvering a car that size into a tight spot tested Harry's skills as a driver, especially with so many thugs watching his every move. But he was up to it. Harry always had a good eye and a deft touch. He wouldn't give himself too much credit though. With the *Mechaiyeh's* power steering, even a lady could have parallel parked using just one hand.

After Harry nestled into the spot, he grabbed his bucket and marched towards the club with a wise-guy escort. Undaunted, he knocked on the door, and a skinny man with a skinny mustache answered.

"What's this?" he said, addressing the gang surrounding Harry. Harry spoke up for himself.

"I'd like to see Mr. Frank Martinelli, please."

"Yeah? Who are you?"

"A friend of Tony Allocco's."

A collective gasp was followed by a collective murmur. The skinny man was taken aback, and then a bit further aback when he caught sight of the baby blue Cadillac convertible parked across the street.

"Who's car is that?"

"It's mine. Now."

Harry was leveling the playing field, and the

MICHAEL VINES

skinny man stood as tall as he could to compensate.

"What's in the bucket?" the skinny man asked, then thrust his hand into the ice and pulled out the plastic bag. "What the fuck's this?"

"It's for Mr. Martinelli. He'll want to have it."

The skinny man dropped the plastic bag back into the bucket and said, "Wait here," before slamming the door in Harry's face.

In a minute he came back out, frisked Harry roughly, and took his bucket. Then he waved for Harry to enter. Harry followed him in, leaving his escort behind to shuffle around outside.

A moment later, Harry found himself in Martinelli's office. The skinny man closed the door behind them, and stayed, leaning against the wall, holding the bucket.

Just as Carlo said, there was a shelf in the room on which sat a row of six glass jars containing human fingers floating in formaldehyde, a name printed on a tag affixed to each. In front of the shelves was a large wooden desk and, sitting behind it, a small, balding man. Frankie Fingers Martinelli.

"You're, uh, who?" Martinelli said in a high, squeaky voice.

"Harry Becker. Friend of Tony's."

"Yeah? How you know Tony?"

"He came to my shop. I paid."

"So, uh, why you here?"

Harry gave him the whole phony spiel. Just as Carlo told him to. How Carlo came to him for help.

How Harry refused because he knew what had gone down. It was on the radio. How Carlo threatened him and how Harry did to him what he had actually done to Tony, Frankie's friend and co-conspirator. Lying like that, in the devil's lair, took balls, and Harry was proving that he had them. He even added a colorful detail, the kind that can make a lie sound like the truth.

"The bloodstain on my floor. I can't get it out."

Frankie listened, taking his measure of Harry. He grilled him, trying to trip him in a lie, but Harry wasn't really lying. He was just coloring outside the lines.

"And you, uh, you stole this punk Barnini's car while you was at it?"

Harry nodded. "Why not?"

Martinelli paused, then asked, "You the pool shark I heard about? Harry the Hebe or somethin'?"

"Harry the Yid," Harry said, but thought to himself, Harry the Hebe, how'd Carlo miss that one? He'd have loved it.

"Yeah, yeah, that's right, Harry the Yid," Martinelli said. "So you're the tough Jew, huh? Ya don't look so tough to me."

Look who's talking, Harry thought. Martinelli looked nasty enough, but not the kind of guy you'd cast as a crime boss. Small, hunched over, and wearing wire rim glasses over his birdlike beak, he reminded Harry of Charles Lane (whose real name Harry knew to be Levison), the sourpuss character

MICHAEL VINES

actor he had seen in countless movies always playing parts like the coldhearted bean counter who can't wait to foreclose on a mortgage and put widows and children out into the street. Harry kept his observations to himself.

"Are you tough?" Martinelli asked, trying to goad him.

"I mind my business," Harry said.

Martinelli snapped his fingers and the skinny man brought him the plastic bag. He took it, opened a desk drawer, and pulled out the things he needed: a sixteen-ounce amber bottle of benzene, a black ink pad, and an official St. Louis Police Department fingerprint card. Then he reached into the plastic bag, unwrapped the bandage covering Carlo's severed finger—undressed it might be a better way to convey the sensuality he brought to his task—and examined it—leered at it might be more precise, his expression revealing something akin to lurid desire. Then he pulled a pristine white handkerchief out of his breast pocket, tipped the bottle of benzene onto it, and used it to caress and clean the tip of the finger. He examined it again and, when he was satisfied, he pressed it onto the ink pad. Then he pressed and rolled the ridges of the ink-stained finger into a square box on the fingerprint card, producing a perfect print. He scrutinized his handiwork, then handed the card to the skinny man.

"Run it down to the precinct," he told him. "Get Rinaldi to check it."

HARRY GETS WISE

The skinny man took the card and went out the door.

Martinelli then turned to Harry with a dead-eyed stare that left him no doubt that though this weird, scrawny little sparrow of a man with the squeaky little voice may not look the part, he was every bit the coldblooded killer he was known to be. A man whose threat was his bond.

"This doesn't check out," he said to Harry, "you're gonna hear from me."

"You know where to find me. Warne Avenue. Liberty Shoe Doctor," Harry said, upping the ante and proving that, though he was scared to death, he had nothing to fear.

* * *

About an hour and a half after putting up his Back-in-20-minutes sign, Harry drove home in the *Mechaiyeh*, a name all the more appropriate with the top down. He was confident that Carlo's print would match—more than confident, he was certain. There was no doubt. Carlo had it all figured out, thinking two, three steps ahead of everybody else. What potential that kid had. And what guts. He'd be okay, Harry thought. He could take care of himself. He could outsmart those good-for-nothings any day of the week.

As Harry guided his new Cadillac convertible up Grand Avenue, the wind blowing cool on his face

MICHAEL VINES

and ruffling his thin hair, he said to himself, aloud, "Carlo the Man. You know, it really does fit."

He breathed in the fresh morning air, smiling, then laughing out loud. He tooted his horn in a jaunty rhythm, trumpeting his hope—not his certainty, but his hope—that now he would finally be left alone.

EPILOGUE

Two years later, Harry received a letter with no return address and unusual, foreign-looking stamps on it. As far as he could make out, it was sent from overseas, somewhere in the South Pacific, maybe. He opened the envelope and inside found a cartoon torn from the funnies section of a newspaper, written in a language he didn't understand or recognize. Scrawled over it in English were the words, "Greetings from the New World."

Eleven years after that, at age seventy-three, Harry Becker died of congestive heart failure. In his final days, Libby would sit by his bedside at the Jewish Hospital and read him the box scores. They brought him comfort when they were good and, that year, they usually were. The 1967 Cardinals won the World Series, but Harry wasn't around to see it. He was buried at Chesed Shel Emeth Cemetery in University City. Goldie had gotten there before him, having died of breast cancer in 1959 when she was forty-four.

Tillie, who had remarried, lived in U. City, as did all the grandchildren, all on the wrong side of the tracks north of Olive Street Road. Still, they attended some of the best public schools in the country.

Libby lived with Paula in a luxurious high rise on Skinker decorated in the finest taste with expansive views of Forest Park. Sometimes she would sit on the custom-built upholstered bench that ran beneath the length of the window sills and gaze out at the World's Fair Pavilion.

By 2017, Harry, Lena, and their three daughters had all been buried in plots close to one another. In late winter of that year, the mood in America had grown dark, hurtling the American Dream into eclipse. During a wave of nativist rage, Harry and Lena's stones were overturned and spray-painted with swastikas, along with those of more than a hundred others who came to this country as immigrants, or were their sons and daughters, grandchildren and great-grandchildren, even great-great-grandchildren.

In their final resting place, they couldn't be left alone.

THE END

ACKNOWLEDGEMENT

I would like to thank Leonard Sherp, whose close reading and brilliant editing helped me so much in preparing this book. Jon Stone for his inspiration and encouragement. Members of my family, especially my late cousin Marshall, whose cascade of vivid childhood memories sparked my own as well as my imagination. Betty Rae Epstein for her indispensable recollections of life as a co-ed at Washington University in the 1940s, as well as fashions of the time. Dr. Ron Stock and Dr. Lawrence Kahn, for their medical expertise. Edwin Pepper for his recollections of interior designer Jack Brandt. Jeff Vines, who did so much to get this novel out of my computer and into the world. And the Columbia Fiction Foundry, the writers group where parts of this novel were workshopped.

ABOUT THE AUTHOR

Michael Vines

Born in St. Louis, he received his Master's degree in English from Columbia University. After grad school he began a career in advertising working as a copywriter and Creative Director for several of New York's most renowned global agencies. He continues to live in New York City with his wife where he enjoys reading, writing, cooking, playing blues and rock guitar, and following politics and the St. Louis Cardinals.

BOOKS BY THIS AUTHOR

Treblinka, Mon Amour

This novel follows the life of Martin Keller (the six-year-old Marty in "Harry Gets Wise"), as an aspiring writer living in New York City in the mid-1970s. When his estranged Holocaust-denying neighbor dies, Martin is surprised to learn that he is both a suspect in her murder and the sole beneficiary in her will. Further complicating his life is his romantic involvement with her granddaughter, a troubled young artist who deals with her internal conflicts by creating disconcerting works of art. An excerpt of this novel was published in the prestigious online literary journal, JewishFiction.net.

A Reason To Believe

The baby of the family in "Harry Gets Wise," Joe Keller becomes a creative director at a large advertising agency in New York City in the early 2000s. Conflicted about telling lies for corporate clients and contributing to the debased values of the popular culture, things seem to hit rock bottom when he gets a new assignment where even the "reason to believe" the product benefit is a lie. They haven't. Various story lines and subplots involving his work and family overlap and resolve in a surprising, rollicking climax at the his son's bar mitzvah.